The Comp[lete] Guide to Connecting Audio, Video, and MIDI Equipment

The Complete Guide to Connecting Audio, Video, and MIDI Equipment

Get the Most Out of Your Digital, Analog, and Electronic Music Setups

José "Chilitos" Valenzuela

Hal Leonard Books
An Imprint of Hal Leonard Corporation

Published in 2015 by Hal Leonard Books
An Imprint of Hal Leonard Corporation
7777 West Bluemound Road
Milwaukee, WI 53213

Trade Book Division Editorial Offices
33 Plymouth St., Montclair, NJ 07042

Printed in the United States of America

Graphic Design: Michael Teborek, Garrett LaBrie
Graphic Editing: Michael Teborek, Roy Sugihara, Garrett LaBrie, Cristian Perez
Technical Editors: Chilitos Valenzuela, Cristian Perez, Roy Sugihara, Dave Hampton
Proofreaders: Marina Valenzuela, Roy Sugihara, Aaron Cervantes
Contributions: Shilpa Patel, José Armenta, Ivan Garcia, Luis Diaz, Alex Lajud, Carolina Limón

Library of Congress Cataloging-in-Publication Data is available upon request.

ISBN 978-1-4803-9145-1

www.halleonardbooks.com

I dedicate this book to my lovely wife

Marina Zapata de Valenzuela

For her patience and understanding, and for believing in me and the project.

Contents

Acknowledgements ix
Introduction xi
How to use this book xiii

Section 1 Home Studios 1

iPad Recording Studio 3
Mbox 3G MIDI Setups 9
Music Production Studio with a Digi 003+ 17
Simple Music Production Studio 33
MOTU 4Pre & Digital Performer Setup 41
Desktop Music Production Studio with Apollo Twin 49
Music Production Studio with MBox Pro 57
Voice-Over Talent Home Studio 65
Music Production Studio with Pro Tools Quartet 73
Live Band Recording with a Digi 003+ 81

Section 2 Professional Studios 91

24-Track Analog Tape Machine Transfer 93
Connecting a Pro Tools HD System 105
Focusrite RedNet to Pro Tools HD 117
Professional Overdub Studio Setup 125
Professional Music Production Setup 137

Section 3 Post Studios 153

Surround Sound Post Setup 155
Avid S6 Post Production Setup 163
Podcast Studio Setup 171
Satellite Link HD & Video Satellite LE Synchronization Setup 179
Video/Audio Synchronization Setup 189

Section 4 Electronic Music Studios (EDM Studios) 201

MIDI Synthesizer Studio 203
Advanced EDM/DJ Production Studio 211
Ableton Live Studio 219
Native Instruments Maschine Studio 227
Propellerhead Reason and Balance Studio 233

Section 5 DJ Studios 243

Vinyl DJ Studio 245
Traktor DJ Studio 251
Serato DJ Studio 257
Basic CDJ Studio 265
Laptop DJ Studio 271
CDJ Studio via Ethernet Link 277

Appendix

A. Cables & Connectors 285
B. Studio Furniture 299
C. Audio Interface Options 301
D. Directory 303

Acknowledgements

I would like to express my thanks and appreciation to those who collaborated with me on this book, and to all my friends and family who patiently supported me and helped me in one way or another throughout the completion of this important book project.

To John Cerullo, Publisher of Hal Leonard Corporation, for giving me the opportunity to publish this book and for his patience. Thanks, John. To my right hand men, Michael Teborek and Roy Sugihara, for their invaluable time, talent, effort, and persistence from the beginning. And to Bill Gibson from Hal Leonard for his patience and understanding in completing this book.

To the AudioGraph International team: Cristian Perez, Michael Teborek, Roy Sugihara, Garrett LaBrie, Marlon Ordoñes, Shilpa Patel, José Armenta, Iván Garcia, Luis Díaz, Carolina Limón, and Alex Lajud.

Also, I want to thank the following people for their help and support:

Michael Prager from Adam-Audio GmbH, Sylvain Missemer and Nathalie Skladanek from Arturia, Jeff Simcox and Karen Emerson from Audio-Technica U.S., Inc., Wynn Morro from Avalon Design, Louis Hernandez Jr., Tim Carroll, Andy Cook, Frank Cook, Jon Connolly, Pepe Reveles, and Angel Ylisastigui from AVID Technology, Inc., Will Kahn from Burl Audio Corp., Cikira from Cikira's "Mushrooms" Studio, Kay Dorrough from Dorrough, DJ Dave Matthias, Robin Eller, Phil Wagner, Hannah Bliss, and Chris Ready of Focusrite Novation Inc., Diana Cartwright, Tawny Kritzman, Dipak Patel, and Rich Harris of G-Technology, Terry Hardin from FXpansion, Lisa Kaufmann from Genelec, Inc., Hoerboard DJ Furniture, Konrad Zukowski of Kaotica Corp., Courtney Killian of DigitalDeck Covers, Scott Turner, Chris Unthank, and Rich Ellis from Larson Studios, Marcus Ryle and Sue Wolf from Line 6, Inc., Salo Loyo and Marlene Loyo, Victoria Kohlhorst from Magma, EveAnna Manley and Humberto Rodríguez from Manley Laboratories, Inc., Tom Kenny from Mix Magazine, Jim Cooper from MOTU, Inc., Fernando Curiel, and Gerardo Porraz from Músico Pro Magazine, Richard Mercado from Native Instruments North America, Inc., Phillip Zittell and David Holland from Omnirax Furniture Company, Gerry Bassermann from Propellerhead Software, Mark Ludmer from Que Audio Inc., Rose Mann-Cherney and Jason Carson from the Record Plant Recording Studios, Tom Hawley and Colin Courtney from Recording Magazine, Dave Hampton from Reftone, Sherry Klein; Anthony Davis, Piers Plaskitt, Fadi Hayek, William Maynard, George Horton, Fernando Guzman, and Max Noach from Solid State Logic, Mick Olesh from Waves, Inc.

Thanks to all of you!
Chilitos

Introduction

The digital audio age has brought us simplicity, accuracy, speed and effectiveness. Today's sound engineers, songwriters, producers and musicians have at their fingertips the ability to create their craft with optimal sound. Of course, knowledge, creativity and sagacity are also required. Now, let's suppose you find yourself alone in your studio, and in front of you are all the necessary elements to create a professional sound, with top professional audio equipment, music instruments and the most sophisticated music software. Then, you ask yourself, what do I do, now? How do I connect all this equipment, and how will I install the software? By this time, you probably have gone through some instructional manuals about your equipment and software, right? Maybe you've found yourself overwhelmed and confused. You've come to discover that instructional manuals sometimes don't explain in detail how to connect your audio interface with your MIDI devices, for example. My question to you is, does having instant access to all this equipment and software make us more efficient and better sounding engineers and producers? Does it make us more valuable and essential? Well, this is how the notion of publishing a book on connecting audio, video and MIDI equipment, like the one you are holding in your hands right now, came about. I wanted to help by making it easier to everyone who has difficulties connecting and understanding his or her own studio.

Technological advancement is a good thing. Every day we witness this process, but what happens when, as soon as we finally understand and learn how to use our "new" music/audio software and hardware, a new software version or hardware comes out in the market? This can be upsetting for many of us, but I think as long as we understand the basic concepts of audio, music, and computers, this should not be a problem. For example, a microphone will always be a microphone, and an audio interface will always be an audio interface, too. The shape or color may change, or maybe the number of inputs and outputs, but that is it. The fundamentals do not change. Because of the nature of this book, it will never be completely outdated, since its contents are based upon basic audio concepts, and not upon a particular software version or hardware model. So, this book should always be handy in any type of studio.

THE COMPLETE GUIDE TO CONNECTING AUDIO, VIDEO AND MIDI EQUIPMENT is divided into five sections or chapters.

The first chapter is dedicated to Home Studio setups, which deals with how to get the best of all the gear you've bought. You will learn how to connect the equipment with the proper cables, and make the proper software assignments so you can introduce audio in your system, and be able to record and mix your music.

The second section is titled Professional Studios, which focuses on the connection of the hardware and the installation of the software in a large-scale studio facility.

Chapter three comprises the Post Production Studios setup. As you may already know, there is a significant difference between a music production studio and a post-production studio. In this chapter, there are setups as simple as a small Podcast setup, to more sophisticated surround sound setups that include control workstations such as the D-Control and the S6 from Avid. Also, there are more complex setups that deal with the synchronization of different types of audio and video machines, including Avid's Satellite Link & Video Satellite LE. Here you will understand and learn how the use of these two options have changed the way of synchronizing digital audio and video.

In chapter four, we will study different studio setups used to produce the current trend of electronic music, often referred to as EDM (Electronic Dance Music).

Finally, chapter five deals with several DJ Studio setups. This particular chapter has inspired me because of the combination between the past and present in DJ Studios today. In other words, even though digital technology has brought the audio industry many changes, the DJing field still uses vinyl records used during the 50's, as well as CDs. I hope you enjoy this section as much as the other ones.

There is quite a bit of useful information in THE COMPLETE GUIDE TO CONNECTING AUDIO, VIDEO AND MIDI EQUIPMENT. Hopefully, you won't have any difficulties understanding and applying the concepts with all the photos and line diagrams included. Please enjoy the book and have a lot of fun connecting your equipment with confidence, and most importantly, creating great sounding music.

Chilitos Valenzuela
www.audiographintl.com

How to Use This Book

In the last twenty years of teaching audio in the United States and in Latin America, I have noticed that a great number of students are visual learners due to their constant use of smartphones, computers, and tablets. For this reason, I've made sure that the contents of THE COMPLETE GUIDE TO CONNECTING AUDIO, VIDEO AND MIDI EQUIPMENT were graphic-based. In this book, you will find a significant number of line diagrams and photographs that make it easier for you to understand the explanations in each studio setup. You will see that on the opposite page of each line diagram, there is a corresponding photograph for the exact audio device, computer, and instrument used in the diagram, including a photo of optional studio furniture to give an idea of what to purchase, and how to organize your equipment. The reason for adding the front panel image of the audio devices, computers, and instruments included on each line diagram was to give you ideas of what to purchase for your studio. Also, this would help you recognize the look of a specific device, instrument, or computer used in a particular studio setup. In addition, I have included these photographs so that a teacher or instructor can ask the student to practice connecting the equipment as an in-class assignment, or you can practice on your own in your studio or home.

Each studio setup in this book follows a certain order. First, you will find the equipment list used in each line diagram, followed by the cable list, and then the computer's system requirements needed to properly run the software used in the setup, whether it be a Macintosh or a PC computer. Also, there is an explanation of how to connect each device in the setup, and what specific type of cable is needed for these hardware connections. Furthermore, there is an explanation of how to setup the software or Digital Audio Workstation (DAW) you are using to introduce audio in your computer or recording device and record and playback what you create. It is important to mention that this book is not going to teach you how to use your software or devices; it will simply show you how to introduce an audio signal in your computer system or recording device.

The brands and models of all the equipment mentioned in this book are a result of a survey I did in a three-month period. In this survey, I asked many of the students I have trained in the last twenty years, from all over the world, what they currently use in their studio setups. Also, I asked them what were the most popular audio devices and software used in their respective countries, and this is how I decided to include the specific audio devices, computers, and instruments in this book. And of course, some of these devices I use in my own studio on a daily basis. Please feel free to acquire whatever equipment from a setup in this book that you think is the right one for you. That is what this book is all about, to help you make a decision to purchase the studio setup you have been dreaming about for a long time. Think of it like you are "window shopping," but with a book. :)

You will also find throughout the book blank pages titled "Notes," which can be used to make your own notes and practice redrawing the connection line diagrams learned in each section. You can also use it as a journal on how to connect your gear, adapt it to your own needs and/or create a layout of your own studio. Every great idea starts by imagining it. Why not sketch it? This will help to enhance your creativity and knowledge.

Finally, I have included a four-part Appendix at the end of the book. The first Appendix comprises the different types of cables and connectors used in this book. It shows the images of the cables and connectors used in each studio setup, as well as the name and description, so you can identify them in any situation. The second Appendix shows photographs of more optional studio furniture, and how equipment is placed and organized in them. The third Appendix shows pictures of audio interfaces as optional substitutions for some of the setup diagrams found in the book. The fourth Appendix is the Directory of all the manufacturers mentioned in this book. This Directory includes the manufacturer's address, phone number, and web address, in case you would like to contact them for more information about their product line.

I hope you enjoy this book and learn how to connect almost any studio setup.

Sincerely,

Chilitos

Home Studios 1

Photo courtesy of composer/keyboardist Salo Loyo

Nowadays, there is no excuse for not being able to produce good-sounding music demos in your bedroom. The cost of the equipment has come to the point that anybody who wants to create music can do it. The only limit is the user's imagination. With a music software, you can literally plug a set of headphones in your laptop and create your own music, using a MIDI keyboard controller and generate sounds out of virtual synthesizers. If you want to use a couple of microphones and effects to make your song sound a bit more sophisticated, you will need to purchase an audio interface to record your voice in the software you're using. And then, you will need help to interconnect all the devices you purchased and make them work properly.

For this reason, I have included in this first section, *Home Studio Setups*, which deals with how to get the best out of all the gear you bought. You will learn how to connect the equipment and make the proper assignments so you can record and mix your music. In this section, you will find setups ranging from the simplest setups to a medium size setups, and get an understanding of how they all get connected to function properly.

iPad Recording Studio

This is a very simple setup that can either be used as a home setup or as an on-the-go setup. It could be used to record a small ensemble of musicians consisting of guitarist, keyboard player, and vocalist.

In this setup we are using the Focusrite iTrack Dock audio interface. This audio interface supports sample rates up to 96kHz and a bit depth up to 24 bits. It has 2 analog inputs, 2 analog outputs, 1 headphones output and a MIDI input via a USB connector. We are also using a Novation Launchkey 25, which is a controller keyboard connected via a USB cable. Also, we are using an iPad 4th generation, because the iTrack Dock audio interface is connected via a Lightning connection, which was introduced with 4th generation iPads. It should be noted that the iTrack Dock audio interface is compatible with either the normal iPad or with the iPad mini.

Equipment List

- 1 – Focusrite iTrack Dock
- 1 – iPad 4th Generation or Later
- 1 – Novation Launchkey 25
- 1 – Microphone
- 1 – Electric Guitar
- 1 – Pair of Speaker Monitors
- 1 – Pair of Headphones

Cable List

- 1 – USB cable
- 2 – 1/4-inch TRS cables
- 1 – 1/4-inch TS cable
- 1 – XLR cable

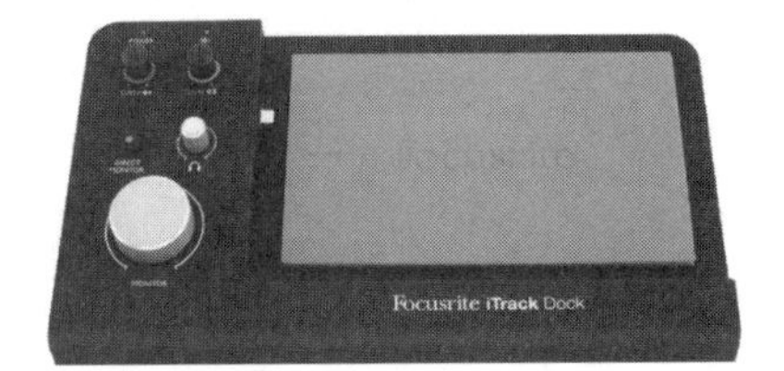

Optional furniture

iPad Recording Studio

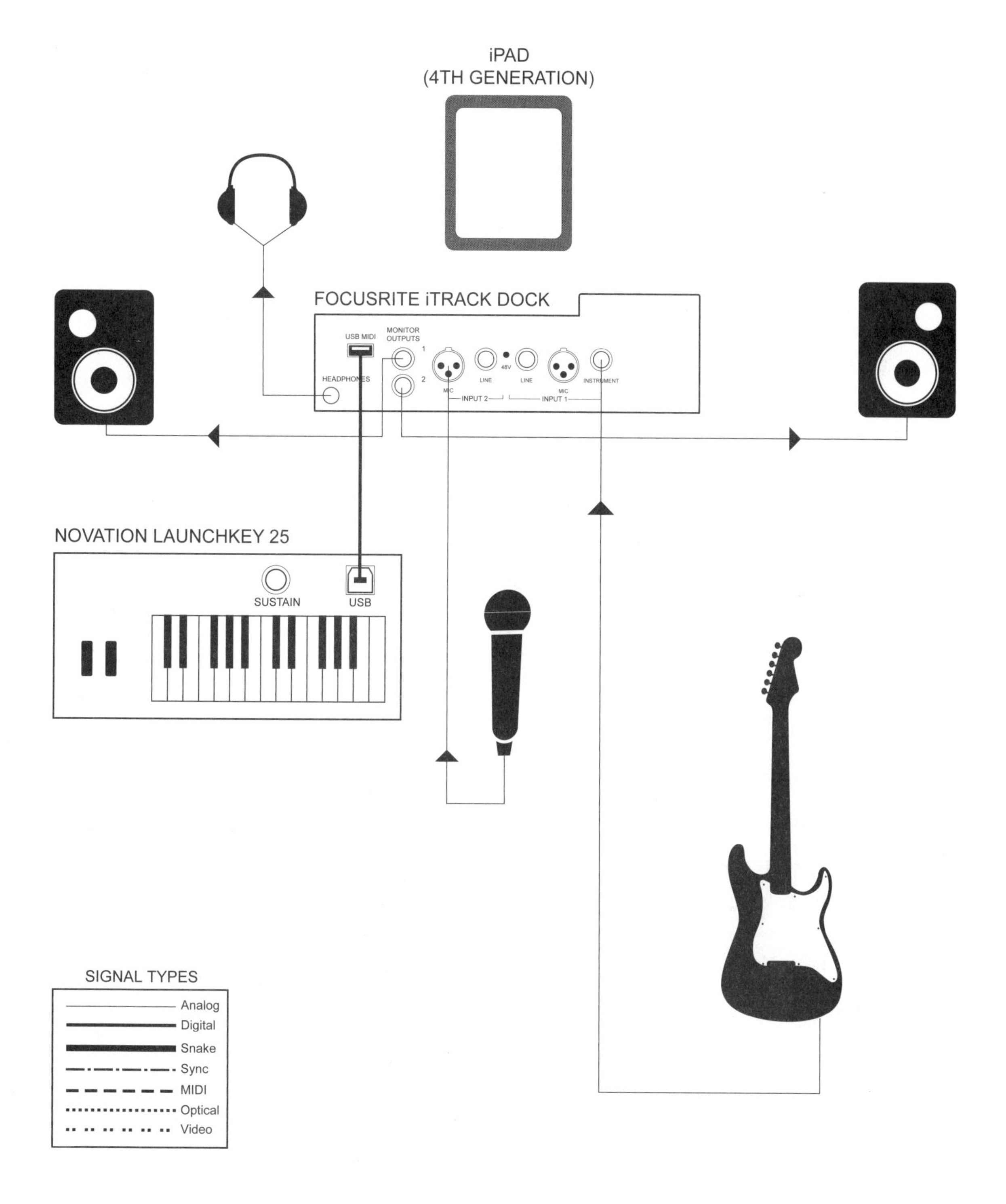

Hardware Connections

Now, let us go through the connections needed for this setup to work:

1. Connecting the iTrack Dock Audio Interface to an iPad 4th Generation

    - For this connection we do not have to use any kind of cable, the way to connect the iTrack Dock audio interface to the iPad is to mount the iPad directly on the iTrack Dock audio interface.

2. Connecting the Guitar to the iTrack Dock Audio Interface

    - Using a 1/4-inch TS cable, connect the output of the guitar to Input 1 of the iTrack Dock audio interface.

3. Connecting the Microphone to the iTrack Dock Audio Interface

    - Using an XLR cable, connect the output of the microphone to the Mic Input 2 of the iTrack Dock audio interface.

4. Connecting the Speaker Monitors and Headphones to the iTrack Dock Audio Interface

    - Using a 1/4-inch to XLR (or a 1/4-inch TRS to 1/4-inch TRS cable), connect Output 1 of the iTrack Dock audio interface to the Left speaker monitor.
    - Using another 1/4-inch to XLR (or a 1/4-inch TRS to 1/4-inch TRS cable), connect Output 2 of the iTrack Dock audio interface to the Right speaker monitor.
    - Connect the headphones to the headphone connector in the iTrack Dock audio interface.

5. Connecting the Novation Launchkey 25 to the iTrack Dock Audio Interface

    - Using a USB cable, connect the USB output of the Novation Launchkey 25 to the iTrack Dock audio interface USB MIDI connector.

System Requirements

GarageBand app for iOS:

- Requires iOS 7.0 or later
- Compatible with iPhone, iPad, and iPod touch

Software Setup

The Focusrite iTrack Dock audio interface works with any CoreAudio iPad app of your choice, for example: Auria, Cubasis, or GarageBand. In this example we are going to use the app, GarageBand, which is available for free in the Apple App Store. So make sure your iPad already has the app installed before starting.

Before launching the app, GarageBand, make sure your iPad is connected to the iTrack Dock audio interface. Once you have launched your app, let´s take a look at how we can get the desired signal.

- In this case we are going to record a small ensemble composed of guitar player, keyboard player, and vocalist.

Setting up iPad and GarageBand

- Once you have launched GarageBand, go to the control bar and touch the "View" button, this will change between the "Touch Instrument" view and the "Tracks" view. For this exercise, we want to work with the "Tracks" view.
- Once we are in the "Tracks" view we need to add 2 Audio Recorder tracks and a Keyboard track.

Assigning all the Audio Tracks in GarageBand

Now you just need to assign the desired outputs to the desired tracks. For example, we could assign Input 1 to Audio Recorder Track #1, Input 2 to Audio Recorder Track #2 and MIDI to the Keyboard track. Now we are ready to record. You can record altogether or separately as you see fit.

Mbox 3G MIDI Setups

This simple music production home studio setup is really powerful and useful for writing songs using a microphone and a guitar and/or to create demos in MIDI using a two-octave MIDI controller and the internal synthesizers in Pro Tools.

This specific setup consists of an Avid Mbox, a Mac Pro computer, an electric guitar, a condenser microphone, a two-octave MIDI controller, and a set of speaker monitors or a pair of headphones. Of course, you will also need a computer monitor, a mouse, and a keyboard, if you don't already have one of each. To avoid having to purchase an external computer monitor, a keyboard, and a mouse when buying a Mac Pro computer, you could just purchase a laptop computer. It all depends on what you already have at home, or not.

Depending on your budget, you have other options for audio interfaces, microphones, software for writing music, etc. Other options for a setup this simple could be: a Duet from Apogee Electronics, the Scarlett 2/2 by Focusrite, M-Audio M-Track, Behringer UFO202, PreSonus AudioBox, and MOTU UltraLite-mk3, among others. Other software packages include Logic, Digital Performer, GarageBand, Cubase, Ableton Live, Studio One, and Propellerhead Reason, among others. As I mentioned before, it all depends on your budget. For example, the cost of the audio interfaces I mentioned above is $500 or less, and the software can be around the same price.

Equipment List

- 1 – Avid Mbox 3G
- 1 – Apple Mac Pro Computer
- 1 – Electric Guitar
- 1 – AT 4050 Condenser Microphone
- 1 – Arturia Keylab 49 Hybrid Synthesizer
- 1 – Pair of Headphones
- 1 – G-Technology 500GB G-Drive Slim Hard Drive
- 1 – PACE USB Smart Key (iLok 2)

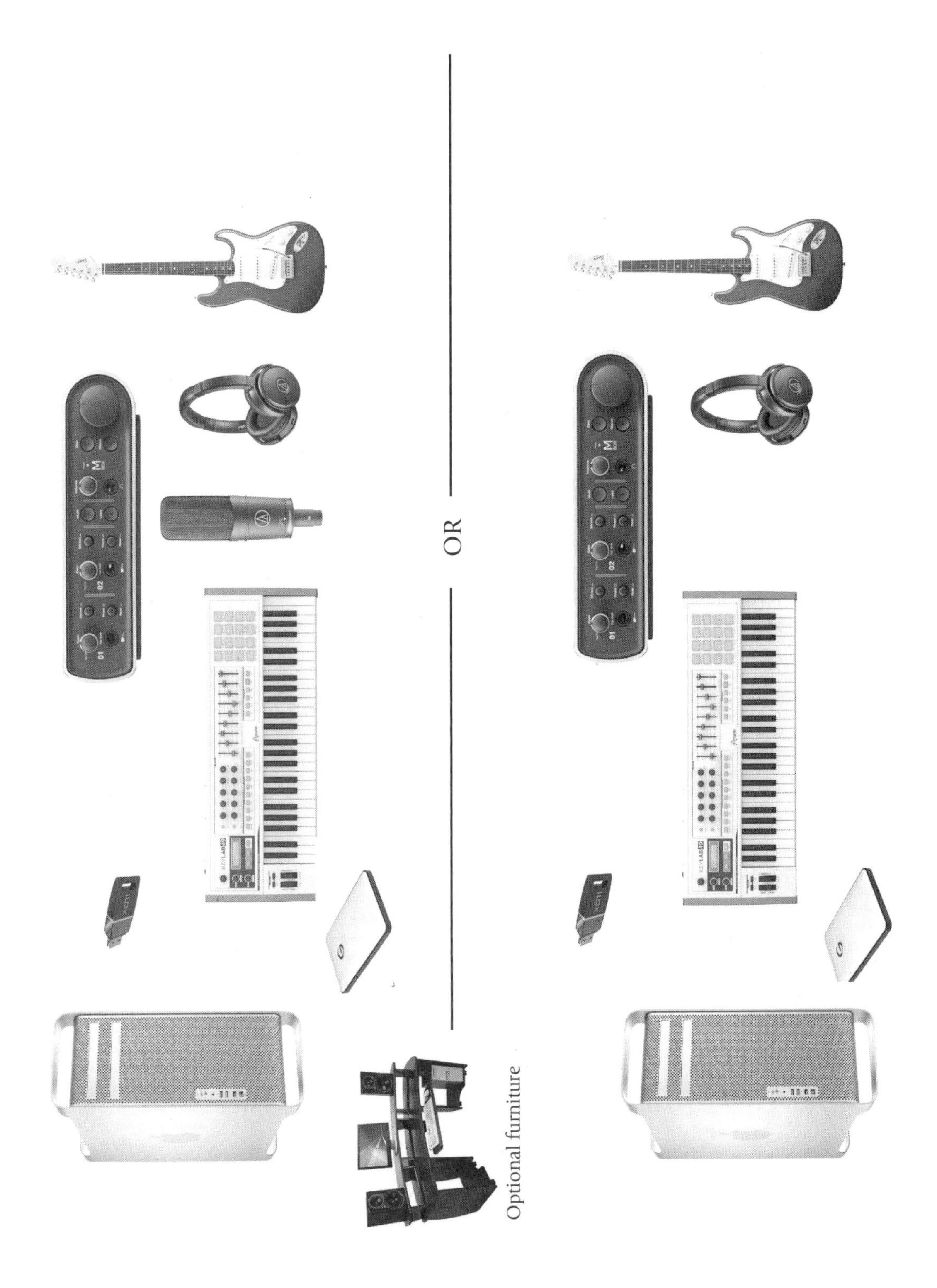
OR
Optional furniture

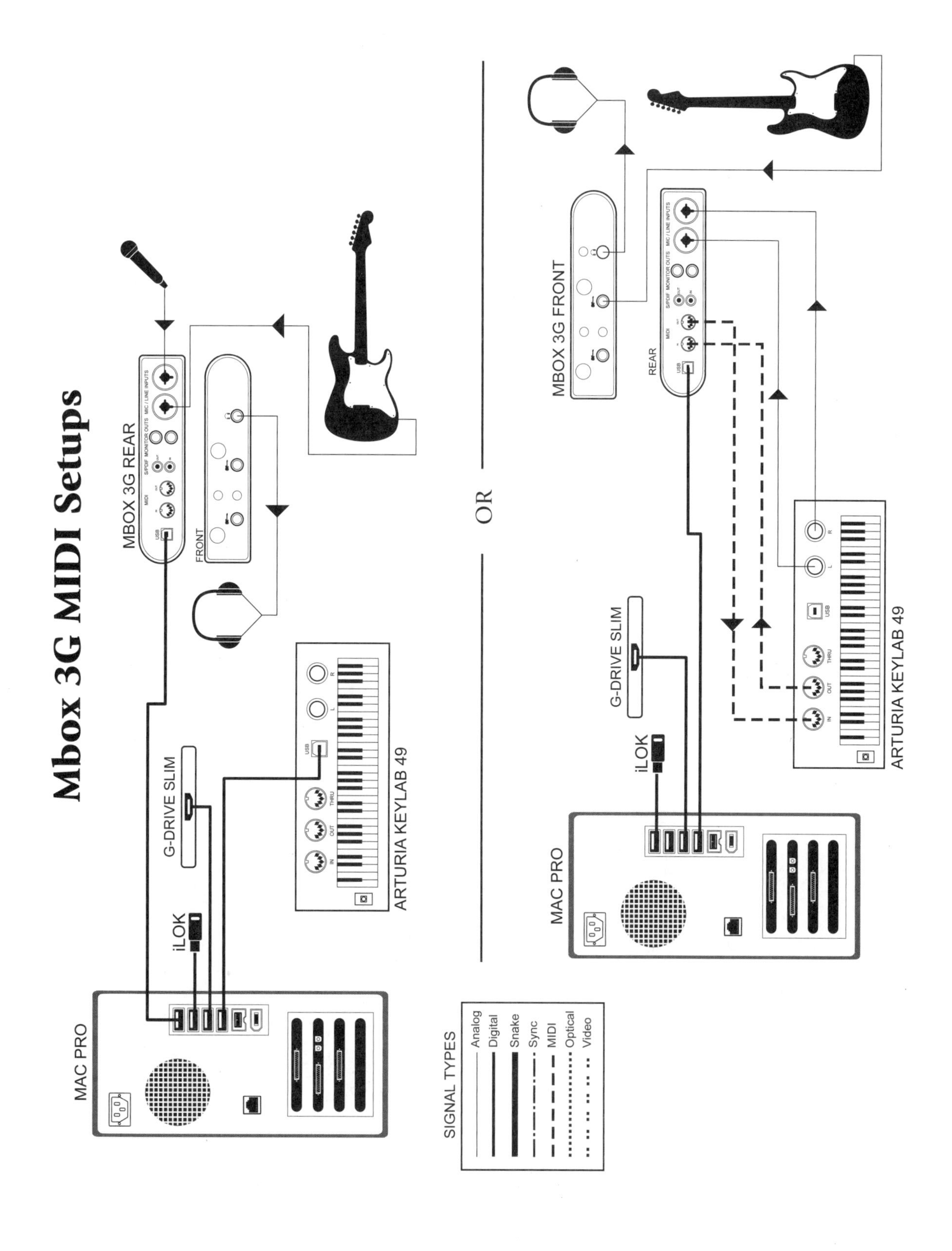
Mbox 3G MIDI Setups
MAC PRO
iLOK
G-DRIVE SLIM
MBOX 3G REAR
USB
MIDI
S/PDIF
MONITOR OUTS
MIC / LINE INPUTS
FRONT
ARTURIA KEYLAB 49
IN
OUT
THRU
USB
L
R
OR
SIGNAL TYPES
Analog
Digital
Snake
Sync
MIDI
Optical
Video
MAC PRO
iLOK
G-DRIVE SLIM
MBOX 3G FRONT
REAR
ARTURIA KEYLAB 49

Cable List

- 3 – USB cables
- 1 – XLR cable
- 1 – 1/4-inch TS cable (unbalanced)
- 1 – 1/4-inch TRS cables
- 2 – MIDI cables

Hardware Connections

1. Connecting the G-Drive Slim External Hard Drive to the System

    - Using a USB cable (depending on your computer), connect an available USB port on your Mac Pro computer to the USB port of the G-Drive Slim external hard drive.

2. Connecting the Mbox 3G to the Mac Pro Desktop Computer

    - Using a USB cable, connect the USB port on the Mbox 3G to an available USB port on the Mac Pro computer.

3. Connecting a Microphone to the Mbox 3G

    - Using an XLR cable, connect the output of the microphone to the "01 Mic/Line" input female XLR jack on the Mbox 3G.
    - When using a microphone on the Mbox 3G, don't forget to select the input source for either "Line" or "Mic" level using the "Front/Rear Source Selector" button on the front panel of the Mbox. When the button is pushed down, the rear panel Mic and balanced Line inputs are active. Notice that when you select the front Line input 1/4-inch jacks, you can plug in instruments (guitars, keyboards, bass) as well. If you do so, then connect a 1/4-inch TS plug. But if you choose to use the rear 1/4-inch concentric connectors (XLR/TRS combo), then connect a 1/4-inch TRS plug. Also, when using a microphone, don't forget to adjust the corresponding gain knob on the front panel. Refer to the Mbox 3G instructional manual for more information.

4. Connecting an Electric Guitar to the Mbox 3G

- Using a 1/4-inch TS cable, connect an electric guitar to the front panel Instrument input jack, or to the "01 Mic/Line" input jack on the Mbox 3G using a 1/4-inch TRS cable. Don't forget to select the corresponding source selection position using the front panel button of the Mbox 3G.

NOTE: If the device you are connecting to any of the inputs has unbalanced outputs (or you are using an unbalanced TS cable), set the line input switch to -10dBv. For balanced outputs (using balanced TRS cables), set the switch to +4dBu. Check on the device's reference guide of the devices you are using in the setups.

5. Connecting the Arturia KeyLab 49 to the Mbox 3G

- Using a MIDI cable, connect the "MIDI OUT" port of the Keylab 49 Hybrid Synth to the "MIDI IN" port of the Mbox audio interface.
- Using another MIDI cable, connect the "MIDI OUT " port of the Mbox audio interface to the "MIDI IN" port of the Keylab 49 Hybrid Synth.
- You want to make sure whether or not the MIDI controller keyboard you are using needs a driver software to be recognized by Pro Tools. If it does need a driver, then you must search by brand and model of the keyboard online for it, download it, and install it. Also, the Arturia Keylab 49 includes the Analog Lab software with an integrated user interface and over 5000 sounds from Arturia's V-Collection line of products. The nice thing about this keyboard is that it is more than a MIDI controller, it is an instrument as well.

6. Connecting Headphones to the Mbox 3G

- Connect the 1/4-inch TRS (stereo) connector of the headphone set to the "Headphone Output" jack on the front of the Mbox 3G. You don't necessarily need to connect a headphone set if you are already using the speaker monitors, it is your choice.

System Requirements

Mbox 3G for Mac OS X (as of this writing):

- Avid-qualified Mac running Mac OS X 10.6.8 or higher
- 4 GB RAM or more recommended
- 15 GB free hard disk space for Pro Tools installation
- Two available USB ports for Mbox and iLok 2 connections
- PACE USB Smart Key (iLok 2) (included, for software authorization)

Mbox 3G for Windows (as of this writing):

- Avid-qualified PC running Windows 7 Home Premium, Professional, or Ultimate (32- or 64-bit) – Service Pack 1
- 4 GB RAM or more recommended
- 15 GB free hard disk space for Pro Tools installation
- Two available USB ports for Mbox and iLok 2 connections
- PACE USB Smart Key (iLok 2) (included, for software authorization)

Software Setup

Assuming all the connections are done correctly and the Pro Tools software is installed properly, with the right Mbox driver and MIDI controller's driver, follow these next steps to configure your hardware in a Pro Tools session.

Setting up Pro Tools

Depending on which version of Pro Tools you are running, don't forget to keep your PACE USB Smart Key (iLok 2) connected in a USB port of your computer if you are running Pro Tools version 9 or higher.

- Once you have launched Pro Tools on your computer, go to the File menu and select "New Session" to create a new session. Let's assign the sample rate to 48 kHz, the Bit Depth to 24 bits, and the Audio File Type to BWF

(.WAV), which is Pro Tools' default audio file type. Once you have the session opened and ready, go to the Track menu and select "New" to create two Mono Audio tracks and one MIDI track, or Instrument track. One audio track for the electric guitar, another for the microphone, and the MIDI track for the MIDI keyboard.

- When working with MIDI, it is a good idea to configure your MIDI studio in Pro Tools. If using external synthesizers, samplers, or sound modules, this will be useful to configure because it will let you assign the model names and brands of your external devices so it will be easier for you to assign them in the Pro Tools Mix window. To accomplish this, go to the menu Setups > MIDI > MIDI Studio, the Audio MIDI Setup (AMS) application, will open. Then go to the Window menu in the AMS, and select the option "Show MIDI Window," the MIDI Setup window will appear. You will notice the MIDI interface you are currently using will be shown on your computer screen. Next, click on the "Add Device" button, a keyboard icon named "new external device" will show up in the window. Double click on it, and the "new external device properties" window appears prompting you to select the external keyboard manufacturer and model that is in your setup. Continue this process until you finish assigning all your external devices. Once you finish your setup, press the "Apply" button to execute the assignments. From now on, every time you create a MIDI or Instrument track in Pro Tools, a list of all the devices you created in the MIDI Studio Setup will show up on the list of inputs and outputs of the corresponding channel strip in the Mix window.
- If you are using only internal software synthesizers, then you don't need to configure the AMS since the name of the synths you are using will automatically be assigned.
- Go to Setups > Hardware Setup and assign the Ch 1-2 Input to Analog. Also, set the Word Clock Mode to "INTERNAL."

Assigning all the Audio Tracks in Pro Tools

Now, let's make the assignments of all the audio tracks you created for our two audio sources in our example:

- In Pro Tools, go to the Setups > I/O Setup menu, and press the "Default" button in the Input and Output tabs. This way, you will be able to see the default names of your inputs and outputs. You can give them different names if that is easier for you. You can also use the I/O Setup dialog window (Setup > I/O) to label the inputs and outputs you are using in Pro Tools and identify them as inserts or sends when working in a session. See the Pro Tools Reference Guide for details.

- Go to the Mix window and assign the inputs and outputs on your tracks, following these directions:

Track (mono)	Input	Inst/Source	Output
Audio track # 1	Analog 1	(Mic)	Analog 1-2
Audio track # 2	Analog 2	(Guitar)	Analog 1-2

- Record enable (arm) the tracks on your Pro Tools session, press the Record and then the Play buttons on the Transport window to start recording. You will notice the audio as waveforms as you are generating sound from either the microphone or the guitar as soon as you start playing or singing.

This concludes this exercise. Again, all the track assignments are arbitrarily chosen so you can understand and learn the process of a recording session. This is by no means the only way to do it, these scenarios are just to practice plugging in your home studio and setting up a session in Pro Tools with your Mbox. These concepts and steps can be applied to other audio interfaces and Digital Audio Workstation software programs. See Appendix C for more audio interface options.

Music Production Studio with a Digi 003+

The following setup line diagram is an example of a music production home studio or a small project studio where you could do an entire music production from the pre-production stage (writing or composing the music), to the production stage (recording, editing, mixing) and finally, to the post-production stage (mastering).

The equipment used in this diagram is only an example of what you might be able to connect to the Avid Digi 003+. It is only a suggestion, a guideline, since you may or may not have the Digi 003+ and all the equipment used in this setup. The process will be similar with other audio interfaces and different equipment.

In this setup, notice there is a modular digital recording machine, known as an ADAT, from Alesis. You might be wondering, what is the deal with this machine in this setup? Do I really need it? What is it for? Well, if you are a new generation engineer, composer, or musician, you may not appreciate the value of this device. There are so many applications in which you may take advantage of this digital recorder. The media used to record audio in this machine is S-VHS video tape.

In the '90s, the ADAT was used for music production all over the world. This machine revolutionized the music industry, and, by the way, I was part of the design group. Consequently, there are so many albums and CDs recorded in that decade. One of the advantages using an ADAT was the fact that the music or audio was kept in its pristine stage, in other words, the audio never deteriorated, and that was one of the reasons to use digital tape, as opposed to magnetic audio tape. Magnetic tape may get a warmer sound, of course, but that is a never-ending debate, so let's leave it alone, shall we?

One reason for having an ADAT machine handy in your studio is for doing digital audio transfers into your Digital Audio Workstation (DAW), whether it is Pro Tools, Logic, Cubase, or Digital Performer session. Maybe one day you will get a call from an artist or record company that wants to digitally remix an entire album that was recorded in the '90s, and to make it sound current using the new audio technology, for example.

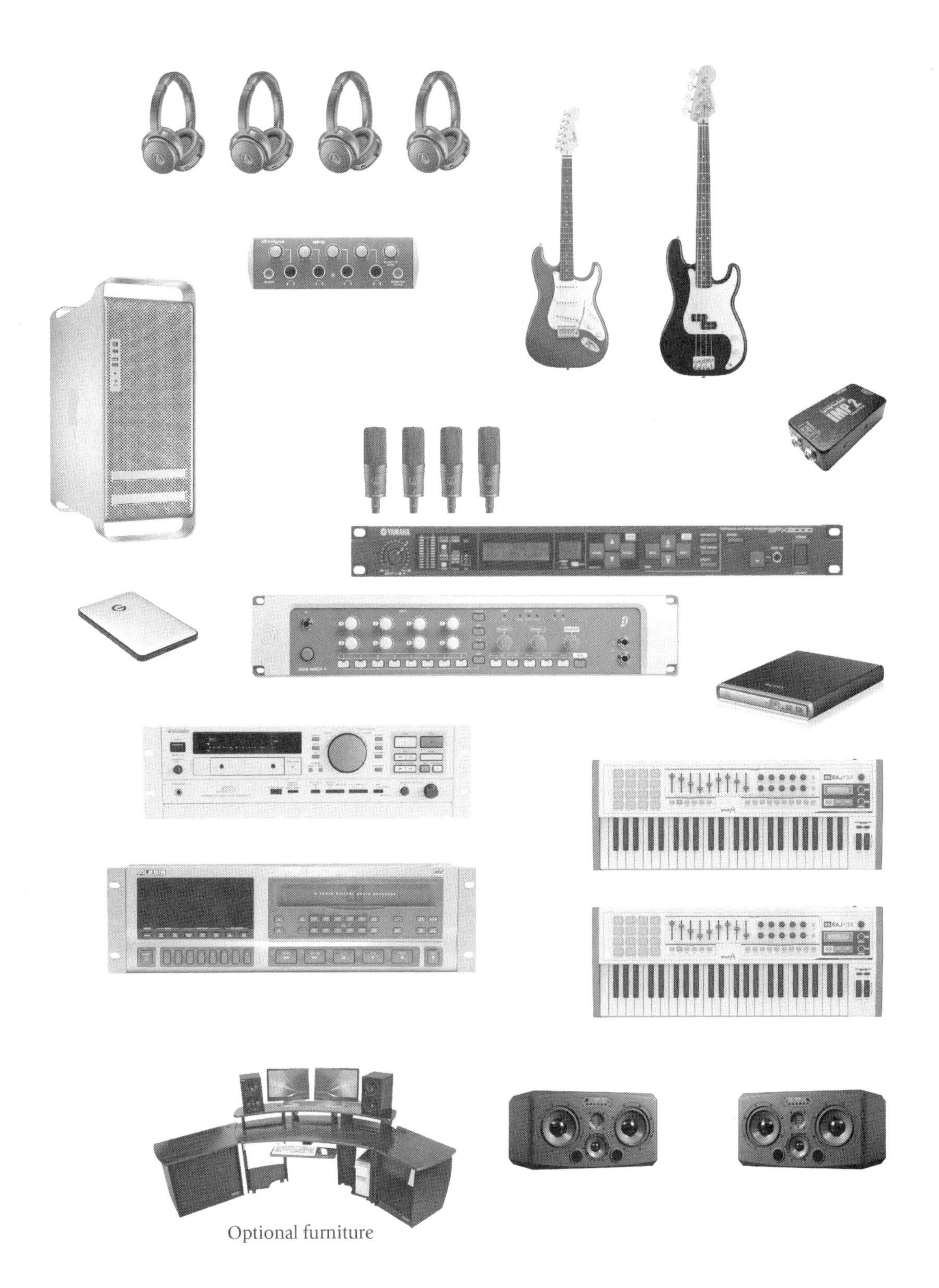

Optional furniture

Music Production Studio with a Digi 003+

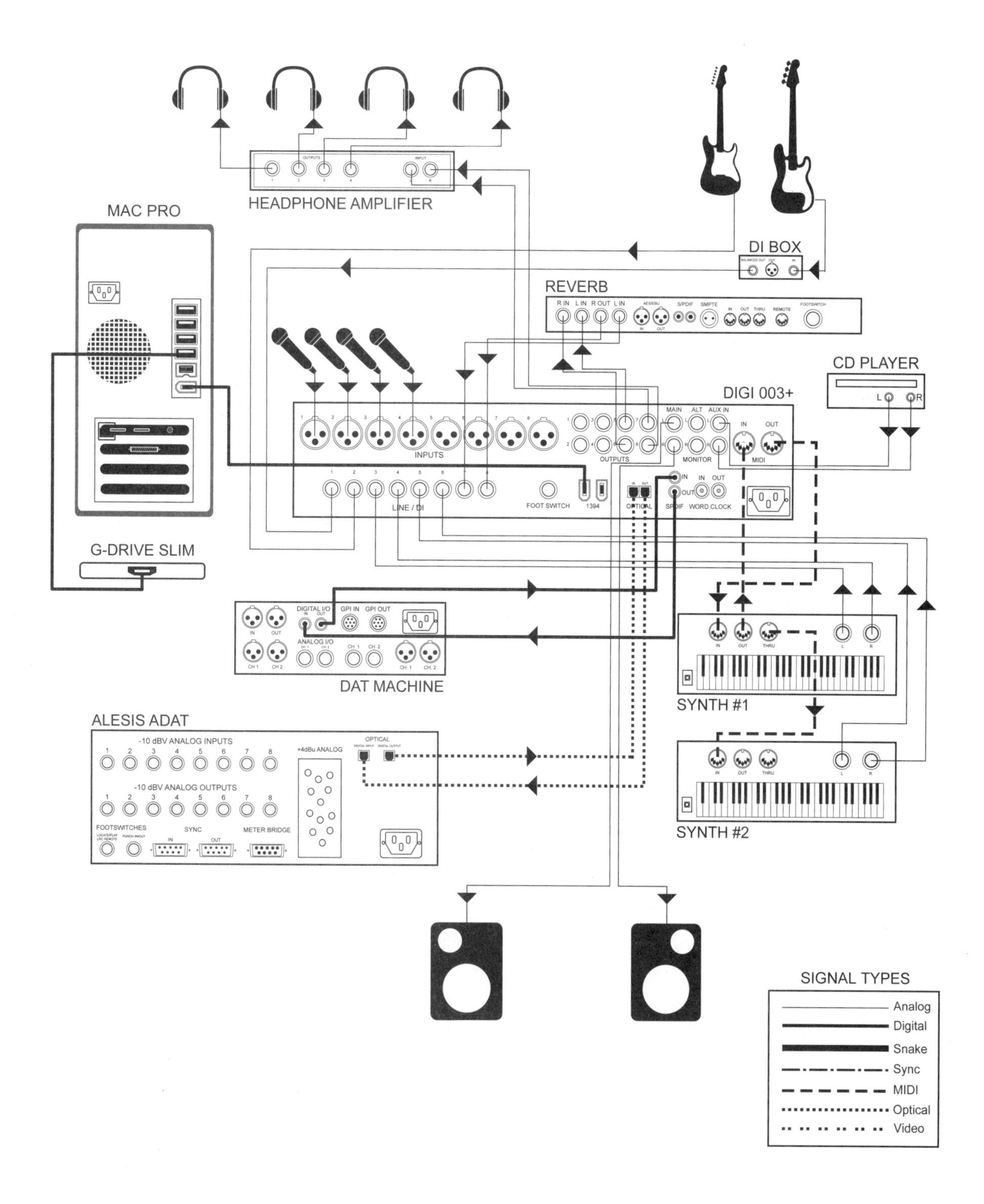

Another situation where you may want to keep an ADAT machine is to record up to sixteen instruments at the same time using the Digi 003+. You may not know this, but your Digi 003+ is capable of accepting up to eighteen channels simultaneously, did you know that? So by having an ADAT in this setup, you can connect eight different audio signals, whether they are line or mic signals. These extra eight signals travel through an optical cable with Toslink connectors (optical connectors) from your ADAT to your Digi 003+. In other words, the cable is used as a digital audio bridge using the audio-to-digital converters in the ADAT. This digital audio transfer format is known as "Lightpipe" in the audio industry. This format is still widely used in some new digital audio devices to carry eight discrete signals via an optical cable.

Continuing with our setup, notice a DAT (Digital Audio Tape) machine is also connected to the Digi 003+ via the digital audio transfer format known as S/PDIF (Sony/Phillips Digital Interface Format). By the way, this digital audio transfer format needs a 75-ohms impedance (Z) type of cable to perform the transfer correctly. Again, this two-track digital recording machine was used in the '90s, continues to be used as a "safety" or backup for your final mixes to keep a copy of it in a safe place. You could also use the connectors to plug the CD recorder or player.

Furthermore, this music production home studio includes an external reverb unit to send your signals via an internal or output bus, or via a hardware insert from your DAW. Also, four microphones and a DI box (Direct Box) are connected in order to record an electric guitar or bass guitar in your session. Also, this setup shows the ability to record MIDI via hardware synthesizers at the same time that you are recording acoustic and electric instruments.

Finally, notice a headphone or cue amplifier is used so the artist and musicians can listen to themselves while recording. And of course, you have your speaker monitors where they can be located in your control room, in your garage, or extra bedroom in your home.

As you can see, this is a complete music production home or project studio where you can create serious sounding music. Now let's take a look at the steps of how you connect this equipment to work together in a recording session:

Equipment List

- 1 – Avid Digi 003+
- 1 – Apple Mac Pro Desktop Computer
- 1 – G-Technology 500GB G-Drive Slim USB 3.0 External Hard Drive

- 1 – Alesis ADAT Modular Digital Recording Machine
- 1 – External Reverb Unit
- 4 – Microphones
- 1 – Direct Box (DI)
- 1 – Electric Guitar/Electric Bass guitar
- 2 – Hardware Synthesizers
- 4 – Headphones
- 1 – Headphone Amplifier
- 1 – Pair of ADAM 3SX-H Speaker Monitors
- 1 – DAT Machine
- 1 – CD Player

Cable List

- 1 – FireWire 400 (or FW 400 to FW 800) cable
- 2 – RCA to 1/4-inch TRS cables
- 2 – RCA 75-ohms cables
- 2 – Toslink (Optical) cables
- 6 – 1/4-inch TRS cables
- 6 – 1/4-inch TS cables (unbalanced)
- 3 – MIDI cables
- 3 – XLR to 1/4-inch TRS cables
- 4 – XLR cables
- 1 – USB cable

Hardware Connections

1. Connecting a G-Technology 500GB G-Drive Slim USB External Hard Drive to the System

    - Using a USB cable, connect an available USB port on your computer to the USB port on your external G-Technology G-Drive Slim external hard drive.

2. Connecting the Apple Mac Pro Desktop Computer to the Digi 003+

    - Using a FireWire 400 cable, connect it to one of the FireWire 1394 port on the rear panel of the Digi 003+ to an available FireWire port located in the back of the computer. If your computer only has FireWire 800 or Thunderbolt connectors, then you will need to use the proper adapter or converter.

3. Connecting the CD Player Analog Outputs to the Digi 003+

    - Using an RCA male connector to a 1/4-inch TRS male connector cable, plug the "ANALOG OUT L" (for the left channel) of the CD player to the "AUX INPUT L" of the Digi 003+.

    - Using another RCA male connector to a 1/4-inch TRS male connector cable, connect the "ANALOG OUT R" (for the right channel) of the CD player to the "AUX INPUT R" of the Digi 003+.

4. Connecting a DAT Machine to the Digital I/O of the Digi 003+

    - Using an RCA 75-ohms Male to Male cable (an RCA cable with gold plated connectors), connect the "DIGITAL I/O IN" of the DAT machine to the "S/PDIF OUT" of the Digi 003+.

    - Using another RCA 75-ohms Male to Male cable, connect the "DIGITAL I/O OUT" of the DAT machine to the "S/PDIF IN" of the Digi 003+.

5. Connecting the ADAT Modular Digital Recording Machine to the Digi 003+

    - Using a cable with Toslink connectors (optical), plug the "OPTICAL OUT" of the ADAT to the "OPTICAL IN" on the Digi 003+.

    - Using another cable with Toslink connectors (optical), plug the "OPTICAL IN" of the ADAT to the "OPTICAL OUT" on the Digi 003+.

6. Connecting a Headphone (Cue) Amplifier to the Digi 003+

- Using a 1/4-inch TRS cable, connect "OUTPUT 7" of the Digi 003+ to the "IN L" (left) jack on the headphone amplifier.
- Using a second 1/4-inch TRS cable, connect "OUTPUT 8" of the Digi 003+ to the "IN R" (right) jack on the headphone amplifier.
- Connect as many headphones as you need in the headphone amplifier.

7. Connecting the External Synthesizers to the Digi 003+

- Using a 1/4-inch TS cable, connect the "OUTPUT L" jack of Synth #1 to "INPUT 3" on the Digi 003+.
- Using another 1/4-inch TS cable, connect the "OUTPUT R" of Synth #1 to "INPUT 4" on the Digi 003+.
- Using a MIDI cable (cable with two 5-pin DIN connectors) connect the "MIDI OUT" on Synth #1 to the "MIDI IN" jack on the Digi 003+.
- Using another MIDI cable, connect the "MIDI IN" jack on Synth #1 to the "MIDI OUT 1" jack on the Digi 003+.
- Using a 1/4-inch TS cable, connect the "OUTPUT L" of Synth #2 to the "LINE 5" jack on the Digi 003+.
- Using another 1/4-inch TS cable, connect the "OUTPUT R"of Synth #2 to the "LINE 6" jack on the Digi 003+.
- Using a MIDI cable, connect the "MIDI THRU" on Synth #1 to the "MIDI IN" on Synth #2.

NOTE: *Use analog inputs 5 to 8 if you need to select a "–10 dBV" (for unbalanced signal), or "+4 dBu" (for balanced signals) operating level for your keyboards. Or, use DI Inputs 1–4 if analog inputs 5 to 8 are not available, or if you do not need to set any operating levels. The DI inputs 1 to 4 are available even if a Microphone is connected to the Mic inputs 1 to 4, just remember, both inputs cannot be active at the same time.*

8. Connecting a Bass Guitar to an External Direct Box (DI)

   - Using a 1/4-inch TS cable, connect the bass guitar to the "LINE IN" of the external Direct Nox.

9. Connecting an External Direct Box to the Digi 003+

   - Using an XLR to 1/4-inch TRS cable, connect the "BALANCED OUT" jack on the Direct box to the "MIC/DI 1" on the Digi 003+. You will need to use the proper adapters for this connection.

10. Connecting an Electric Guitar to the Digi 003+

    - Using a 1/4-inch TS cable, connect the electric guitar to the "MIC/DI 2" input on the Digi 003+.

NOTE: *The XLR connectors on Inputs 1 to 4 of the Digi 003+ are wired specifically to match the impedance of microphones. Do not use these XLR connectors for line inputs; use the 1/4-inch connectors instead.*

11. Connecting 4 Microphones to the Digi 003+

    - Using three XLR-Male to XLR-Female cables, make the following connections:
    - The first microphone to the "MIC/DI 1".
    - The second microphone to the "MIC/DI 2".
    - The third microphone to the "MIC/DI 3".
    - The fourth microphone to the "MIC/DI 4".

NOTE: *Notice the electric guitar and the first microphone are connected to the "MIC/DI 2" of the Digi 003+ at the same time, the mic on the XLR jack, and the guitar on the 1/4-inch jack. When you have this situation, don't forget to press the Mic/DI switch located on the top panel of the Digi 003+ to select the corresponding signal input, so when you are using the electric guitar on the second DI input, you need to press the MIC/DI button until it is lit, meaning that it is in the DI position. If it is unlit, then it will mean that it is in the MIC position. The DI 1 to 4 inputs are balanced inputs. If you connect a 1/4-inch TS or unbalanced connector such an unbalanced guitar connector (phono plug), it will just short the negative signal side of the unbalanced connector to ground.*

Also, remember to turn on the phantom power (+48V) for any condenser microphone you are using. Dynamic microphones do not require phantom power. Furthermore, although phantom power can be used safely with most microphones, ribbon microphones can be damaged by it. Advice from Avid: always turn off the phantom power and wait at least 30 seconds before connecting a ribbon microphone.

12. Connecting an External Reverb Unit to the Digi 003+

    - Using a 1/4-inch TRS cable, connect the "OUTPUT 5" jack on the Digi 003+ to "L IN" on the reverb unit.
    - Using another a 1/4-inch TRS cable, connect the "OUTPUT 6" jack on the Digi 003+ to "R IN" on the reverb unit.
    - Using yet another ¼-inch TRS cable, connect "INPUT 7" on the Digi 003+ to the "L OUT" jack on the reverb unit.
    - Using one last 1/4-inch TRS cable, connect "INPUT 8" on the Digi 003+ to the "R OUT" jack on the reverb unit.

13. Connecting the ADAM 3SX-H Speaker Monitors to the Digi 003+

    - Using a 1/4-inch TRS cable, connect the "MONITOR OUT R" on the Digi 003+ to the right speaker.
    - Using another 1/4-inch TRS cable, connect "MONITOR OUT L" on the Digi 003+ to the left speaker.

NOTE: *All inputs and outputs of the Digi 003+ are balanced lines, which means that you need to use 1/4-inch TRS connectors. Be aware of this in case of undesirable noise. Consult the reference manuals of your devices to make sure you are using the proper balanced/unbalanced connectors.*

System Requirements

Pro Tools 11 for Mac (as of this writing):

- Avid-qualified Apple computer
- 4 GB RAM or more, 8GB or more is recommended
- 15 GB minimum free hard disk space
- Mac OS X 10.8 or later
- Monitor with at least 1024 x 768 resolution
- One or more Hard Disk Drives dedicated for audio recording and playback
- USB 2.0 port available to connect the PACE USB Smart Key (iLok 2)

Pro Tools 11 for Windows (as of this writing):

- Avid-qualified Windows-based computer
- 4 GB RAM or more, 8GB or more is recommended
- 15 GB minimum free hard disk space
- Windows 7 Home Premium, Professional or Ultimate only with Service Pack 1, Windows 8 Standard or Pro edition
- Requires 64-bit Windows operating system
- Monitor with at least 1024 x 768 resolution
- One or more Hard Disk Drives dedicated for audio recording and playback\
- USB 2.0 port available to connect the PACE USB Smart Key (iLok 2)

NOTE: PACE USB Smart Key (iLok 2) with valid license is required for Pro Tools 11 to work, without it Pro Tools will not launch.

Software Setup

In this particular example, we will be using Pro Tools as our DAW. Regardless of what version of Pro Tools you are using, you should already have installed the software and other files required to run Pro Tools properly. Also, it is very important that you check which operating system is installed in your computer, whether you are using a Macintosh (Mac OS X) or a PC running on Windows. If you are not sure you have the proper software versions for both your computer system and Pro Tools, or any other digital device you are using in your setup, such as MIDI controllers, audio interfaces, etc., then check the compatibility information on the software versions you are running in the respective websites of the company's devices you are using. For example, if you are using Pro Tools, then you can visit www.avid.com to check on the latest compatibility information.

Getting back to our setup, assuming all the connections are done properly, let's take a look at how we can get a specific signal, such as an electric guitar signal in your Pro Tools session and what kind of software settings and assignments have to be made to accomplish this process. The software settings may vary depending on your Pro Tools software version.

- Keep in mind that having all the equipment displayed in this particular line diagram connected does not mean you will record or use everything at the same time. For example, you can either use DI #2 or Mic #2, but cannot use both at the same time since is not possible (it has to be either or). The same applies for DI #3 or Mic #3 and for DI #4 or Mic #4, according to our diagram at the beginning of this setup.
- Now, let's assume that we are going to record a rhythm section using all the MIDI equipment, Bass on DI 1 input, Guitar and Synth #2 on inputs DI 2 to 4, Master Synth #1 on Inputs 3 and 4, Drum Loop from the CD on the ALT input, and the ADAT (drums previously recorded in another studio). We will record all this in Pro Tools first, then we will use the Mic Inputs 1 to 4 to record voices and Inputs 7 and 8 will be used as the returns from the reverb unit. Finally, we will transfer the recording into the DAT machine.

Setting up Pro Tools

To accomplish everything I mentioned above, let's make all the assignments now in the Pro Tools software:

- Once you have launched Pro Tools in your computer, go to the File menu and select "New Session" to create a new session. Let's assign the sample rate to 48 kHz, since we are digitally transferring the drums from the ADAT tape. The Bit Depth set it at 16 bits again, this is because the ADAT's bit resolution is 16 bits in this example, even though we could have used the 20-bit version. Also, set the Audio File Type to BWF (.WAV) which is Pro Tools default audio file type. Once you have the session open and ready, go to the Track menu and select "New" to create 16 Mono Audio tracks and one MIDI track, or Instrument track. You can also create 12 Mono Audio tracks, 2 Stereo Audio tracks and 1 MIDI or Instrument track, just to practice using different types of tracks.

- When working with MIDI, it is a good idea to configure your MIDI studio in Pro Tools. This will be useful because it will let you assign the model names and brands of your external synthesizers and samplers so it will be easier for you to assign them in the Pro Tools Mix window. To accomplish this, go to the menu Setups > MIDI > MIDI Studio, and the Audio MIDI Setup (AMS) application will open. Then go to the Window menu in the AMS and select the option Show MIDI Window, the MIDI Setup window will appear. You will notice the MIDI interface you are currently using will be shown on your computer screen. Next, click on the "Add Device" button, and a keyboard icon named "new external device" will show up in the window. Double click on it, and the "new external device properties" window will appear prompting you to select the external keyboard manufacturer and model that is in your setup. Continue this process until you finish assigning all your external devices. Once you finish your setup, press the "Apply" button to execute the assignments. From now on, every time you create a MIDI or Instrument track in Pro Tools, a list of all the devices you created in the MIDI Studio Setup will show up in the list of inputs and outputs of the corresponding channel strip in the Mix window.

Setting up the Digital Inputs and Outs in Pro Tools

Since we are using a Digital Audio Tape (DAT) machine in our setup to record and keep a digital "safety" copy of the final mix in the DAT machine after finishing the project, then it is time to make the proper settings in Pro Tools to accept digital audio. Since the Digi 003+ can accept RCA S/PDIF, Optical S/PDIF, and ADAT Lightpipe digital audio transfer formats, we need to make sure that they are assigned properly. Follow the next steps to accomplish this:

- Go to the menu Setups > Hardware Setup and assign the Digital Input to "RCA = S/PDIF" to accept digital audio data from the DAT machine. Also, set the OPTICAL option to ADAT (not to S/PDIF optical) to accept digital audio information via "Lightpipe" from the ADAT modular recorder.

- Since we are using external digital devices, it is important to set the proper clock reference in Pro Tools for a successful digital audio transfer.

The Digi 003+ provides two BNC connectors to plug a 75-ohm cable for the Word Clock In and another BNC cable for the Word Clock Out jack on the back panel. We need the proper word clock signal to synchronize, or "clock" Pro Tools and the Digi 003+ to the industry standard Word Clock. Word clock is used to synchronize a wide range of digital devices, such as non-linear video systems and other types of equipment typically found in professional audio facilities.

So make sure to set the right word clock setting when doing a digital audio transfer. Also, make sure all connections are correct between the Digi 003+ and the external devices we are using in our setup. Since the ADAT and DAT machine don't have physical Word Clock connectors like the Digi 003+, then, we have to assign the correct Word Clock setting in Pro Tools via the Setup > Hardware menu.

> *NOTE: You always have to be sure to match the sample rate setting of the Pro Tools session, as well as to verify the termination requirements and other internal settings for the device; see the manufacturer's documentation if you need more information on the particular requirements for your other equipment.*

When finishing setting up the proper digital inputs and Word Clock reference in Pro Tools, it is then time to do the digital audio transfer from ADAT first to record all the drums in our project into Pro Tools. Once the final mix is completed, send it then to the DAT machine to keep a safe copy of it.

Assigning all the Audio Tracks in Pro Tools

Now, let's make the assignments of all the audio tracks you created for our different audio sources in our example:

- In Pro Tools, go to the Setups > I/O Setup menu, and press the "Default" button in the Input and Output tabs. This way, you will be able to see the default names of your inputs and outputs. You can give them different names if that is easier for you. You can also use the I/O Setup dialog window (Setup > I/O) to label the inputs and outputs you are using in Pro Tools and identify them as inserts or sends when working in a session. See the Pro Tools Reference Guide for details.

- Also in Pro Tools, go to the Mix window and assign the inputs and outputs on the audio tracks you created earlier. If it makes it easier for you, follow the next table:

Track (mono)	Input	Inst/Source	Output
Audio track # 1	Analog 1	(Bass)	Analog 1-2
Audio track # 2	Analog 2	(Electric Guitar)	Analog 1-2
Audio track # 3	Analog 3	(Synth #1 L)	Analog 1-2
Audio track # 4	Analog 4	(Synth #1 R)	Analog 1-2
Audio track # 5	Analog 5	(Synth #2 L)	Analog 1-2
Audio track # 6	Analog 6	(Synth #2 R)	Analog 1-2
Audio track # 7	Analog 7	(CD Player L)	Analog 1-2
Audio track # 8	Analog 8	(CD Player R)	Analog 1-2
Audio track # 9-16	ADAT 1-8	(Drum Set)	Analog 1-2
MIDI track # 1	MIDI 1	(Synthesizers)	MIDI OUT *

NOTE: You can select any MIDI channel number for your synths.

- If you choose to use 2 Stereo tracks instead of 4 Mono tracks for the synthesizers, assign Input Analog 3-4 to one of them, and Input Analog 5-6 to the other.

- Remember to set the format for Inputs 1-4 on your Digi 003+ to their corresponding status, set the levels for the analog inputs, and remember to press the "Aux IN 7/8" button on the front of the Digi 003+.

- In your Pro Tools session, record enable (arm) the tracks you are going to record first. For example, you can record enable audio tracks 9-16 to record the drums coming from the ADAT machine, according to our setup example. Then press the Record and then the Play buttons on the Transport window, and press Play on your ADAT. After finishing recording the drums, disable the Record Enable button on audio tracks 9-16. Next, record enable track #1 to record the Bass guitar, and so on until you finish recording your instruments. If you have several musicians playing at the same time, then record enable all the tracks you need to record the instruments at the same time.

Continuing with our example, let's set four audio tracks to record the voices using the four mics we connected in our setup earlier. We are also going to set up an Aux Input track to use it as the return track for the reverb unit so the singers can have a little bit of reverberation in their headphones.

Follow the next steps:

- Create 4 Mono Audio Tracks. They will appear as Audio 17, 18 19 and 20.
- Create a Stereo Aux Input track.
- Go to the Mix window and assign the inputs/outputs as follows:

Track	Input	Inst/Source	Output
Audio track # 17	Analog 1	(Mic 1)	Analog 1-2
Audio track # 18	Analog 2	(Mic 2)	Analog 1-2
Audio track # 19	Analog 3	(Mic 3)	Analog 1-2
Audio track # 20	Analog 4	(Mic 4)	Analog 1-2
Stereo Aux Input	Analog 7-8	(Reverb)	Analog 1-2

- Next, assign a send on all the tracks and set their outputs to "Analog 7-8." This would be the mix sent to the Headphone amplifier so the musicians and singers can hear themselves.
- On tracks 17, 18, 19 and 20 (or on the tracks you want to have the Reverb effect), assign a second Send and set its output to Interface "Analog 5-6," so the voices can be routed to the reverb unit. The reverb return will be inputs "Analog 7-8" already set in the Stereo Aux Input track. Don't forget to label your tracks so it will be easier to identify them.
- Remember to set the format for Inputs 1-4 on your Digi 003+ to their corresponding status, that is, changed from DI to Mic, to let the microphone signal in. Set the preamp levels for the analog inputs, and remember to disable the "Aux Input to Ch 7-8" button on the front of the Digi 003+; otherwise, instead of having the return of the Reverb, you will have the CD Player again on the Stereo Aux Input track and you will not hear any Reverb at all.

- Record enable only tracks 17, 18, 19 and 20 in your Pro Tools session; press the Record button and then the Play button on the Transport window. Now the singers can sing along with the music and record it.

Sending all recorded and mixed tracks into the DAT machine

- Go to the Setups > Hardware Setup menu and assign the Digital Input to "RCA = S/PDIF, OPTICAL = ADAT." Set the Clock Source to RCA (S/PDIF).
- Create a Stereo Master Fader track. Set the Master Fader to the automation mode "auto write." While playing the mix, start moving down slowly the fader of the Master Fader track to make a nice and smooth fade out to the end of the song.
- Go to the Mix window and assign the Output of the Master Fader track from "Analog 1-2" to S/PDIF L-R (Stereo). This will send the mix to the DAT machine via S/PDIF.
- Enable the REC button on your DAT Machine, and then press the Play button on the transport window in Pro Tools to start digitally transferring your final mix to the DAT machine.

This concludes this exercise. Again, all the track assignments are arbitrarily chosen so you can understand and learn the process of a recording session. This is by no means the only way to do it, these scenarios are meant to practice plugging in your home studio and setting up a session in Pro Tools with your Digi 003+. These concepts and steps apply to other audio interfaces and Digital Audio Workstations. See Appendix C for more audio interface options.

Simple Music Production Studio

This is a simple setup that can be either used as a home studio or as an "on the go" setup. It could be used by a solo artist singing and playing keyboard. We are using the Focusrite Scarlett 2i4 audio interface, this is a USB 2.0 audio interface that supports sample rates up to 96kHz and a Bit Depth up to 24 bits. It has 2 analog inputs with microphone preamplifiers included, 4 analog outputs, two of which can be either balanced or unbalanced and the other two are unbalanced, and one headphone output and MIDI in and out.

We are also using a MIDI keyboard controller, which is connected to the Scarlett 2i4 via USB to the computer. In this example we are using an Apple MacBook Pro, and a foam on top of the microphone known as the EyeBall by Kaotica Corp. (www.kaoticaeyeball.com). This foam is sort of a "mobile studio" whether you work from home, or go on the road, you can take it with you, and simply put it over your microphone. It also includes a pop filter to avoid those annoying explosive words.

Equipment List

- 1 – Focusrite Scarlett 2i4 Audio Interface
- 1 – Apple MacBook Pro
- 1 – MIDI Keyboard Controller
- 1 – AT 4050 Condenser Microphone
- 1 – Kaotica EyeBall
- 1 – Pair of Speaker Monitors
- 1 – Pair of Headphones
- 1 – PACE USB Smart Key (iLok 2)

Cable List

- 1 – XLR cable

Optional furniture

Simple Music Production Studio

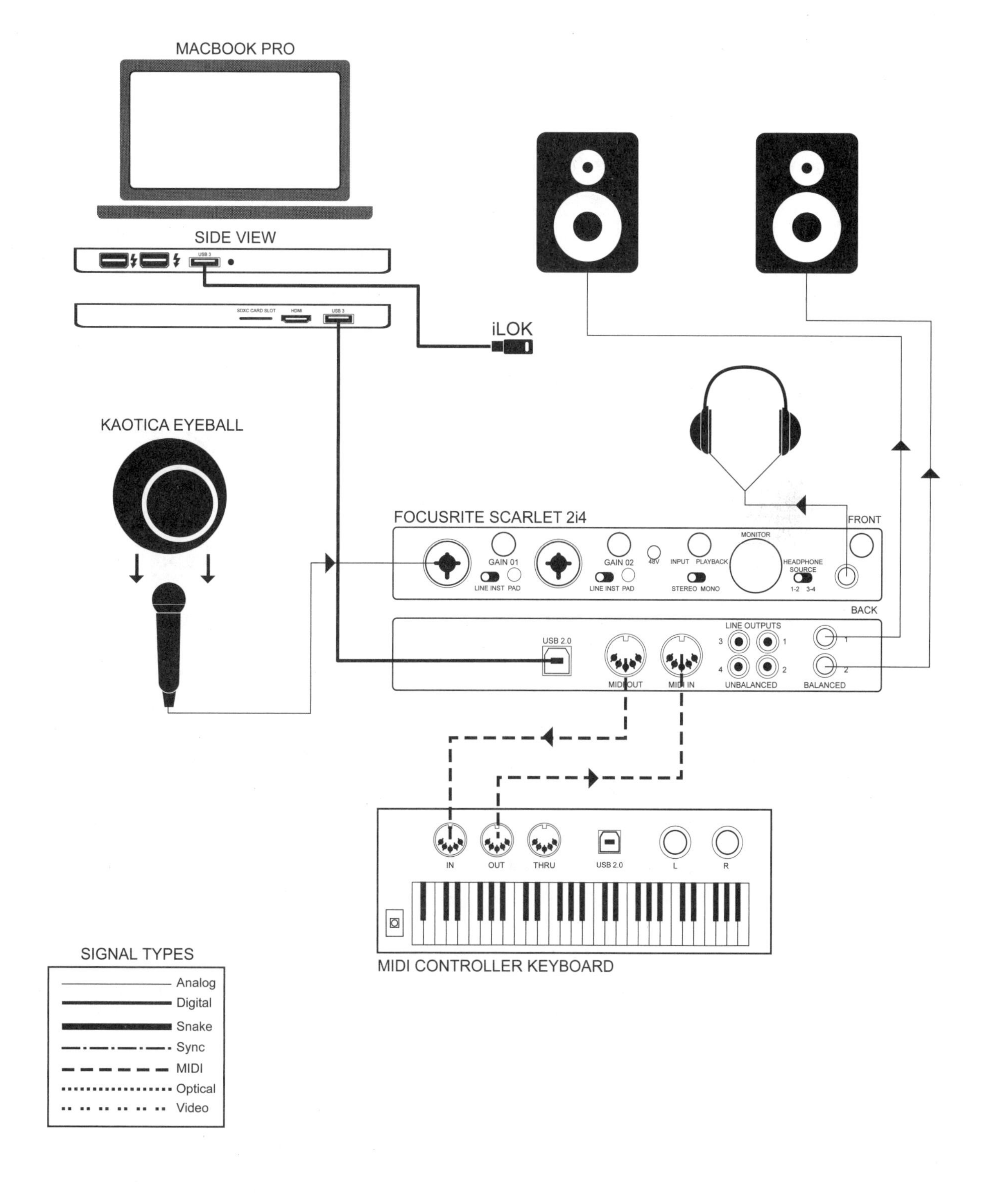

- 2 – 1/4-inch to XLR (or 1/4-inch to 1/4-inch cables)
- 2 – USB cables

Hardware Connections

Let's take a look at the connections you have to do in order to get this setup working properly:

1. Connecting the Scarlett 2i4 Audio Interface to a MacBook Pro Computer
    - Using a USB cable, connect the USB 2.0 output of the Scarlett 2i4 audio interface to an available USB connector on the MacBook Pro.

2. Connecting a Microphone to the Scarlett 2i4 Audio Interface
    - Using an XLR cable, connect the microphone to Input 1 of the Scarlett 2i4 audio interface. This is done from the front panel of the interface.

3. Connecting the Speaker Monitors and Headphones to the Scarlett 2i4 Audio Interface
    - Using a 1/4-inch to XLR or a 1/4-inch to 1/4-inch cable (depending on the connectors of your speakers), connect the balanced Output 1 of the Scarlett 2i4 audio interface to the Left speaker monitor.
    - Using another 1/4-inch to XLR or a 1/4-inch to 1/4-inch cable (depending on the connectors of your speakers), connect the balanced Output 2 of the Scarlett 2i4 audio interface to the Right speaker monitor.
    - For the headphones, you can plug them in to the 1/4-inch headphone jack in the Scarlett 2i4 audio interface, use a 1/8-inch to 1/4-inch adapter if necessary.

4. Connecting the MIDI Keyboard Controller to the MacBook Pro and to the Scarlett 2i4 Audio Interface
    - Using a MIDI cable, connect the "MIDI OUT" port of the MIDI synthesizer to the "MIDI IN" connector of the Scarlett 2i4 audio interface.
    - Using a second MIDI cable, connect the "MIDI OUT" connector of the

Scarlett 2i4 audio interface to the "MIDI IN" port of the MIDI synthesizer.

NOTE: If your computer has more than 2 available USB ports, you can use a USB standard A to USB standard B cable to connect the USB port of the MIDI keyboard controller to an available USB port on the computer. If necessary, you may purchase a USB hub to accomodate all 3 USB connections.

System Requirements

Pro Tools 11 for Mac (as of this writing):

- Avid-qualified Apple computer
- 4 GB RAM or more, 8GB or more is recommended
- 15 GB minimum free hard disk space
- Mac OS X 10.8 or later
- Monitor with at least 1024 x 768 resolution
- One or more Hard Disk Drives dedicated for audio recording and playback
- PACE USB Smart Key (iLok 2)
- USB 2.0 port available to connect the PACE USB Smart Key (iLok 2)
- USB 2.0 port available to connect the Scarlett 2i4 audio interface
- USB 2.0 port available to connect the MIDI controller keyboard
- Dedicated graphics card is recommended

Pro Tools 11 for Windows (as of this writing):

- Avid-qualified Windows-based computer
- 4 GB RAM or more, 8GB or more is recommended
- 15 GB minimum free hard disk space
- Windows 7 Home Premium, Professional or Ultimate only with Service

Pack 1, Windows 8 Standard or Pro edition

- Requires 64-bit Windows operating system
- Monitor with at least 1024 x 768 resolution
- One or more Hard Disk Drives dedicated for audio recording and playback
- PACE USB Smart Key (iLok 2)
- USB 2.0 port available to connect the PACE USB Smart Key (iLok 2)
- USB 2.0 port available to connect the Scarlett 2i4 audio interface
- USB 2.0 port available to connect the MIDI controller keyboard
- Dedicated graphics card is recommended

NOTE: PACE USB Smart Key (iLok 2) with valid license is required for Pro Tools 9 or higher to work, without it Pro Tools will not launch.

Software Setup

The DAW used in this example is Pro Tools. You should already have installed the software and other files required to run Pro Tools. You should also have installed the required drivers to use the Scarlett 2i4 as an audio interface. In case you do not have the required software or drivers installed, you could visit the site of the software and hardware developer. In this case you could visit www.avid.com and www.focusrite.com to download them, or for other types of information.

NOTE: Don't forget to always keep the PACE USB Smart Key (iLok 2) with a valid license connected to the computer; otherwise you will not be able to launch the Pro Tools software.

To explain this setup, we are using Pro Tools 11, but you can use earlier versions of Pro Tools, or other compatible DAWs that work with the Focusrite Scarlett 2i4. For more information visit www.focusrite.com.

Setting up Pro Tools

First, launch the Pro Tools software. Once Pro Tools has launched go to File menu and select "New Session" to create a new session. Select the sample rate and the Bit Depth; remember that the Scarlett 2i4 audio interface supports sample rates up to 96kHz and a Bit Depth up to 24 bits. In this case let's select a sample rate of 48kHz and a Bit Depth of 24 bits to achieve better sounding recordings. Set the Audio File Type to BWF (.WAV). Once the session is open, go to the Track menu and select "New" and create 1 Mono Audio track and one MIDI or Instrument track.

Assigning all the Audio Tracks in Pro Tools

- In Pro Tools, go to the Setups > I/O Setup menu, and press the "Default" button in the Input and Output tabs, by doing so, you will be able to see the default names of your inputs and outputs.
- In Pro Tools, go to the Mix window and assign the inputs and outputs on the audio and MIDI or Instrument tracks you created earlier. You could make these assignments in the Edit window as well, but in order to assign the track's ins and outs, you have to show the I/O section in the Edit window. To show the I/O in the Edit window, go to the View > Edit Window Views > I/O.
- In your Pro Tools session record enable (arm) the track that you are going to record.
- Set the recording level from the microphone using the Scarlett 2i4 GAIN 01 knob to adjust the signal level from the mic. If you are using a condenser type of microphone, don't forget to turn the 48V button on (on the front panel) to activate the phantom power so the condenser mic can function properly.

Setting up to record MIDI

- Create an Instrument track to record MIDI in your session. First go to the "Track " menu and select "New Track." Choose a stereo Instrument track.
- Select an available internal virtual synthesizer via an insert in the Instrument track. This could be Xpand2 or Vacuum, or any other available virtual instrument.
- Go to the MIDI input selector and assign the MIDI keyboard controller

you have connected to your computer. Select the "All" option. This means that Pro Tools will accept MIDI in all sixteen MIDI channels available.

- Next, assign the MIDI output in the Instrument track to the Xpand2 or any other virtual instrument you have selected.
- Record Enable the Instrument track and play the keys on your MIDI keyboard controller. You will notice MIDI information coming in and shown in the track's meter. You should be able to hear in your speaker monitors or headphones the sound produced by the virtual instrument you assigned in the Instrument track. Now, you are ready to record MIDI.

This concludes this exercise. Remember, all the track assignments are arbitrarily chosen so you can understand and learn the process of a recording session. By no means is this the only way to do it; these scenarios are just to practice plugging in your studio and setting up a session in Pro Tools 11 with your Scarlett 2i4 audio interface. See Appendix C for more audio interface options.

MOTU 4pre & Digital Performer Setup

This is another example of a simple and affordable music production home studio recording station where the only limit is the user's imagination. It is designed for those who would like to create demo songs in their bedroom to then take them to the next production level.

This specific setup is based on MOTU's 4pre audio interface and Digital Perfomer as the DAW. Also, included in this setup, there is an electric bass and guitar as well as a microphone. All these elements will give the opportunity to create a song idea. Notice, an iMac is used in this setup, but you can use any Apple or Windows-based computer system. Other alternatives for an Apple computer is the Mac Mini and the MacBook Pro laptop. It all depends on what you already have at home, or not.

Again, depending on your budget, you have other options for audio interfaces, microphones, software for writing, recording and mixing music. The other options for a setup like this could be: a Duet from Apogee Electronics, the Scarlett 2/2 by Focusrite, M-Audio's M-Track, Behringer's UFO202, PreSonus' AudioBox, and MOTU's UltraLite-mk3, among others. Other software packages include Logic from Apple, GarageBand from Apple, Yamaha's Cubase, Ableton Live, Studio One from PreSonus, and Propellerhead's Reason, among others. As I mentioned before, it all depends on your budget.

Equipment List

- 1 – MOTU 4pre Audio Interface
- 1 – Pair of KRK Speaker Monitors
- 1 – Pair of Headphones
- 1 – AT 4050 Condenser Microphone
- 1 – Electric Guitar
- 1 – Electric Bass Guitar
- 1 – Digital Performer 8
- 1 – Apple iMac Desktop Computer

Optional furniture

MOTU 4pre & Digital Performer Setup

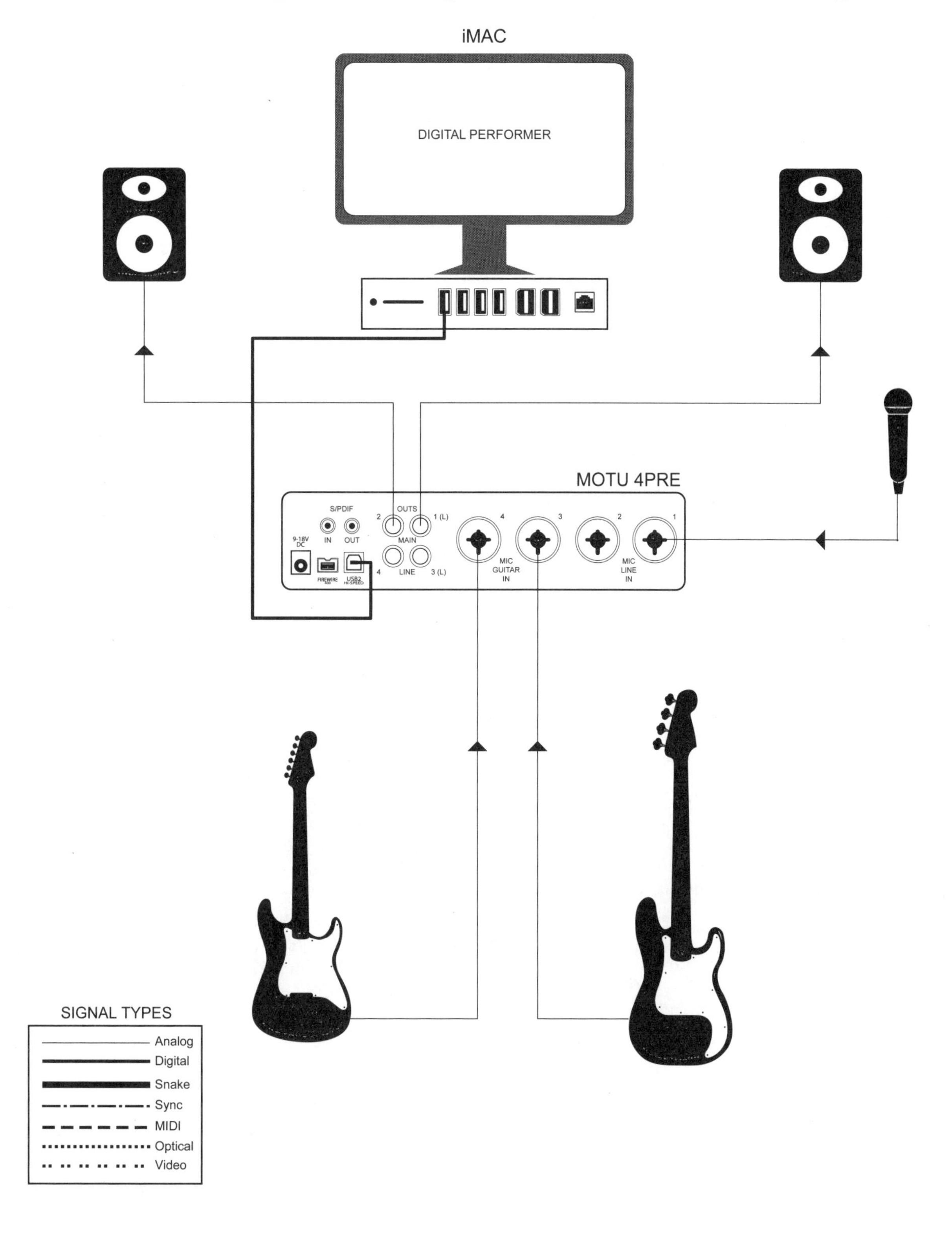

Cable List

- 1 – FireWire 400 or USB cable (depending on your computer)
- 1 – XLR cable
- 2 – 1/4-inch TS cables (unbalanced)
- 2 – 1/4-inch to XLR (or 1/4-inch to 1/4-inch cables)

Hardware Connections

1. Connecting the MOTU 4pre Audio Interface to the Apple's iMac Computer

    - Using either a FireWire cable or a USB cable, connect the respective port on the back of your 4pre interface to an available port on the iMac computer.

2. Connecting the Speakers and/or Headphones to the MOTU's 4pre

    - Using a 1/4-inch TRS to XLR cable (or a 1/4-inch TRS to 1/4-inch TRS cable, depending on the input jacks of your speaker monitors), connect the "MAIN OUT 1" output jack of the MOTU 4pre audio interface to the Left speaker monitor.
    - Using a 1/4-inch TRS to XLR cable (or a 1/4-inch TRS to 1/4-inch TRS cable, depending on the input jacks of your speaker monitors), connect the "MAIN OUT 2" output jack of the 4pre audio interface to the Right speaker monitor.
    - If you are using only headphones for monitoring your music, then just plug the 1/4-inch TRS (stereo) headphone connector to the headphone jack located on the front of the MOTU's 4pre. Use the "Phones" knob to adjust the headphone level. Be careful when you wear the headphones as the knob can be set to its highest position and it can hurt your ears.

3. Connecting an Electric Bass Guitar to the MOTU's 4pre

    - Using a 1/4-inch TS to 1/4-inch TS cable, connect the output of the electric bass guitar to Input 3 labeled as "MIC/GUITAR IN."

NOTE: Inputs 3 and 4 1/4-inch jacks on the MOTU's 4pre are high impedance (Hi-Z) which are suitable for DI guitar or bass inputs.

4. Connecting an Electric Guitar to the MOTU's 4pre

- Using a 1/4-inch TS to 1/4-inch TS cable, connect the output of the electric guitar to Input 4 labeled as "MIC/GUITAR IN."

NOTE: The inputs 3 and 4 1/4-inch jacks on the MOTU's 4pre, are high impedance (Hi-Z) which are suitable for DI guitar or bass inputs. Also, if your guitar or bass uses active electronics, you should activate the -20 dB Pad feature to attenuate the signal.

You can also set the input levels for a Mic and a Line TRS instrument input using the Trim mode on the MOTU 4pre. This trim control provides +60dB and +22 dB of boost, respectively. To accomplish this, do the following:

- Push the MIX knob (on the front panel) repeatedly until the green trim LED is illuminated on the front panel.
- Turn the TRIM/MIX knob to adjust the trim.

5. Connecting the Microphone to the MOTU's 4pre Audio Interface

- Using an XLR cable, connect the output of the microphone to Input 1 of the "MIC LINE IN" section of the MOTU's 4pre audio interface. If you are using a condenser microphone, don't forget to activate the Phantom Power (+48V). To do this, push the TRIM/MIX knob (on the front panel) repeatedly until the green trim LED is illuminated. Then, push and hold the corresponding TRIM/MIX knob for a few seconds to toggle the 48V phantom power. The red 48V LED will turn on or off accordingly. If you don't have a condenser microphone, do not turn this button on, you could damage the microphone.
- In the event that your mic signal is too strong, you will need to activate the -20 dB Pad. Each XLR mic input is equipped with a -20 dB Pad switch.
- Push the MIX knob repeatedly until the green trim LED is illuminated on the front panel.

- Push the TRIM/MIX knob to toggle the pad- the amber Pad LED will turn on or off accordingly.

System Requirements

Digital Performer 8 for Mac OS X and Windows (as of this writing):

- Mac OS X version 10.6.8 or later
- Windows 7 (32- and 64-bit)
- 4GB RAM or more recommended
- Computer display resolution 1024 x 768 required, 1280 x 1024 or higher recommended
- Mac: built-in audio, any Core Audio compatible hardware, any Core MIDI compatible hardware

MOTU 4Pre for Mac (as of this writing):

- Mac OS X version 10.5, 10.6, 10.7 or later required
- All Intel processor Macs
- 2 GB RAM or more recommended
- Available FireWire or high-speed USB 2.0 port
- A large hard drive (preferably at least 250 GB)

MOTU 4Pre for Windows (as of this writing):

- 1 GHz Pentium-based PC compatible or faster equipped with at least one USB2 or FireWire port
- 2 GB RAM or more recommended
- Windows 8, Windows 7 or Vista, 32- or 64-bit; Vista SP 2 or later required
- Available FireWire or high-speed USB 2.0 port

- A large hard drive (preferably at least 250 GB)

Software Setup

Installing all necessary drivers and complementary files

NOTE: Before you connect the 4pre to your computer, you should run the 4pre software installer.

- Insert the MOTU Audio Installer disc or run the file you have downloaded from www.motu.com.
- If necessary, read the Read Me file for installation assistance and other important information.
- Open the MOTU Installer application and follow the instructions.

Once you have connected all the devices, it is time to set some software features in order to get your recording station ready.

1. After you have launched Digital Performer 8
   - Create a new session by clicking on the DP8 icon on the dock or Applications folder, and then click on "New > Save as > Save"

2. Setting up the 4Pre settings
   - From Digital Performer 8, go to Setup > Configure Audio System > Configure Hardware Driver. Choose the MOTU 4pre from the list of drivers.

3. Setting up tracks to record in Digital Performer 8
   - To create a new track, go to Project > Add Track > Mono/Stereo Track. If DP8 new session has already created some tracks, you can either configure one of them, or create new ones. Do as you desire.
   - To route the instrument or a mic signal to the track, you will have to click on "input" on the track window and select the correct MOTU 4pre input.
   - Click on record enable, and then you should be able to record on DP8 through your MOTU 4pre. Remember to avoid clipping by adjusting the

levels on the front panel of the audio interface once signal is coming in to DP8.

This concludes this exercise. Again, all the track assignments are arbitrarily chosen so you can understand and learn the process of a recording session. By no means is this the only way to do it; these scenarios are just to practice plugging in your studio and setting up a session in Digital Performer 8 with your MOTU 4pre audio interface. See Appendix C for more audio interface options.

Desktop Music Production Studio with Apollo Twin

This high resolution desktop music production home studio setup is perfect for an artist who likes to put down his/her musical ideas with a classic analog sound using any of the major Digital Audio Workstation software programs such as: Avid Pro Tools 10 and Pro Tools 11, Apple Logic Pro X, Steinberg Cubase 7.5, and Ableton Live 9. In this simple setup we are using the Apollo Twin audio interface by Universal Audio. This desktop Thunderbolt audio interface has two premium mic/line preamps; two line outputs; front-panel Hi-Z instrument input and headphones output for monitoring. It can record in sample rates of up to 192kKz and in 24-bits of resolution giving you amazing clarity in your recordings.

This particular audio interface uses a technology known as Unison™, which offers incredible models of classic tube and transformer-based preamplifiers. It also has up to eight additional digital inputs via a Toslink (optical) connector, in which it can internally be set to accept two digital channels of S/PDIF or eight digital channels of Lightpipe from any ADAT compatible device. We are also using a microphone, an electric bass guitar, and a Fender Super Bassman bass amplifier. Additionally, we are also using an Apple iMac computer in this setup.

Be aware that this particular audio interface has to be connected to a Thunderbolt connector in your computer. If your computer does not have a Thunderbolt interface connector, this audio interface won't work, and as of this writing, the Apollo Twin does not work on Windows-based computers either. If this is your situation, then, you can purchase another type and model of a FireWire or USB audio interface. Among other companies that have audio interfaces are Apogee, Propellerhead, Focusrite, Avid, and PreSonus.

Equipment List

- 1 – Universal Audio Apollo Twin Thunderbolt Audio Interface
- 1 – Apple iMac Desktop Computer
- 1 – Fender Super Bassman Bass Mmplifier
- 1 – Microphone

Optional furniture

Desktop Music Production Studio with Apollo Twin

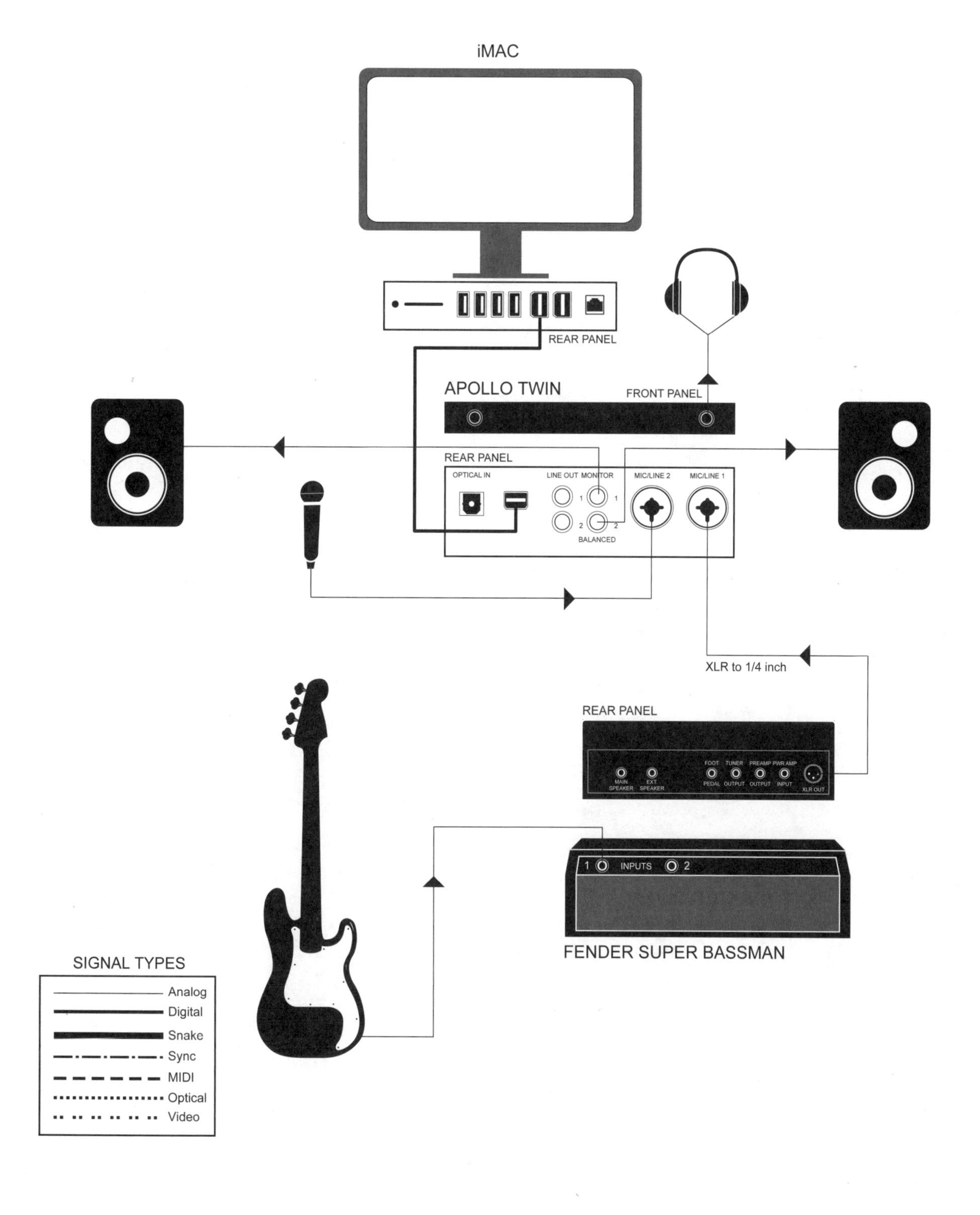

- 1 – Electric Bass Guitar
- 1 – Pair of Powered Speaker Monitors
- 1 – Pair of Headphones
- 1 – PACE USB Smart Key (iLok 2)

Cable List

- 1 – XLR cable
- 3 – 1/4-inch to XLR or 1/4-inch to 1/4-inch TRS cables
- 1 – 1/4-inch to 1/4-inch TS cable
- 1 – Thunderbolt cable

Hardware Connections

Let's take a look at the connections you have to do in order to get this setup working properly:

1. Connecting the Apollo Twin Audio Interface to an Apple iMac Computer
    - Using a Thunderbolt cable, connect the thunderbolt port of the Apollo Twin audio interface to an available thunderbolt connector on the iMac.
2. Connecting the Microphone to the Apollo Twin Audio Interface
    - Using an XLR cable, connect the microphone to the "MIC/LINE 2" input in Apollo Twin audio interface.
3. Connecting the Fender Super Bassman Amplifier to the Apollo Twin Audio Interface
    - Using a female XLR cable to 1/4-inch cable, connect the XLR output jack of the Fender Super Bassman to the "MIC/LINE 1" Input of the Apollo Twin audio interface. Don't forget to assign "Input 1" for a Line level signal.

4. Connecting the Bass to the Fender Super Bassman Amplifier

    • Using a 1/4-inch to 1/4-inch TS cable, connect the bass to Input 1 on the front panel of the Fender Super Bassman amplifier.

5. Connecting the Speaker Monitors and Headphones to the Apollo Twin Audio Interface

    • Using a 1/4-inch to XLR or a 1/4-inch to 1/4-inch TRS cable, connect the monitor Output L of the Apollo Twin to the Left powered speaker monitor.

    • Using another 1/4-inch to XLR or a 1/4-inch to 1/4-inch TRS cable, connect the monitor Output R of the Apollo Twin audio interface to the Right powered speaker monitor.

    • If you are using your headphones to monitor your sound, just connect the Headphones to the 1/4-inch headphone jack in the Apollo Twin audio interface, use an 1/8-inch to 1/4-inch adapter if necessary.

System Requirements

For Pro Tools 11 for Mac OS X (as of this writing):

- Avid-qualified Apple computer
- 4 GB RAM or more, 8GB or more is recommended
- 15 GB minimum free hard disk space
- Mac OS X 10.8 or later
- Monitor with at least 1024 x 768 resolution
- One or more Hard Disk Drives dedicated for audio recording and playback
- PACE USB Smart Key (iLok 2)
- USB 2 port available to connect the PACE USB Smart Key (iLok 2)
- USB 2 port available to connect the Apollo Twin audio interface
- Dedicated graphics card is recommended

NOTE: PACE USB Smart Key (iLok 2) with valid license is required for Pro Tools 9 or higher to work, without it Pro Tools will not launch.

Apollo Twin for Mac OS X (as of this writing):

- Apple Mac computer with available Thunderbolt or Thunderbolt 2 port
- Mac OS X 10.8 Mountain Lion, 10.9 Mavericks, or later
- Internet connection to download software and authorize UAD plug-ins
- Compatible VST, Audio Units, RTAS, or AAX 64 plug-in host application software
- 3 GB available disk space

Software Setup

In this example, we will be using Pro Tools 11 as our DAW. You should already have installed the software and other files required to run Pro Tools. Also, you should have installed the required software to use the Apollo Twin audio interface. In case you do not have the required software or drivers installed you could visit the site of the software and hardware developer. In this case you could visit www.avid.com and www.uaudio.com to check for them or for other types of information.

NOTE: Don't forget to always keep the PACE USB Smart Key (iLok 2) with a valid license connected to the computer; otherwise you will not be able to launch the Pro Tools software.

Getting the desired bass guitar signal once you have launched the Pro Tools 11 software in your computer.

- In this case, let's suppose that a bass player is going to add an overdub of his/her bass guitar and a background vocal. The bass signal is going to be generated through a Fender Super Bassman Bass Amplifier. Also, let's suppose he or she is going to record a section of the chorus of a song that was previously recorded.

Setting up Pro Tools

First, launch Pro Tools 11 and go to File menu and select "Open Session" to open the previously recorded session. Once you have the session open and ready, go to the Track menu and select "New" and create 2 Mono Audio Tracks.

Assigning the Inputs and Outputs for the Audio Tracks in Pro Tools

- The next step is to make the input and output assignments for the two audio tracks you created for the audio sources in this example.
- In Pro Tools, go to the Setups > I/O Setup menu, and press the "Default" button in the Input and Output tabs, by doing so you will be able to see the default names of your inputs and outputs.
- Now in Pro Tools, go to the Mix window and assign the inputs and outputs on the audio tracks you created earlier. You could follow the next table:

Track (mono)	Input	Inst/Source	Output
Audio track # 1	Analog 1	(Amplifier Output)	Analog 1-2
Audio track # 2	Analog 2	(Microphone)	Analog 1-2

- In your Pro Tools session record enable the Bass guitar track (Audio Track #1). Play the session with the song and adjust the input recording level for the bass sound. When you are ready to record the bass, press the Record button and then the Play button on the Transport window in Pro Tools. Once you have recorded the bass guitar, set the bass guitar audio track out of the record enable mode. Now, set the Audio Track #2 in the record enable mode, and adjust the recording input level coming from the microphone. If you would like to add some reverb effect in your voice, then simply insert an available reverb plug-in in your Pro Tools and select a preset. Maybe a Medium or Small Vocal Plate preset in the plug-in. Once you have set the recording level for your vocal, press the Record and Play buttons on the Transport window in Pro Tools to start recording your voice track. You will notice the quality of your recordings using the Apollo Twin audio interface.

This concludes this exercise. Remember, all the track assignments are arbitrarily chosen so you can understand and learn the process of a recording session using the Apollo Twin from Universal Audio. By no means is this the only way to do it, these scenarios are just to practice plugging in your studio and setting up a session in Pro Tools. You could use other DAWs and bass amplifiers from other companies if you desire. See Appendix C for more audio interface options.

Music Production Studio with Mbox Pro

This simple setup can be used either as a home setup or a portable setup and is designed to record a guitarist with his amp, playing by himself, or accompanied by a Drum Machine.

In this setup we are recording the guitar through the Fender Twin Reverb amp. One way is with a microphone placed in front of the amp, and the other way is through the line output of the amp. In this case we will use a mic to capture the guitar sound.

We are also using the Avalon V5 preamplifier. This is a solid-state preamp with a very compact design. You can choose between line and microphone inputs, and it comes with a tone-shaper function, which are basically equalization presets that come with the V5. You can choose to use the tone-shaping presets or bypass them.

The audio interface we are using in this setup is the Mbox Pro by Avid. This 4-Input by 6-Outputs FireWire 400 audio interface is capable of recording at a bit resolution up to 24-bits and sample rates up to 192 kHz. It can be connected to the computer via FireWire 1394. In this example we are using a Mac mini computer, but the Mbox Pro audio interface can also be used with a Windows-based computer, if this computer has the required FireWire connector.

The Mbox Pro has 6 analog outputs, from which you can connect the speakers. It also has 2 independent headphones outputs, meaning that you can either work by using a pair of headphones or a pair of speakers. In this setup we are going to use a pair of speakers.

Equipment List

- 1 – Avid Mbox Pro Audio Interface
- 1 – Electric Guitar
- 1 – Fender Twin Reverb Guitar Amplifier
- 1 – Microphone
- 1 – Avalon V5 Preamplifier

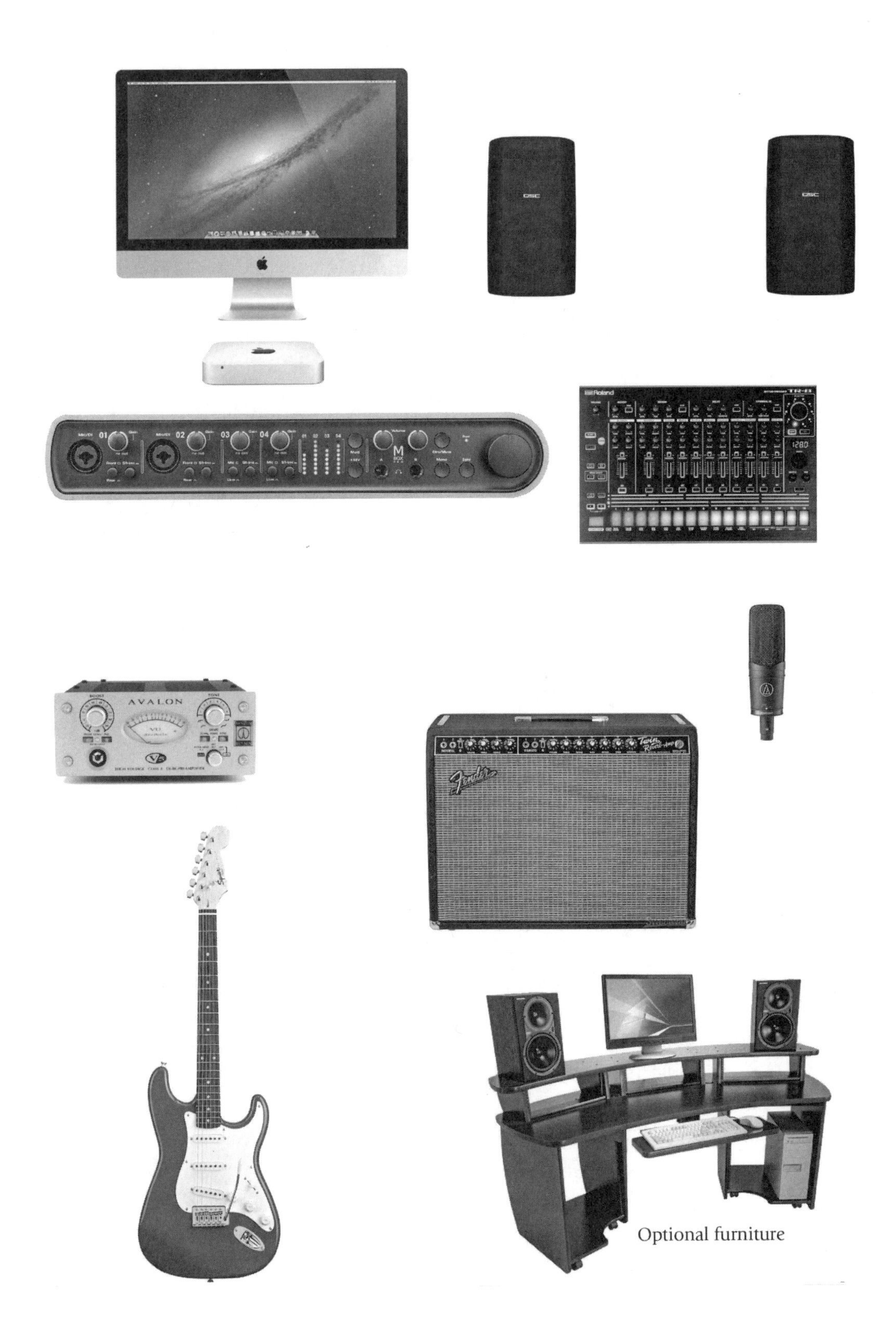

Optional furniture

Music Production Studio with Mbox Pro

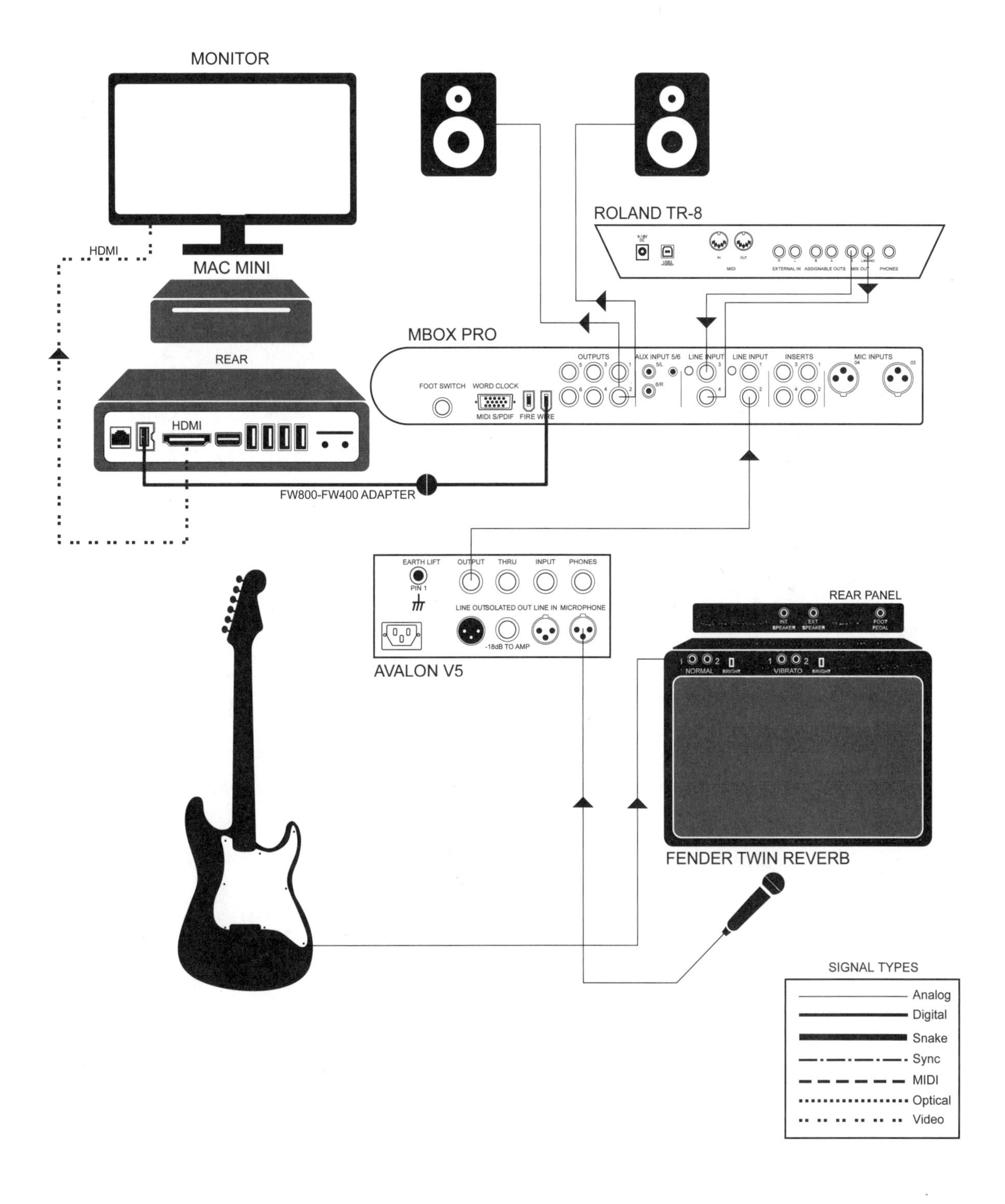

- 1 – Roland TR-8 Drum Machine
- 1 – QSC Powered Speaker Monitors
- 1 – Apple Mac Mini Desktop Computer
- 1 – PACE USB Smart Key (iLok 2)

Cable List

- 1 – 1/4-inch TS cable
- 1 – XLR cable
- 5 – 1/4-inch TRS cables
- 1 – FireWire 400 to FireWire 800 cable
- 1 – HDMI cable

Hardware Connections:

Now, let us go through the connections needed for this setup to work:

1. Connecting the Computer Video Monitor to the Apple Mac Mini Computer

    - Using an HDMI cable, connect the HDMI port on the back of your Mac Mini to the HDMI port on your computer video monitor. If you don't have an HDMI port in your computer monitor, then use the proper cable adapter and cable to connect the Thunderbolt port of the Mac Mini to the VGA connector in your computer monitor.

2. Connecting the Mbox Pro Audio Interface to the Apple Mac Mini Computer

    - Using a FireWire 400 to FireWire 800 cable, connect the FireWire 800 port on the back of your Mac Mini to either of the FireWire 400 ports on the Mbox Pro audio interface. It should be noted that the Mbox Pro can not be powered solely from the FireWire connection; it needs to be connected to its own power supply to function.

3. Connecting the Avalon V5 Preamp to the Mbox Pro Audio Interface

    - Using a 1/4-inch TRS Male to Male cable, connect the Line Out 1/4-inch output of the Avalon V5 to the 1/4-inch Line Input 2 of the Mbox Pro audio interface. Remember to choose to use the line input in the Mbox Pro.

4. Connecting the Drum Machine to the Mbox Pro Audio Interface

    - Using a 1/4-inch TRS cable, connect the Left Output of the Drum Machine to Line Input 3 of the Mbox Pro audio interface.
    - Using another 1/4-inch TRS cable, connect the Right Output of the Drum Machine to Line Input 4 of the Mbox Pro audio interface.

5. Connecting the Speaker Monitors to the Mbox Pro Audio Interface

    - Using a 1/4-inch to XLR or a 1/4-inch to 1/4-inch cable, connect Output 1 of the Mbox Pro audio interface to the Left powered speaker monitor.
    - Using another 1/4-inch to XLR or a 1/4-inch to 1/4-inch cable, connect Output 2 of the Mbox Pro audio interface to the Right powered speaker monitor.

6. Connecting the Fender Twin Reverb Amplifier to the Avalon V5 Preamplifier

    - Using an XLR cable, connect the microphone to the "Microphone" input of the Avalon V5. Place the microphone in front of the Fender Twin Reverb guitar amp.

7. Connecting the Guitar to the Fender Twin Reverb Amplifier

    - Using a 1/4-inch TS cable, connect the guitar output to the Normal 1 Input of the Fender Twin Reverb guitar amplifier.

System Requirements

Mbox Pro for Mac OSX (as of this writing):

- Avid-qualified Mac running Mac OS X 10.6.8 or higher (32- or 64-bit)

- 4 GB RAM or more recommended
- 15 GB free hard disk space for Pro Tools installation
- Two available USB ports for Mbox and iLok 2 connections
- PACE USB Smart Key (PACE USB Smart Key (iLok 2) - included, for software authorization)

Mbox Pro for Windows (as of this writing):

- Avid-qualified PC running Windows 7 Home Premium, Professional, or Ultimate (32- or 64-bit) – Service Pack 1
- 4 GB RAM or more recommended
- 15 GB free hard disk space for Pro Tools installation
- Two available USB ports for Mbox and iLok 2 connections
- PACE USB Smart Key (iLok 2) (included, for software authorization)

Software Setup

In this example, we will be using Pro Tools as our DAW. You should already have installed the software and other files required to run Pro Tools, as well as the required drivers to use the Mbox Pro audio interface. In case you do not have the required software or drivers installed, you could visit the site of the software and hardware developer. In this case, you could visit www.avid.com to check for drivers and other information.

Getting the desired guitar signal:

- In this case we are going to record a guitar player accompanied by a Drum Machine, and use the signal that comes from the Fender Twin Reverb guitar amplifier.

Setting up Pro Tools

First you should launch Pro Tools. Once Pro Tools has launched go to File menu and select "New Session" to create a new session. Now we can choose the sample rate and the Bit Depth, remember that the Mbox Pro audio interface supports sample rates up to 192kHz and a Bit Depth up to 24 bits. In this case, let´s choose a sample rate of 44.1kHz and a Bit Depth of 16 bits. Set the Audio File Type to BWF (.WAV). Once you have the session opened and ready, go to the Track menu and select "New" and create 3 Mono Audio Tracks.

Assigning the Audio Track in Pro Tools

- The next thing is to make the input and output assignments of all audio tracks you created for our different audio sources in this example.
- In Pro Tools, go to the Setups > I/O Setup menu, and press the "Default" button in the Input and Output tabs, by doing so you will be able to see the default names of your inputs and outputs.
- Now in Pro Tools, go to the Mix window and assign the inputs and outputs on the audio tracks you created earlier, you could follow the next table:

Track (mono)	Input	Inst/Source	Output
Audio track # 1	Analog 2	(Amplifier)	Analog 1-2
Audio track # 2	Analog 3	(Drum Machine L)	Analog 1-2
Audio track # 3	Analog 4	(Drum Machine R)	Analog 1-2

- In your Pro Tools session Record Enable (arm) the tracks that you are going to record. For example, you could record enable tracks 3 and 4 to listen to the drum's sound, adjust the recording levels, and record the Drum Machine in stereo (Left and Right) on tracks 3 and 4. At the same time you could Record Enable track 1 to listen to the guitar, adjust levels, and finally record it. You could be adding more tracks as you need them and repeat the same process for each track you create.

This concludes this exercise. Again, all the track assignments are arbitrarily chosen so you can understand and learn the process of a recording session in an Avid Mbox Pro. By no means is this the only way to do it, these scenarios are just to practice plugging in your studio and setting up a session in Pro Tools. You could use other DAWs and preamplifiers from other companies if you desire. See Appendix C for more audio interface options.

Voice-Over Talent Home Studio

In the past, a Voice Over Talent had to drive a long distance to a studio to record his/her voice for a commercial job, or for an audition. Technology has changed all that. Nowadays, most Voice Over Talents have a small studio at home where they can record and send via Internet their auditions or jobs without leaving their house. This very simple setup is designed for that specific purpose. In this setup, we are using a Duet 2 audio interface by Apogee Electronics. These desktop USB 2-ins and 4-outs audio interface can record in sample rates to up to 192 kHz and in 24-bits of resolution giving you amazing clarity in your recordings.

The microphone preamplifiers in the Duet 2 are great, but if you would like to give a little more warmth and body to your voice, a nice external preamplifier would give you that quality. In this example we are using a V5 from Avalon Design, of course, you can use any other preamp you desire. We are also using an Apple Mac Mini computer, but if you were going to be traveling, then a better choice would be an Apple MacBook Pro laptop. Be aware that the Apogee audio interfaces are only compatible with Apple computers so if you are planning on using this setup with a Windows based computer you should use another audio interface with similar features, like an Avid Mbox or a Focusrite Scarlett 2i4, for example.

Furthermore, notice in the line diagram we are using a foam on top of the microphone know as the EyeBall by Kaotica Corp. (www.kaoticaeyeball.com). The Eyeball reduces the undesirable external noise leaving only the sound and tone that is introduced into the microphone. By reducing the external noise, phase problems and cancellation are diminished within an acoustically untreated room. This foam is sort of a "mobile studio." Whether you work from home, or go on the road, you can take it with you, and simply put it over your microphone. It also includes a pop filter to avoid recording those annoying explosive words.

Equipment List

- 1 – Apogee Duet 2 Audio Interface
- 1 – Apple Mac Mini Desktop Computer
- 1 – Avalon V5 Preamplifier

AVALON
Optional furniture

Voice-Over Talent Home Studio

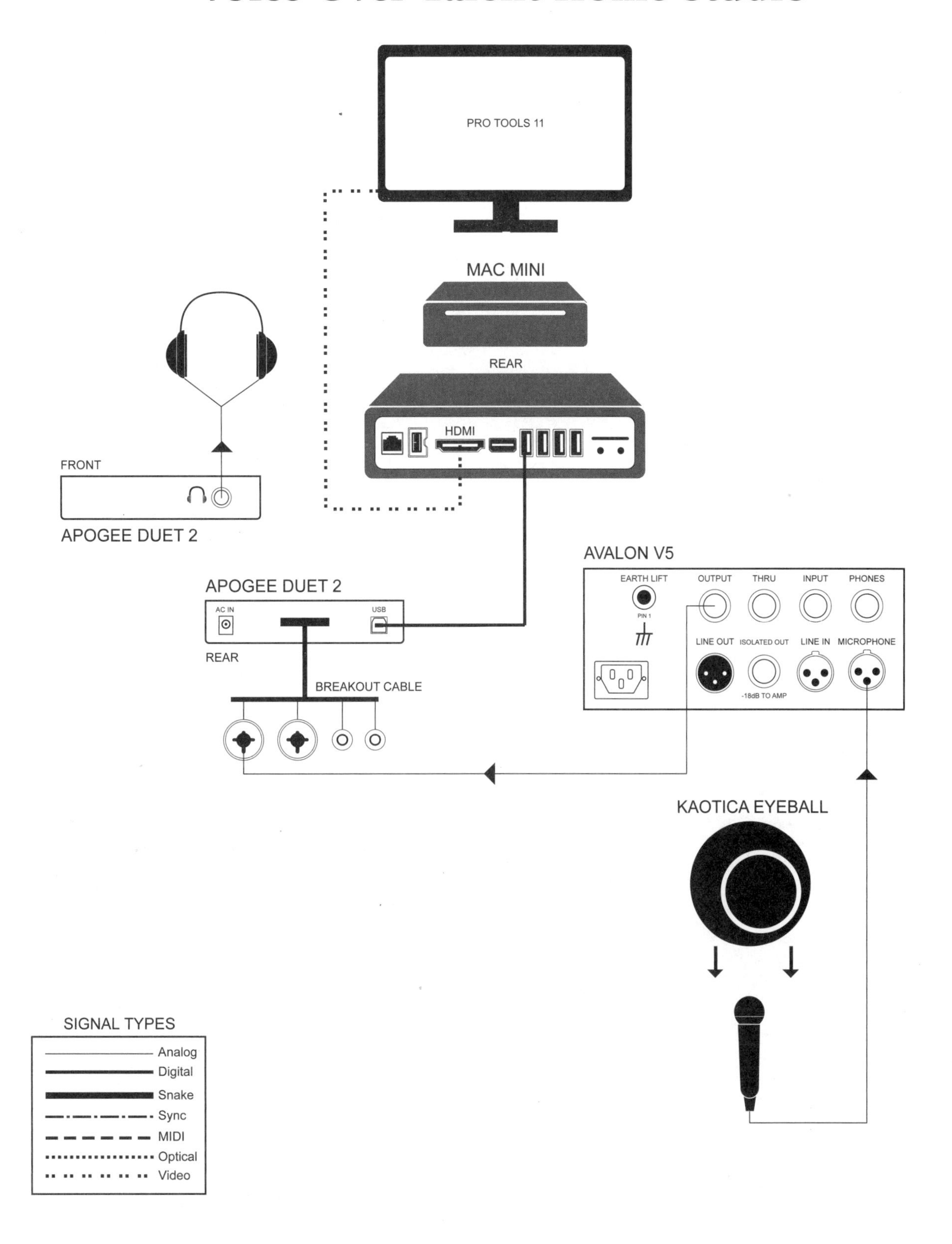

- 1 – Audio-Technica 4050 Condenser Microphone
- 1 – Kaotica EyeBall
- 1 – Pair of Headphones

Cable List

- 1 – XLR cable
- 1 – 1/4-inch TRS cable
- 1 – USB cable
- 1 – Apogee Duet 2 breakout cable
- 1 – HDMI cable

Hardware Connections

Let's take a look at the connections you have to do in order to get this setup working properly:

1. Connecting the Apogee Duet 2 Audio Interface to a Mac Mini Computer
    - Using a USB cable, connect the USB 2.0 port of the Apogee Duet 2 audio interface to an available USB port on the Mac Mini.

2. Connecting the Microphone to the Avalon V5 Preamplifier
    - Using an XLR cable, connect the microphone to the microphone input on the Avalon V5 preamplifier.

    NOTE: If you happen to purchase the EyeBall from (www.kaoticaeyeball.com)*, now is the time to put it over the microphone.*

3. Connecting the Avalon V5 to the Apogee Duet 2 Audio Interface
    - Using a 1/4-inch TRS cable, connect the "Line Out" 1/4-inch output of the Avalon V5 to the XLR-1/4-inch (connector combination) Input 1 of the breakout cable of the Apogee Duet 2 audio interface.

4. Connecting the Headphones to the Apogee Duet 2 Audio Interface

    - Just connect the headphones to the 1/4-inch headphone jack located on the front of the Apogee Duet 2 audio interface, use a 1/8-inch to 1/4-inch adapter if necessary.

System Requirements

Pro Tools 11 for Mac (as of this writing):

- Avid-qualified Apple computer
- 4 GB RAM or more, 8GB or more is recommended
- 15 GB minimum free hard disk space
- Mac OS X 10.8 or later
- Monitor with at least 1024 x 768 resolution
- One or more Hard Disk Drives dedicated for audio recording and playback
- PACE USB Smart Key (iLok 2)
- USB 2 port available to connect the PACE USB Smart Key (iLok 2)
- USB 2 port available to connect the Apogee Duet 2 audio interface
- Dedicated graphics card is recommended

NOTE: PACE USB Smart Key (iLok 2) with valid license is required for Pro Tools 11 to work, without it Pro Tools will not launch.

Duet 2 for Mac (as of this writing):

- Computer: Intel Mac 1.5GHz or faster
- Memory: 2 GB RAM minimum, 4 GB recommended
- OS: 10.6.4 or greater
- Connection and Power: USB, powered by any available USB port on the computer (DC power optional)

Software Setup

In this example, we will be using Pro Tools 11 as our DAW. You should already have installed the software and other files required to run Pro Tools. You should also have installed the required Apogee "Maestro 2" software to control the Apogee Duet 2 audio interface. In case you do not have the required software or drivers installed you could visit the site of the software and hardware developer. In this case you could visit www.avid.com and www.apogeedigital.com to check for them or for other types of information.

> *NOTE: Don't forget to always keep the PACE USB Smart Key (iLok 2) with a valid license connected to the computer; otherwise you will not be able to launch the Pro Tools software.*

Setting up Pro Tools

First, launch Pro Tools 11, once Pro Tools is open go to File menu and select "New Session" to create a new session. Select the sample rate and the Bit Depth, remember that the Apogee Duet 2 audio interface supports sample rates up to 192kHz and a Bit Depth up to 24 bits, but for this example, select a sample rate of 48kHz and a Bit Depth of 16 bits. Set the Audio File Type to BWF (.WAV).

1. Assigning the Duet 2 audio interface in your Pro Tools session

    - In Pro Tools, go to the menu Setups > Playback Engine, and select the Duet 2 as your audio interface engine. This pop-up menu is located on the top of the Playback Engine dialog window. Also, while in this window, set the buffer to 64, for lower latency you can set it to 32, but you may need to adjust the buffer higher depending on the size of the project you are working on. Once you have selected the Duet 2 as your audio interface, and have selected the buffer size, click on the OK button to execute the selection.

2. Assigning the inputs and outputs of the Audio Tracks in Pro Tools

    - In Pro Tools, go to the Setups > I/O Setup menu, click on the Input tab, and press "Delete Path". You will notice the all the inputs from the Duet 2 audio interface will be shown. Do the same with the Output tab. This way, you will be able to see the default names of your inputs and outputs. You can also use the I/O Setup dialog window (Setup > I/O) to label the inputs and outputs you are using in Pro Tools so you can easily identify them when working in a session. See the Pro Tools Reference Guide for details. .

- Open "Maestro 2" found in the Applications folder in the Mac computer.
- Select the inputs from the Input tab in the "Maestro 2" application.
- Select the proper input signal, a microphone or an instrument. If you are using a condenser microphone, then turn the phantom power on (48V).
- Go to the Output tab in "Maestro 2" and select the outputs to be routed to Pro Tools.
- Once you have selected these parameters, go to the Track menu and select "New" to create one Mono Audio track.
- In Pro Tools select the proper inputs coming from Duet 2.
- Show the Mix window in the Window menu, and assign Input 1 and Outputs 1 and 2 on the audio track you created earlier. If you don't see any signal activity in the track's meter when you record enable the track and speak on the microphone, then check that the 48V phantom power is on.
- If you are using the Avalon V5 preamplifier, then turn the selector knob to the right to select the 48V. Of course, assuming that you are using a condenser microphone. If signal still not coming in your Pro Tools session, then check the mic cable or your input assignments in Pro Tools.
- Adjust recording levels of your voice in the Pro Tools session, either via the external preamplifier (the V5 in this example) or the Duet 2's preamplifier.
- Record enable (arm) the track that you are going to record on. Press the Record button on the Transport window of Pro Tools, followed by the Play button. You should be able to notice Pro Tools started to record, so go ahead and speak over the mic to start recording your voice.

This concludes this exercise. Again, all the track assignments are arbitrarily chosen so you can understand and learn the process of a recording session. By no means is this the only way to do it, these scenarios are just to practice plugging in your studio and setting up a session in Pro Tools 11 with the Apogee Duet 2 audio interface. You could use other DAWs and preamplifiers from other companies if you desire. See Appendix C for more audio interface options.

Music Production Studio with Pro Tools Quartet

This simple music production home studio setup is really powerful and useful to write songs using a microphone and a guitar and/or create demos in MIDI using a two-octave MIDI controller and the internal synthesizers in Pro Tools.

This specific setup consists of a Pro Tools | Quartet, a Mac Mini computer, an electric guitar, a condenser microphone, a two-octave MIDI controller, and a set of speaker monitors or a pair of headphones. Of course, you will also need a computer monitor, a mouse, and a keyboard, if you don't already have one of each. To avoid having to purchase an external computer monitor, a keyboard, and a mouse when buying a Mac Mini computer, you could just purchase a laptop computer. It all depends on what you already have at home, or no.

Depending on your budget, you have other options for audio interfaces, microphones, software for writing music, etc. Other options for a setup this simple could be: the Scarlett 2/2 by Focusrite, M-Audio M-Track, Behringer UFO202, PreSonus AudioBox, and MOTU UltraLite-mk3, among others. Other software packages include Logic, Digital Performer, GarageBand, Cubase, Ableton Live, Studio One, and Propellerhead Reason, among others. As I mentioned before, it all depends on your budget. For example, the cost of the audio interfaces I mentioned above is $500 or less, and the software can be around the same price.

Equipment List

- 1 – Apogee Pro Tools | Quartet
- 1 – Apple Mac Mini Desktop Computer
- 1 – Electric Guitar
- 1 – Audio-Technica 4050 Condenser Microphone
- 1 – Arturia Keylab 49 Hybrid Synthesizer
- 1 – Pair of ADAM A7X Speaker Monitors

Optional furniture

Music Production Studio with Pro Tools Quartet

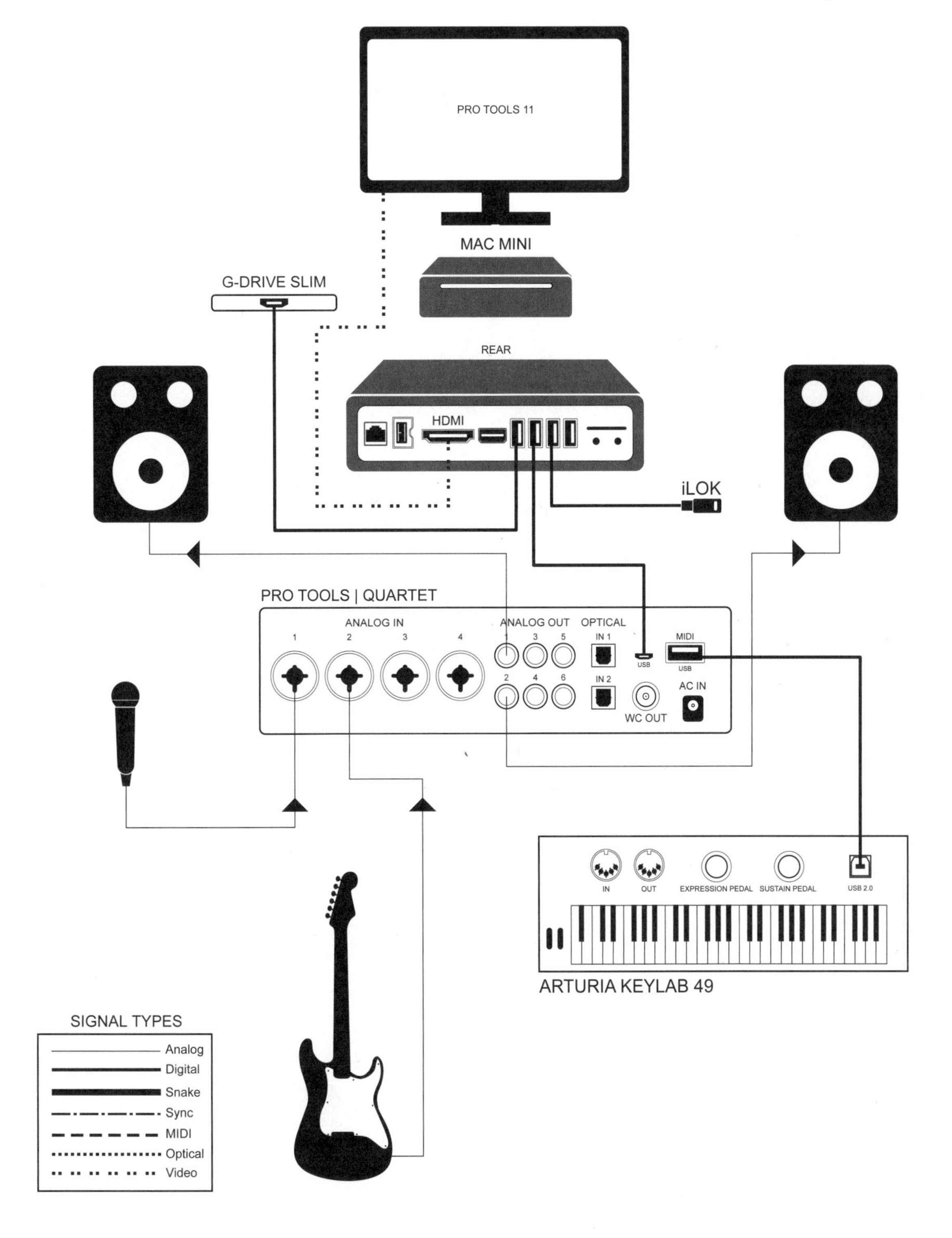

- 1 – Pair of Headphones
- 1 – G-Technology 500GB G-Drive Slim hard drive
- 1 – PACE USB Smart Key (iLok 2)

Cable List

- 1 – HDMI cable
- 1 – MIDI (USB) cable
- 2 -- USB to Micro USB cables
- 1 – XLR cable
- 1 – 1/4-inch TS cable (unbalanced)
- 2 – 1/4-inch TRS cables

Hardware Connections

1. Connecting the G-Drive Slim External Hard Drive to the System
    - Using a USB to Micro USB cable (included with the G-Drive Slim), connect an available USB port on your Mac Mini computer to the Micro USB port of the G-Drive Slim external hard drive.
2. Connecting the Mac Mini Computer to the Computer Video Monitor
    - If applicable, use an HDMI cable and connect the computer video monitor to the HDMI port of the Mac Mini computer. If your video monitor does not have an HDMI port, then use a Thunderbolt to VGA video adapter and connect your computer video monitor.
3. Connecting the Pro Tools Quartet to the Apple Mac Mini Desktop Computer
    - Using a USB to Micro USB cable, connect the Micro USB port on the Pro Tools Quartet to an available USB port on the Mac Mini computer.

4. Connecting a Microphone to the Pro Tools Quartet

 - Using a male XLR to female XLR cable, connect the male XLR end from the microphone to the "ANALOG IN 1" input female XLR jack on the Quartet.

5. Connecting an Electric Guitar to the Pro Tools Quartet

 - Using a 1/4-inch TS cable, connect an Electric Guitar to the "ANALOG IN 2" input female XLR/TS on the back of the Quartet.

NOTE: If the device you are connecting to any of the inputs has unbalanced outputs (or you are using an unbalanced TS cable), set the line input switch to -10dBv. For balanced outputs (using balanced TRS cables), set the switch to +4dBu. Check on the device's reference guide of the devices you are using in the setups.

6. Connecting the Arturia KeyLab 49 to the Pro Tools Quartet

 - Using a MIDI (USB) cable, connect the "USB 2.0" port of the Keylab 49 Hybrid Synth to the "MIDI USB" port on the rear of the Quartet.
 - You want to make sure whether or not the MIDI controller keyboard you are using needs a driver software to be recognized by Pro Tools. If it does need a driver, then you must search by brand and model of the keyboard online for it, download it, and install it. Also, the Arturia Keylab 49 includes the Analog Lab software with an integrated user interface and over 5000 sounds from Arturia's V-Collection line of products. The nice thing of this keyboard, is that is more than a MIDI controller, it is an instrument as well.

7. Connecting the ADAM A7X Speaker Monitors to the Pro Tools Quartet

 - Using a 1/4-inch TRS Male to Male cable, connect the "ANALOG OUT 1" on the rear of the Quartet to the Left speaker.
 - Using a 1/4-inch TRS Male to Male cable, connect the "ANALOG OUT 2" on the rear of the Quartet to the Right speaker.

8. Connecting Headphones to the Pro Tools Quartet

- Connect the 1/4-inch TRS (stereo) connector of the headphone set to the "Headphone Output" jack on the right side of the Quartet. You don't necessarily need to connect a headphone set if you are already using the speaker monitors, it is your choice.

System Requirements

Quartet for Mac OS X (as of this writing):

- Avid-qualified Mac running Mac OS X 10.6.8 or higher
- 2 GB RAM (4 GB or more recommended)
- 15 GB free hard disk space for Pro Tools installation
- Two available USB ports for Quartet and iLok 2 connections
- PACE USB Smart Key (iLok 2) (included, for software authorization)

Software Setup

Assuming all the connections are done correctly and the Pro Tools software is installed properly, with the right Pro Tools|Quartet driver and MIDI controller driver, follow the next steps to configure your hardware in a Pro Tools session.

Setting up Pro Tools

Depending of which version of Pro Tools you are running, don't forget to keep your PACE USB Smart Key (iLok 2) connected in a USB port of your computer if you are running Pro Tools version 9 or higher.

- Once you have launched Pro Tools on your computer, go to the File menu and select "New Session" to create a new session. Let's assign the sample rate to 48 kHz, the Bit Depth to 24 bits, and the Audio File Type to BWF (.WAV), which is Pro Tools' default audio file type.

Assigning the Pro Tools | Quartet audio interface in Pro Tools

- In Pro Tools, go to the menu Setups > Playback Engine, and select the

Quartet as your audio interface engine. This pop-up menu is located on the top of the Playback Engine dialog window. Also, while in this window, set the buffer to 64, for lower latency you can set it to 32, but you may need to adjust the buffer higher depending on the size of the project you are working on. Once you have selected the Pro Tools | Quartet as your audio interface, and have selected the buffer size, click on the OK button to execute the selection.

- In Pro Tools, go to the Setups > I/O Setup menu, click on the Input tab, and press "Delete Path". You will notice the all the inputs from the Quartet audio interface will be shown. Do the same with the Output tab. This way, you will be able to see the default names of your inputs and outputs. You can also use the I/O Setup dialog window (Setup > I/O) to label the inputs and outputs you are using in Pro Tools so you can easily identify them when working in a session. See the Pro Tools Reference Guide for details.
- Open the Pro Tools IO Control application. This application is an interface control application made for Mac and Windows. Featuring a single window design, and multiple tab interface for quick access to all device and system settings, Pro Tools IO Control makes software control of Pro Tools | Quartet easy. The software works the same on Mac and Windows.
- Select the desired inputs from the Input tab in the "Pro Tools IO Control" application.
- Select the proper input signal, a microphone or an instrument. If you are using a condenser microphone, then turn the phantom power on (48V).
- Go to the Output tab in the "Pro Tools IO Control" and select how you want to route the Pro Tools | Quartet outputs.
- Once the Pro Tools session is open and ready, go to the Track menu and select "New" to create two Mono Audio tracks and one Instrument track. One audio track for the electric guitar, another for the microphone.

Assigning all the Audio Tracks in Pro Tools

Go to the Mix window and assign the inputs and outputs on your tracks following these directions:

Track (mono)	Input	Inst/Source	Output
Audio track # 1	Analog 1	(Mic)	Analog 1-2
Audio track # 2	Analog 2	(Guitar)	Analog 1-2

- Record enable (arm) the tracks on your Pro Tools session, press the Record and then the Play buttons on the Transport window to start recording. You will notice the audio as waveforms as you are generating sound from either the microphone or the guitar as soon as you start playing and singing.

NOTE: Pro Tools 11 includes a new Avid Audio Engine and low latency record buffer allowing you to record and monitor tracks within Pro Tools with low latency (latency is the a slight delay between when you play a note and when you hear it with a record enabled track). In many cases, as with other DAWs, this latency is low enough to not be noticeable. However the latency depends on the speed of your computer, the size of the session, and the number of recorded tracks and effects you have assigned. If you notice latency when recording, you can use Pro Tools IO Control mixer to solve the problem. Audio signals from mics, guitars, etc., going into the Quartet interface can be monitored directly using Pro Tools IO Control mix software from the interface, without having to pass through Pro Tools record enabled tracks, and can be mixed with the playback output from Pro Tools for very low latency playing and recording. For more detailed information on the Pro Tools | Quartet please refer to the Reference Guide.

This concludes this exercise. Remember, all the track assignments are arbitrarily chosen so you can understand and learn the process of a recording session. This is by no means the only way to do it, these scenarios are just to practice plugging in your home studio and setting up a session in Pro Tools with Pro Tools | Quartet. These concepts and steps can be applied to other audio interfaces and Digital Audio Workstation software programs. See Appendix C for more audio interface options.

Live Band Recording with a Digi 003+

This setup is an example of how to organize and setup a recording session using sixteen different microphones at once with a Digi 003+ audio interface and Pro Tools. Again, the equipment used in this diagram is only an example of what you might be able to connect to the Avid Digi 003+. It is only a guideline since you may or may not have the same computer, all the equipment, and microphones used in this setup. The process will be similar using other audio interfaces, different equipment and microphones.

In this scenario, we are using the Digi 003+, an Apple Mac Pro desktop computer, an external G-Technology FireWire hard drive, sixteen microphones, a DAT machine, an analog mixing board used as a sub-mixer, two external synthesizers, an external Drum Machine, a MIDI interface, an 8-channel preamplifier with digital outputs, a pair of speaker monitors, a headphone or cue amplifier, and some headphones for the musicians.

Equipment List

- 1 – Avid Digi 003+
- 1 – PreSonus DigiMax Preamplifier
- 1 – Apple Mac Pro Desktop Computer
- 1 – G-Technology G-Drive Slim Hard Drive
- 1 – Avid MIDI I/O
- 1 – Hardware Drum Machine
- 1 – 8-Channel Analog Line Mixing Board
- 1 – DAT machine
- 2 – Hardware Synthesizers
- 16 – Microphones
- 1 – Headphone Amplifier

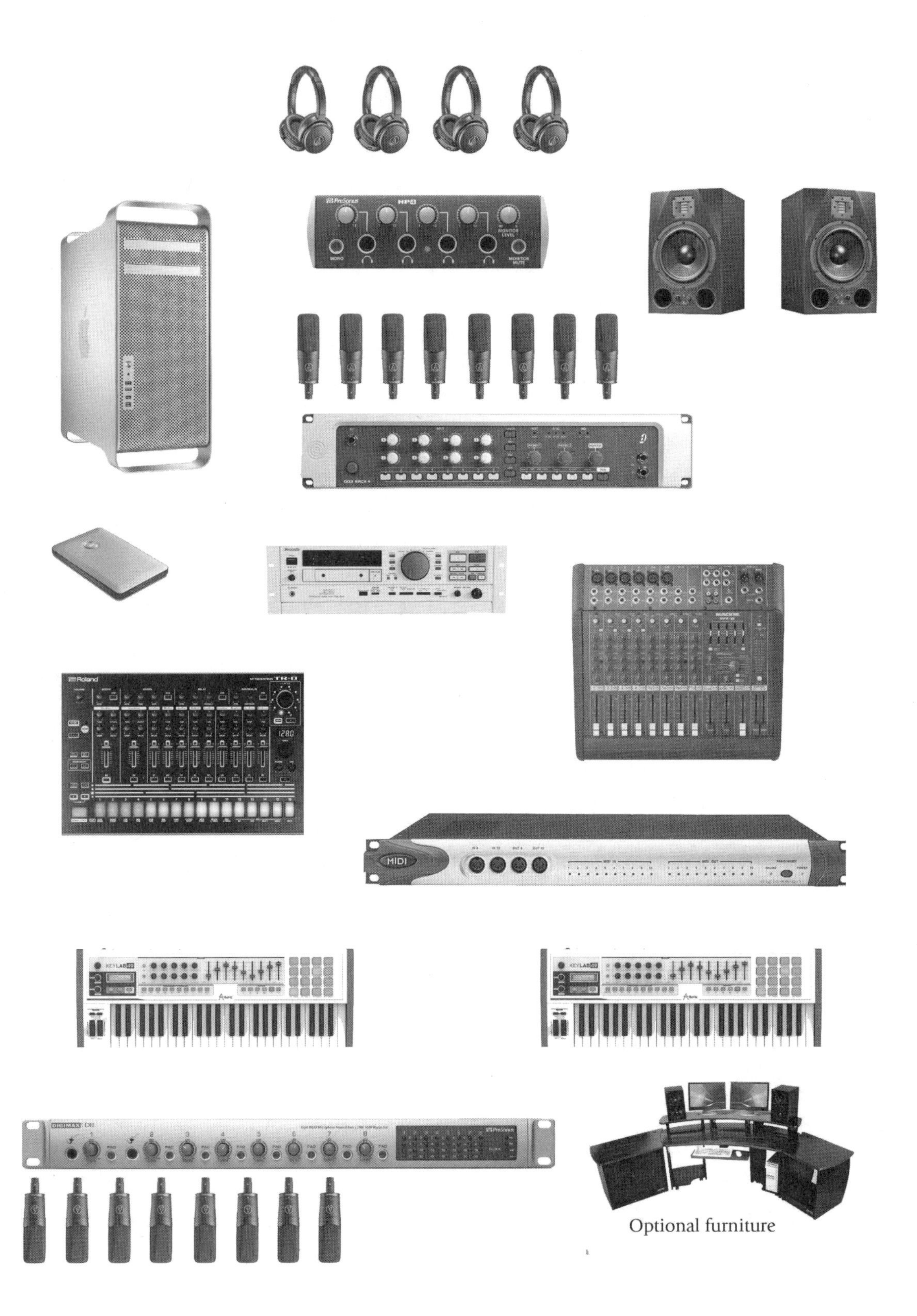
Roland
MIDI
Optional furniture

Live Band Recording with a Digi 003+

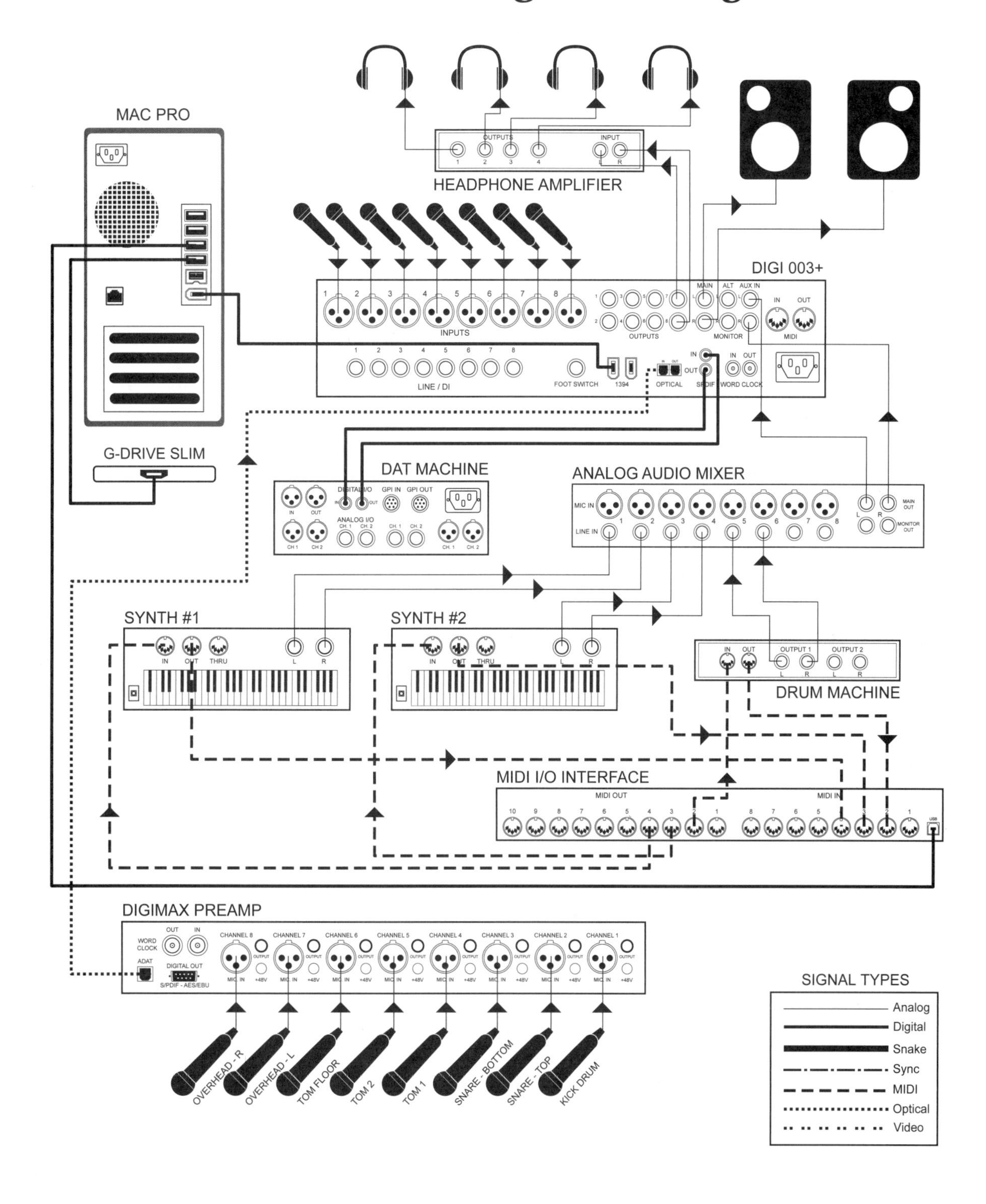

- 4 – Pairs of Headphones
- 1 – Pair of ADAM A7X Speaker Monitors

Cable List

- 1 – FireWire 400 cable (with FireWire 800 to FireWire 400 adapter)
- 16 – XLR cables
- 6 – 1/4-inch TS cables
- 6 – 1/4-inch TRS cables
- 1– Optical cable
- 6 – MIDI 5-pin DIN cables
- 2 – USB cables
- 2 – RCA 75-ohms cables

Hardware Connections

1. Connecting a G-Drive Slim External Hard Drive to the Mac Pro Computer
   - Using a USB cable (depending on your computer), connect an available USB port on your computer to the USB port on your external G-Drive Slim external hard drive.

2. Connecting the Mac Pro Computer to the Digi 003+
   - Using a FireWire 400 cable, connect the FireWire 1394 port on the rear panel of the Digi 003+ to an available FireWire port located in the back of your the computer. If your computer only has FireWire 800 or Thunderbolt connectors, then you will need to use the proper adapter from FireWire 400 to FireWire 800.

3. Connecting a DAT Machine to the Digital I/O of the Digi 003+
   - Using an RCA 75-ohms cable (an RCA cable with gold plated connectors),

connect the "DIGITAL OUT" of the DAT machine to the "S/PDIF IN" of the Digi 003+.

- Using another RCA 75-ohms cable, connect the "S/PDIF OUT" of the Digi 003+ to the "DIGITAL IN" of the DAT machine.

4. Connecting a Headphone (Cue) Amplifier to the Digi 003+

    - Using a 1/4-inch TRS cable, connect "OUTPUT 7" of the Digi 003+ to the "IN L" (left) jack on the headphone amplifier.
    - Using a second 1/4-inch TRS cable, connect "OUTPUT 8" of the Digi 003+ to the "IN R" (right) jack on the headphone amplifier.
    - Connect as many headphones as your headphone amplifier allows.

5. Connecting the Synthesizers to the Audio Mixer (The mixer in this case is used as a sub-mixer of the external synthesizers and the external Drum Machine in this setup)

    - Using a 1/4-inch TS cable, connect the "OUTPUT L" of Synth #1 to "INPUT 1" on the audio mixer.
    - Using another 1/4-inch TS cable, connect the "OUTPUT R" of Synth #1 to "INPUT 2" on the audio mixer.
    - Using a 1/4-inch TS cable, connect the "OUTPUT L" of Synth #2 to "INPUT 3" on the audio mixer.
    - Using another a 1/4-inch TS cable, connect the "OUTPUT R" of Synth #2 to "INPUT 4" on the audio mixer.

6. Connecting the Synthesizers to a MIDI Patcher

    - Using a MIDI cable, connect the "MIDI OUT" on Synth #1 to "MIDI IN 4" on the MIDI Patcher.
    - Using another MIDI cable, connect the "MIDI IN" on Synth #1 to "MIDI OUT 4" on the MIDI Patcher.
    - Using a MIDI cable, connect the "MIDI IN" on Synth #2 to "MIDI OUT 3" on the MIDI Patcher.

- Using a MIDI cable, connect the "MIDI OUT" on Synth #2 to "MIDI IN 3" on the MIDI Patcher.

7. Connecting the Drum Machine to the Audio Mixer

   - Using a 1/4-inch TS Male to Male cable, connect the "OUTPUT 1 L" of the Drum Machine to "INPUT 5" on the audio mixer.
   - Using another 1/4-inch TS Male to Male cable, connect the "OUTPUT 1 R" of the Drum Machine to "INPUT 6" on the audio mixer.

8. Connecting the Drum Machine to the MIDI Patcher

   - Using a MIDI cable, connect the "MIDI OUT" on the Drum Machine to "MIDI IN 2" on the MIDI Patcher.
   - Using another MIDI cable, connect the "MIDI IN" on the Drum Machine to "MIDI OUT 2" on the MIDI Patcher.

9. Connecting 8 Microphones to the Digi 003+

   Using XLR-Male to XLR-Female, make the following connections:

   - Mic 1 to the "MIC IN 1" of the Digi 003+.
   - Mic 2 to the "MIC IN 2" of the Digi 003+.
   - Mic 3 to the "MIC IN 3" of the Digi 003+.
   - Mic 4 to the "MIC IN 4" of the Digi 003+.
   - Mic 5 to the "MIC IN 5" of the Digi 003+.
   - Mic 6 to the "MIC IN 6" of the Digi 003+.
   - Mic 7 to the "MIC IN 7" of the Digi 003+.
   - Mic 8 to the "MIC IN 8" of the Digi 003+.

10. Connecting 8 Microphones to a DigiMax Preamplifier for a Drum Set

    Using XLR-Male to XLR-Female, make the following connections:

    - "MIC IN 1" to the Kick microphone.

- "MIC IN 2" to the Snare Top microphone.
- "MIC IN 3" to the Snare Bottom microphone.
- "MIC IN 4" to the Tom 1 microphone.
- "MIC IN 5" to the Tom 2 microphone.
- "MIC IN 6" to the Floor Tom microphone.
- "MIC IN 7" to the Overheads Left microphone.
- "MIC IN 8" to the Overheads Right microphone.

11. Connecting the Preamp to the Digi 003+
    - Using an optical cable, connect the "ADAT" (optical) port on the preamp to the "OPTICAL IN" on the Digi 003+.

12. Connecting an Analog Audio Mixer to the Digi 003+
    - Using a 1/4-inch TRS Male to Male cable, connect the "AUX IN L" on the Digi 003+ to the "STEREO OUT L" on your Analog Audio Mixer.
    - Using another 1/4-inch TRS Male to Male cable, connect the "AUX IN R" on the Digi 003+ to the "STEREO OUT R" on your Analog Audio Mixer.

13. Connecting the Digi 003+ to the Speaker Monitors
    - Using a 1/4-inch TRS cable, connect "MAIN OUT R" on the Digi 003+ to the right speaker.
    - Using another 1/4-inch TRS cable, connect "MAIN OUT L" on the Digi 003+ to the left speaker.

NOTE: *Your speaker monitors might have 1/4-inch TRS cable XLR jacks or Banana type connectors in its inputs, if this is the case, use the correct cables with the connectors you need for your situation.*

System Requirements

Pro Tools 11 for Mac (as of this writing):

- Avid-qualified Apple computer
- 4 GB RAM (8GB or more is recommended)
- 15 GB minimum free hard disk space
- Mac OS X 10.8 or later
- Monitor with at least 1024 x 768 resolution
- One or more Hard Disk Drives dedicated for audio recording and playback
- PACE USB Smart Key (iLok 2)
- USB 2 port available to connect the PACE USB Smart Key (iLok 2)
- Dedicated graphics card is recommended

NOTE: PACE USB Smart Key (iLok 2) with valid license is required for Pro Tools 11 to work, without it Pro Tools will not launch.

Software Setup

Assuming all the connections are ready, follow these steps to configure your hardware in your Pro Tools session:

- Create a new session and then create 18 Mono Audio tracks and 3 MIDI tracks, or 14 Mono Audio tracks, 2 Stereo Audio tracks and 3 MIDI tracks.
- When working with MIDI, it is a good idea to configure your MIDI studio in Pro Tools. This will be useful because it will let you assign the model names and brands of your external synthesizers and samplers so it will be easier for you to assign them in the Pro Tools Mix window. To accomplish this, go to the menu Setups > MIDI > MIDI Studio, the Audio MIDI Setup (AMS) application will open. Then go to the Window menu in the AMS, and select the option Show MIDI Window, the MIDI Setup window will appear. You will notice the MIDI interface you are currently using will be shown in your computer screen. Next, click on the "Add Device" button,

a keyboard icon named "new external device" will show up in the window. Double click on it, and the "new external device properties" window appears prompting you to select the external keyboard manufacturer and model that is in your setup. Continue this process until you finish assigning all your external devices. Once you finish your setup, press the "Apply" button to execute the assignments. From now on, every time you create a MIDI or Instrument track in Pro Tools, a list of all the devices you created in the MIDI Studio Setup will show up in the list of inputs and outputs of the corresponding channel strip in the Mix window.

- When using a DAT machine or an external CD Burner, via S/PDIF, you need to set up the digital inputs in Pro Tools. To do this, go to the Setups > Hardware Setup menu and assign the Digital Input to "RCA = S/PDIF, not to OPTICAL = ADAT," and don't forget to set the Clock Source to S/PDIF (RCA).

Assigning all the Audio Tracks in Pro Tools

Now, let's make the assignments of all the audio tracks you created for the different audio sources in our example:

- In Pro Tools, go to the Setups > I/O Setup menu, and press the "Default" button in the Input and Output tabs. This way, you will be able to see the default names of your inputs and outputs. You can also use the I/O Setup dialog window (Setup > I/O) to label the inputs and outputs you are using in Pro Tools and identify them as inserts or sends when working in a session. See the Pro Tools Reference Guide for details.

- In Pro Tools, go to the Mix window and assign the inputs and outputs on the audio tracks you created earlier. If it makes it easier for you, follow the next table:

Track (mono)	Input	Inst/Source	Output
Audio track # 1-8	Analog 1-8	(Mic 1-8)	Analog 1-2
Audio track # 9-16	ADAT 1-8	(Digimax)	Analog 1-2
Audio track # 13-14	S/PDIF 1	(DAT)	Analog 1-2
MIDI track #1	S#1 IN CH 1	(Synth #1)	S#1 OUT (CH 1)
MIDI track #2	S#2 IN CH 2	(Synth #2)	S#2 OUT (CH 2)
MIDI track #3	DM IN	(Drum Machine)	DM OUT (CH 3)

- Remember to set the format for the eight inputs on your Digi 003+ to their corresponding status, meaning they must be set to Mic inputs since we are using only microphones. Also, set the preamp levels in the Digi 003+ for the mic inputs to get a good recording signal.
- Now, assign a Send on all the tracks and set their output to "Analog 7-8" and that would be the mix sent to the headphones so the musicians can listen to themselves.
- Record enable the tracks on your Pro Tools session, press the Record and then the Play buttons on the Transport window to start recording all the instruments you set the microphones to.

This concludes this exercise. Remember, all the track assignments are arbitrarily chosen so you can understand and learn the process of a recording session. This is by no means the only way to do it; these scenarios are just for practicing plugging in your home studio and setting up a session in Pro Tools with your Digi 003+. These concepts and steps apply to other audio interfaces and Digital Audio Workstations. See Appendix C for more audio interface options.

Professional Studios 2

Photo courtesy of The Record Plant Recording Studios, SSL-1, Los Angeles, CA

It is no secret that the audio industry has changed dramatically over the last 20 years. You may think that the sound you get from a home studio is comparable to or better than the sound from a professional studio. While both are "good" sounds, there is a stark difference between a "good" sound and a professional sound. Several factors to take in consideration are the acoustically designed space, the quality of the equipment, the experience and the ability of the sound engineer, etc. For now, this chapter will focus on the equipment, the hardware connections, and the software installations required in large-scale professional studios.

24-Track Analog Tape Machine Transfer

If you are working or have worked in a large format recording studio such as The Record Plant, Westlake or the Village in Los Angeles or any other large format recording studio on a another city or country, you may or may not have performed the task of transferring audio from a 2-inch tape analog recording machine to a Pro Tools HD system. This is a typical job in a studio when the situation is that, an entire record was recorded on tape few year ago, and perhaps, the entire record or just a song needs to be remixed to be used as a soundtrack for a film, or another artist wants to do a new version of a particular song, for example.

If you have never have performed this task, this setup diagram and assignment process will help you to do the job properly. In this particular setup we are using a 2-inch analog tape machine, a Pro Tools HDX system with three Avid HD I/O audio interfaces, among other devices. For an easier visual explanation purposes of this setup, I have use three audio interfaces, but you can only use two to do the transfer.

Also, I have included three Avid PRE preamplifiers to show how you connect them and set them up in the diagram and the description. You don't need to have the preamps if you are doing a straight transfer, but I case you need to increase the levels of the recorded signals on the tape, you can do so. In other words, the preamps are optional.

Equipment List

- 3 – Avid HD I/O Audio Interfaces
- 3 – Avid PRE MIDI Controlled Preamplifiers
- 1 – Avid Sync HD Synchronizer
- 1 – Avid MIDI I/O 10-Port MIDI Patcher
- 1 – HDX PCIe Card
- 1 – 24-Track 2-inch Analog Tape Machine
- 1 – Pair of Dorrough 40-A Analog Loudness Meters

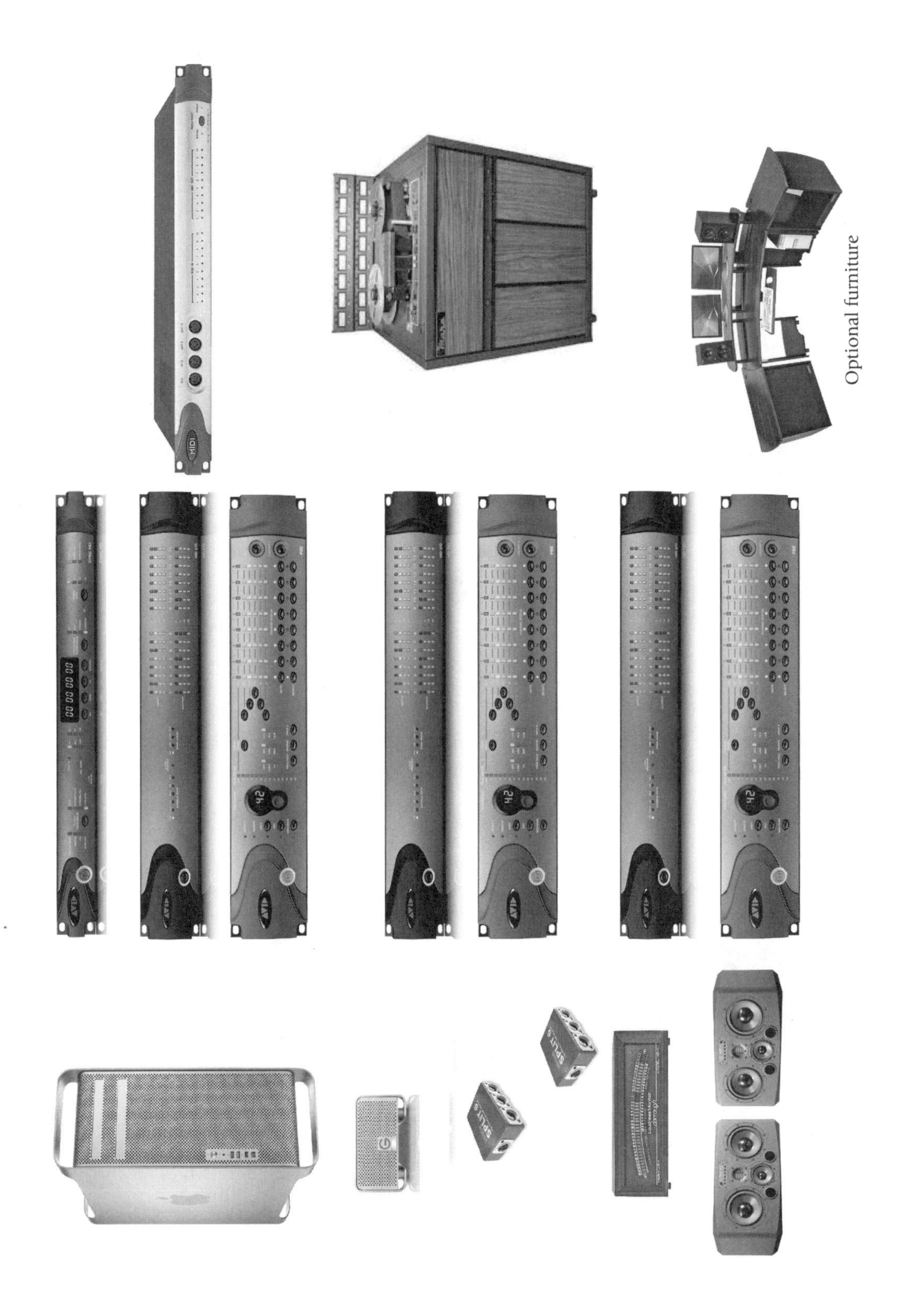
Optional furniture
MIDI

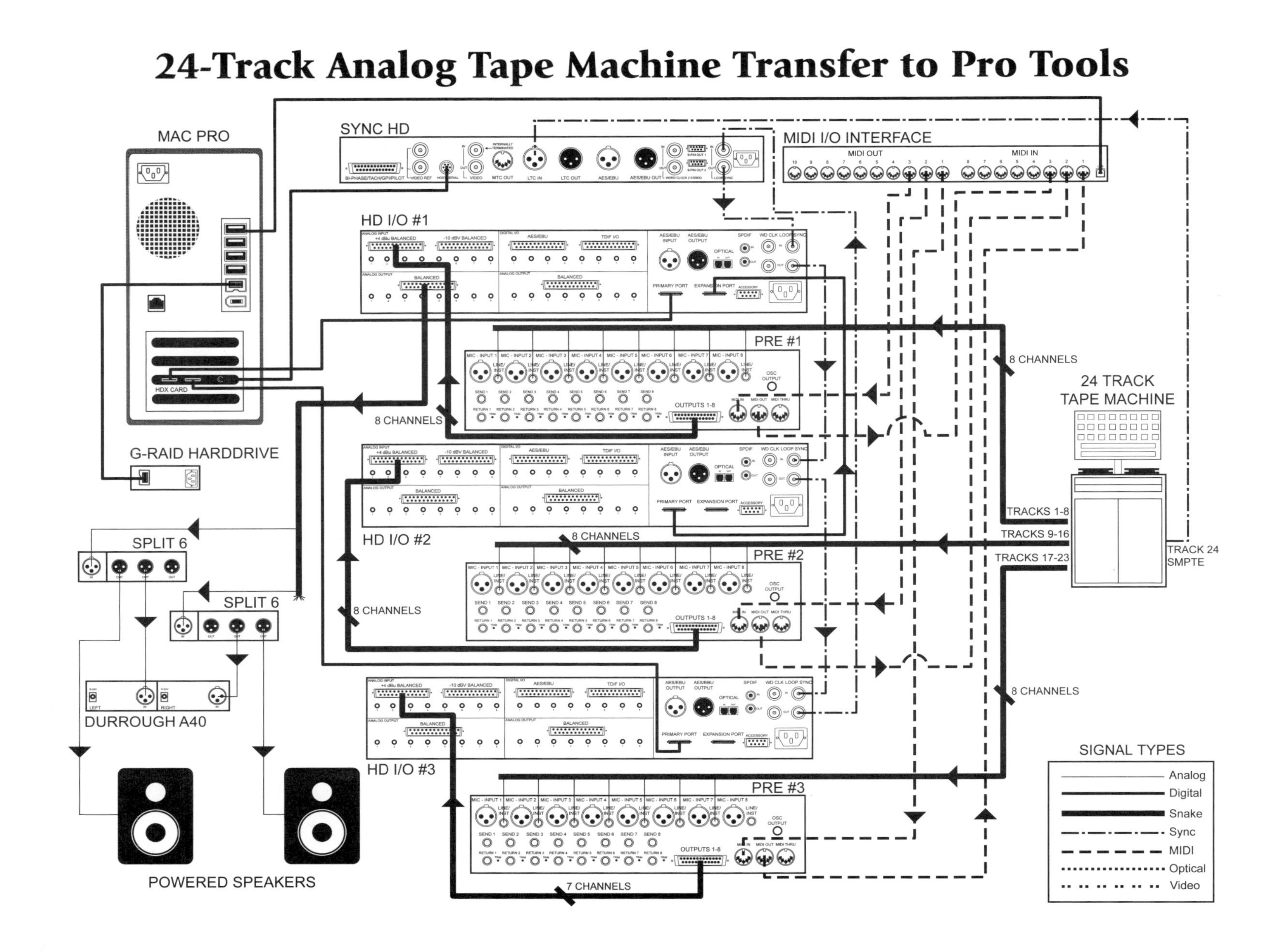
24-Track Analog Tape Machine Transfer to Pro Tools
MAC PRO
HDX CARD
SYNC HD
MIDI I/O INTERFACE
MIDI OUT
MIDI IN
HD I/O #1
PRE #1
8 CHANNELS
8 CHANNELS
24 TRACK
TAPE MACHINE
G-RAID HARDDRIVE
HD I/O #2
8 CHANNELS
TRACKS 1-8
TRACKS 9-16
TRACKS 17-23
TRACK 24
SMPTE
PRE #2
SPLIT 6
SPLIT 6
8 CHANNELS
DURROUGH A40
8 CHANNELS
HD I/O #3
PRE #3
POWERED SPEAKERS
7 CHANNELS
SIGNAL TYPES
Analog
Digital
Snake
Sync
MIDI
Optical
Video

- 2 – Whirlwind Split 6 Line Level Parallel Splitters
- 1 – Pair of ADAM S3X-H Powered Speaker Monitors
- 1 – Apple Mac Pro Desktop Computer
- 1 – 12 TB G-RAID FireWire 800 External Hard Drive

Cable List

- 3 – Avid DigiLink mini cables
- 3 – 8x8 XLR to 1/4-inch TRS cable snakes
- 3 – 8x8 DB-25 to DB-25 cable snakes
- 1 – 8x8 DB-25 to XLR cable snake
- 5 – XLR cables
- 6 – 5-Pin DIN MIDI cables
- 1 – 8-pin Mini DIN Serial cable
- 4 – BNC cables
- 1 – USB cable
- 1 – FireWire 800 cable

Hardware Connections

Once you have all the cables and the Pro Tools hardware components, is time to connect all these elements together. To get you started, I have assembled a sample connection diagram and explanations that shows how this is done. Of course, these are just examples, you are not likely to have the exact system list of components and processors discussed here, but hopefully, this diagram and explanation will give you an idea of how to connect a similar system. For example, the Inputs and outputs of the audio interfaces were arbitrarily selected, you can choose any Input and/or output you desire for your situation.

1. Connecting a 12 TB G-RAID FireWire 800 External Hard Drive to the Apple Mac Pro Desktop Computer
   - Using a FireWire 800 cable (depending in your computer), connect an

available FireWire 800 port on your Apple Mac Pro desktop computer to an available FireWire 800 port on your external G-RAID 12 TB FireWire 800 hard drive.

2. Connecting the HD I/O Audio Interfaces to the Apple Mac Pro Computer

- Using a DigiLink Mini Cable, connect PORT 1 of the HDX PCIe card [located at the back of your computer] to the PRIMARY PORT on the rear panel of the HD I/O #1 audio interface.
- Using another DigiLink Mini Cable, connect the EXPANSION PORT on the HD I/O #1 audio interface to the PRIMARY PORT on HD I/O #2 audio interface.
- Using a third DigiLink Mini Cable, connect the HD I/O #3 audio interface PRIMARY PORT to PORT 2 of the HDX PCIe card located in the Apple Mac Pro desktop computer.
- In case you are using two HDX PCI cards, don't forget to connect the HDX TDM Flex cable (a SATA cable) between the two HDX PCIe cards so they can share data along the TDM bus.

3. Connecting the Loop Sync among the HD I/O Audio Interfaces

- Using a BNC cable, connect the LOOP SYNC OUT of the HD I/O #1 audio interface to the LOOP SYNC IN of the HD I/O #2 audio interface.
- Using another BNC cable, connect the LOOP SYNC OUT of the HD I/O #2 audio interface to the LOOP SYNC IN of the HD I/O #3 audio interface.

4. Connecting the Sync HD to the HD I/O Audio Interfaces

- Using a BNC cable, connect LOOP SYNC OUT of the SYNC HD to the LOOP SYNC IN of the HD I/O #1 audio interface.
- Using a BNC cable, connect LOOP SYNC OUT" of the HD I/O #3 audio interface to the LOOP SYNC IN of the SYNC HD.

5. Connecting the Sync HD to the Apple Mac Pro Computer

- Using a serial cable provided with the SYNC HD, connect the DigiSerial port on the HDX PCIe card to the HOST SERIAL port on the rear panel of the SYNC HD. In the event that you are using more than one HDX cards, or an older Pro Tools HD 3 system, the SYNC HD always goes connected to the first HDX or HD Core PCIe cards installed in your computer.

6. Connecting the MIDI I/O Interface to the Apple Mac Pro Computer

- Using a USB cable, connect to an available USB port on the computer to the USB port on the Avid MIDI I/O Interface.

7. Connecting SMPTE (LTC) from the 2-inch Tape Machine to the SYNC HD

- Using an XLR Female to Male cable, connect the output of Track 24 on the 2-inch Tape Machine to the LTC IN jack of the Sync HD located in the rear panel.

8. Connecting the 2-inch Tape Machine to the Avid PRE #1

Using an 8x8 XLR to 1/4-inch TRS cable snake, connect the following:

- TRACK 1 OUT of the 2- inch Tape Machine to LINE/INST IN 1 of PRE #1
- TRACK 2 OUT of the 2- inch Tape Machine to LINE/INST IN 2 of PRE #1
- TRACK 3 OUT of the 2- inch Tape Machine to LINE/INST IN 3 of PRE #1
- TRACK 4 OUT of the 2- inch Tape Machine to LINE/INST IN 4 of PRE #1
- TRACK 5 OUT of the 2- inch Tape Machine to LINE/INST IN 5 of PRE #1
- TRACK 6 OUT of the 2- inch Tape Machine to LINE/INST IN 6 of PRE #1
- TRACK 7 OUT of the 2- inch Tape Machine to LINE/INST IN 7 of PRE #1
- TRACK 8 OUT of the 2- inch Tape Machine to LINE/INST IN 8 of PRE #1

9. Connecting the 2-inch Tape Machine to the Avid PRE #2

Using an 8x8 XLR to 1/4-inch TRS cable snake, connect the following:

- TRACK 9 OUT of the 2- inch Tape Machine to LINE/INST IN 1 of PRE #2
- TRACK 10 OUT of the 2- inch Tape Machine to LINE/INST IN 2 of PRE #2

- TRACK 11 OUT of the 2- inch Tape Machine to LINE/INST IN 3 of PRE #2
- TRACK 12 OUT of the 2- inch Tape Machine to LINE/INST IN 4 of PRE #2
- TRACK 13 OUT of the 2- inch Tape Machine to LINE/INST IN 5 of PRE #2
- TRACK 14 OUT of the 2- inch Tape Machine to LINE/INST IN 6 of PRE #2
- TRACK 15 OUT of the 2- inch Tape Machine to LINE/INST IN 7 of PRE #2
- TRACK 16 OUT of the 2- inch Tape Machine to LINE/INST IN 8 of PRE #2

10. Connecting the 2-inch Tape Machine to the Avid PRE #3

    Using an 8x8 XLR to 1/4-inch TRS cable snake, connect the following:

    - TRACK 17 OUT of the 2- inch Tape Machine to LINE/INST IN 1 of PRE #3
    - TRACK 18 OUT of the 2- inch Tape Machine to LINE/INST IN 2 of PRE #3
    - TRACK 19 OUT of the 2- inch Tape Machine to LINE/INST IN 3 of PRE #3
    - TRACK 20 OUT of the 2- inch Tape Machine to LINE/INST IN 4 of PRE #3
    - TRACK 21 OUT of the 2- inch Tape Machine to LINE/INST IN 5 of PRE #3
    - TRACK 22 OUT of the 2- inch Tape Machine to LINE/INST IN 6 of PRE #3
    - TRACK 23 OUT of the 2- inch Tape Machine to LINE/INST IN 7 of PRE #3

11. Connecting the Avid PRE #1 to the HD I/O Audio Interface #1

    - Using an 8x8-DB25 to DB25 cable snake, connect the "OUTPUTS 1-8" DB-25 connector on the rear panel of the PRE #1 to the Analog Input DB-25 connector labeled "+4dBu BALANCED" of the HD I/O audio interface #1.

12. Connecting the Avid PRE #2 to the HD I/O Audio Interface #2

    - Using an 8x8-DB25 to DB25 cable snake, connect the "OUTPUTS 1-8" DB-25 connector on the rear panel of the PRE #2 to the Analog Input DB-25 connector labeled "+4dBu BALANCED" of the HD I/O audio interface #2.

13. Connecting the Avid PRE #3 to the HD I/O Audio Interface #3

   - Using an 8x8-DB25 to DB25 cable snake, connect the "OUTPUTS 1-8" DB-25 connector on the rear panel of the PRE #3 to the Analog Input DB-25 connector labeled "+4dBu BALANCED" of the HD I/O audio interface #3.

14. Connecting the Avid PRE to the Avid MIDI I/O Interface

   - Using a MIDI cable, connect the MIDI OUT Port 3 from the MIDI I/O interface to the MIDI IN port of PRE #1.
   - Using a MIDI cable, connect the MIDI OUT port of the PRE #1 to the MIDI IN Port 3 of the MIDI I/O interface.
   - Using a MIDI cable, connect the MIDI OUT Port 2 from the MIDI I/O interface to the MIDI IN port of PRE #2.
   - Using a MIDI cable, connect the MIDI OUT port of the PRE #2 to the MIDI IN Port 2 of the MIDI I/O interface.
   - Using a MIDI cable, connect the MIDI OUT Port 1 from the MIDI I/O interface to the MIDI IN port of the PRE #3.
   - Using a MIDI cable, connect the MIDI OUT port of the PRE #3 to the MIDI IN Port 1 of the MIDI I/O interface.

15. Connecting Output 1 and 2 of the HD I/O Audio Interface #1 to the two Whirlwind Split 6 Line Level Parallel Splitters

   - Using an 8x8 DB25 to XLR cable snake, connect the XLR cables labeled Output 1 and Output 2 from the 8x8 DB25 to XLR cable snake plugged in to the ANALOG OUTPUT BALANCED DB-25 connector on the rear panel of the HD I/O audio interface #1 to the INPUT jack of each Whirlwind Splitter 6, one for the LEFT channel, and another for the RIGHT channel.

16. Connecting the Whirlwind Split 6 Line Level Parallel Splitters to the Dorrough 40-A Analog Loudness Meters

   - Using an XLR cable, connect one of the outputs of the Left channel splitter to the Left channel of the Dorrough meter.

- Using another XLR cable, connect one of the Outputs of the Right channel splitter to the Right channel of the Dorrough meter.

17. Connecting the Whirlwind Split 6 Line Level Parallel Splitters to the Powered Speaker Monitors

    - Using an XLR cable, connect another one of the Outputs of the Left channel splitter to the Left channel powered speaker.

    - Using another XLR cable, connect another one of the Outputs of the Right channel splitter to the Right channel powered speaker.

NOTE: You should consult the manufacturer's documentation for information of all your equipment in your studio to select the proper cables and cable snakes for your units.

System Requirements

Since the system requirements for Pro Tools is constantly being updated, and depending on the Pro Tools HD hardware and software versions you are using in your studio, it is best to visit www.avid.com and search for the "Avid Knowledge Base – Pro Tools System Requirements," for both Mac OS and Windows OS and look for your specific Pro Tools and operating system in your computer.

Software Setup

Regardless of what version of Pro Tools you use in your studio, version 9, 10 or 11 (as of this writing), you should already have installed the software and other files required to run Pro Tools properly. Also, it is very important that you check which operating system is installed in your computer, whether you are using a Macintosh (Mac OSX) or a PC running on Windows. You can always search the Internet for any software updates for all your devices and visit www.avid.com to check for the latest compatibility information.

Setting Up Pro Tools

First, you should launch Pro Tools, and once Pro Tools has launched, select "Create New Session" from the QuickStart dialog box to create a new session. Now, choose the sample rate of 48kHz, the Bit Depth to 24 bits, and set the Audio File Type to BWF (.WAV). Once you have the session open and ready, go to the "Track" menu and select "New," a dialog window will prompt you to enter the information for the tracks you want to create. So go ahead and create 24 Mono Audio tracks for each track of the 2-inch tape machine. Notice we are also recording the SMPTE time code in Pro Tools.

Configuring the Avid PREs

To remote control your Avid PREs preamplifiers from the Pro Tools software, you need to configure them first following the steps described below:

- When working with MIDI, it is a good idea to configure your MIDI studio in Pro Tools. This will be useful because it will let you assign the model names and brands of your external devices such as synthesizers, samplers, etc., so it will be easier for you to assign them in the Pro Tools Mix window. To accomplish this, go to the Setups > MIDI > MIDI Studio menu, the Audio MIDI Setup (AMS) application will open. Then go to the "Window" menu in the AMS, and select the option "Show MIDI Window"- the MIDI Setup window will appear. You will notice the icon of the MIDI interface you are currently using will be shown in your computer screen which in this case is the Avid MIDI I/O. Next, click on the "Add Device" button, a keyboard icon named "New External Device" will appear on your computer screen. Double click on it, and the "New External Device Properties" window appears prompting you to select the external device's manufacturer and model that is in your setup, which in this example, the manufacturer will be Avid, and the Model will be PRE.
- Next, click on the "IN" and the "OUT" small arrows on the PRE icon you have just created and drag them to Port 1 Input and to Port 1 Output of the MIDI I/O. You will create two more PREs and drag them to Port 2 IN and OUT , and Port 3 IN and OUT, respectively. You should end up with three PREs connected to the first three ports of the MIDI I/O icon. Once you finish with the setup, press the "Apply" button to execute the assignments. From now on, every time you create a MIDI or Instrument track in Pro Tools, a list of all the devices you created in the MIDI Studio Setup will show up in the list of Inputs and outputs of the corresponding channel strip in the Pro Tools Mix window.

On each PRE front panel, press "MIDI CHAN" and use the "GAIN/PARM" control to set the MIDI channel from 1-16. In this case set the MIDI channel to 1.

- Each PRE must be declared in the Pro Tools "Peripherals" dialog. To do so, go to Setups > Peripherals menu, and click on the "Mic Preamps" tab. From the "Type" pop-up menu, select PRE. From the "Receive From" menu, select the PRE's source port and a MIDI channel to receive data (this will be the MIDI device you configured in the AMS. For PRE #1 will be PRE 1-1, for the #2 will be PRE 1-2, and for #3 will be PRE 1-3). From the "Send To" pop-up menu, choose a destination port and a MIDI channel to transmit data (this will be the same device as you have selected above, so for PRE #1 will be 1-1, for the #2 will be 1-2, and for the #3 will be 1-3). Click the OK button on the screen.

- Lastly, from the Mic Preamp tab of the I/O setup, map the PRE's outputs.

Verifying the Sync HD is properly connected and configured

- In Pro Tools, go to the Setup > Peripherals menu, and select the "Synchronization" tab. Verify the box is checked for "Enable Sync HD". Set any of the other options as desired.

Configuring the HD I/O audio interfaces and PRE

- This particular setup has three HD I/O audio interfaces. The HD I/O #1 is attached to the first port (Port 1) of the Avid HDX PCIe card, so it will appear in the "Peripherals" list on the "Hardware Setup" window, as well as the HD I/O #3, which is attached to the second port (Port 2) of the Avid HDX PCIe card, but HD I/O #2 needs to be declared because it is connected thru the Expansion port of the HD I/O #1. To do this, go to Setups > Hardware Setup menu, select the first HD I/O in the Peripherals list, and make the proper assignment. Set the Inputs 1-8 of the three audio interfaces to "Analog 1-8" and make sure the Clock Source is set to "Loop Sync." Then click OK.

- Go to Setups > I/O Setup menu, and press the "Default" button in the Input and Output tabs. This way, you will be able to see the default names of your Inputs and outputs. (You can also give them different names). Choose the Mic Preamps tab and click in the path row under the audio interface's Input channel you want to assign the PRE. Do this for the three of them. This was the last step for the PRE configuration. If you go to View

> Mix Window Shows > Mic Preamps menu, you should see the Preamp controls on the top most section of controls of each channel strip of the Mix window to remotely control the preamplifiers from Pro Tools.

Configuring Pro Tools to record

- To be able to record any track for the transfer, you must record enable (press the red record button) all 24 audio tracks in your Pro Tools session. Also, you need to set the Session Start time in the Session Setup window located in the Setup > Session menu. This is to have a time reference in Pro Tools for future tasks needed to be done after the transfer is finished, you never know.
- Test to see if you are getting audio coming from the 2-inch tape machine on each Pro Tools audio track, do this by pressing the Play button on the tape machine to start the playback.
- Once you know audio is getting on each audio track, click on the "Online" button on Pro Tools Transport window. This will allow Pro Tools to accept time code to be able to synchronize with the 2-in tape machine.
- If you are ready to transfer all 24 tracks (track 24 is the SMPTE track, remember?), press the Record button on Pro Tools Transport window. You will notice the ONLINE button will start flashing, then, press the Play button on the tape machine. If everything is working fine, Pro Tools should be in "Pause-Record" mode, and it won't start recording until it reaches the time you specified earlier as the "Session Start Time" in the Session Setup window. Once it reaches the specific location time, Pro Tools will start recording, and the analog audio transfer will be completed once you press Stop in the 2-inch tape machine transport since Pro Tools is acting as a "slave" machine (that is, it's been controlled by the tape machine transport).

Congratulations, you did it!

This concludes this exercise. Remember, all the track assignments are arbitrarily chosen so you can learn and understand the process of transfering 24 analog tracks from a 2-inch tape machine to a Pro Tools HD session. By no means this is the only way to do it, these scenarios are just to practice connecting your studio and assigning external devices in your Pro Tools HD studio.

Connecting a Pro Tools HD System

In this professional Pro Tools HD studio setup, we are using the Avid HD I/O audio interface and the 96 I/O. The 96 I/O became a "Legacy" machine when Avid released the new generation of audio interfaces such as the HD I/O, HD OMNI, and HD MADI. "Legacy" audio interfaces are still found in many studios, so this setup is for those who still have these interfaces or had just purchased them used, and have the need to learn how to connect their music production studio. With this specific setup one can produce some good sounding 96 kHz/24-bit recordings and mixdowns using external outboard gear as well as internal digital signal processors via TDM plug-ins.

Equipment List

- 1 – Avid HD I/O Audio Interface
- 1 – Avid 96 I/O Audio Interface
- 1 – Avid HD Core PCIe Card
- 1 – Avid HD Accel PCIe Card
- 2 – External Reverb Processors
- 1 – Delay Processor
- 1 – Compressor Processor
- 1 – Gate Processor
- 1 – Equalizer (EQ)
- 1 – Four-channel Analog Mixer
- 1 – QSC GX7 Power Amplifier
- 1 – Pair of Speaker Monitors
- 1 – Apple Mac Pro Desktop Computer
- 1 – 12TB G-RAID FireWire 800 External Hard Drive

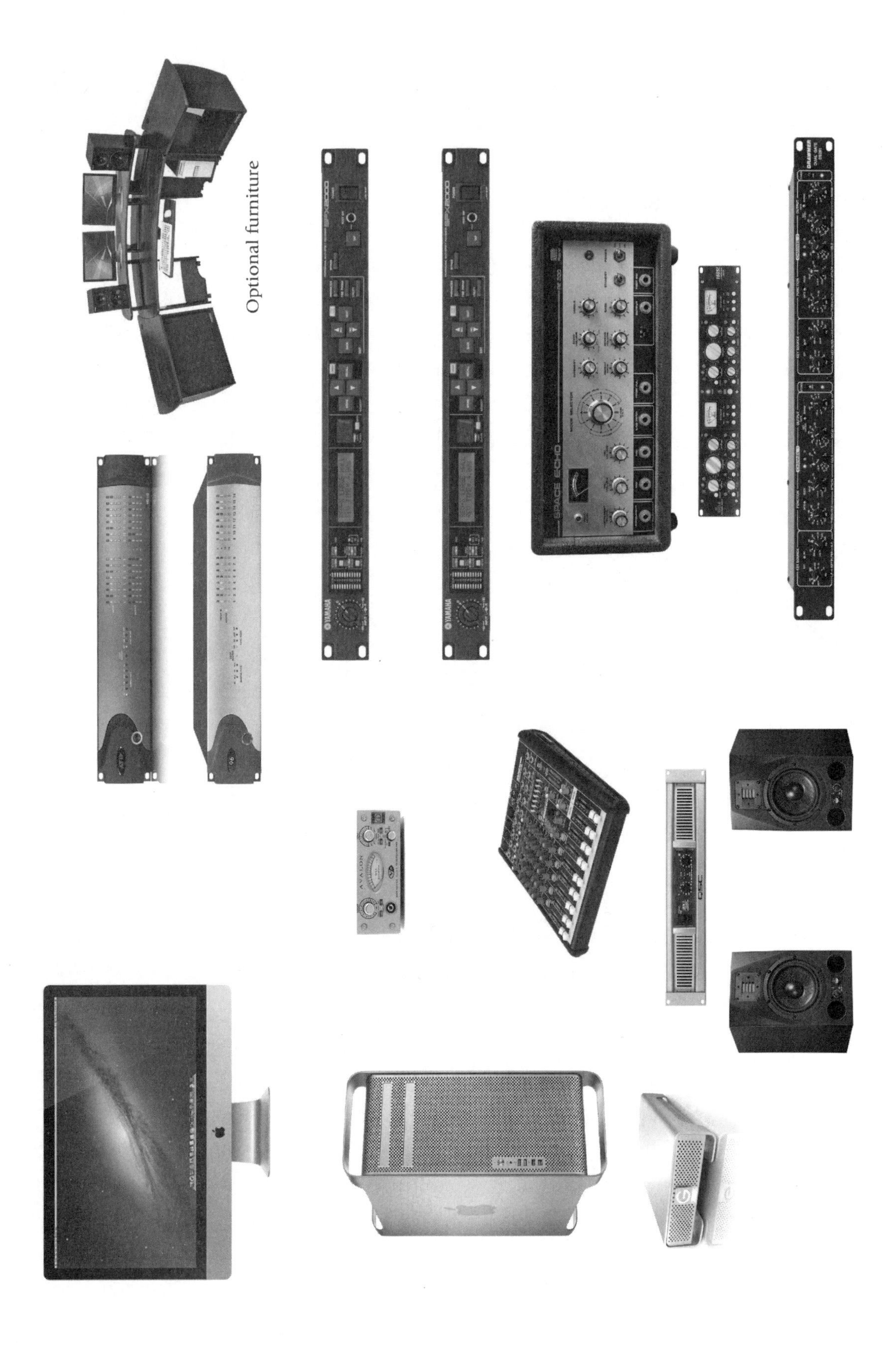
Optional furniture
SPACE ECHO

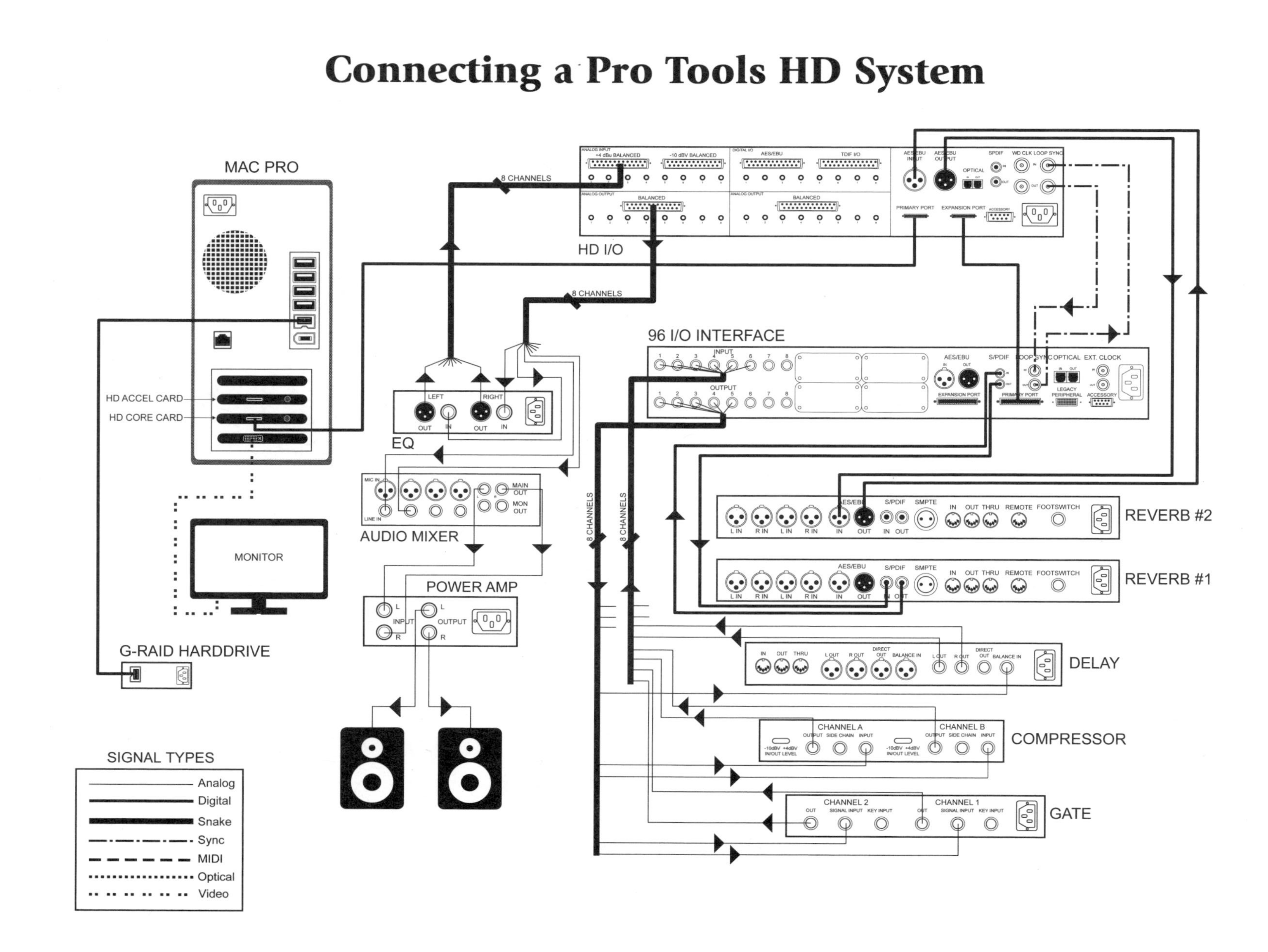
Connecting a Pro Tools HD System
MAC PRO
HD ACCEL CARD
HD CORE CARD
MONITOR
G-RAID HARDDRIVE
HD I/O
8 CHANNELS
8 CHANNELS
8 CHANNELS
8 CHANNELS
96 I/O INTERFACE
EQ
AUDIO MIXER
POWER AMP
REVERB #2
REVERB #1
DELAY
COMPRESSOR
GATE
SIGNAL TYPES
Analog
Digital
Snake
Sync
MIDI
Optical
Video

Cable List

- 2 – Avid DigiLink cables
- 2 – DigiLink to DigiLink Mini adapters
- 4 – 8x8 DB-25 to XLR (or 1/4-inch TRS) cable snakes
- 4 – 1/4-inch TRS Cables
- 2 – BNC Cables
- 2 – 75-ohm RCA Cables
- 2 – 110-ohm AES/EBU Cables
- 2 – FireWire 800 cables

Hardware Connections

Once you have gathered all the components of your studio, the next trick is to connect all these elements together. To get you started, I have assembled a sample line diagram and a step-by-step explanation that shows how this is done. Of course, these are just examples, you are not likely to have the exact system list of components and processors discussed here. Hopefully, this section will give you a rough idea of how to connect systems similar to those shown here. For example, the Input and output of the audio interfaces are picked arbitrarily, you can select any input and output you desire.

1. Connecting a 12TB G-RAID FireWire 800 External Hard Drive to the Apple Mac Pro Dsktop Computer

    - Using a FireWire 800 cable (depending on your computer), connect an available FireWire 800 port on your Apple Mac Pro desktop computer to an available FireWire 800 port on your 12TB G-RAID FireWire 800 external hard drive.

2. Connecting the Avid HD I/O Audio Interface to the Apple Mac Pro Desktop Computer

    - Connect the HD Core Card (located on the back of your computer) to the PRIMARY PORT of the Avid HD I/O audio interface (located on its rear panel) using the 12-foot DigiLink cable provided when you purchased your Pro Tools HD system. If you need a DigiLink cable longer than 12 feet in length, you may purchase it from Avid or any other professional audio vendor. The available lengths are: 1.5ft, 12ft, 25ft, 50ft, 100ft, and 200ft. If you are running sessions higher than 96 kHz of Sample Rate, don't use cable lengths higher than 50ft. DigiLink cables 100ft and 200ft don't support rate above 96kHz. You will also need a DigiLink to DigiLink Mini adapter.

3. Connecting the Avid HD I/O Audio Interface to the 96 I/O

    - Connect the EXPANSION PORT of the Avid HD I/O audio interface (located on the rear panel) to the PRIMARY PORT of the 96 I/O using the 1.5ft. DigiLink cable provided with your audio interfaces.

4. Connecting the LOOP SYNC

    - Connect the LOOP SYNC OUT of the Avid HD I/O audio interface to the LOOP SYNC IN of the 96 I/O audio interface, using the 1.5ft. BNC cable provided with your interfaces.
    - Connect the LOOP SYNC OUT of the 96 I/O audio interface to the LOOP SYNC IN of the Avid HD I/O audio interface, using another 1.5ft. BNC cable.

5. Connecting the Reverb Unit #2 to the Avid HD I/O Audio Interface using the AES/EBU Digital Audio Transfer Format

    - Using a 110-ohm AES/EBU cable, connect the AES/EBU OUT of Reverb unit #2 to the AES/EBU INPUT of the Avid HD I/O audio interface.
    - Using another 110-ohm AES/EBU Cables, connect the AES/EBU OUTPUT of the Avid HD I/O audio interface to the AES/EBU IN of Reverb unit #2.

6. Connecting the Reverb Unit #1 to the 96 I/O Audio Interface using the S/PDIF Digital Audio Transfer Format

    - Using a 75-ohm RCA-Male to RCA-Male cable, connect the S/PDIF OUT of the 96 I/O audio interface to the S/PDIF IN of Reverb unit #1.
    - Using another 75-ohm RCA-Male to RCA-Male cable, connect the S/PDIF

OUT of Reverb unit #1, to the S/PDIF IN of the 96 I/O audio interface.

7. Connecting the Delay, the Compressor, and the Gate Processors to the 96 I/O Audio Interface Inputs

    - In this example, we are using the 96 I/O audio interface's analog Ins and Outs to route all the external signal processors for this we are using an 8x8 – 1/4-inch TRS-Male to 1/4-inch TRS-Male cable snake. You should consult your manufacturer's documentation for information to select the proper snake for your units, that is, if they have balanced or unbalanced Inputs and Outputs.
    - Connect the OUT L jack of the delay unit to the ANALOG INPUT 1 of the 96 I/O audio interface. Remember, these Input assignments on the 96 I/O are arbitrary; you can connect them as you desire, or as your equipment is capable of.
    - Connect the OUT R jack on the delay unit to the ANALOG INPUT 2 of the 96 I/O audio interface.
    - Connect the CHANNEL A output jack of the compressor to the ANALOG INPUT 3 on the 96 I/O audio interface.
    - Connect the CHANNEL B output jack of the compressor to the ANALOG INPUT 4 of the 96 I/O audio interface.
    - Connect the CHANNEL 1 OUT jack of the gate unit to the ANALOG INPUT 5 of the 96 I/O audio interface.
    - Connect the CHANNEL 2 OUT jack on the gate unit to the ANALOG INPUT 6 of the 96 I/O audio interface.

8. Connecting the Delay, the Compressor, and the Gate Processors to the 96 I/O Audio Interface Outputs

    - In this example, we are using another 8x8 – 1/4-inch TRS to 1/4-inch TRS-Male cable snake. Again, you should consult your manufacturer's documentation for information to select the proper cable snake for your units.
    - Connect the ANALOG OUTPUT 1 of the 96 I/O audio interface to the BALANCE IN jack of the delay unit.

- Connect the ANALOG OUTPUT 3 of the 96 I/O audio interface to the CHANNEL A IN jack of the compressor.
- Connect the ANALOG OUTPUT 4 of the 96 I/O audio interface to the CHANNEL B IN jack of the compressor.
- Connect the ANALOG OUTPUT 5 of the 96 I/O audio interface to the CHANNEL 1 SIGNAL INPUT jack of the gate unit.
- Connect the ANALOG OUTPUT 6 of the 96 I/O audio interface e to the CHANNEL 2 SIGNAL INPUT jack of the gate unit.

NOTE: Notice we did not use the output 2 jack of the 96 I/O audio interface; this is to keep the same inputs and output orders on the 96 I/O audio interface. The reason we only use output one is because in this example we are injecting a mono signal to the delay unit to get a delayed stereo signal output.

9. Connecting the Equalizer Unit (EQ) Outputs to the Avid HD I/O Audio Interface Inputs
    - Connect the LEFT OUT jack of the EQ to INPUT #5 of the Avid HD I/O audio interface, using an 8x8 – DB-25 to XLR-Female or 1/4-inch TRS-Male cable snake, depending on your EQ unit.
    - Connect the RIGHT OUT jack of the EQ to INPUT #6 of the Avid HD I/O audio interface, using another 8x8x DB-25 – XLR-Male or 1/4-inch combination cable snake, again, depending on your EQ unit.

10. Connecting the Avid HD I/O Audio Interface Outputs to the EQ Inputs
    - Connect OUTPUT #5 of the Avid HD I/O audio interface to the LEFT IN jack of the EQ, using an 8x8 – DB-25 to XLR-Female or 1/4-inch TRS-Male cable snake, depending on your EQ unit.
    - Connect OUTPUT #6 of the Avid HD I/O audio interface to the RIGHT IN jack of the EQ, using an 8x8 – DB-25 to XLR-Female or 1/4-inch TRS-Male cable snake, depending on your EQ unit.

11. Connecting the Output of the Avid HD I/O Audio Interface to the Analog Audio Mxer

- Connect OUTPUT #1 on the Avid HD I/O audio interface to LINE IN #1 jack of the analog audio mixer using the same cable snakes as above.
- Connect OUTPUT #2 on the Avid HD I/O audio interface to LINE IN #2 jack of the analog audio mixer using the same cable snakes as above

12. Connecting the Mixer to the QSC GX7 Power Amplifier

- Connect the MONITOR OUT L on the analog audio mixer to the INPUT L jack of the GX7 power amplifier, using a 1/4-inch TRS-Male to 1/4-inch TRS-Male cable.
- Connect the MONITOR OUT R on the analog audio mixer to the INPUT R jack of the GX7 power amplifier, using a 1/4-inch TRS-Male to 1/4-inch TRS-Male cable.

13. Connecting the QSC GX7 Power Amplifier to the Speaker Monitors

- Connect the OUTPUT L jack of the power amplifier to the LEFT speaker monitor, using a 1/4-inch TRS-Male to XLR-Male cable. (This is the type of cable that most speakers use. However, some speakers require other types of cables, so check the manufacturer's documentation of your speakers and power amplifier for more information).
- Connect the OUTPUT R jack of the power amplifier to the RIGHT speaker monitor, using a 1/4-inch TRS-Male to XLR-Male cable. (This is the type of cable that most speakers use. However, some speakers require other types of cables, so check the manufacturer's documentation of your speakers and power amplifier for more information).
- If your monitor speakers are powered (meaning they already have a power amplifier built in), you do not need to connect them to an external power amplifier. In this case, you may go back to step 12 and connect the MONITOR OUT L and R of the analog audio mixer to the speaker monitors.

NOTE: You should consult the manufacturer's documentation for information of all your equipment in your studio to select the proper cables and cable snakes for your units.

System Requirements

Since the system requirements for Pro Tools is constantly being updated, and depending on the Pro Tools HD hardware and software versions you are using in your studio, it is best to visit www.avid.com and search for the "Avid Knowledge Base – Pro Tools System Requirements," for both Mac OS and Windows OS and look for your specific Pro Tools and Operating system in your computer.

Software Setup

In this particular example, we will be using a Pro Tools HD 2 system. Regardless of what version of Pro Tools you in your system, you should already have installed the software and other files required to run Pro Tools properly. Also, it is very important that you check which operating system is installed in your computer, whether you are using a Macintosh (Mac OSX) or a PC running on Windows. If you are not sure you have the proper software versions for both your computer system and Pro Tools, along with any other digital device you are using in your setup, such MIDI controllers, audio interfaces, etc., then check the compatibility information on the software versions you are running in the respective websites of the company's device you are using. For example, if you are using Pro Tools, then you can visit www.avid.com to check on the latest compatibility information.

Setting up Pro Tools

Let's simulate mixing a 16-track Pro Tools session you recorded earlier. In this simulation we will integrate all the external signal processors shown in the diagram at the beginning of this setup. Let's make all the proper assignments in the Pro Tools software:

- Once you have launched Pro Tools in your computer, go to the File menu and select "Open Session" to open the session you recorded earlier. I recommend to save a copy of your original session just in case something happens to the file or you got lost in the assignment process and you would rather start from the beginning again. Use the SAVE AS command located in the FILE menu, and give the session another name when prompted and click on the OK button to save it. It should be routed inside the folder you saved the original session.

Assigning the External Signal Processors in Pro Tools

Now, let's make the proper assignments in Pro Tools for all the external signal processors in the Mix window:

- Since we are using six external devices in our example (two reverb units, one delay, one compressor, one gate, and one equalizer or EQ), let's create two stereo Aux Input tracks to use them as reverb . The other devices we will assign them as hardware inserts in the Pro Tools audio tracks, just to show the process of how to assign them, again, all these examples are just a guide and a way for you to see the process of how to do it with your own studio equipment.
- You can label the Inputs, outputs, Inserts and busses (internal or output) in Pro Tools to make it easier for you to assign them in your session. This avoids confusion when assigning track Inputs, outputs and sends, especially when you are working on a large session.
- To do this, go to the Setups > I/O Setup menu, you should see the Avid HD I/O and the 96 I/O icons in the I/O Setup window. Press the "Default" button on each tab of each interface shown. First, default the Input, then the Output, the Bus, and finally the Insert tab. This way, you will be able to see the default names Pro Tools gives to each tab so you will be able to identify where you plugged all your external devices.
- Next, let's label the Input tab of the first interface, the Avid HD I/O audio interface, so click once on this tab. You probably will see different names or assignments from prior sessions and/or interfaces used before in your Pro Tools system.
- Double click on Input 5 and Input 6, notice the name will be selected (highlighted) and ready to be renamed. Go ahead and rename them as "EQ IN LEFT" and "EQ IN RIGHT," respectively. While the name is still highlighted, click on the Tab key on your computer keyboard once, this will move the cursor down and be ready to rename the next set of Inputs. Go ahead and rename Inputs 7 and 8 as "REVERB 1 LEFT IN" and "REVERB 1 RIGHT IN." If you notice in the diagram, the reverb #1 unit is

connected to the S/PDIF digital Ins and Outs of the Avid HD audio interface. You need to set Input and output 7 and 8 to accept digital signals via the S/PDIF Enclosure port. Do this in the menu Setup > Hardware to select the digital I/O.

- Now, click on the Output tab and double click on Output 1 and 2. Rename these outputs as "MAIN SPEAKERS." While the name is still selected (highlighted), click on the Tab key of your computer keyboard, this will move the cursor down and be ready to rename the next set of outputs, in this case will be Outputs 3 and 4. Rename them as "SPEAKERS B," in case you have a second pair of speaker monitors in your studio. Again, while the name is still selected (highlighted), click on the Tab key and rename Outputs 5 and 6 as "EQ OUT L" and "EQ OUT R," and one more time, click the Tab key to rename Outputs 7 and 8 as "REVERB 1 LEFT OUT" and "REVERB 1 RIGHT OUT." Don't forget to label the name plates of the 2 stereo Aux Input track as "REV 1 Return" and "REV 2 Return."

- Continuing with labeling your external devices in Pro Tools, go back to the Input tab of the I/O Setup window in Pro Tools, and select Input 1 of the 96 I/O audio interface and rename it as "DELAY IN" only for Input 1, Input 2 leave it as is. In the example diagram notice we are only using a mono Input of the delay unit. In the table below, please follow the name assignments for the rest of the inputs and outputs for the 96 I/O.

Input	Name	Output	Name
Analog 1	DELAY IN	Analog 1	DELAY OUT L
Analog 2	INPUT 2	Analog 2	DELAY OUT R
Analog 3	COMPRESSOR IN L	Analog 3	COMPRESSOR OUT L
Analog 4	COMPRESSOR IN R	Analog 4	COMPRESSOR OUT R
Analog 5	GATE IN L	Analog 5	GATE OUT L
Analog 6	GATE IN R	Analog 6	GATE OUT R55
S/PDIF L	REVERB #2 IN L	S/PDIF L	REVERB #2 OUT L
S/PDIF R	REVERB #2 IN R	S/PDIF R	REVERB #2 OUT R

- You will notice that the digital inputs and outputs 7 and 8 must be assigned to S/PDIF Enclosure on the 96 I/O audio interface, and in the same manner you assigned inputs and outputs 7 and 8 on the Avid HD I/O audio interface AES/EBU through the Setup > Hardware menu. You can also check the Reference Guide for the Avid HD I/O audio interface and 96 I/O for more information of how to assignh the digital ports.

Assigning Hardware Inserts and Sends in your session:

As I mentioned above, in this exercise we are using hardware Inserts in the audio tracks themselves, as well as a couple of Sends and stereo Aux Input tracks to use them as the reverb returns. Now that the inputs and outputs are labeled, it is going to be much easier to assign the Inserts, sends and returns to and from the external devices. Let's simulate the following scenario, we will assign the reverb #1 to the voice track, and the reverb #2 to the snare track. Also, let's suppose we are adding a compressor to the bass track, the delay to an electric guitar track , the gate to the snare to get rid of the hi-hat bleeding, and the equalizer to EQ the lead vocal. Take a look at the following assignment table. By the way, all these assignments are done in the Pro Tools Mix window:

Track (mono)	Insert	Send	Return	Input/Output
Bass	COMP (96 I/O)			Analog 3-4
Snare	(96 I/O)	Rev 1	REV 1 Ret	S/PDIF 7-8
Snare	GATE (96 I/O)			Analog 5-6
Electric Guitar	DELAY (96 I/O)			Analog 1-2
Vocal	EQ (192 I/O)			Analog 5-6
Vocal	(HD I/O)	Rev 2	REV 2 Ret	AES/EBU 7-8

NOTE: It may take a little bit of time analyzing this process, but it is normal. It is not easy, so go ahead and read two or three times until you understand it, and apply it in one of your sessions, it works great!

This concludes this exercise. Again, all the track assignments are arbitrarily chosen so you can learn and understand the process of adding external signal processors in your mixing session. By no means this is the only way to do it, these scenarios are just to practice connecting your studio and assigning external devices in your Pro Tools HD studio.

Focusrite RedNet To Pro Tools HD

Focusrite RedNet is a near zero latency system of modular Ethernet-networked audio interfaces that brings Audinate's Dante digital audio networking system to the studio environment. In this setup, five Focusrite RedNet units are interfaced with Pro Tools HDX and the SSL Matrix 2 mixing board. The Focusrite RedNet 1 is an 8-channel A-D/D-A. Two of these units make 16 channels of audio interfaced with the SSL Matrix 2. The Focusrite RedNet 4 is an 8-channel Mic/Line preamp unit. Two of these units provide 16 microphone sources to our setup. The Focusrite RedNet 5 connects the Focusrite RedNet system to an Avid Pro Tools HD system and routes up to 32 input and 32 output channels between Pro Tools and the Focusrite RedNet network.

Equipment List

- 1 – Solid State Logic (SSL) Matrix 2 Mixing Board
- 1 – AVID HDX PCIe Card
- 1 – Ethernet Switch
- 1 – Apple Mac Pro Desktop Computer
- 2 – Focusrite RedNet 1 Units
- 2 – Focusrite RedNet 4 Units
- 1 – Focusrite RedNet 5 Unit
- 16 – Microphones

Cable List

- 4 – 8x8 DB-25 to DB-25 cable snakes
- 7 – Ethernet cables
- 16 – XLR cables
- 1 – DigiLink Mini cable

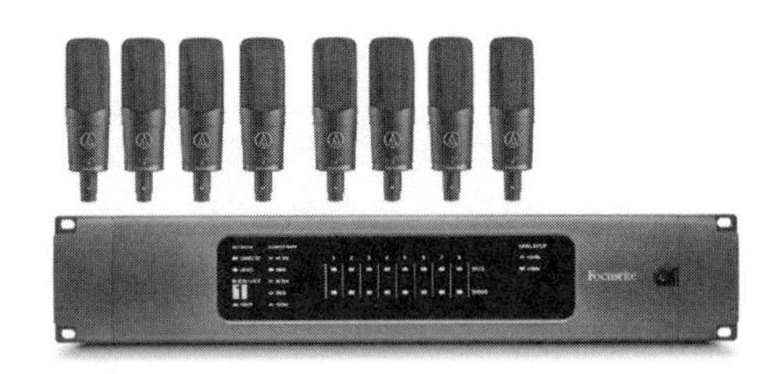

Optional furniture

Focusrite RedNet to Pro Tools HD

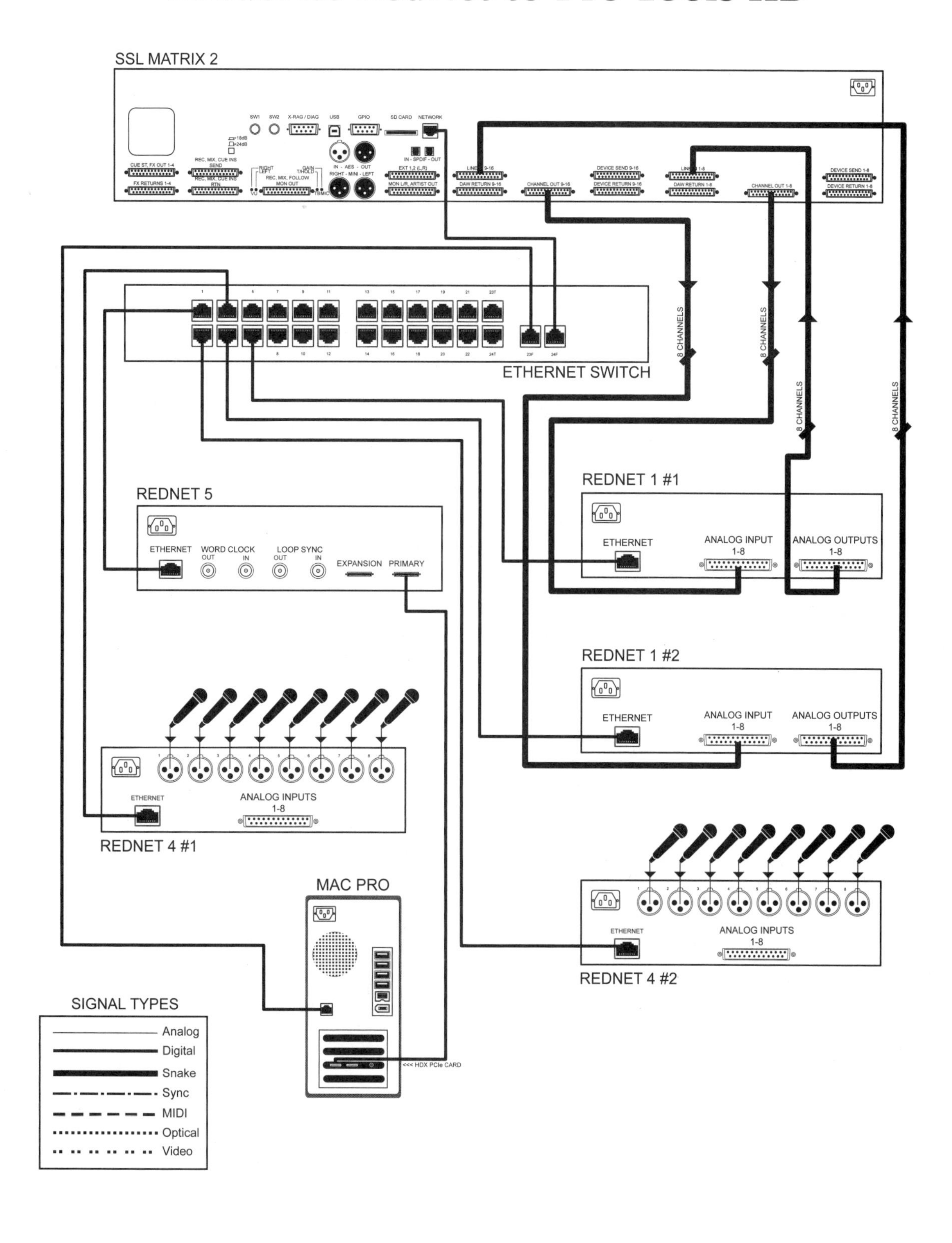

Hardware Connections

1. Connecting the SSL Matrix 2 to the two Focusrite RedNet 1 Units
   - Using a 8x8 DB-25 to DB-25 cable snake, connect the "ANALOG OUTPUTS 1-8" from the rear panel of the Focusrite RedNet 1 #1 unit to the "LINE IN 1-8" on the rear panel of the SSL Matrix 2.
   - Using another 8x8 DB-25 to DB-25 cable snake, connect the "CHANNEL OUT 1-8" on the rear panel of the SSL Matrix 2 to the "ANALOG INPUT 1-8" on the rear panel of the Focusrite RedNet 1 #1 unit.
   - Using the third 8x8 DB-25 to DB-25 cable snake, connect the "ANALOG OUTPUTS 1-8" from the rear panel of the Focusrite RedNet 1 #2 unit to the "LINE IN 9-16" on the rear panel of the SSL Matrix 2.
   - Using the fourth 8x8 DB-25 to DB-25 cable snake, connect the "CHANNEL OUT 9-16" on the rear panel of the SSL Matrix 2 to the "ANALOG INPUT 1-8" on the rear panel of the Focusrite RedNet 1 #2 unit.

2. Connecting the SSL Matrix 2 to the Ethernet Switch
   - Using an Ethernet cable, connect the "NETWORK" Ethernet port on the rear panel of the SSL Matrix 2 to the "24F" port on the Ethernet Switch.

3. Connecting all the Focusrite RedNet Units to the Ethernet Switch
   - Using an Ethernet cable, connect the "ETHERNET" port on the Focusrite RedNet 1 #1 unit to the "6" port on the Ethernet switch.
   - Using a second Ethernet cable, connect the "ETHERNET" port on the Focusrite RedNet 1 #2 unit to the "4" port on the Ethernet switch.
   - Using a third Ethernet cable, connect the "ETHERNET" port on the Focusrite RedNet 4 #1 unit to the "3" port on the Ethernet switch.
   - Using a fourth Ethernet cable, connect the "ETHERNET" port on the Focusrite RedNet 4 #2 unit to the "2" port on the Ethernet switch.
   - Using a fifth Ethernet cable, connect the "ETHERNET" port on the Focusrite RedNet 5 unit to the "1" port on the Ethernet switch.

4. Connecting the Focusrite RedNet 5 Unit to the Apple Mac Pro Quad-Core Desktop Computer HDX PCIe Card

    - Using a standard DigiLink Mini cable, connect the "PRIMARY PORT" on the rear panel of the Focusrite RedNet 5 unit to the DigiLink mini port on the HDX PCIe card inside the Apple Mac Pro Quad-Core desktop computer.

5. Connecting the Microphones to the Focusrite RedNet 4 #1 Unit

    - Using an XLR cable, connect the output of the first microphone to "XLR IN 1" of the Focusrite RedNet 4 #1 unit.
    - Using a second XLR cable, connect the output of the second microphone to "XLR IN 2" of the Focusrite RedNet 4 #1 unit.
    - Using a third XLR cable, connect the output of the third microphone to "XLR IN 3" of the Focusrite RedNet 4 #1 unit.
    - Using a fourth XLR cable, connect the output of the fourth microphone to "XLR IN 4" of the Focusrite RedNet 4 #1 unit
    - Using a fifth XLR cable, connect the output of the fifth microphone to "XLR IN 5" of the Focusrite RedNet 4 #1 unit.
    - Using a sixth XLR cable, connect the output of the sixth microphone to "XLR IN 6" of the Focusrite RedNet 4 #1 unit.
    - Using a seventh XLR cable, connect the output of the seventh microphone to "XLR IN 7" of the Focusrite RedNet 4 #1 unit.
    - Using the eighth XLR cable, connect the output of the eighth microphone to "XLR IN 8" of the Focusrite RedNet 4 #1 unit.

6. Connecting the Microphones to the Focusrite RedNet 4 #2 Unit

    - Using an XLR cable, connect the output of the first microphone to "XLR IN 1" of the Focusrite RedNet 4 #2 unit.
    - Using a second XLR cable, connect the output of the second microphone to "XLR IN 2" of the Focusrite RedNet 4 #2 unit.
    - Using a third XLR cable, connect the output of the third microphone to

"XLR IN 3" of the Focusrite RedNet 4 #2 unit.

- Using a fourth XLR cable, connect the output of the fourth microphone to "XLR IN 4" of the Focusrite RedNet 4 #2 unit.
- Using a fifth XLR cable, connect the output of the fifth microphone to "XLR IN 5" of the Focusrite RedNet 4 #2 unit.
- Using a sixth XLR cable, connect the output of the sixth microphone to "XLR IN 6" of the Focusrite RedNet 4 #2 unit.
- Using a seventh XLR cable, connect the output of the seventh microphone to "XLR IN 7" of the Focusrite RedNet 4 #2 unit.
- Using the eighth XLR cable, connect the output of the eighth microphone to "XLR IN 8" of the Focusrite RedNet 4 #2 unit.

System Requirements

Focusrite RedNet Control for Mac OS X (as of this writing)

- Apple Mac with OSX 10.7 (Lion), 10.8 (Mountain Lion) or later. Please note that Focusrite RedNet is not supported by Mac PPC.
- Min. 2 GB RAM
- Dual core Intel Processor (Quad core recommended)
- Focusrite RedNet Control for Windows (as of this writing):
- PC running Windows 7 or Windows 8 (32- or 64-bit). Please note that Focusrite RedNet is not supported by Windows Vista.
- Min. 2 GB RAM
- Dual Core processor (Quad core recommended)

NOTE: Users should check the Focusrite website for the latest information regarding specifications of suitable computers for the RedNet system.

Software Setup

- Go to www.focusrite.com/register, and follow the instructions on the software card to register your product and download Focusrite RedNet Control and associated software.
- When all downloads are complete, install the Focusrite RedNet drivers and Focusrite RedNet Control application in the usual manner.

Configuring Focusrite RedNet Control

- Click Settings > Select Network Interface and select the network adapter that is connected to the Dante network.
- Click Settings > Host Mode and select "Focusrite RedNet 5," since we are interfacing the Focusrite RedNet system with Pro Tools HDX.

NOTE: The default sample rate of the Focusrite RedNet units is 48 kHz. To change this rate, select the sample rate in Settings > Sample Rate.

- On the Pro Tools Hardware Setup page (click Setup > Hardware), select each Focusrite RedNet 5 unit in turn and click the Set to Default button. This will ensure that the Focusrite RedNet 5 is correctly configured for use with Pro Tools.
- Activate "Pro Tools Mode" in Focusrite RedNet Control. The Focusrite RedNet PCIe card will be detected automatically by Pro Tools and added to the list of available audio sources. The input and output channels available via the Focusrite RedNet PCIe card will be listed in Pro Tool's Audio I/O Setup as "Input N" or "Output N" (where n will have a value of between 1 and 128).

This concludes this exercise. Remember, all the track assignments are arbitrarily chosen so you can know and understand the process of setting up a session to set up your Focusrite RedNet units with Pro Tools HDX. By no means is this the only way to do it, these scenarios are just to practice plugging in your studio and configuring your Focusrite RedNet system with Pro Tools HDX.

Professional Overdub Studio Setup

Overdubbing is a technique in which a performer/artist listens to pre-recorded tracks and records a new performance along with the existing one in order to create a mix of both recordings. Usually a rhythm section (drums, bass, rhythm guitar, and piano, along with a guide vocal track) will be the first recorded tracks. Then, solo instruments such as keyboards, guitars, strings, horns, and final vocals will be added (overdubbed) in order to complete the project.

It is a very common practice to start on a music production in one studio, and continue with the overdub process in another one, in a different city, or even in a different country. So, overdubbing is the example of how we will use this particular setup.

To explain, let's suppose that in this scenario, a Pro Tools session was previously created in a studio in Dallas, Texas. And, let's suppose the artist, who started the pro -ject there, did not have the time to record his final vocals and his electric guitar solo parts. Now, the artist had to be in Los Angeles for a week doing promotion for his new production, but his record label contacted him and told him they needed the completed song project within three days. Therefore, he will have to do overdubs of his voice and electric guitar in LA using the professional studio setup shown in this example. Remember, I am only showing the recording of the overdub, not the mix, consequently, you will notice in the line diagram that there is no mixing board.

Although the setup used in this example consists of a small amount of equipment, it is still a very powerful one, capable of achieving high quality results. We are using some of the best pro audio equipment available today, including one of the most powerful computer Apple has released to date. Also, a couple of high quality Avalon Preamps are going through a Mytek Digital 8x192 A-D/D-A converter. And, a Burl B26 Orca control room monitor system is being used as our monitor section. Let's take a look at how one will connect this equipment.

Equipment List

- 1 – Apple Mac Pro Quad-Core Desktop Computer
- 2 – Computer Monitors

BURL
STUDIO MONITOR
CONTROL ROOM MONITOR
B26
ORCA
AVALON
VU
AVALON
VU
Optional furniture

Professional Overdub Studio Setup

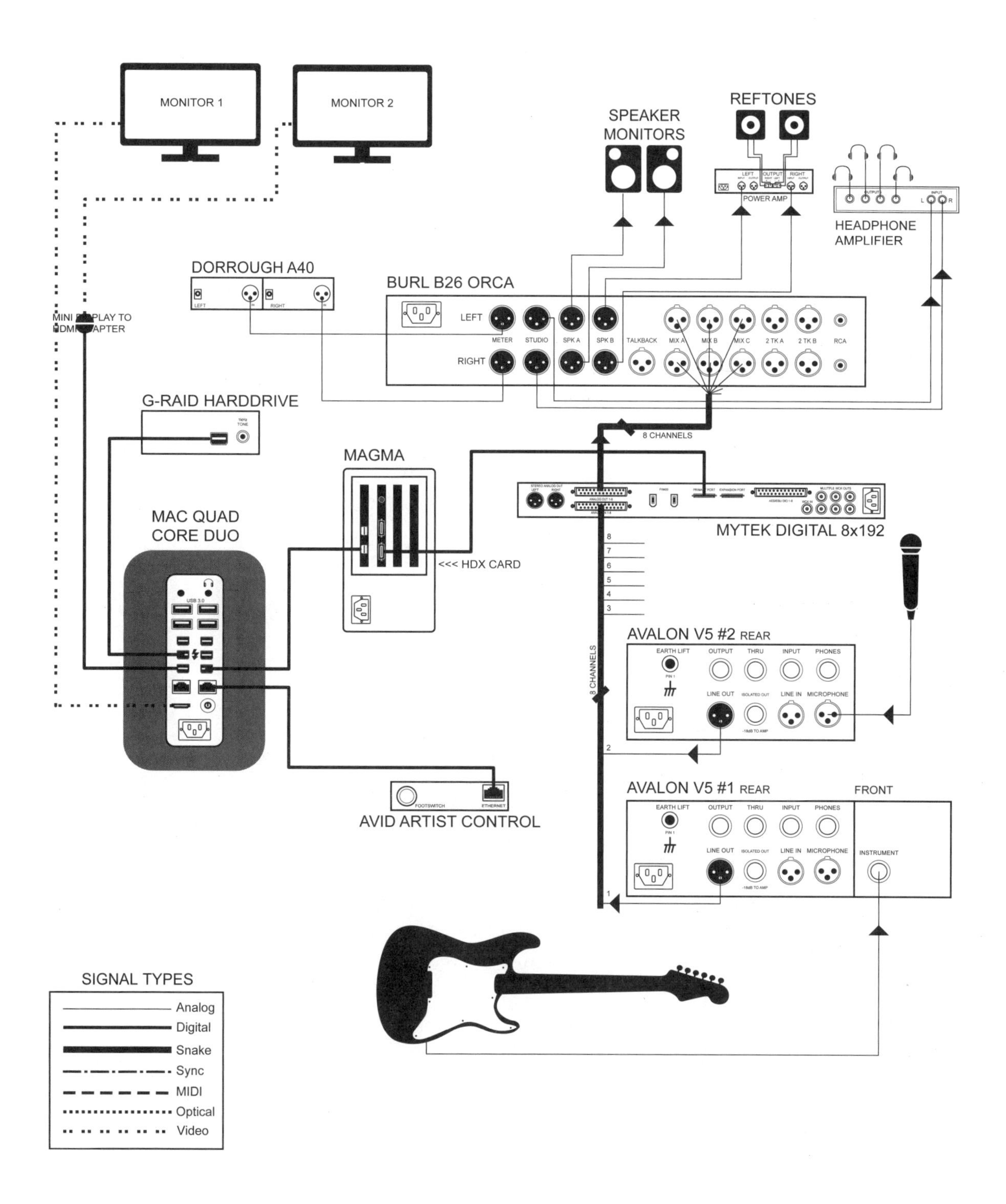

- 1 – 12TB G-Technology G-RAID STUDIO External Hard Drive
- 1 – Avid HDX PCIe Card
- 1 – Magma ExpressBox 3T Expansion Chassis
- 1 – Avid Artist Control Fader Control Surface
- 1 – Burl Audio B26 Orca Control Room Monitor System
- 1 – Mytek Digital 8X192 AD/DA Audio Interface
- 2 – Pairs of Powered Speaker Monitors
- 2 – Reftone Speaker Monitors
- 2 – Dorrough 40-A Loudness Meter
- 2 – Avalon V5 Preamplifiers
- 1 – Microphone
- 1 – Electric Guitar

Cable List

- 3 – Thunderbolt cables
- 2 – HDMI cables
- 1 – Mini Display to HDMI adapter
- 1 – Ethernet cable
- 1 – Avid DigiLink Mini cable
- 1 – 8x8 DB-25 to Female XLR cable snake
- 1 – 8x8 DB-25 to Male XLR cable snake
- 7 – XLR cables
- 1 – 1/4-inch TS to 1/4-inch TS cable
- 2 – Dual Banana to Banana male speaker cables
- 2 – XLR Female to 1/4-inch male TS cables

Hardware Connections

Once you have gathered all the components of the studio, the next trick is to connect all these elements together. To get you started, I have assembled a sample connection diagram and explanation that show how this is done. Of course, these are just examples, you are not likely to have the exact system list of components and processors discussed here, but hopefully, this diagram and explanation will give you an idea of how to connect a similar system. The inputs and outputs of the audio interfaces were arbitrarily selected, but you can choose any input and/or output you desire for your situation.

1. Connecting a 12TB G-Technology G-RAID Hard Drive to the Apple Mac Pro Quad-Core Desktop Computer

    - Using a Thunderbolt cable, connect an available Thunderbolt port on the back of the Apple Mac Pro Quad-Core desktop computer to the Thunderbolt port on the external G-Technology 12TB G-RAID STUDIO hard drive.

2. Connecting the Avid Artist Control to the Apple Mac Pro Quad-Core Computer

    - Using an Ethernet cable, connect an available Ethernet port on the back of the Apple Mac Pro Quad-Core desktop computer to the Ethernet port on the back of the Avid Artist Control fader control surface.

3. Connecting the Magma ExpressBox 3T Expansion Chassis (with an Avid HDX PCIe card) to the Apple Mac Pro Quad-Core Desktop Computer

    - Using a Thunderbolt cable, connect the Thunderbolt on the back of your Apple Mac Pro Quad-Core desktop computer to an available Thunderbolt port on the Magma ExpressBox 3T expansion chassis.

4. Connecting the Magma ExpressBox 3T Expansion Chassis to the Mytek Digital 8x192 AD/DA Converter

    - Using an Avid DigiLink Mini cable, connect the DigiLink port 1 on the HDX PCIe card in the Magma expansion chassis to the DigiLink Mini Primary port on the back of the Mytek Digital 8x192 AD/DA.

5. Connecting a Microphone to the Avalon V5 #2 Preamplifier in the Diagram

    - Using an XLR cable, connect the output of the microphone to the "MICROPHONE IN" jack on the rear panel of the top Avalon V5#2 preamplifier.

6. Connecting the Electric Guitar to the Avalon V5 #1 Preamplifier in the Diagram

    - Using a 1/4-inch to 1/4-inch TS cable, connect the 1/4-inch output jack of the Guitar to the "INSTRUMENT" 1/4-inch input jack in the front panel of the Avalon V5 #1 preamplifier.
    - Don't forget to set the input selector on the right of the V5 #1 preamp, to the "Instrument Hi-Z Line" position to be able to get the guitar signal in.

7. Connecting both Avalon V5 Preamplifiers to the Mytek Digital 8x192 AD/DA Converter

    - Using the DB-25 to Female XLR cable snake, connect the XLR cable labeled "1" on the 8x8 DB-25 to Female XLR cable snake to the "LINE OUT" of the Avalon V5 #1 preamplifier.
    - Using the DB-25 to Female XLR cable snake, connect the XLR cable labeled "2" on the 8x8 DB-25 to Female XLR cable snake to the "LINE OUT" of the Avalon V5 #2 preamplifier.
    - Using the same DB-25 to XLR Female cable snake, connect the DB-25 connector to the "ANALOG IN 1-8" port on the rear panel of the Mytek Digital 8x192 AD/DA converter.

8. Connecting the Mytek Digital 8x192 AD/DA to the Burl Audio B26 Orca Control Room Monitor

    Using an 8x8 DB-25 to Male XLR cable snake, make the following connec tions:

- Connect XLR OUT 1 and XLR OUT 2 of the 8x8 DB-25 to Male XLR cable snake to MIX A LEFT and MIX A RIGHT of the Burl B26 Orca.
    - Connect XLR OUT 3 and XLR OUT 4 of the 8x8 DB-25 to Male XLR cable snake to MIX B LEFT and MIX B RIGHT of the Burl B26 Orca.

- Connect XLR OUT 5 and XLR OUT 6 of the 8x8 DB-25 to Male XLR cable snake to MIX C LEFT and MIX C RIGHT of the Burl B26 Orca.

9. Connecting the Burl Audio B26 Orca Control Room Monitor to the Speaker Monitors

   - Using an XLR cable, connect the SPEAKER A LEFT OUT of the Burl B26 Orca to the Left Powered Speaker Monitor.

   - Using an XLR cable, connect the SPEAKER A RIGHT OUT of the Burl B26 Orca to the Right Powered Speaker Monitor.

   - Using an XLR cable, connect the SPEAKER B LEFT OUT of the Burl B26 Orca to the LEFT INPUT channel of the power amplifier.

   - Using an XLR cable, connect the SPEAKER B RIGHT OUT of the Burl B26 Orca to the RIGHT INPUT channel of the power amplifier.

   - Using a Dual Banana to Banana Male speaker cable, connect the Left Output channel of the power amplifier to the Banana Input jack of the Left REFTONE speaker monitor.

   - Using a Dual Banana to Banana Male speaker cable, connect the Right Output channel of the power amplifier to the Banana Input jack of the Right REFTONE speaker monitor.

10. Connecting the Headphone Distribution Amplifier to the Burl B26 Orca Control Room Monitor:

    - Using an XLR Female to a 1/4-inch TRS cable, connect the STUDIO LEFT OUTPUT jack on the rear of the Burl B26 to the Left channel of the headphone distribution amplifier.

    - Using an XLR Female to a 1/4-inch TRS cable, connect the STUDIO RIGHT OUTPUT jack on the rear of the Burl B26 to the Right channel of the headphone distribution amplifier.

11. Connecting the Burl B26 Orca Control Room Monitor to the Dorrough 40-A Loudness Meters

    - Using an XLR cable, connect the LEFT METER OUTPUT connector on the rear panel of the Burl B26 to the LEFT XLR connector on the rear of the

Dorrough 40-A Loudnesss Meter.

- Using an XLR cable, connect the RIGHT METER OUTPUT connector on the rear panel of the Burl B26 to the RIGHT XLR connector on the rear of the Dorrough 40-A Loudnesss Meter.

System Requirements

Since the system requirements for Pro Tools are constantly being updated, and depending on the Pro Tools HD hardware and software versions you are using in your studio, it is best to visit www.avid.com and search for the "Avid Knowledge Base – Pro Tools System Requirements," for both Mac OS and Windows OS and look for your specific Pro Tools and Operating system in your computer.

NOTE: In our example we are connecting the Mytek 8x192 directly to the HDX PCIe card, but you can also connect it using the FireWire port. If this is the case, then the FireWire option drivers and the Mytek Control Panel software should be installed before the first connection to the computer. Make sure you check the Mytek website for the most current drivers and detail instructions at www.mytekdigital.com.

Software Setup

Getting back to our setup, assuming all the hardware connections were done properly, and that all the Pro Tools software and extra files were already installed, let's take a look at how we can get the microphone and electric guitar signals to the previously recorded Pro Tools session. Also, let's see what kind of software settings and assignments have to be made to accomplish this overdub process.

Setting up the front panel of the Mytek Digital 8X192 AD/DA Converter:

- Set the SOURCE TO DIGITAL OUT (ADC) to ANALOG – The Mytek uses the SOURCE TO DIGITAL OUT (ADC) button to select audio signals received and passed through the 8X192 AD/DA converter to the Pro Tools system and converter's digital outputs. In this case, we are using the signals coming from the analog inputs; therefore we select the analog option.

- Set the SOURCE TO ANALOG OUT (DAC) to DIOCARD 1 – The Mytek uses SOURCE TO ANALOG OUT (DAC) to select signals passed through the converter's analog outputs (i.e. from Pro Tools to the analog outputs). Since we have the HDX option installed in card slot #1, we choose the option, "DIOCARD 1."

- Set the converter to internal clock. If the "EXT. LED" is lit, press and hold the EXT CLOCK button to come out of external mode. Once the Pro Tools session is open and set to internal, the Mytek unit will follow that sample rate and display accordingly.

- The Meters button gives you the option to display the input or output signals.

- The Stereo XLR/Phones button allows you to choose what you are listening to when connected to the headphones jack or the XLR output on the back panel. One can choose to listen to specific stereo outputs or a mix of all eight channels serving as an 8-channel summing mixer.

Setting up Pro Tools with the Mytek 8x192 Audio Interface

- Turn the converters on.

- Once you have launched Pro Tools in your computer, go to Hardware > Setup and make sure that Pro Tools is detecting the audio interface (converters). Pro Tools recognizes the Mytek 8x192 with a DIO-HDX card as an Avid HD I/O audio interface. You should see a HD I/O in the peripherals section of the Hardware Setup window. Select the HD I/O and set it to Default.

- Set the Clock Source to Internal.

- Now go to the Setup > I/O menu and configure it according to your needs.

Setting Pro Tools for recording the overdubs

Now that all the cable connections and software installations were made correctly, is time to set the audio tracks to record in Pro Tools for our overdubbing session:

- In Pro Tools, go to the Setups > I/O menu, and press the "Default" button in the Input and Output tabs. This way, you will be able to see the default names of the inputs and outputs given by Pro Tools. You can also use the I/O Setup dialog window (Setup > I/O) to label the inputs and outputs you are using in your Pro Tools session. See the Pro Tools Reference Guide for more details.

- Launch Pro Tools.
- Locate and open the Pro Tools session to which we need to add the vocal and the guitar solo tracks.
- Once the session is opened, listen to the previously recorded tracks to get familiarized with the song. If it is not done yet, I highly recommend inserting markers throughout the song to identify all the sections of the song, that is, the Intro, the Verse, the Chorus, etc. By the way, don't forget to assign the outputs of all the previously recorded tracks to the output default settings, that is Output 1 and 2 in Pro Tools, so you can listen to them through the main powered speaker monitors. Of course, if the speaker monitors in your studio are connected to different outputs, then assign them accordingly.
- Create a new track and assign the input of that track accordingly. For example, if the V5 #2 preamp where the microphone is connected to, is plugged in into Input #2 of the Mytek 8x192, then select Input 2 as the microphone input in your newly created Pro Tools audio track.
- Enable the "Input Monitor" button (the green "I" button) on the audio track to set the recording input level of the vocal using the Avalon V5 #2 preamp in our line diagram example.
- Once you set the recording level of the microphone, press the "Record Enable" button (the button with a "dot" inside that turns red when on) on the microphone's audio track.
- Press the Record button on the Pro Tools Transport window and then press the Play button to start the recording. By this time, the singer should be able to listen to the previously recorded tracks in his headphone mix and start singing to record his vocal track needed for the song project.
- If the vocal track was recorded right on the first take, then create a second audio track in the Pro Tools session for the electric guitar. If the output of the Avalon V5 #1 preamp is connected to Input #1 of the Mytek 8x192, then make the appropriate assignment in Pro Tools.

- Enable the "Input Monitor" button (the green "I" button) on the audio track to set the recording line level of the electric guitar so the solo guitar part in our scenario can be recorded.
- Once the recording line input level of the electric guitar is set using the Avalon V5 #1 preamp in our line diagram example, press the Record button on the Pro Tools Transport window and then press the Play button to start the recording. By this time, the same singer playing the guitar now, should be able to listen to the previously recorded tracks in his headphone mix and start playing his guitar solo part to be recorded. Now, the song project is completed and ready to be sent to the record label so they can mix it down.

This concludes this exercise. Again, all the track assignments are arbitrarily chosen so you can understand and learn the process of setting up a session using the Mytek audio interface with Pro Tools HDX. By no means is this the only way to do it, these scenarios are just to practice plugging in studios like the one in the example above.

Professional Music Production Setup

In the past, when I was asked to record a band in a studio, I remember I always had to arrive much earlier than anybody else. The first thing I did, besides having the first cup of fresh coffee, was turn the machines on so they would warm up, since most of the studios I worked at in those days were analog with 24-track 2-inch tape machines and tube outboard gear. I also remember having to demagnetize the recording machine's heads and align them to an operating level using a certain magnetic tape model and brand. Next, I had to make all the necessary connections on the patchbay to route the instrument signals to where I needed to send them. Now all that seems to be a thing of the past, now, most of the sessions are done in home studios. This is why I wanted to include a setup using patchbays. Even though this setup is not completely analog, it is good to know how it is done, especially for the new generation of audio engineers who have not had the opportunity to make connections like the one I will discuss ahead. This particular studio setup is designed to record and mix music projects.

Equipment List

- 1 – Solid State Logic (SSL) Matrix 2 Mixing Console
- 1 – SSL X-Rack Effects Processor
- 1 – SSL MadiXtreme PCIe Card
- 1 – SSL Alpha-Link MADI SX 24 I/O Audio Interface
- 1 – Avid PRE Preamplifier
- 1 – Apple Mac Pro Quad-Core Desktop Computer
- 1 – Magma ExpressBox 3T Expansion Chassis
- 4 – 24-Point Audio Patchbays
- 1 – 16-input Drum Room Tie Line Plate
- 1 – 6-Slot API Lunchbox

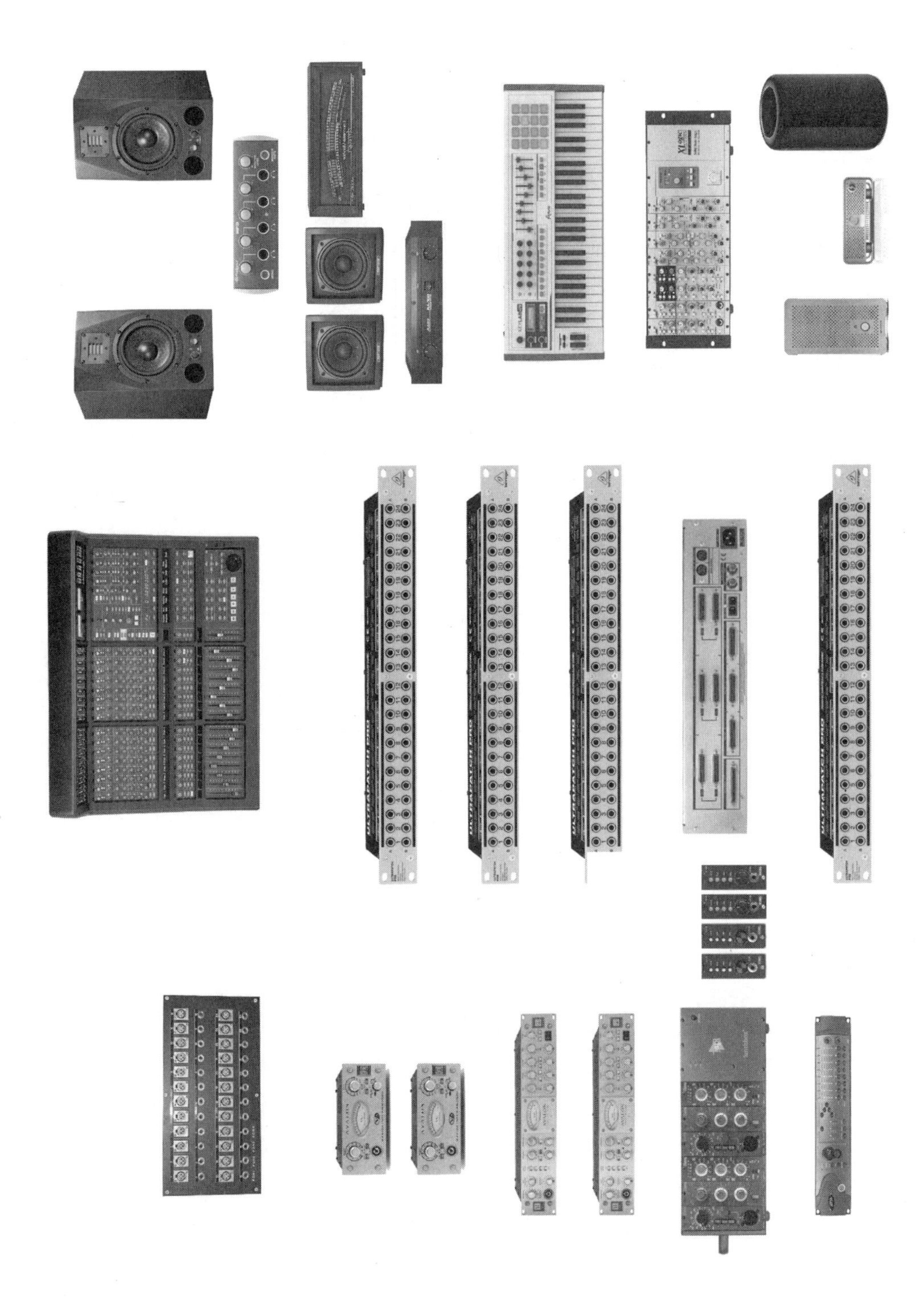

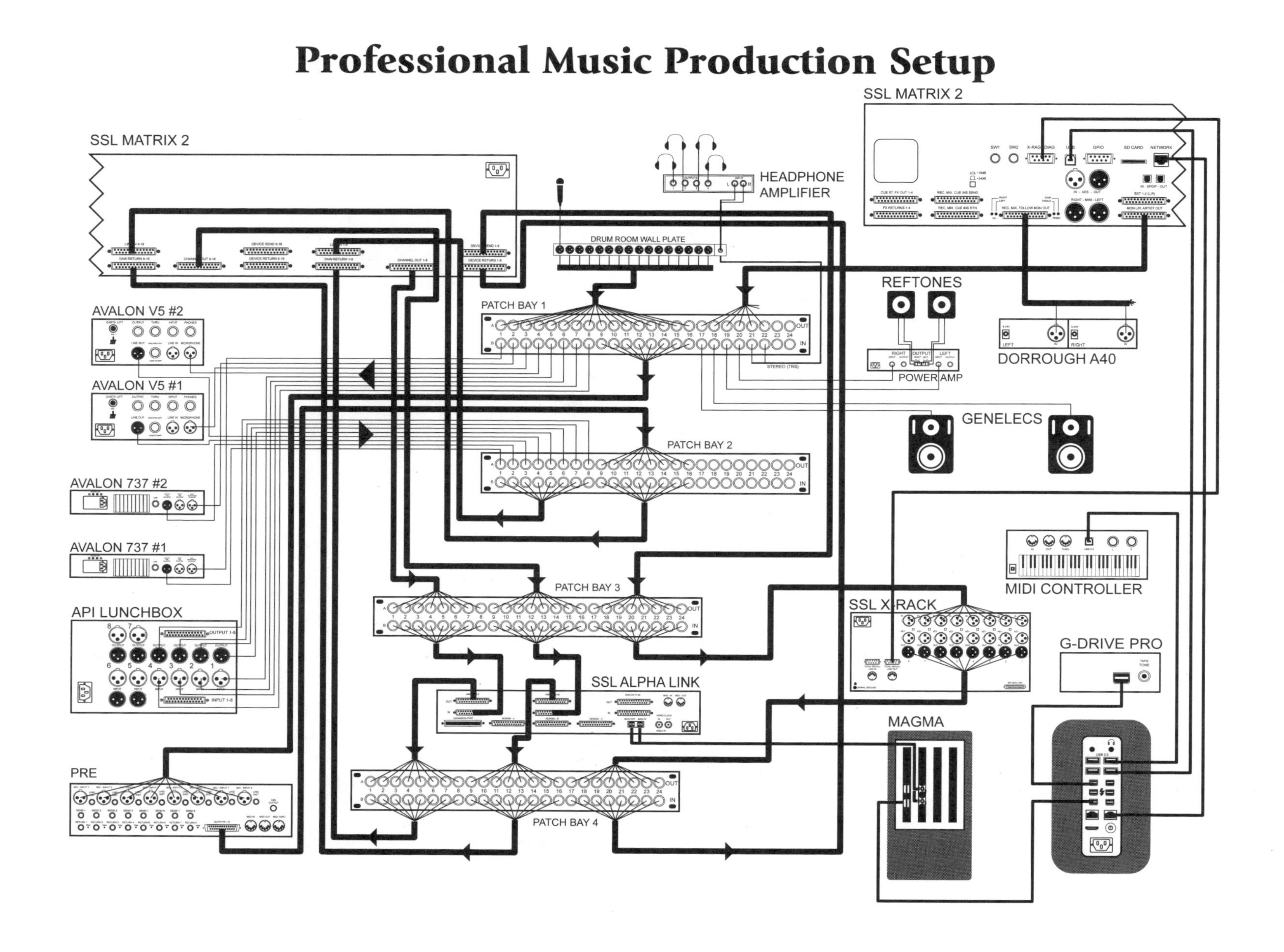
Professional Music Production Setup
SSL MATRIX 2
SSL MATRIX 2
HEADPHONE AMPLIFIER
DRUM ROOM WALL PLATE
REFTONES
POWER AMP
DORROUGH A40
GENELECS
PATCH BAY 1
STEREO (TRS)
PATCH BAY 2
PATCH BAY 3
PATCH BAY 4
AVALON V5 #2
AVALON V5 #1
AVALON 737 #2
AVALON 737 #1
API LUNCHBOX
PRE
SSL ALPHA LINK
SSL X-RACK
MIDI CONTROLLER
G-DRIVE PRO
MAGMA

- 2 – Avalon VT 737SP Tube Preamplifiers
- 2 – Avalon V5 Preamplifiers
- 1 – Headphone Amplifier
- 1 – G-Technology 4TB G-Drive Pro External Hard Hrive
- 1 – Alesis RA-100 Power Amplifier
- 1 – Pair of ADAM A7X Speaker Monitors
- 2 – Reftone Speaker Monitors
- 4 – AudioTechnica Headphones
- 2 – Dorrough 40-A Loudness Meters
- 1 – MIDI Keyboard Controller

Cable List

- 13 – 8x8 DB-25 to 1/4-inch TRS cable snakes
- 4 – 8x8 XLR Male to 1/4-inch TRS cable snakes
- 2 – 8x8 XLR Female to 1/4-inch TRS cable snakes
- 1 – 8x8 DB-25 to XLR Male cable snake
- 1 – XLR Male to XLR Female cable
- 2 – XLR Male to 1/4-inch TRS cables
- 1 – 1/4-inch TRS to a Dual 1/4-inch TS cable
- 2 – 1/4-inch TRS to 1/4-inch TS cable
- 2 – Dual Banana to Banana Male speaker cables
- 1 – 9-pin Serial cable
- 2– Thunderbolt cable
- 1 – Fiber Optic MADI cable
- 3 – USB cable
- 1 – Ethernet cable

Hardware Connections

Once all the equipment and cables are gathered, is time to connect them together. This setup looks a little bit intimidating and complex, but is not, if you do it logically and step-by-step as I will describe it. To get started, I have assembled a line diagram with the connections and explanations that shows how this is done. Of course, these are just examples, you are not likely to have the exact system list of components discussed here, but hopefully, this line diagram and explanation will give you an idea of how to connect a similar system, which is this book's purpose. For example, the inputs and outputs connections on the patchbays were arbitrarily selected, you can choose a different order of the inputs and outputs you desire for your studio situation.

1. Connecting the Apple Mac Pro Quad-Core Dual GPU Desktop Computer to the G-Technology 4TB G-DRIVE PRO External Hard Drive.

    - Using a Thunderbolt cable, connect an available Thunderbolt port on the G-DRIVE PRO external hard drive to an available port on the back of the Apple Mac Pro Quad-Core Dual GPU desktop Computer.

2. Connecting the Apple Mac Pro Quad-Core Dual GPU Desktop Computer to the Solid State Logic (SSL) Matrix 2 Mixing Board.

    - Using a USB cable, connect the USB port on the rear panel of the SSL Matrix 2 to an available USB port on the back of the Apple Mac Pro Quad-Core Dual GPU desktop computer.
    - Using an Ethernet cable, connect the Ethernet port on the rear panel of the SSL Matrix 2 to an available Ethernet port on the back of the Apple Mac Pro Quad-Core Dual GPU desktop computer.

3. Connecting the Apple Mac Pro Quad-Core Dual GPU Desktop Computer to the Magma ExpressBox 3T Expansion Chassis with an SSL MadiXtreme PCIe card inside.

    - Using a second Thunderbolt cable, connect an available Thunderbolt port on the Magma expansion chassis to another available Thunderbolt port on the back of the Apple Mac Pro Quad-Core Dual GPU desktop computer.

4. Connecting the SSL MadiXtreme PCIe Card located inside the Magma ExpressBox 3T Expansion Chassis to the SSL Alpha-Link SX 24 I/O Audio Interface.

- Using a dual Fiber Optic MADI cable, connect the SSL MadiXtreme PCIe card MADI port on the back of the Magma expansion chassis to the MADI port on the rear panel of the SSL Alpha-Link SX 24 I/O audio interface.

5. Connecting the SSL X-Rack Effects Rack to the SSL Matrix 2 Mixing Board.

   - Using a 9-pin serial cable, connect the "TOTAL RECALL LINK IN" serial port connector on the rear panel of the SSL X-Rack to the "X-RACK/DIAG" serial port connector located on the rear panel of the SSL Matrix 2 mixing board.

6. Connecting a MIDI Keyboard Controller to the Mac Pro Quad-Core Dual GPU Desktop Computer.

   - Using an USB cable, connect the USB port on the rear panel of the MIDI keyboard controller to an available USB port on the back of the Mac Pro desktop computer.

7. Connecting the SSL Alpha-Link MADI SX Outputs to PATCHBAY #4

   - Using an 8x8 DB-25 to 1/4-inch TRS cable snake, connect the "ANALOG OUT 1-8" DB-25 connector from the rear panel of the SSL Alpha-Link SX to points "1-8" on the rear of the top row (Outputs) of PATCHBAY #4.
   - Using an 8x8 DB-25 to 1/4-inch TRS cable snake, connect the "ANALOG OUT 9-16" DB-25 connector from the rear panel of the SSLAlpha-Link SX to points "9-16" on the rear of the top row (Outputs) of PATCHBAY #4.

NOTE: For the purposes of clarity in the line diagram, the top row sockets are the OUTPUTS and the lower row are the INPUTS. Also, notice we are using balanced ¼-inch connectors and not Bantam or TTY. This is for the practical purposes of using the ¼-inch TRS connectors in this example. I personally, prefer using the Bantam type of connectors as supposed to the ¼-inch balanced. One of the reasons why, is the size, you get more "points" or jacks in one row than a ¼-inch TRS plug. Also, they stay tight longer, avoiding any non-desired extra connection noise in the patchbay. Although, one of the disadvantages of using the Bantam or TTY connectors in a patchbay, is that they are more expensive than using balanced ¼-inch patchbays.

NOTE: *The two most common configuration modes to hooking up a patch-bay are Normalled and Half-Normalled. In this sample setup, all the patchbays are configured as Normalled, in other words, whatever signal is on the top row (outputs) of the patchbay, it automatically goes through the button row (inputs) without the need of using patch cords to make a connection between the top and lower rows. Furthermore, in a single Normalled patchbay, by inserting a patch cord in either, the output or the input jack, it will break the signal path, but in double Normalled patch bay the signal path is going to be broken only when inserting a patch cord in both jacks. Whereas in a Half-Normalled patchbay, by inserting a patch cord into the top jack (output) of a patchbay, it allows the source signal to be heard without breaking the connection to the mixer channel, for example; the only way to break the connection of the direct signal is by inserting a patch cord into the lower jack (input) of a patchbay.*

8. Connecting the SSL X-Rack Outputs to PATCHBAY #4

- Using an 8x8 XLR Female to 1/4-inch TRS cable snake, connect the "OUT 1-8" on the rear panel of the SSL X-Rack to points "17-24" on the rear of the top row (Outputs) of PATCH BAY #4.

t• Using an 8x8 DB-25 to 1/4-inch TRS cable, connect the "DAW RETURN 1-8" DB-25 port on the rear panel of the SSL Matrix 2 to points "1-8" on the rear of the bottom row (Inputs) of PATCHBAY #4.

- Using a second 8x8 DB-25 to 1/4-inch TRS cable, connect the "DAW RETURN 9-16" DB-25 port on the rear panel of the SSL Matrix 2 to points "9-16" on the rear of the bottom row (Inputs) of PATCHBAY #4.

- Using a third 8x8 DB-25 to 1/4-inch TRS cable, connect the "DEVICE RETURN 1-8" DB-25 port on the rear panel of the SSL Matrix 2 to points "17-24" on the rear of the bottom row (Inputs) of PATCHBAY #4.

10. Connecting SSL Alpha-Link MADI SX Inputs to PATCHBAY #3

- Using an 8x8 DB-25 to 1/4-inch TRS cable, connect the "ANALOG IN 1-8" DB-25 port on the rear panel of the SSL Alpha-Link MADI SX to points "1-8" on the rear of the bottom row (Inputs) of PATCHBAY #3.
- Using another 8x8 DB-25 to 1/4-inch TRS cable, connect the "ANALOG IN 9-16" DB-25 port on the rear panel of the SSL Alpha-Link MADI SX to points "9-16" on the rear of the bottom row (Inputs) of PATCHBAY #3.

11. Connecting the SSL X-Rack Inputs to PATCHBAY #3

- Using an 8x8 XLR Male to 1/4-inch TRS cable snake, connect the "1-8" on the rear of the SSL X-Rack to points "17-24" on the rear of the bottom row (Inputs) of PATCHBAY #3.

12. Connecting SSL Matrix 2 Outputs to PATCHBAY #3

- Using an 8x8 DB-25 to 1/4-inch TRS snake, connect the "CHANNEL OUT 1-8" DB-25 port on the rear panel of the SSL Matrix 2 to points "1-8"on the rear of the top row (Outputs) of PATCHBAY #3.
- Using an 8x8 DB-25 to 1/4-inch TRS cable snake, connect the "CHANNEL OUT 9-16" DB-25 port on the rear panel of the SSL Matrix 2 to points "9-16" on the rear of the top row (Outputs) of PATCHBAY #3.
- Using another 8x8 DB-25 to 1/4-inch TRS cable snake, connect the "DEVICE SEND 1-8" on the rear panel of the SSL Matrix 2 to points "17-24" on the rear of the top row (Outputs) of PATCHBAY #3.

13. Connecting the SSL Matrix 2 Inputs to PATCHBAY #2

- Using an 8x8 DB-25 to 1/4-inch TRS cable snake, connect the "LINE IN 1-8" DB-25 port on the rear panel of the SSL Matrix 2 to points "1-8" on the rear of the bottom row (Inputs) of PATCHBAY #2.
- Using another 8x8 DB-25 cable to 1/4-inch TRS snake, connect the "LINE IN 9-16" DB-25 port on the rear panel of the SSL Matrix 2 to points "9-16" on the rear of the bottom row (Inputs) of PATCHBAY #2.

14. Connecting the Avid PRE preamplifier Outputs to PATCHBAY #2

- Using an 8x8 DB-25 to 1/4-inch TRS cable snake, connect the "OUTPUTS 1-8" DB-25 port on the rear panel of the Avid PRE to points "9-16" on the rear of the top row (Outputs) of PATCHBAY #2.

15. Connecting the API Lunchbox Outputs to PATCHBAY #2

    - Using 4 XLR to 1/4-inch TRS cables, connect "OUTPUTS 1-4" on the rear panel of the API Lunchbox to points "5-8" on the rear of the top row (Outputs) of PATCHBAY #2.

16. Connecting the Avalon VT 737SP Preamplifiers Outputs to PATCHBAY #2

    - Using an XLR to 1/4-inch TRS cable, connect the "OUTPUT LINE BALANCED" of the Avalon VT 737SP #1 to point "1" on the rear of the top row (Outputs) of PATCHBAY #2.
    - Using an XLR to 1/4-inch TRS cable, connect the "OUTPUT LINE BALANCED" of the Avalon VT 737SP #2 to point "2" on the rear of the top row (Outputs) of PATCHBAY #2.

17. Connecting the Avalon V5 Preamplifiers Outputs to PATCHBAY #2

    - Using an XLR to 1/4-inch TRS cable, connect the "LINE OUT" of the Avalon V5 #1 to point "3" on the rear of the top row (Outputs) of PATCHBAY #2.
    - Using an XLR to 1/4-inch TRS cable, connect the "LINE OUT" of the Avalon V5 #2 to point "4" on the rear of the top row (Outputs) of PATCHBAY #2.

18. Connecting the SSL Matrix 2 Monitor Out to PATCH BAY #1

    - Using an 8x8 DB-25 to to 1/4-inch TRS cable snake, connect the "MON L/R, ARTIST OUT" DB-25 conenctor on the rear panel of the SSL Matrix 2 to points "17-24" on the rear of the top row (Outputs) of PATCHBAY #1.

19. Connecting the drum room wall plate (Tie Line) to PATCHBAY #1

    - Connecting the hard-wired 16x16 cable snake of the drum room wall plate to points "1-16" on the rear of the top row (Outputs) of PATCHBAY #1.

20. Connecting the API Lunchbox Inputs to PATCHBAY #1

    - Using 4 XLR to 1/4-inch TRS cables, connect "INPUTS 1-4" on the rear panel of the API Lunchbox to points "5-8" on the rear of the bottom row (Inputs) of PATCHBAY #1.

21. Connecting the Avalon VT 737SP Preamplifiers Inputs to PATCHBAY #1

    - Using an XLR to 1/4-inch TRS cable,, connect the "INPUT LINE BALANCED" of the Avalon VT 737SP #1 to point "1" on the rear of the bottom row (Inputs) of PATCHBAY #1.
    - Using an XLR to 1/4-inch TRS cable,, connect the "INPUT LINE BALANCED" of the Avalon VT 737SP #2 to point "2" on the rear of the bottom row (Inputs) of PATCHBAY #1.

22. Connecting the Avalon V5 Preamplifiers Inputs to PATCHBAY #1

    - Using an XLR to 1/4-inch TRS cable, connect the "LINE IN" of Avalon V5 #1 to point "3" on the rear of the bottom row (Inputs) of PATCHBAY #1.
    - Using an XLR to 1/4-inch TRS cable, connect the "LINE IN" of Avalon V5 #2 to point "4" on the rear of the bottom row (Inputs) of PATCHBAY #1.

23. Connecting the Avid PRE Preamplifier Inputs to PATCHBAY #1

    - Using an 8x8 XLR Male to 1/4-inch TRS cable snake, connect "MIC INPUTS 1-8" on the rear panel of the Avid PRE preamplifier to points "9-16" on the rear of the bottom row (Inputs) of PATCHBAY #1.

24. Connecting the Headphone Amplifier Inputs to the Drum Room Wall Plate (Tie Line)

    - Using a 1/4-inch Stereo TRS to a Dual Mono 1/4-inch TS cable, connect the "HEADPHONE OUT" of the drum room wall plate to "INPUT L & R" of the Headphone Amplifier.

25. Connecting the Hard-Wired Headphone cable from the Drum Room Wall Plate to PATCHBAY #1

- Connect the hard-wired Stereo TRS to Dual Mono 1/4-inch cable from the Drum Room Wall Plate to points "21 & 22" on the rear of the bottom row (Inputs) of PATCHBAY #1

26. Connecting the Headphones to the Headphone Amplifier

- Connect the 1/4-inch TRS connector of the first pair of Headphones to the first Output of the Headphone Amplifier.
- Connect the 1/4-inch TRS connector of the second pair of Headphones to the second Output of the Headphone Amplifier.
- Connect the 1/4-inch TRS connector of the third pair of Headphones to the third Output of the Headphone Amplifier.
- Connect the 1/4-inch TRS connector of the fourth pair of Headphones to the fourth Output of the Headphone Amplifier.

NOTE: If your Headphones do not have a 1/4-inch TRS connector, you will have to use a 1/8-inch TRS to 1/4-inch TRS adapter for the Headphones.

27. Connecting the Genelecs 1031A to PATCHBAY #1

- Using an XLR Male to 1/4-inch TRS cable, connect point "17" on the rear of the bottom row (Inputs) of PATCHBAY #1 to the Left Genelec speaker monitor.
- Using an XLR Male to 1/4-inch TRS cable, connect point "18" on the rear of the bottom row (Inputs) of PATCHBAY #1 to the Right Genelec speaker monitor.

28. Connecting the Alesis RA-100 Power Amplifier to PATCHBAY #1

- Using a 1/4-inch TRS to 1/4-inch TRS cable, connect point "19" on the rear of the bottom row (Inputs) of PATCHBAY #1 to the "LEFT INPUT" of the Alesis RA100 power amplifier.
- Using another 1/4-inch TRS to1/4-inch TRS cable, connect point "20"

on the rear of the bottom row (Inputs) of PATCH BAY #1 to the "RIGHT INPUT" of the Alesis RA100 power amplifier.

29. Connecting the SSL Matrix 2 to the Dorrough 40-A Loudness Meters
    - Using an 8x8 DB-25 to XLR Male cable snake, connect the DB-25 connector of the Master I/O on the rear panel of the SSL Matrix 2.
    - Using the XLR cable labeled "1" from the 8x8 DB-25 to XLR Male cable snake used above, connect the "LEFT IN" of the pair of Dorrough loudness meters.
    - Using the XLR cable labeled "2" from the 8x8 DB-25 to XLR Male cable snake used above, connect the "RIGHT IN" of the pair of Dorrough loudness meters.

30. Connecting the Reftone Reference Speaker Monitors to the Alesis RA-100 Power Amplifier
    - Using a Dual Banana to Banana Male speaker cable, connect the Left Output channel of the power amplifier to the Banana Input jack of the Left Reftone speaker monitor.
    - Using a Dual Banana to Banana Male speaker cable, connect the Right Output channel of the power amplifier to the Banana Input jack of the Right Reftone speaker monitor.

System Requirements

Pro Tools HD

Since the system requirements for Pro Tools is constantly being updated, and depending on the Pro Tools HD hardware and software versions you are using in your studio, is best to visit www.Avid.com and search for the "Avid Knowledge Base – Pro Tools System Requirements", for both, Mac OS and Windows OS and look for your specific Pro Tools and Operating system in your computer.

Matrix 2

Matrix Remote is a Java application and will run under Java Version 5 or higher. PC users can download the latest version from www.java.com.

ipMIDI is compatible with Mac OS X 10.5, 10.6, 10.7 and 10.8; Windows 2000, XP, Vista, 7 and 8. Check the SSL website for the latest versions of the ipMIDI virtual MIDI interface driver and the Matrix Remote application. These can be found at www.solidstatelogic.com/support/consoles/matrix/downloads.asp

Software Setup

As I mentioned before, the Pro Tools system we are using in this example, is a Pro Tools 11. Regardless what version of Pro Tools you use in your studio, you should already have installed the software and other files required to run Pro Tools properly. Also, it is very important that you check which operating system is installed in your computer, whether you are using a Macintosh (Mac OSX) or a PC running on Windows. You can always search in the internet for any software updates for all your devices. For example, if you are using Pro Tools, then you can visit www.Avid.com to check for the latest compatibility information.

Also, we are using an SSL Matrix 2 as our mixing board and Pro Tools control surface. This machine also needs software to be installed. To install the software correctly, please follow the next steps:

- On the USB stick which came with Matrix you will find two programs to install. Install the program called MatrixRemote on the computer from which you intend to control the Matrix 2, and install the program called ipMIDI on any computers which have a DAW installed which you intend to use with the Matrix 2.

Matrix Remote

- Mount the MatrixRemote.dmg disk image and open it. Drag the enclosed Matrix Remote application to the Applications folder, then to the Dock or any other convenient location.

ipMIDI

- Mount the ipMIDI.dmg disk image and open it. Double click on the ipMIDI.pkg file to run the installation program. Note that you will be asked to log out and in again once you have completed the installation.

Once you have logged back in open Audio MIDI Setup and double click on the ipMIDI icon. Set the number of MIDI ports to 9 in the resulting pop-up.

NOTE: if you are upgrading an older copy of ipMIDI you must uninstall it before running the installer. To uninstall ipMIDI simply delete: '/Library/Audio/MIDI Drivers/ipMIDIDriver.plugin'. You should empty the Trash after deleting the '.plugin' file before running the installer.

NOTE: There are two versions of ipMIDI for Mac; V1.5 is suitable for OS X 10.5 whilst V1.6 runs on OS X 10.6, 10.7, 10.8 and 10.9. Please choose the correct version for your Mac.

Assuming all the connections were done properly and the software was installed correctly in both Pro Tools and the Matrix 2, follow the steps below to configure your hardware in your Pro Tools session.

- First, launch the Pro Tools software, the QuickStart dialog box will appear on the screen. Select the "Create Blank Session" option to create a new session. Now, choose the sample rate of 48kHz, the Bit Depth to 24 bits, and set the Audio File Type to BWF (.WAV). The next step is to give it a name to your session, so go ahead and give it a name and save it on the Desktop of your computer. You will notice the Edit and Mix window will appear on the screen.
- Once you have the new session opened, go to the "Track" menu and select "New", a dialog window will prompt you to enter the information for the number and type tracks you want to create. Go ahead and create 16 Mono Audio Tracks. You should be able to see sixteen channel strips on the Pro Tools Mix window.
- Go to the Setups > I/O Setup menu, and press the "Default" button in the Input and Output tabs. Since we are using the SSL Alpha-Link MADI SX 24 I/O as our audio interface, you will notice the input and output names associated with the Alpha Link SX 24 I/O. You can also give every input and output a different name if that is easier for you to recognize them. Check the Pro Tools Reference Guide for more details.

- Plug in some microphones and instruments through the patch bays and make the proper input and output assignments in the Pro Tools Mix window. Make sure you are seeing signal activity in each channel of the Matrix 2 mixing board, and adjust a reasonable recording level on each channel. Go ahead and have some fun recording and mixing. Check the Matrix 2 Manual in case you have trouble using the board.

This concludes this exercise. Remember, all the track assignments and patchbay connections are arbitrarily chosen so you can understand and learn the process of setting up a studio like the one we just covered. By no means is this, the only way to do it, these scenarios are just to practice plugging in a studio of this magnitude and configuring a Matrix 2 system with Pro Tools 11.

Post Studios 3

Photo courtesy of Larson Studios, Stage 3, Hollywood, CA

Post Production studio setups are different than Music Production studio setups. Depending on the kind of projects a particular Post Production studio offers, the type of equipment varies. A Post studio can specialize in Sound Editing, Music Editing, ADR, Sound Design, Foley, or Mixing for Film and/or TV, or all of the above. For example, if a post studio offers Mixing for Film and TV, then a "Dubbing Stage" would be necessary. A dubbing stage is a theater-like studio, with a mixing board or control surface, theater seats, big video screens and projectors. Here is where final decisions are made and executed on a Film or TV series. As an example of a Dubbing Stage, take a look at the photo above, this studio is equipped with an Avid Pro Tools system, two-32 fader Avid D-Control surfaces, an Avid Satellite Link Synchronization, loudness meters, and a multi-channel monitor system, among other equipment.

Surround Sound Post Setup

This setup can be used as a professional Post-Production studio and is designed to record, mix, and monitor multiple sources. This setup is based around an Avid HD Native system with a D-Control work surface. This work surface is better known as an ICON system. ICON stands for Integrated CONsole environment.

We are also using the Apogee Symphony 8x8 I/O as our audio interface. The Symphony I/O comes in different configurations. The configuration used in this example, is an 8-in by 8-out analog, and is capable of recording at a bit resolution of 24-bits and in sample rates up to 192kHz. In this case, the Symphony is connected to an Avid HD Native PCIe card inside of an Apple Mac Pro desktop computer.

A single "CONTROL" cable connects the work surface to the Avid XMon. The XMon provides all the monitoring connections for the D-Control. The XMon provides 2 sets of 7.1 Analog Inputs and 2 sets of 7.1 Analog Outputs to which you can connect different sets of surround speakers.

Equipment List

- 1 – Apogee Symphony 8x8 Analog I/O Audio Interface
- 1 – Apple Mac Pro desktop Computer
- 1 – Avid PRE Preamplifier
- 1 – Avid Sync HD Synchronizer
- 1 – Avid HD|Native PCIe Card
- 1 – Avid D-Control
- 1 – Avid XMON
- 8 – Genelec Powered Speakers for 7.1 Surround
- 1 – MOTU Fast Lane MIDI Interface
- 1 – NETGEAR ProSafe Ethernet switch
- 1 – PACE USB Smart Key (iLok 2)
- 4 – Audio-Technica 4050 Condenser Microphones

Optional furniture

Surround Sound Post Setup

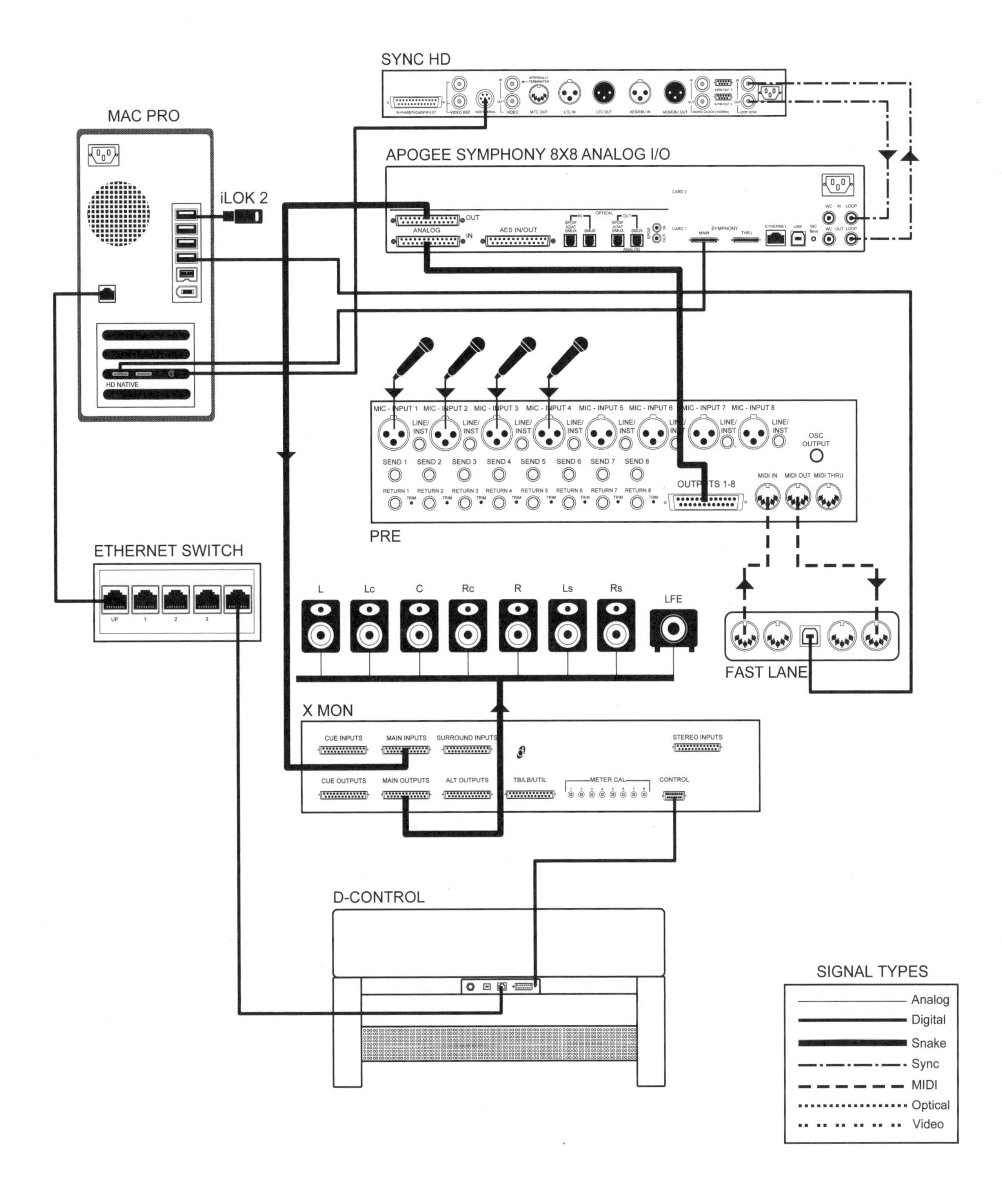

Cable List

- 2 – 8x8 DB-25 to DB-25 cable snakes
- 1 – 8x8 DB-25 to XLR male cable snake
- 2 – Ethernet cables
- 1 – 15-pin control cable
- 1 – DigiLink Mini cable
- 1 – DigiSerial cable
- 2 – BNC cables
- 4 – XLR cables
- 2 – MIDI cables
- 1 – USB cable

Hardware Connections

Let's take a look at the connections you have to do in order to get this studio setup working properly:

1. Installing an HD Native PCIe card into an Apple Mac Pro desktop computer

    - Open the Apple Mac Pro desktop computer and install the HD Native PCIe card in the lowest number slot (closest to the graphics card).

2. Connecting the Apogee Symphony 8x8 Analog I/O audio interface to the HD Native card

    - Using a DigiLink Mini cable, connect Port 1 on the back on your HD Native PCIe card to the MAIN port on the Apogee Symphony 8x8 Analog I/O audio interface,

NOTE: The Symphony I/O does not have any preamps built into it, so a separate stand-alone preamplifier, such as the Avid PRE will be needed. You can connect up to 4 interfaces to the HD Native card.

- If you are using additional audio interfaces, Loop Sync connections will also have to be made (see Step #4).

3. Connecting the Avid PRE to the Apogee Symphony 8x8 Analog I/O

   - Using a DB-25 to DB-25 cable, connect the OUPUTS 1-8 of the Avid PRE preamplifier to the ANALOG IN of the Symphony I/O audio interface.
   - Using a MIDI cable, connect the MIDI OUT on the rear panel of the PRE preamplifier to an Input on the Fast Lane MIDI interface.
   - Using a MIDI cable, connect the corresponding MIDI Output of the Fast Lane MIDI interface to the MIDI IN on the rear panel of the PRE.
   - Using a USB cable, connect the USB port of the Fast Lane MIDI interface to an available USB port on the Apple Mac Pro computer.
   - Using an XLR cable, connect the first microphone to the MIC INPUT 1 port on the rear of the PRE
   - Using an XLR cable, connect the second microphone to the MIC INPUT 2 port on the rear of the PRE
   - Using an XLR cable, connect the third microphone to the MIC INPUT 3 port on the rear of the PRE
   - Using an XLR cable, connect the forth microphone to the MIC INPUT 4 port on the rear of the PRE

4. Connecting the Sync HD to the HD Native card

   - Connect the supplied DigiSerial cable, from the DigiSerial port on the HD Native card to the HOST SERIAL port on the back of the Sync HD.
   - Using a BNC cable, connect the Loop Sync OUT of the Sync HD to the Loop Sync IN of the Symphony audio interface.
   - Using a second BNC cable, connect the Loop Sync OUT of the Symphony audio interface to the Loop Sync IN of the Sync HD.

5. Connecting the Avid D-Control

   - Using a standard Ethernet cable, connect the D-Control Fader unit to the

Ethernet switch. Any additional fader units will require their own Ethernet connection.

- Connect one of the Ethernet ports on your Apple Mac Pro desktop computer to the Ethernet switch as well.

6. Connecting the Apogee Symphony 8x8 Analog I/O Audio Interface to the Avid XMON

- Using a DB-25 to DB-25 cable, connect the ANALOG OUT of the Symphony I/O to the MAIN INPUTS on the rear panel of the XMON.

7. Connecting the D-Control to the XMON

- Using the supplied 15-pin control cable, connect the D-Control to the connector labeled "CONTROL" on the XMON.

8. Connecting the speakers

- Using a DB-25 to XLR male cable, connect the main output of the XMON to the input of the speakers.
- The XMON is permanently wired for 7.1 surround and follows the format of:

1	2	3	4	5	6	7	8
L	Lc	C	Rc	R	Ls	Rs	LFE

System Requirements

Pro Tools 11 for Mac (as of this writing):

- Avid-qualified Apple computer
- 8 GB RAM or more, 16GB or more is recommended
- 15 GB minimum free hard disk space
- Mac OS X 10.8 or later
- Monitor with at least 1024 x 768 resolution
- One or more hard disk drives dedicated for audio recording and playback

- PACE USB Smart Key (iLok 2)
- USB 2 port available to connect the PACE USB Smart Key (iLok 2)
- Ethernet port available

NOTE: PACE USB Smart Key (iLok 2) with valid license is required for Pro Tools 11 to work, without it Pro Tools will not launch.

Software Setup

In this example, we will be using Pro Tools 11 as our DAW. You should already have installed the software and other files required to run Pro Tools. In case you do not have the required software or drivers installed you could visit the website of the software and hardware developer, in this case you could visit www.avid.com and www.apogeedigital.com to check for them or for other type of information.

NOTE: Don't forget to always keep the PACE USB Smart Key (iLok 2) with a valid license connected to the computer, otherwise you will not be able to launch the Pro Tools software.

Once you have launched the Pro Tools 11 software in your computer:

1. Setting up Pro Tools

   - First, you should launch Pro Tools, and once Pro Tools has launched, select "Create Blank Session" from the QuickStart dialog box to create a new session. Now we can choose the sample rate and the Bit Depth, remember that Pro Tools 11 supports sample rates up to 192kHz and a Bit Depth up to 32-bit float, in this case let´s choose a sample rate of 48kHz and a Bit Depth of 32-bit float. Set the Audio File Type to BWF (.WAV). Once you have the session opened and ready, go to the Track menu and select "New" and create the desired number and format of tracks.

2. Check the I/O Setup

   - In Pro Tools, go to the Setup > I/O menu, and press the "Default" button on the Input and Output tabs, by doing so you will be able to see the default names of your inputs and outputs. Make sure the "Default Path" setting is set for D-Control/D-Command.

3. Enable the D-Control

    - In Pro Tools, go to the Setup > Peripherals menu, and select the Ethernet Controllers tab. Check the box to "Enable".

    - Make sure to select the units in the order they are physically laid out from Left to Right. For instance if the left most unit is a Fader unit then select the Fader unit first, followed by the Main unit.

4. Verify the Sync HD is properly connected and configured

    - In Pro Tools, go to the Setup > Peripherals menu, and select the Synchronization tab. Verify the box is checked for "Enable Sync HD". Set any of the other options as desired.

5. Configure the Avid PRE

    - On the PRE front panel, press "MIDI CHAN" and use the "GAIN/PARM" control to set the MIDI channel from 1-16.

    - Configure AMS (Mac) or MSS (Windows) from within Pro Tools by going to Setup > MIDI > MIDI Studio

    - In Pro Tools, go to the Setup > Peripherals menu, and select the Mic Preamps tab. Choose PRE from the "Type" pop-up menu. Set the "Receive From" and "Send To" as you configured from your MIDI Setup.

    - Lastly, from the Mic Preamp tab of the I/O setup, map the PRE's outputs.

This concludes this exercise. Again, all the track assignments are arbitrarily chosen so you can understand and learn the process of setting up a session. By no means is this the only way to do it, these scenarios are just to practice plugging in your studio and setting up a session in Pro Tools 11 with an ICON system.

Avid S6 Post Production Setup

This example can be used as a professional post-production studio setup and is designed to record and monitor multiple sources. This Professional Post Production setup is based around an HDX system with an Avid S6 control surface. With this console, Avid combines the best of the ICON and System 5 product families in a revolutionary new modular design.

The audio interface we are using is the HD OMNI by Avid. The HD OMNI is an all-in-one professional preamp, I/O, and monitoring interface. This audio interface is 4-in by 8-out and is capable of recording in a resolution of 24-bits and in sample rates up to 192kHz. The interface is connected to Port 1 on the HDX card. We are also using an Apple Mac Pro Quad-Core desktop computer, but the HDX cards and HD OMNI audio interface can also be used with a Windows-based computer. The Avid S6 connects via Ethernet to a hub or switch, which is also connected to your computer. The S6 features high-speed EUCON Ethernet connectivity, this enables the surface to communicate directly with Pro Tools and other EUCON-enabled DAW's.

Equipment List

- 1 – Avid HD OMNI Audio Interface
- 1 – Apple Mac Pro Quad-Core Desktop Computer
- 1 – Avid Sync HD Synchronizer
- 1 – Avid HDX PCIe Card
- 1 – Avid S6 Control Surface
- 1 – AVID XMON S6 Monitoring System
- 1 – XMON app
- 1 – Set of ADAM A7X Speakers Monitors for 7.1 Surround
- 1 – Ethernet Switch

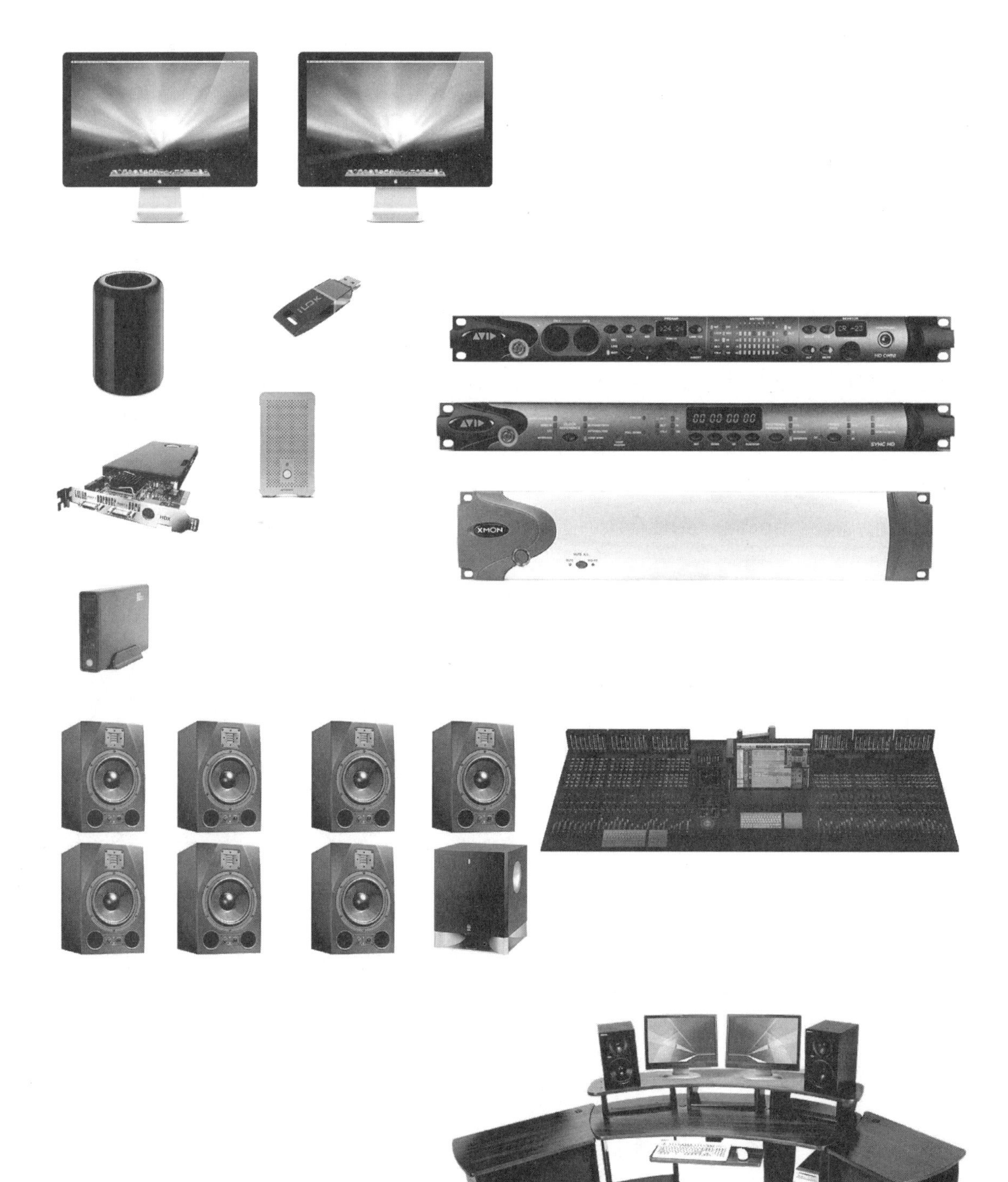

Optional furniture

Avid S6 Post Production Setup

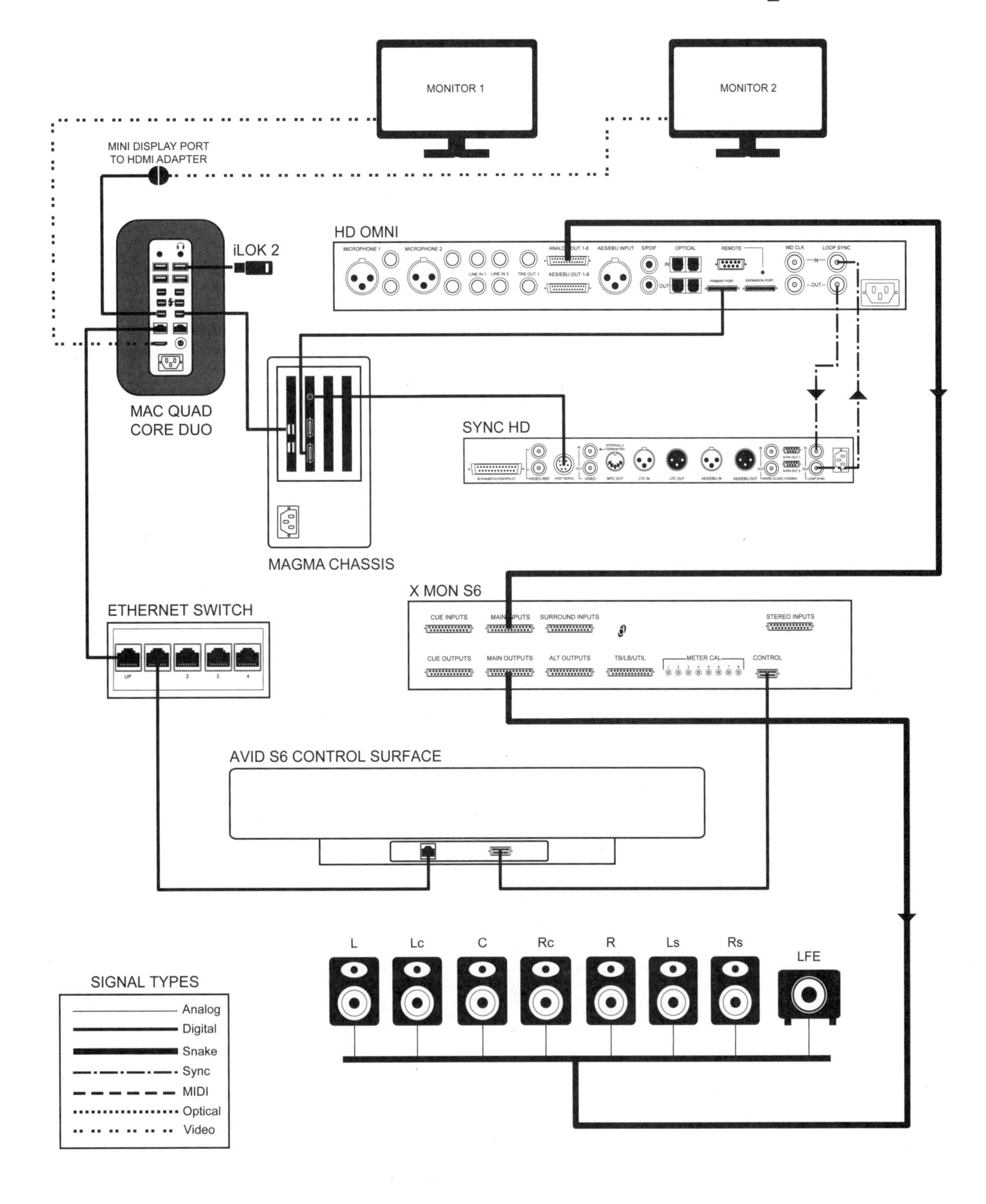

Cable List

- 1 – DB-25 to DB-25 cable snake
- 1 – DB-25 to XLR male cable snake
- 2 – Ethernet cables
- 1 – 15-pin control cable
- 1 – DigiLink Mini cable
- 1 – DigiSerial cable
- 2 – BNC cables
- 2 – Thunderbolt cables
- 2 – Thunderbolt to mini display adapters (for video monitors)
- 1– HDMI cable

Hardware Connections

Let's take a look at the connections you have to do in order to get this setup working properly:

1. Connecting the Magma ExpressBox 3T Expansion Chassis (with an Avid HDX PCIe card) to the Apple Mac Pro Quad-Core desktop computer

    - Using a Thunderbolt cable, connect a Thunderbolt jack on the back of your computer to an available Thunderbolt port on the Magma ExpressBox 3T expansion chassis.

2. Connecting the HD OMNI Audio Interface to the Magma ExpressBox 3T Expansion Chassis with an Avid HDX PCIe Card

    - Using a DigiLink Mini cable, connect port 1 on the back on the HDX card (inside of the chassis) to the PRIMARY PORT on the HD OMNI audio interface, it should be noted that the HD OMNI has 2 mic preamps built into it.

3. Connecting the Sync HD to the HDX Card

- Connect the supplied DigiSerial cable, from the DigiSerial port on the HDX card to the HOST SERIAL port on the back of the Sync HD.
- Using a BNC cable, connect the Loop Sync OUT of the Sync HD to the Loop Sync IN of the audio interface, HD OMNI.
- Using a BNC cable, connect the Loop Sync OUT of the HD OMNI to the Loop Sync IN of the Sync HD.

NOTE: If additional audio interfaces are used, continue to connect the Loop Sync OUT to the Loop Sync In of each successive interface. The last audio interface will Loop Sync to the Sync HD to complete the chain.

4. Connecting the Avid S6 Control Surface

- Using a standard Ethernet cable, connect the main Ethernet cable from the console to the Ethernet switch.
- Connect one of the Ethernet ports on your Apple Mac Pro Quad-Core desktop computer to the Ethernet switch as well.

5. Connecting the S6 to the Avid XMON 6

- Using the supplied 15-pin control cable, connect the S6 to the connector labeled "CONTROL" on the XMON.

6. Connecting the speaker monitors

- Using a DB-25 to XLR male cable, connect the main output of the XMON to the input of the speaker monitors.
- The XMON is permanently wired for 7.1 surround and follows the format of:

1	2	3	4	5	6	7	8
L	Lc	C	Rc	R	Ls	Rs	LFE

System Requirements

Pro Tools 11 for Mac OS X (as of this writing):

- Avid-qualified Apple computer
- 8 GB RAM or more, 16GB or more is recommended
- 15 GB minimum free hard disk space
- Mac OS X 10.8 or later
- Monitor with at least 1024 x 768 resolution
- One or more hard disk drives dedicated for audio recording and playback
- PACE USB Smart Key (iLok 2)
- USB 2 port available to connect the PACE USB Smart Key (iLok 2)
- Ethernet port available
- Dedicated graphics card is recommended

Pro Tools 11 for Windows (as of this writing):

- Avid-qualified Windows-based computer
- 8 GB RAM or more, 16GB or more is recommended
- 15 GB minimum free hard disk space
- Windows 7 Home Premium, Professional or Ultimate only with Service Pack 1, Windows 8 Standard or Pro edition
- Requires 64-bit Windows operating system
- Monitor with at least 1024 x 768 resolution
- One or more hard disk drives dedicated for audio recording and playback
- PACE USB Smart Key (iLok 2)
- USB 2 port available to connect the PACE USB Smart Key (iLok 2)
- Ethernet port available
- Dedicated graphics card is recommended

Software Setup

In this example, we will be using Pro Tools as our DAW. You should already have installed the S6 software, and other files required to run Pro Tools. In case you do not have the required software or drivers installed you could visit the site of the software and hardware developer, in this case you could visit www.avid.com to check for them or for other type of information.

> NOTE: *Don't forget to always keep the PACE USB Smart Key (iLok 2) with a valid license connected to the computer, otherwise you will not be able to launch the Pro Tools software.*

The S6 control surface should always be started up before launching the Pro Tools software:

1. Setting up the S6

    - From the Master Module, choose Settings > Workstations > Config. Then, select the frame depth and width of your console. Next, drag the modules down to the empty frame to match your configuration.
    - Confirm the location of the flashing module by touching any control on it. Repeat for the additional modules in order. Drag the numbered display modules down to the matching frame locations. Then, press DONE to complete the process.
    - You must also configure the Monitor section of the S6 and the XMON app before launching Pro Tools. Please refer to the S6 documentation for detailed instructions.

2. Setting up Pro Tools

    - First you should launch Pro Tools, and once Pro Tools has launched, select "Create New Session" from the QuickStart dialog box to create a new session. Now we can choose the sample rate and the Bit Depth, remember that Pro Tools 11 supports sample rates up to 192kHz and a Bit Depth up to 32-bit float, in this case let´s choose a sample rate of 96kHz and a Bit Depth of 32-bit. Set the Audio File Type to BWF (.WAV). Once you have the session opened and ready, go to the Track menu and select "New" and create the desired number and format of tracks.

3. Enable the S6

   - In Pro Tools, go to the Setup > Peripherals menu, and select the Ethernet Controllers tab. Check the box to "ENABLE EUCON SUPPORT" at the bottom of the dialog box.

4. Verify the Sync HD is properly connected and configured

   - In Pro Tools, go to the Setup > Peripherals menu, and select the Synchronization tab. Verify the box is checked for "Enable Sync HD". Set any of the other options as desired.

5. Configure the HD OMNI

   - In Pro Tools, go to the Setup > Hardware menu, and from the Peripherals list on the left, select HD OMNI if not already selected.

   - Select the Monitor tab. Since the settings on this tab are reflected on the Main tab as well as the I/O Setup, it should be configured first.

This concludes this exercise. Again, all the track assignments are arbitrarily chosen so you can understand and learn the process of setting up a session. By no means is this the only way to do it, these scenarios are just to practice plugging in your studio and setting up a session in Pro Tools 11 with your S6 control surface.

Podcast Studio Setup

The audio landscape is constantly changing and one of the new facets of technology has become the ever increasing popularity of podcasts. From comedy to news to entertainment, it seems that everyone who is anyone these days has their own podcast. The term 'podcast' is derived from the Apple iPod combined with the term 'broadcast.' Their popularity is a direct result of the ease of which one can record, distribute and maintain their own podcast, from anywhere on the globe to anywhere on the globe. This particular setup showcases 2 microphones in the event that you would like to have guests or a co-host for your podcast.

Equipment List

- 1 – Universal Audio Apollo Twin Audio Interface
- 1 – Behringer MDX 4600 Microphone Preamplifier
- 1 – Pair of Headphones
- 2 – AudioTechnica AT4050ST Microphones
- 1 – PACE USB Smart Key (iLok 2)
- 1 – Apple MacBook Pro Laptop Computer

Cable List

- 1 – Thunderbolt cable
- 4 – XLR cables

Hardware Connections

1. Connecting the Apollo Twin Audio Interface to a MacBook Pro Computer
    - Using a Thunderbolt cable, connect the Thunderbolt port on the back of the Apollo Twin interface to an available port on the Apple MacBook Pro.

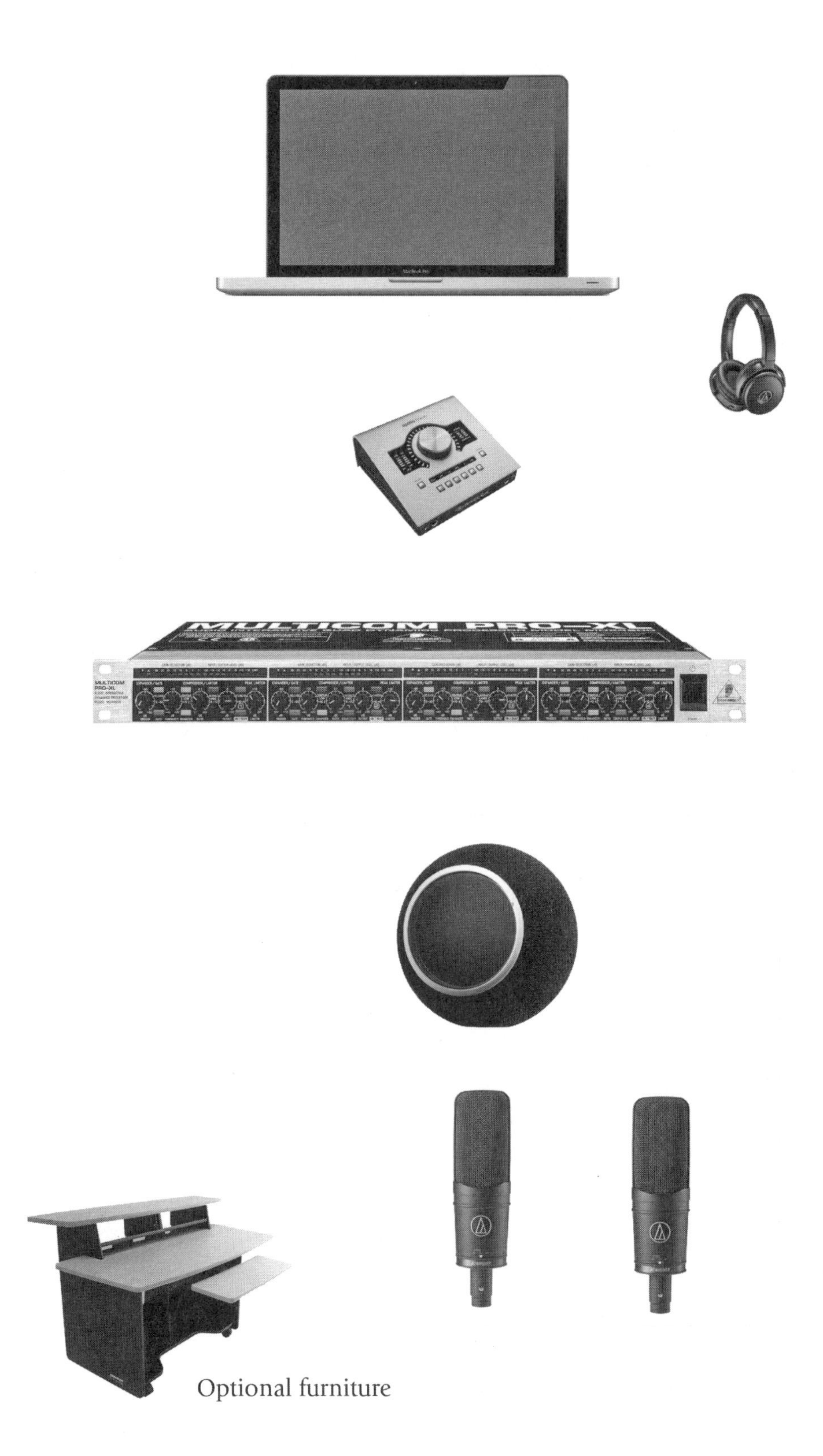
MULTICOM PRO-XL
Optional furniture

Podcast Studio Setup

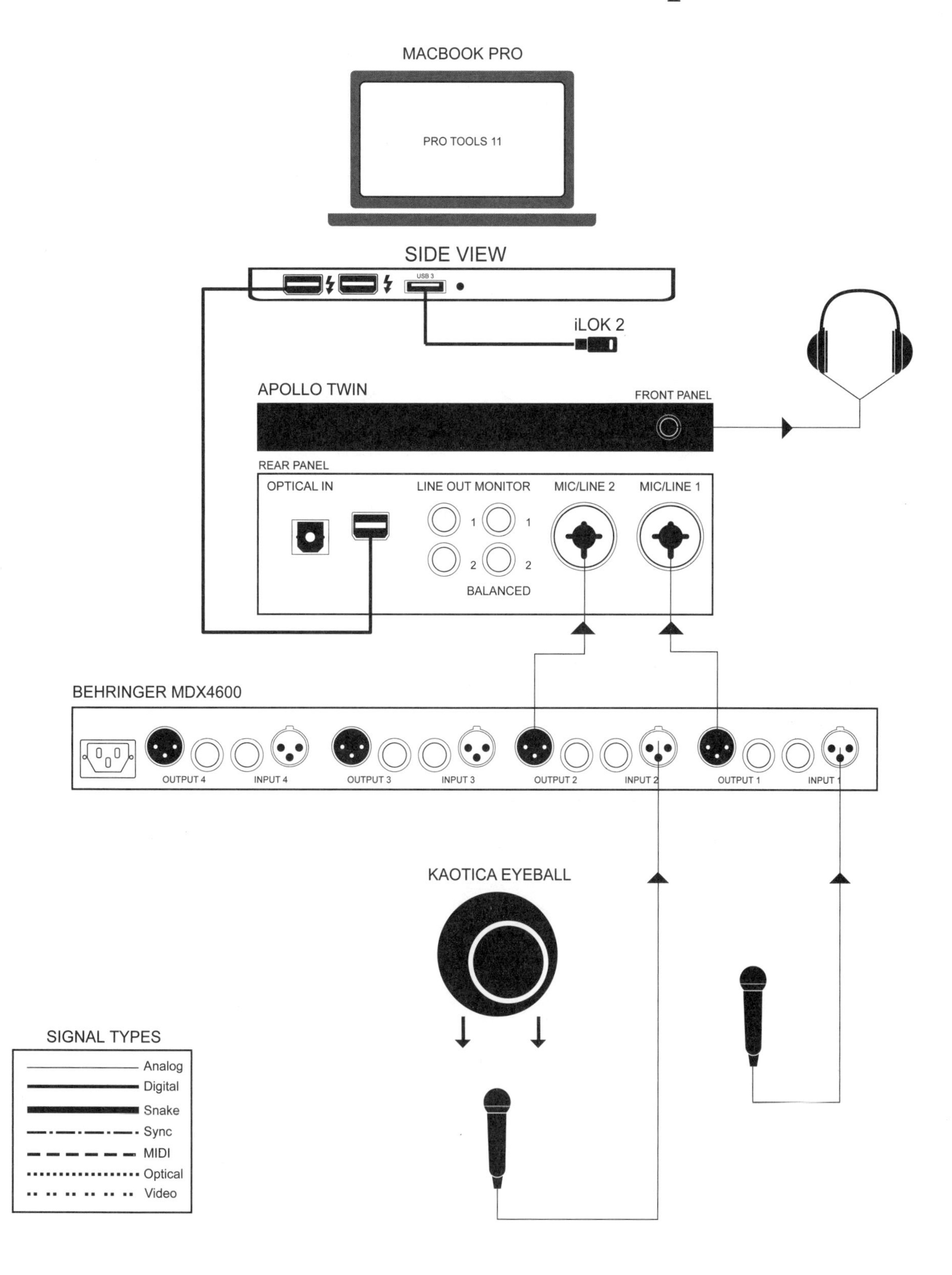

2. Connecting a pair of Headphones to the Apollo Twin Audio Interface

    - Connect the 1/4-inch TRS (stereo) headphone connector to the headphone jack located on the front panel of the Apollo Twin. Use the "phones" knob to adjust the headphone level. Be careful when you wear the headphones as the knob can be set to its highest level and it can hurt your ears.

3. Connecting the Apollo Twin Audio Interface to the Behringer MDX4600

    - Using an XLR cable, connect "Output 1" of the Behringer MDX4600 to the "MIC/LINE 1 " input jack of the Apollo Twin interface.
    - Using another XLR cable, connect "Output 2" of the Behringer MDX4600 to the "MIC/LINE 2" input jack of the Apollo Twin interface.

4. Setting up the Kaotica Eyeball to the Microphone

    - Remove the pop filter on the Eyeball and insert the microphone.
    - Place the microphone with the EyeBall on the mic stand.
    - Position the mic with the EyeBall about 1-3" from the center of the pop filter to your mouth.

5. Connecting the Microphones to the Behringer MDX4600

    - Using an XLR cable, connect the output of one microphone to "Input 1" of the Behringer MDX4600 mic preamplifier.
    - Using another XLR cable, connect the output of the other microphone to "Input 2" of the Behringer MDX4600 mic preamplifier.

System Requirements

Apollo Twin for Mac OS X (as of this writing):

- Apple Mac computer with available Thunderbolt port
- Mac OS X 10.8 Mountain Lion or 10.9 Mavericks

- Internet connection to download software and authorize UAD plug-ins
- Compatible VST, Audio Units, RTAS, or AAX 64 plug-in host application software
- 2 GB available disk space

Pro Tools for Mac OS X (as of this writing):

- Mac OS X 10.8 Mountain Lion or 10.9 Mavericks
- 4GB minimum, 8GB required for video playback

Software Setup

Installing all necessary drivers and complementary files:

> *NOTE: Before you connect the Apollo Twin to your computer, you should run the software installer first. Go to www.uaudio.com and download the UAD for Mac system.*

- Launch the assistant and follow the instructions in order to install the UAD.
- After the installation is done, restart your computer.

Once you have connected all the devices, it is time to set some software features in order to get your podcast station ready. Also, after you have turned on your Apollo Twin audio interface, the system will now recognize it, if prompted, complete the firmware update.

1. Launch Pro Tools 11
   - To create a new session, click on Create Blank Session option on the Quick Start dialog box, select the parameters you desire, and then save your session.

2. Setting up tracks for recording
   - To create a new track, go to Track > New and set two mono/audio tracks.

- To route the mic signal to the tracks, go to the I/O selector and choose the corresponding input from the interface for each track.

- Click on the record enable buttons of each track. Adjust your mic recording level to start recording your podcast.

NOTE: Other common DAW to work for podcasts is Audacity, which is free, easy to use and similar to Pro Tools.

Uploading your Podcast

Once you have recorded your podcast, the next step should be to share it on a platform. The way we are going to do this is by using a Pro Tools 11 feature that allows you to link your material via SoundCloud. It is a very fast and easy way to upload it to the cloud:

Uploading your podcast:

- In Pro Tools 11, go to Setup > Connect to SoundCloud. In the pop up window capture your login and password information to sign in into SoundCloud.

- Then, select the clip where the podcast has been recorded with the Grabber tool in Pro Tools.

- Go to File > "Bounce to Disk" and in the pop up window select File type: "mp3." And in the "Share With" option select SoundCloud.

- Choose the directory where the file will be stored and then click on "Bounce."

On the "mp3" pop up window, you should select the encoding speed and bit rate for the file; also you will have to introduce some file information such as Title, Artist, Album, etc.

- Finally, on the "Share with SoundCloud" window, give a "title," "description," and "license" type for your SoundCloud file. Click on "Share" and you are done.

Another way to submit a podcast is with iTunes, here is a general explanation of what you have to do:

- Create your audio podcast episode, which can be an MP3 audio format.
- Create an RSS feed (an XML file) that:
  - Conforms to the RSS 2.0 specification
  - Includes the recommended iTunes RSS tags
  - Contains pointers to your episode with the <enclosure> tag
- Create your cover art, which must be a JPEG or PNG file in the RGB color space with a minimum size of 600 x 600 pixels. For best results, and to be considered for promotion in the iTunes Store or the Podcasts app, cover art must be at least 1400 x 1400 pixels.
- Post the RSS feed, cover art, and your episodes on a server that supports "byte-range" requests and a publicly accessible URL. Support for byte-range requests allows users to stream your episodes.
- In iTunes, submit your RSS podcast feed URL to the iTunes Store.

Also there are some options that you can use in order to host your podcast, some of them are:

- SoundCloud
- Archive.org
- Amazon S3
- Ourmedia.org
- Podomatic
- Podbean

This concludes this exercise. Remember, all the track assignments are arbitrarily chosen so you can understand and learn the process of setting up your own podcast with your specific equipment. By no means this is the only way to do it, this scenario is just to give you a model to work from. See Appendix C for more audio interface options.

Satellite Link HD & Video Satellite LE Synchronization Setup

This post-production studio arrangement is typically used in dub stages where mixing film and TV is the specialty, among other applications. The use of the Satellite Link HD and Video Satellite LE software options from Avid has changed the way to synchronize audio and video machines making the post-production workflow much easier, faster, and less costly. With this technology, you can synchronize multiple Pro Tools systems via a simple Ethernet connection making them act as one system. To be exact (as of this writing), you can link up to twelve Pro Tools HD systems, or eleven Pro Tools HD systems with an additional Video Satellite LE option on a separate CPU to manage all the video playback and having the rest of the systems playing back only the audio of a Pro Tools session.

In this particular setup, we are using three Apple Mac Pro Quad-Core desktop computers connected via Ethernet so that they can each control transport functions, make clip selections, and Solo tracks in Pro Tools across any of the systems linked. Also, we are synchronizing an Apple MacBook Pro laptop computer to handle all HD and SD video playback using the Video Satellite LE software option from Avid.

> *NOTE: Please note that Satellite Link HD and Video Satellite LE are now part of the Pro Tools 11 installation process. In prior Pro Tools software versions, this option was installed separately.*

Equipment List

- 1 – Apple MacBook Pro Laptop Computer
- 3 – Apple Mac Pro Quad-Core Duo Desktop Computers
- 3 – Avid HDX PCIe Cards
- 4 – PACE USB Smart Keys (iLok 2)

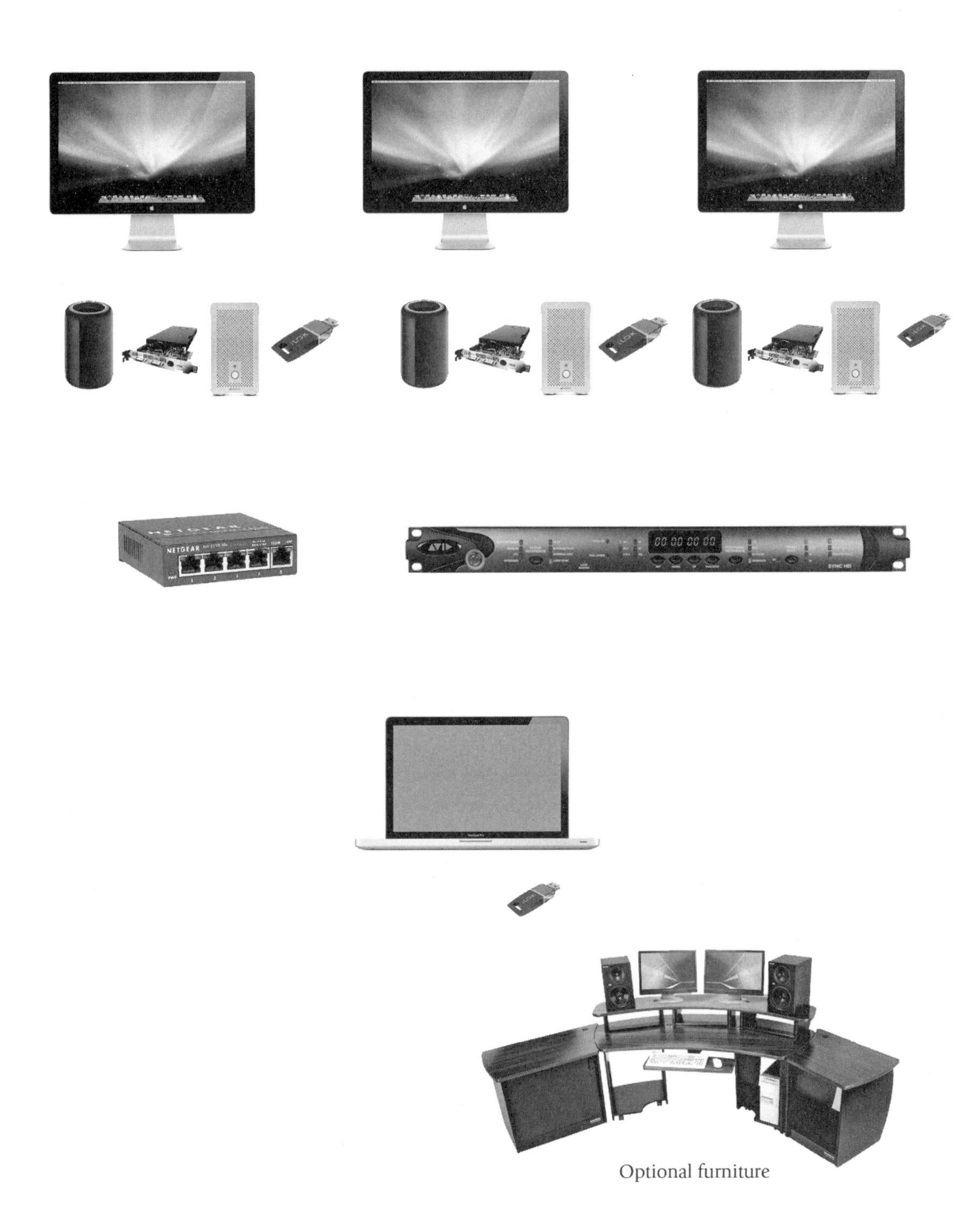

Optional furniture

Satellite Link HD & Video Satellite LE Synchronization Setup

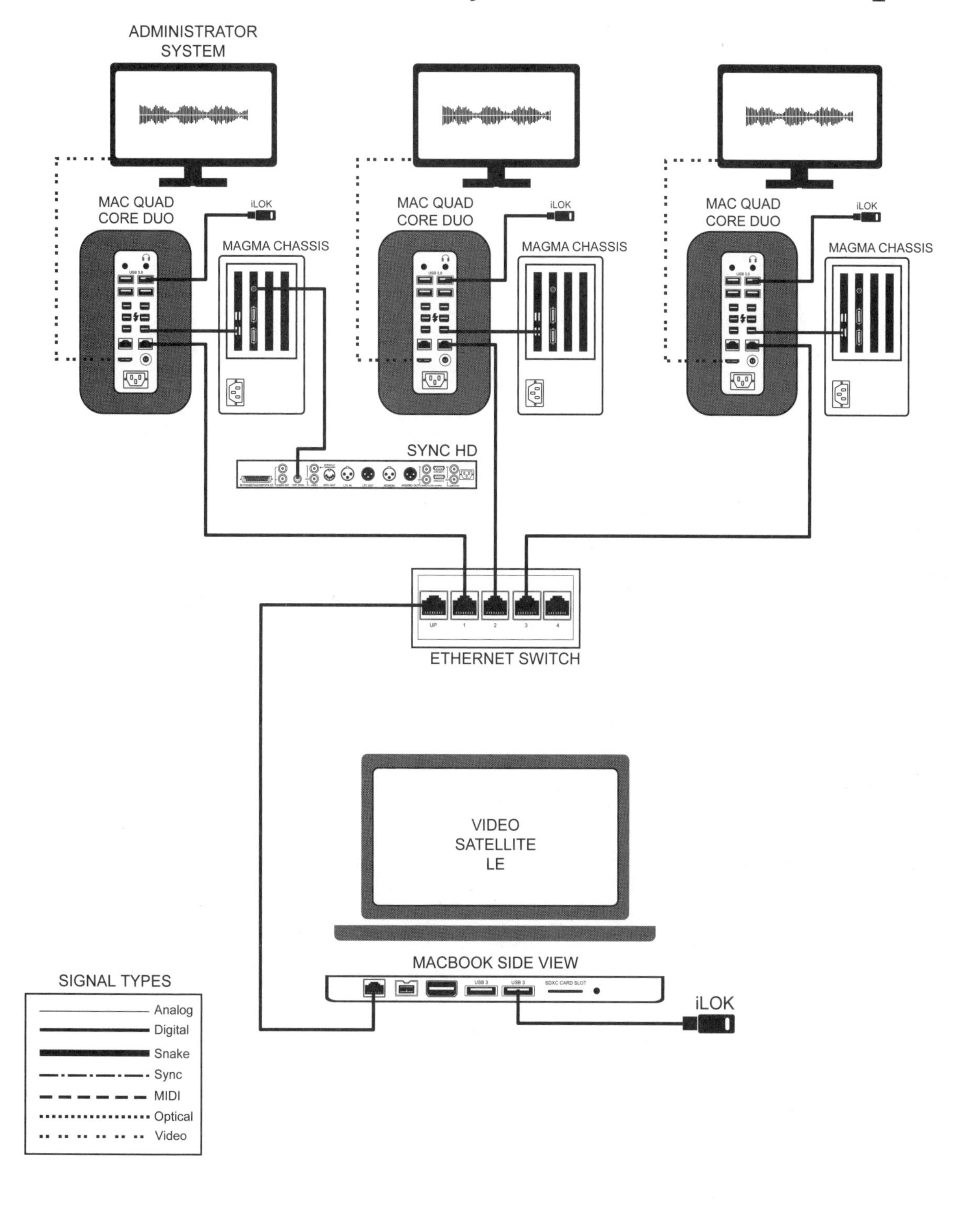

- 3 – Magma ExpressBox 3T Expansion Chassises
- 1 – Ethernet Switch
- 1 – Avid Sync HD Synchronizer

Cable List

- 4 – Ethernet cables
- 3 – Thunderbolt cables
- 1 – 8-pin serial cable

Hardware Connections

1. Connecting the Apple MacBook Pro Laptop to the Ethernet Switch
    - Using an Ethernet cable, connect the "UP" port (see line diagram) on the Ethernet switch to the Ethernet port on the Apple MacBook Pro.

2. Connecting the Mac Pro Quad-Core desktop computer to the Ethernet switch
    - Using an Ethernet cable, connect the respective ethernet port on each Mac Pro Quad-Core desktop computer into the Ethernet switch.
    - Make sure the Mac Pro Quad-Core desktop computer that will be acting as the Administrator System is plugged into Port 1 on the Ethernet Switch. Each subsequent Apple Mac Pro desktop computer should be connected in the proper order in line.

3. Connecting the Magma ExpressBox 3T Expansion Chassis to the Apple Mac Pro Quad-Core desktop computer
    - Using a Thunderbolt cable, connect the respective port on the back of the Magma ExpressBox 3T expansion chassis to an available Thunderbolt port on the Apple Mac Pro. Repeat for each Apple Mac Pro desktop computer.

NOTE: Make sure that each computer in this setup is equipped with a PACE USB Smart Key (iLok 2) that is plugged into an available USB port otherwise Pro Tools 11 will not open.

4. Connecting the Sync HD to the "Administrator System" Mac Pro Quad-Core Desktop Computer

   - Using a 8-pin serial cable, connect the "HOST SERIAL" port from the rear panel of the Sync HD to the DigiSerial port of the Avid HDX card in the Magma ExpressBox 3T expansion chassis.

System Requirements

Since the system requirements for Pro Tools is constantly being updated, and depending on the Pro Tools HD hardware and software versions you are using in your studio, it is best to visit www.avid.com and search for the "Avid Knowledge Base – Pro Tools System Requirements," for both Mac OS and Windows OS and look for your specific Pro Tools and operating system in your computer. But I did want to include the system requirements as of this writing. Please find below the system requirements needed to use Satellite Link HD and Video Satellite LE.

For Administrator System:

- Avid-qualified computer running Pro Tools HD software
- Avid Pro Tools|HD, HDX or HD Native hardware
- Avid SYNC HD or SYNC I/O peripheral
- Ethernet connection to a Local Area Network (LAN)

For Satellite Link HD:

- Avid-qualified computer running Pro Tools HD software
- Avid Pro Tools|HD, HDX or HD Native hardware
- Avid SYNC HD or SYNC I/O peripheral
- PACE USB Smart Key (iLok 2) with Satellite Link authorization
- Ethernet connection to a Local Area Network (LAN)

NOTE: All Pro Tools systems in a Satellite Link network must be synchronized or resolved to a common video reference, or "house sync," using the Avid SYNC HD or SYNC I/O peripheral.

For Video Satellite LE:

- Avid-qualified Mac OS X computer
- Avid Pro Tools or Pro Tools HD software
- Ethernet connection to a Local Area Network (LAN)
- PACE USB Smart Key (iLok 2) with authorization for the Video Satellite LE option

Software Setup

Regardless of what version of Pro Tools you are running in your system (Pro Tools 8, 9, 10 or 11), you should already have installed the software and other files required to run Pro Tools properly. Also, it is very important that you check which operating system is installed in your computer, whether you are using a Macintosh (Mac OSX) or a PC running on Windows. If you are not sure you have the proper software versions for both your computer system and Pro Tools (along with any other digital device you are using in your setup, such MIDI controllers, audio interfaces, etc.) then check the compatibility information on the software versions you are running in the respective websites of the company's device you are using. For example, if you are using Pro Tools, then you can visit www.avid.com to check on the latest compatibility information.

Setting up Pro Tools:

For this example, let's simulate that we are using a dubbing stage to mix a 75-track Pro Tools session from a film that was recorded and edited earlier. The job requires three Pro Tools operators, one to mix the dialog, a second one to mix the music and a third one to mix all the sound effects in the movie. Also, let's suppose the dubbing stage has the three Pro Tools HD systems required for the job, including an Avid ICON (D-Control). See the photo in the beginning of this section so you have an idea of what a dubbing stage looks like. Notice in the diagram at the beginning of this setup, we are using three Pro Tools HDX systems for the Satellite Link, and one Pro Tools 11 software for the Video Satellite LE. Let's make all the proper assignments in the Pro Tools software:

- Before Pro Tools is launched to work in the project, you need to load the same session on the three Pro Tools HDX systems, and the video file on the Video Satellite LE computer system. This is so the same session runs at the same time synchronized with all four computer systems, and each mixer (Pro Tools operator) will have the opportunity to work on their part of the project at the same time.

- Once the session has been loaded on all the systems, and you have launched Pro Tools on each of them, go to the File menu and select "Open Session" to open the session that will be mixed on all the computers. I recommend, to save a copy of your original session just in case something happens to the file or you got so lost in the assignment process that you rather start from the beginning again. Use the Save As command located in the FILE menu, give the session another name when prompted, and click on the OK button to save it. It should be routed inside the folder you saved the original session.

Configuring Satellite Link and Video Satellite LE in Pro Tools:

- To begin using the Satellite Link option, the basic network settings and the Satellite network must be configured on each Pro Tools system, which in this case, you would have to do it four times, one for each computer, including the Video Satellite LE. In the event that the computers you are using, have multiple Ethernet interfaces, then, select the one you want to use for the Satellite Link communication. To do this, in Pro Tools, go to the Setup > Peripherals menu, and click on the Satellites tab. Then, under the Advanced Network Settings, choose the Ethernet interface from the interface pop-up menu, and then click on the "OK" button to execute the selection.

Selecting the TCP/UDP port for Satellite Link communication:

Systems in a Satellite Link network need to use the same TCP/UDP port to communicate. Available satellite systems will only appear on the other satellite systems using the same port. By default, Satellite Link uses TCP/UDP port 28282. If you choose not to use this default port, then choose a port between 1024 and 65534.

To select the TCP/UDP port for Satellite Link communication, do the following:

- Select the Setup > Peripherals menu and click on the Satellites tab.

- Under Advanced Network Settings option, enter the TCP/UDP port number you want the system to use.
- Select a port between 1024 and 65534.
- When you are done, click on the OK button.

Configuring a Satellite Link Network

- To set up Pro Tools systems or Video Satellite LE for Satellite Link operation, one Pro Tools system on the network must be designated an "Administrator" system. Other systems on the network are configured as "Satellite" systems, and are added to the network from the "Administrator" system.

To configure the main Pro Tools system as an "Administrator" do the following:

- On the main Pro Tools system, select the Setup > Peripherals menu and click on the Satellites tab.
- In the System Name text box, enter a desired name for the system.
- Under the Mode section, select Administrator.
- Under "Administrator," select the current system from the one of the system pop-up menus.
- When you are done, click on the OK button.

To configure a Satellite System do the following for each Pro Tools system you want to configure as a Satellite Link "Satellite," different from the "Administrator" system:

- Select the Setup > Peripherals menu and click on the Satellites tab.
- In the System Name text box, enter the desired name for a specific system.
- Under the Mode section, select Satellite.
- When you are done, click on the OK button.

To configure a Video Satellite LE system as a "Satellite" do the following:

- On the "Satellite" Pro Tools system, select the Setup > Peripherals menu and click on the Satellites tab.
- In the System Name text box, enter the desired name for the system.
- Under the Mode section, select Enable Satellite Mode.
- When you are done, click on the OK button.

Authorizing Video Satellite LE

Video Satellite LE is automatically installed with Pro Tools, but requires a valid Video Satellite LE authorization in order to be enabled in Pro Tools. The Video Satellite LE feature set for Pro Tools is automatically enabled if a valid Video Satellite LE authorization is detected on your PACE USB Smart Key (iLok 2). The PACE USB Smart Key (iLok 2) is manufactured by PACE Anti-Piracy and is included with certain Pro Tools systems or can be purchased separately. The software is authorized using the PACE USB Smart Key (iLok 2).

NOTE: In order for audio and video playback to be frame edge aligned, it is recommended that a SYNC HD or SYNC I/O (if working in previous Pro Tools versions) peripheral be connected to the administrator Pro Tools system, and that the SYNC be locked to black burst or tri-level sync. For tri-level sync, a SYNC HD is required. SYNC peripherals are only for use with Pro Tools systems with Pro Tools HD hardware. If using a qualified PCIe video card or Avid video peripheral on the Video Satellite LE system, the video hardware should also be locked to the same video reference signal that the SYNC peripheral is referencing.

Assigning the Video Satellite LE system

When the Video Satellite LE system has already been configured as a "Satellite," it becomes available on the "Administrator" system. The satellite system is then declared to connect to the main Pro Tools.

To declare the satellite system on the "Administrator" system:

- On the Pro Tools "Administrator" system, select the Setup > Peripherals menu and click on the Satellites tab.
- Under the Administrator section, assign the system you want to use as a "Satellite" from the pop-up menus.
- When you are done, click on the OK button.

NOTE: In the Synchronization section of the Pro Tools Transport window, the declared or assigned "Satellite" systems will appear, in order, from left to right. Only one Video Satellite LE system can be connected to a main "Administrator" Pro Tools system at a time. If the "Administrator" system is configured to Transmit Play Selections, those selections will be transmitted to the Video Satellite LE system. However, selections made on the Video Satellite LE system will not be transmitted to the "Administrator" system.

Once you have assigned and declared all four Pro Tools systems (in this example), you will notice that when you press the Play button on any Pro Tools system, whether is the "Administrator" or a "Satellite" system, all four Pro Tools sessions on all four computer systems will play back in perfect synchronization making the mixing job more enjoyable.

This concludes this exercise. Again, all the system assignments are arbitrarily chosen so you can understand and learn the process of setting up your own Avid Satellite Link with Video Satellite LE network with your specific equipment. This scenario is just to give you an idea, and a model to work from.

Video/Audio Synchronization Setup

There have been situations when a film or TV series was finalized and as a result of time passing and technology changing, a part of the audio, for example, the sound effects, the dialog and music was saved in a Hi-8mm video tape using a Tascam DA-88 digital audio recording machine. For those who still remember, this machine was used in the '90s, in mostly post studios. Some studios still have this type of machine for the purpose of making digital transfers. Well, let's suppose that a particular film or TV series needed to be released in another language, and the job is to do a digital audio transfer to capture the music and effects tracks (M & E) only, as the dialog will be translated, edited, and conformed to the linear video coming from a 3/4-inch Video Tape Recorder (VTR).

This is a common job in a post studio, so let's see what equipment is needed to do the job, how it is connected, and what would be the process to accomplish the project. In this particular setup we are using an Avid Pro Tools HDX system with one Avid HD I/O audio interface. Notice the HD I/O is an 8x8x8, that is, 8-Analog Inputs, 8-Analog Outputs, and 8-Digital Inputs and Outputs with several digital audio transfer formats: AES/EBU, T-DIF, ADAT Lightpipe. Also, notice I have included one Avid SYNC HD to use it as a positional reference to synchronize all the machines together. We will also be using an Apogee Big Ben Master Word Clock generator and a Black Burst generator for clock and video reference. Remember, we are supposing this film or TV series was done a few years ago, so the video is still in a 3/4-inch video tape machine. For this reason, I have included a Video Tape Recorder (VTR) and a video monitor to watch the video as the audio transfer is being done. And finally, I implemented an analog mixing board to monitor the audio.

Equipment List

- 1 – Avid 8x8x8x HD I/O Audio Interface
- 1 – Avid Sync HD Synchronizer
- 1 – Avid HDX PCIe Card
- 1 – 3/4-inch Video Tape Recorder

Optional furniture

Video/Audio Synchronization Setup

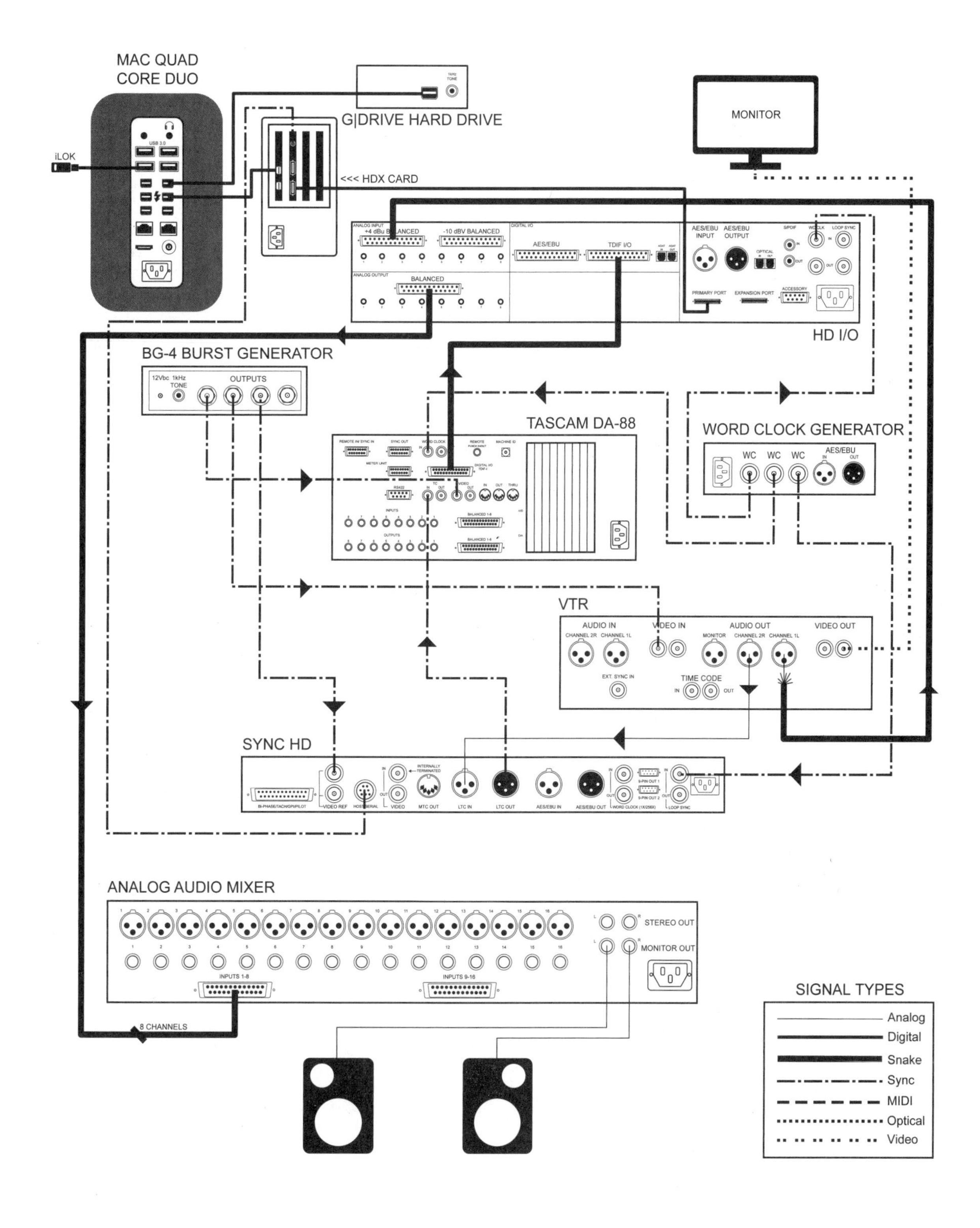

- 1 – Tascam DA-88 digital recording machine
- 1 – Analog mixing board
- 1 – Apogee Big Ben Master Word Clock generator
- 1 – Burst Electronics Black Burst generator
- 1 – Pair of powered speaker monitors
- 1 – Apple Mac Pro desktop computer
- 1 – G-Technology 24TB G|SPEED Studio hard drive
- 1 – Magma ExpressBox 3T expansion chassis
- 1 – PACE USB Smart Key (iLok 2)

Cable List

- 1 – Avid DigiLink Mini cable
- 1 – 8x8 DB-25 to DB-25 cable snake
- 1 – Tascam PW-88D 8x8 DB-25 to DB-25 cable snake
- 1 – 8x8 DB-25 to Male XLR cable snake
- 1 – XLR cable
- 1 – XLR to RCA cable
- 1 – RCA Video cable
- 1 – 8-Pin Mini DIN Serial cable
- 2 – 1/4-inch TRS cables
- 6 – 75-ohm BNC cables
- 2 – Thunderbolt cables

Hardware Connections

Once you have all the cables and the Pro Tools hardware components, it's time to connect all these elements together. To get you started, I have assembled a sample connection diagram and explanations that shows how this is done. Of course, these are just examples, you are not likely to have the exact system list of components discussed here, but hopefully, this diagram and explanation will give you an idea of how to connect a similar system. For example, the inputs and outputs of the audio interfaces were arbitrarily selected, you can choose any input and/or output you desire for your situation.

1. Connecting the G-Technology's G|SPEED Studio external hard drive to the Apple Mac Pro desktop computer

    - Using a Thunderbolt 2 cable (depending in your computer), connect an available Thunderbolt 2 port on your Apple Mac Pro desktop computer to a Thunderbolt 2 port on the G|SPEED Studio external hard drive.

2. Connecting the Magma ExpressBox 3T expansion chassis to the Apple Mac Pro desktop computer

    - Using a Thunderbolt 2 cable (depending in your computer), connect an available Thunderbolt 2 port on your Apple Mac Pro desktop computer to a Thunderbolt 2 port on the Magma ExpressBox 3T expansion chassis.

3. Connecting the Avid HD I/O audio interface to the Avid HDX PCIe card

    - Using a DigiLink Mini cable, connect PORT 1 of the HDX PCIe card [located inside of the Magma ExpressBox 3T expansion chassis] to the PRIMARY PORT on the rear panel of the HD I/O audio interface.
    - In case you are using two HDX PCIe cards inside of the Magma ExpressBox 3T expansion chassis, don't forget to connect the HDX TDM Flex cable (a SATA cable) between the two HDX PCIe cards so they can share data along the TDM bus.

4. Connecting the Apogee's Big Ben Word Clock generator to the Avid HD I/O audio interface

    - Using a 75-ohm BNC cable, connect one of the Big Ben Word Clock Output jack to the Word Clock Input of the HD I/O audio interface. Notice we are not using the Loop Sync connector of the HD I/O, this is because we are using an external word clock generator for the clock reference on all the devices that need external clocking.

5. Connecting the Big Ben Word Clock generator to the Avid Sync HD

    - Using a 75-ohm BNC cable, connect one of the Big Ben Word Clock generator output jack to the Word Clock Input of the Sync HD.

6. Connecting the Big Ben Word Clock generator to the Tascam DA-88

    - Using a 75-ohm BNC cable, connect one of the Big Ben Word Clock generator output jack to the Word Clock Input of the DA-88.

7. Connecting the Burst Electronics Black Burst generator to the Avid Sync HD

    - Using a 75-ohm BNC cable, connect one of the Black Burst generator Output jack to the Video REF Input of the Sync HD.

8. Connecting the Burst Electronics Black Burst generator to the Tascam DA-88

    - Using a 75-ohm BNC cable, connect one of the Black Burst generator Output jack to the Video REF Input of the DA-88.

9. Connecting the Black Burst generator to the DA-88

    - Using a 75-ohm BNC cable, connect one of the Black Burst Output jack of the external Black Burst generator to the Video REF Input of the DA-88.

10. Connecting the Burst Electronics Black Burst generator to the VTR

    - Using a 75-ohm BNC cable, connect one of the Black Burst generator Output jack to the Video Input of the Video Tape Recorder (VTR).

11. Connecting the Avid Sync HD to the Avid HDX PCIe card

    - Using an 8-pin Mini DIN serial cable provided with the SYNC HD, connect the DigiSerial port on the HDX PCIe card inside of the Magma ExpressBox 3T expansion chassis to the HOST SERIAL port on the rear panel of the SYNC HD. In the event that you are using more than one HDX cards, or an older Pro Tools HD 3 system, the SYNC HD always goes connected to the first HDX or HD Core PCI cards installed in your computer.

12. Connecting SMPTE (LTC) from the VTR to the Avid SYNC HD

- Using an XLR Female to Male cable, connect the analog output of Track 2 on the VTR to the LTC IN jack of the Sync HD located in the rear panel.

13. Connecting SMPTE (LTC) from the SYNC HD to the Tascam DA-88

- Using an XLR Female to an RCA Male cable, connect the LTC OUT jack of the Sync HD located in the rear panel to the TIME CODE IN jack of the DA-88.

14. Connecting the Avid HD I/O to the analog audio mixer

- Using an 8x8 DB-25 to DB-25 cable snake, connect the BALANCED (+4dBu) ANALOG OUTPUTS of the HD I/O to the Inputs 1-8 DB-25 connector of the analog audio mixer.

15. Connecting the VTR analog audio output to the Avid HD I/O

- Using an 8x8 DB-25 to a Male XLR cable snake, connect the Analog Output of Track 1 of the VTR to the BALANCED (+4dBu) ANALOG INPUTS of the HD I/O.

16. Connecting the VTR to the video monitor

- Using an RCA Video cable, connect the Video Out of the VTR to the Input to the Video IN jack of the video monitor.

17. Connecting the output of the analog audio mixer to the powered speaker monitors

- Using a 1/4-inch TRS cable, connect the Left Monitor Output jack of the analog audio mixer to the Left powered speaker monitor.
- Using a 1/4-inch TRS cable, connect the Right Monitor Output jack of the analog audio mixer to the Right powered speaker monitor.

System Requirements

Since the system requirements for Pro Tools are constantly being updated, and depending on the Pro Tools HD hardware and software versions you are using in your studio, it is best to visit www.avid.com and search for the "Avid Knowledge Base

– Pro Tools System Requirements," for both Mac OS and Windows OS and look for your specific Pro Tools and operating system in your computer.

Software Setup

As I mentioned before, the Pro Tools system we are using in this example is a Pro Tools 11 system. Regardless of what version of Pro Tools you use in your studio, version 9, 10 or 11 (as of this writing), you should already have installed the software and other files required to run Pro Tools properly. Also, it is very important that you check which operating system is installed in your computer, whether you are using a Macintosh (Mac OSX) or a PC running on Windows. If you are using Pro Tools, then you can visit www.avid.com to check for the latest compatibility information.

Assuming all the connections were done properly, follow the steps below to configure your hardware in your Pro Tools session.

- First, launch the Pro Tools software, the QuickStart dialog box will appear on the screen. Select the "Create Blank Session" option to create a new session. Now, choose the sample rate of 48kHz, the Bit Depth to 16 bits, and set the Audio File Type to BWF (.WAV). The next step is to give it a name to your session, so go ahead and name it "DA-88 Transfer" and save it on the Desktop of your computer. You will notice the Edit and Mix window will appear on the screen.
- Once you have the new session open, go to the "Track" menu and select "New," a dialog window will prompt you to enter the information for the number and format of the audio tracks you want to create. Create 8 Mono Audio Tracks, one for each track of the DA-88 digital recording machine. Create a ninth audio track to record the reference dialog (Production Audio) that is recorded on the analog audio Track 1 of the VTR. This track is used as a dialog guide or reference track when conforming the dialog that will be recorded in another language, according to our example. If necessary, you could also create track number 10 in Pro Tools to record the SMPTE time code coming in from the analog Track 2 out of the VTR, but only if necessary.

Setting the digital inputs to T-DIF in Pro Tools

Since the DA-88 uses the T-DIF (Tascam Digital Interface Format) digital audio transfer format, and we made the T-DIF connections in our setup, we need to set the format for the inputs in Pro Tools to T-DIF. To do so, follow the next steps:

- In Pro Tools, go to the Setups > Hardware menu, and click on the Digital tab and set the format to be T-DIF (you must have at least one digital card in your HD I/O audio interface). Once you assign the digital tab to T-DIF, click now on the Main tab and assign inputs 1-8 to accept T-DIF digital audio signals. Refer to the Pro Tools Reference Guide for more details to how to make these assignments.

- Also, in Pro Tools, go to the Setups > I/O Setup menu, and press the "Default" button in the Input and Output tabs. This way, you will be able to see the default names of your inputs and outputs. You can also give every input a different name if that is easier for you to recognize your inputs, which in this case you could label your inputs as "DA-88-1," "DA-88-2," "DA-88-3," and so on. You can also label your outputs 1 and 2 to "Monitors" to remember those outputs are your speaker monitors, for example. See the Pro Tools Reference Guide for more details.

- Next, go to the Mix window and practice assigning the inputs and outputs on the audio tracks you created earlier. If it makes it easier for you, follow the next table:

Track (mono)	Input	Source	Output
Audio track # 1	DA-88-1	(Sound FX 1)	Monitors
Audio track # 2	DA-88-2	(Sound FX 2)	Monitors
Audio track # 3	DA-88-3	(Sound FX 3)	Monitors
Audio track # 4	DA-88-4	(Sound FX 4)	Monitors
Audio track # 5	DA-88-5	(Sound FX 5)	Monitors
Audio track # 6	DA-88-6	(Sound FX 6)	Monitors
Audio track # 7	DA-88-7	(Music Mix L)	Monitors
Audio track # 8	DA-88-8	(Music Mix R)	Monitors
Audio track # 9	VTR CH-1	(Reference Dialog)	Monitors

NOTE: *Remember that your outputs 1 and 2 are connected to the Analog Audio Mixer from the HD I/O, so make sure to bring up the corresponding faders in your mixing board so you can listen and monitor what is coming out of your Pro Tools system during the transfer.*

Verifying the Sync HD is properly connected and configured

It is important to check if your Sync HD is being read by Pro Tools. Otherwise, Pro Tools won't be able to synchronize to the rest of the machines. Follow the next checklist to successfully synchronize Pro Tools to other devices:

- In Pro Tools, go to the Setup > Peripherals menu, and select the Synchronization tab. Verify the box is checked for "Enable Sync HD." Set the Sync HD to read any of the other options as desired.
- In Pro Tools, go to the Setup > Session menu, the Session dialog window will appear. There are several things you need to setup in this window:
- Make sure your Clock Source is set correctly. Remember we are using an external Master Clock generator, so check your connections to be sure you are getting the correct Word Clock reference. You need to do the same with the DA-88 and Sync HD.
- Make sure the Session Start Time is set correctly so when initiating the transfer, Pro Tools starts recording on the right start time.
- Check that the Time Code Frame Rate is set to the right speed. You must know which frame rate the video is in, so select the correct one. Just to refresh your mind, the different frames in Pro Tools are: 23.976 fps (frames per second) for Hi-Def, 24 fps for Film, 29.97 fps ndf (non drop frame), 29.97 fps df (drop frame), both for NTSC color video, and 30 fps ndf, and 30 fps df, both for NTSC black and white video.
- Make sure the Incoming Time field in the Session Setup menu window in Pro Tools is reading the same time code numbers (hours:minutes:seconds:-frames) as the Sync HD peripheral. If this is not the case, then check your connections. Also, check that you don't have a cable that is defected, if so, try a different cable, you never know.
- Check that the Sync HD is set to accept LTC (Longitudinal Time Code) and not VITC (Vertical Interval Time Code).
- Make sure the Black Burst is connected to the Video Ref Input of the Sync HD, as well as the VTR and the DA-88. Otherwise, your video will start drifting away from the audio within minutes after the video playback has started.

Setting Pro Tools to record the digital transfer from DA-88 & VTR

- Once you have tested that all your machines are working properly and in synchronization with Pro Tools, and that you made the proper input assignments in the Mix window, then it is time to start the digital transfer from the DA-88. Before you record, press the Input Monitoring button (green "I" button) in all the audio tracks in Pro Tools to make sure you are getting the proper signals, including the analog audio coming from the VTR. Do this by pressing the Play button on the VTR to start the audio and video playback. By the way, if you take a look at the line diagram, notice the VTR is acting as the "Master" machine, the one generating the SMPTE time code. This means that in order for Pro Tools to start recording, the VTR has to start playing back first. Pro Tools will start recording when it reads the proper Incoming Time set during the original recording on the VTR.

- Once you are seeing signal levels on each audio track of Pro Tools, then it is time to start the recording process. Press the "Record Enable" button on all audio tracks in the session. Also, double check the Session Time field located in the Setup > Session menu is the correct one. At the same time, make sure the ONLINE button on the Transport window of Pro Tools (first button on the left with a small clock icon) is enabled (flashing). This function will allow Pro Tools to accept time code to be able to synchronize with the VTR.

- To start the digital transfer, press the Record button in Pro Tools, then press the Play button on the VTR. Pro Tools should be in "Pause-Record" mode (the green playback and the red recording buttons will start flashing), and it won't start recording until it reaches the time you specified earlier as the Session Start field in the Session Setup window. Once it reaches the specific location time, Pro Tools will start recording, as well as the analog audio coming from the VTR. The digital transfer will be completed once you press the Stop button on the VTR transport. Remember, in this setup Pro Tools is acting as the "Slave" machine, that is, it is being controlled by the tape machine transport.

This concludes this exercise. Again, all the track assignments are arbitrarily chosen so you can understand and learn the process of setting up a session to do the digital transfer. By no means is this the only way to do it, these scenarios are just to practice plugging in a setup similar to this one.

EDM Studios 4

Photo courtesy of Cikira's "Mashrooms" Studio, Central WA, USA

It was not that long ago that the equipment needed for Electronic Music Production was beyond the reach of the average music composer and keyboard player. The hardware back then was not only expensive but also large and robust, not to mention a physical location was needed to house all those keyboards. The digital revolution has changed that scenario completely, and the computer has become the center of Electronic Music Production. Contrary to what was needed years ago to produce electronic music, all that's needed now is your computer, a Digital Audio Workstation (DAW), a MIDI keyboard controller, and a pair of headphones to do the job. In this chapter we will study the different setups currently used to facilitate the creation of Electronic Music.

MIDI Synthesizer Studio

This MIDI Synthesizer setup involves the use of 2 hardware synthesizers, an Apple Mac Pro desktop computer, a G-Technology G-RAID Mini 2 TB external hard drive, Avid Digi 003+, MIDI I/O interface, Roland TR-8, and an analog audio mixer. This setup can nicely accommodate a composer, whether that composer works in music, television, or film. With two hardware synthesizers connected to the Avid Digi 003+, a composer has many options when it comes to his musical palette. For example, one synthesizer can provide the ground-shaking sub bass for a composition, while the other synthesizer can contribute its unique string patches. Or, synthesizer #1 can be used to play virtual instruments within your DAW, while synthesizer #2 can add analog sounds from its own banks.

Also, with the Roland TR-8 Drum Machine in this setup, the composer has access to two legendary Roland Drum Machines: the TR-909 and the TR-808. The TR-8 contains 16 kits made up of 11 instrument types. In addition to MIDI, it also has USB connectivity to synchronize with external devices in your setup. Through MIDI or USB, the TR-8 will sync to your project's tempo.

Both synthesizers and the Roland TR-8 connect to the MIDI I/O interface, which connects to the Apple Mac Pro desktop computer. Their audio outputs will go to the Digi 003+, and into your DAW (in this case to Pro Tools). Instead of monitoring the mix from the Digi 003+, the main outputs of the Digi 003+ will go to an external audio mixer in order to sum the digital mix to analog. Then, once the sound is summed, the signal will go out to the monitors. If the mix is to the user's liking, the analog mix could go back into the Digi 003+.

Equipment List

- 1 – Apple Mac Pro Desktop Computer
- 1 – G-Technology G-RAID Mini 2TB external hard drive
- 1 – Avid Digi 003+ Audio Interface
- 2 – External MIDI Synthesizers
- 1 – Roland TR-8 External Drum Machine

Optional furniture

MIDI Synthesizer Studio

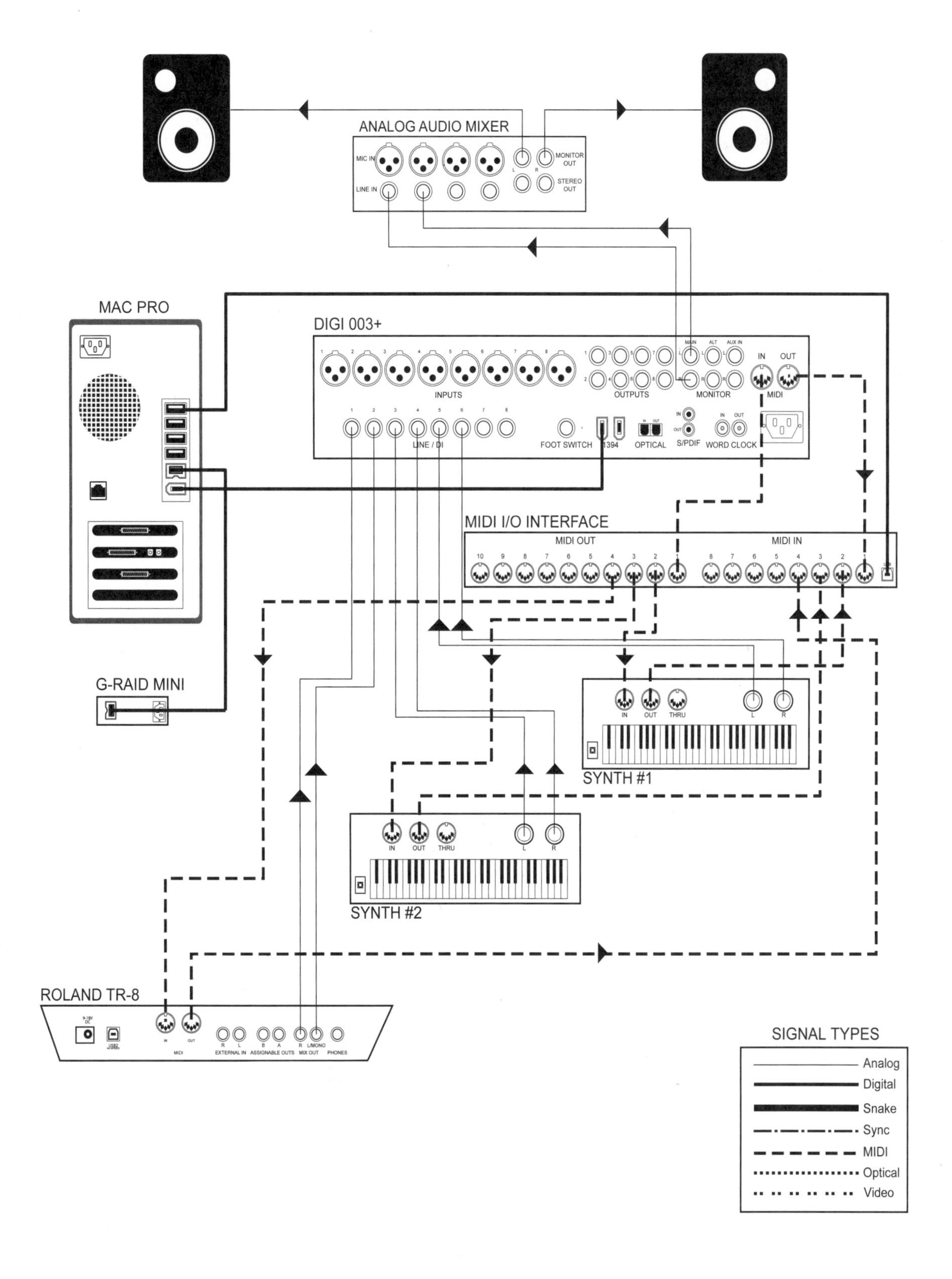

- 1 – Avid MIDI I/O Interface
- 1 – Analog Audio Mixer
- 1 – Pair of ADAM A7X Powered Speaker Monitors

Cable List

- 1 – FireWire 800 cable
- 1 – FireWire 800 to 400 cable
- 8 – MIDI cables
- 1 – USB cable
- 8 – 1/4-inch TRS cables
- 2 – 1/4-inch TRS to XLR cables

Hardware Connections

1. Connecting the Digi 003+ to the Apple Mac Pro Computer

   - Using a FireWire 400 cable, connect a "FIREWIRE 1394" port on the rear panel of the Digi 003+ to an available "FIREWIRE" port located on the back of the Apple Mac Pro computer.

   NOTE: If your computer has a FireWire 800 port only, then you will have to use a FireWire 400 to 800 adapter to connect the Digi 003+ to your computer.

2. Connecting the G-RAID Mini to the Apple Mac Pro Computer

   - Using a FireWire 800 cable, connect the FireWire port from the back of the G-RAID Mini to the FireWire 800 port on the back of your computer.

3. Connecting the Digi 003+ to the MIDI I/O Interface

   - Using a MIDI cable, connect the "MIDI OUT 1" port of the MIDI I/O interface to the "MIDI IN" of the Digi 003+.

- Using another MIDI cable, connect the "MIDI OUT " of the Digi 003+ to "MIDI IN 1" port of the MIDI I/O interface.

4. Connecting the External Synths and Roland TR-8 to the MIDI I/O Interface

Using the six MIDI cables, connect the following:

- "MIDI OUT 2" from the MIDI I/O interface to "MIDI IN" on Synth #1.
- "MIDI OUT 3" from the MIDI I/O interface to "MIDI IN" on Synth #2.
- "MIDI OUT 4" from the MIDI I/O interface to "MIDI IN" on the Roland TR-8.
- "MIDI OUT" from Synth #1 to "MIDI IN 2" of the MIDI I/O interface.
- "MIDI OUT" from Synth #2 to "MIDI IN 3" of the MIDI I/O interface.
- "MIDI OUT" from Roland TR-8 to "MIDI IN 4" of the MIDI I/O interface.

5. Connecting the MIDI I/O Interface to the Apple Mac Pro Computer

- Using a USB cable, connect the USB port on the MIDI I/O interface to any available "USB" port on the back of the Mac Pro computer.

6. Connecting the Digi 003+ to the Audio Mixer

- Using a 1/4-inch TRS-Male to 1/4-inch TRS-Male cable, connect the "MAIN OUT LEFT" on the Digi 003+ to the "LINE IN LEFT" on your audio mixer.
- Using another 1/4-inch TRS-Male to Male cable, connect the "MAIN OUT RIGHT" on the Digi 003+ to the "LINE IN RIGHT" on your audio mixer.

7. Connecting the Roland TR-8 and the External Synths Audio to the Digi 003+

Using 1/4-inch TRS-Male to Male cables, make the following connections.

- "MIX OUT L" on the Roland TR-8 to "Input 5" on the Digi 003+.
- "MIX OUT R" on the Roland TR-8 to "Input 6" on the Digi 003+.
- "OUTPUT L" on Synth #2 to "LINE/INST 3" on the Digi 003+.

- "OUTPUT R" on Synth #2 to "LINE/INST 4" on the Digi 003+.
- "OUTPUT L" on Synth #1 to "LINE/INST 2" on the Digi 003+.
- "OUTPUT R" on Synth #1 to "LINE/INST 1" on the Digi 003+.

8. Connecting the Adam A7X Speaker Monitors to the Audio Mixer

   - Using a 1/4-inch TRS-Male to XLR-Male cable, connect the "MONITOR OUT L" on the audio mixer to the left powered speaker. (This is the type of cable that most speakers use. However, some speakers require other types of cables, so check your manufacturer's documentation for more information).
   - Connect the "MONITOR OUT R" on the audio mixer to the right powered speaker, using another 1/4-inch TRS-Male to XLR-Male.

System Requirements

Since the system requirements for Pro Tools are constantly being updated, and depending on the Pro Tools hardware and software versions you are using in your studio, it is best to visit www.avid.com and search for the "Avid Knowledge Base – Pro Tools System Requirements," for both Mac OS and Windows OS and look for your specific Pro Tools and Operating system in your computer.

Software Setup

Assuming all the connections are ready, follow these steps to configure your hardware in your Pro Tools session.

- Launch the Pro Tools software and create a new session. After you named the session, create at least 6 Stereo Audio tracks and six or more Stereo Instrument tracks or as many as you need.
- If you are working with external MIDI devices in Pro Tools, it will be beneficial to configure your MIDI Studio. To accomplish this in Pro Tools, go to the menu Setups > MIDI > MIDI Studio, and the Audio MIDI Setup (AMS) application will open. Then go to the Window menu in the AMS and select the option Show MIDI Window, the MIDI Setup window will appear. You will notice the MIDI interface you are currently using will be shown on your computer screen. Next, click on the "Add Device" button, and a

keyboard icon named "new external device" will show up in the window. Double click on it, and the "new external device properties" window will appear prompting you to select the external keyboard manufacturer and model that is in your setup. Continue this process until you finish assigning all your external devices. Once you finish your setup, press the "Apply" button to execute the assignments. From now on, every time you create a MIDI or Instrument track in Pro Tools, a list of all the devices you created in the MIDI Studio Setup will show up in the list of inputs and outputs of the corresponding channel strip in the Mix window.

- In Pro Tools, go to the Mix window and assign the MIDI inputs and MIDI outputs on the Instrument tracks you created earlier, to the MIDI channels corresponding to the devices you want.
- Since the Instrument tracks have audio inputs and outputs, besides MIDI ins and outs, you must assign the respective audio inputs coming from the external synthesizers and drum machine. Also, in order to record these external devices sounds into Pro Tools, you must assign the audio outputs of the Instrument tracks to the Stereo Audio tracks inputs you created earlier. Make sure that the outputs of all the Audio and Instrument tracks in your session are assigned to Analog 1 and 2. This assures that you will be able to listen to your external devices sounds when you record them, and when you playback the Pro Tools session with the instruments you have recorded.
- Next, push the Record Enable button on each track you want to record to be able to see if you are getting a good signal coming from your devices. Then, press the Record button in the Pro Tools Transport window and finally, press the Play button to start recording the MIDI devices you desire.

This concludes this exercise. Remember, all the track assignments are arbitrarily chosen so you can understand and learn the process of a recording session using synthesizers. By no means is this the only way to do it, these scenarios are just to practice plugging in your electronic music studio and setting up a session in Pro Tools with an Avid Digi 003+ audio interface. These concepts and steps apply to other audio interfaces and Digital Audio Workstation software programs. See Appendix C for more audio interface options.

Advanced EDM/DJ Production Studio

This Advanced Producer/DJ setup is for the creative producer whose priority is to get a very clean signal out of his mixes. There are two identical systems in this setup, comprising two Apple MacBook Pro laptop computers running Ableton Live, connected to two PreSonus Audiobox USB audio interfaces and 2 M-Audio Trigger Finger MIDI controllers. The two M-Audio Trigger Finger MIDI controllers give the user plenty of tactile control in Ableton Live.

The DAW mix coming from each MacBook Pro goes out through the PreSonus AudioBox, and then gets processed by the Avalon VT 737SP preamplifier with the options of compressor/limiter/EQ.

There are two Avalon VT 737SPs in this setup. Together, they can be linked in stereo, where they can take both the left and right of the DAW mix, adding clarity to the mix. Once the mixes from both MacBook Pros are treated with the Avalon VT 737SPs, the signal continues to the Pioneer DJM-900SRT audio mixer. From here, you can further process the overall mix, and in real time.

A Pioneer CDJ-2000 adds to this setup the ability to "throw in" samples over the mix, or play full recordings side by side with the mix.

Equipment List

- 2 – Apple MacBook Pro Laptop Computers
- 2 – PreSonus AudioBox USB Audio Interfaces
- 2 – M-Audio Trigger Finger MIDI Controllers
- 4 – Avalon VT 737SP Preamplifiers
- 1 – Pioneer DJM-900SRT DJ Mixer
- 1 – Pioneer CDJ-2000 Multi Format Player
- 1 – QSC GX7 Power Amplifier
- 1 – Pair of QSC Speaker Monitors

Optional furniture

Advanced EDM/DJ Production Studio

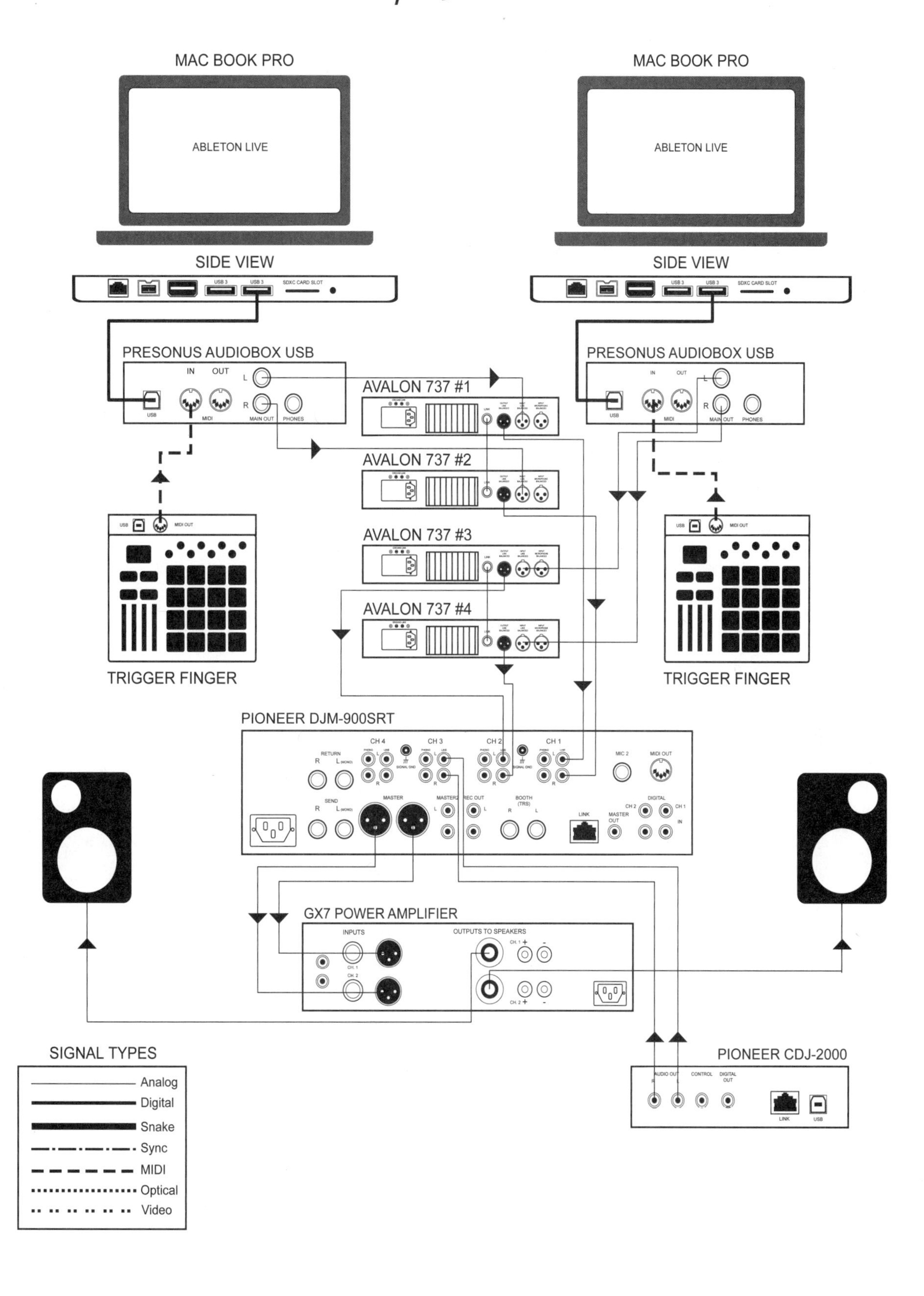

Cable List

- 2 – USB cables
- 2 – MIDI cables
- 4 – 1/4-inch TRS to XLR-Male cables
- 4 – XLR-Female to RCA Male cables
- 4 – 1/4-inch TS cables
- 2 – RCA cables
- 2 – XLR cables

Hardware Connections

1. Connecting the PreSonus AudioBox USB Audio Interface to the MacBook Pro
    - Using a USB cable, connect the USB port on the side of the MacBook Pro to the USB port on the rear panel of the PreSonus AudioBox USB audio interface.

2. Connecting the M-Audio Trigger Finger to the PreSonus Audiobox USB Audio Interfaces
    - Using a MIDI cable, connect the "MIDI OUT" of each M-Audio Trigger Finger to the "MIDI IN" of the PreSonus AudioBox USB audio interface.

3. Connecting the PreSonus AudioBox USB Audio Interface to the two Stereo-Linked Avalon 737SPs
    - Using a 1/4-inch TRS to XLR-Male cable, connect the "MAIN OUT L" of the PreSonus AudioBox USB audio interface on the left, to the "INPUT LINE BALANCED" of the first Avalon VT-737SP (#1).
    - Using a 1/4-inch TRS to XLR-Male cable, connect the "MAIN OUT R" of the PreSonus AudioBox USB audio interface on the left, to the "INPUT LINE BALANCED" of the second Avalon VT-737SP (#2).

- Using a 1/4-inch TS cable, connect the "LINK" jack of VT-737SP #1 to the "LINK" jack of Avalon VT-737SP #2.
- Using another 1/4-inch TRS to XLR-Male cable, connect the "MAIN OUT L" of the PreSonus AudioBox USB audio interface on the right, to the "INPUT LINE BALANCED" of the third Avalon VT-737SP (#3) .
- Using one more 1/4-inch TRS to XLR-Male cable, connect the "MAIN OUT R" of the PreSonus AudioBox USB audio interface on the right, to the "INPUT LINE BALANCED" of the fourth Avalon VT-737SP (#4).
- Using a 1/4-inch cable, connect the "LINK" jack of VT-737SP #3 to the "LINK" jack of Avalon 737 #4.

4. Connecting the two Stereo-Linked VT-737SPs to the Pioneer DJM-900SRT Audio Mixer
   - Using an XLR-Female to RCA cable, connect the "OUTPUT LINE BALANCED" of the first VT-737SP (#1) to the "CH-1 LINE L" of the Pioneer DJM-900SRT audio mixer.
   - Using an XLR-Female to RCA cable, connect the "OUTPUT LINE BALANCED" of the second VT-737SP (#2) to the "CH-1 LINE R" of the Pioneer DJM-900SRT audio mixer.
   - Using another XLR-Female to RCA cable, connect the "OUTPUT LINE BALANCED" of the third VT-737SP (#3) to the "CH-2 LINE L" of the Pioneer DJM-900SRT audio mixer.
   - Using one more XLR-Female to RCA cable, connect the "OUTPUT LINE BALANCED" of the fourth VT-737SP (#4) to the "CH-2 LINE R" of the Pioneer DJM-900SRT audio mixer.

5. Connecting the Pioneer CDJ-2000 Multi Format Player to the Pioneer DJM-900SRT Audio Mixer
   - Using an RCA to RCA cable, connect the "AUDIO OUT L" of the CDJ-2000 to the "CH-3 LINE IN L" of the DJM-900SRT audio mixer.
   - Using another RCA to RCA cable, connect the "AUDIO OUT R" of the CDJ-2000 to the "CH-3 LINE IN R" of the DJM-900SRT audio mixer.

6. Connecting the Pioneer DJM-900SRT Audio Mixer to the QSC GX7 Power Amplifier

   - Using an XLR cable, connect the "MASTER OUT L" of the Pioneer DJM-900SRT to the "CH 1 IN" of the QSC GX7 power amplifier.

   - Using another XLR cable, connect the "MASTER OUT R" of the Pioneer DJM-900SRT to the "CH 2 IN" of the QSC GX7 power amplifier.

7. Connecting the QSC GX7 Power Amplifier to the QSC Speaker Monitors

   - Using a 1/4-inch TS cable, connect the "OUTPUTS TO SPEAKER CH 1" of the GX7 to the 1/4-inch input jack of the Left speaker.

   - Using a 1/4-inch TS cable, connect the "OUTPUTS TO SPEAKER CH 2" of the GX7 to the 1/4-inch nput jack of the Right speaker.

System Requirements

For PreSonus Audiobox for Mac OS X (as of this writing):

- Mac OS X 10.8 or later
- Intel Core Duo processor (Intel Core 2 Duo or Intel Core i3 or better recommended)
- 4 GB RAM or more recommended

For PreSonus Audiobox for Windows (as of this writing):

- Windows 7 x64/x32 SP1, Windows 8 x64/x32
- Intel Core Duo or AMD Athlon X2 processor (Intel Core 2 Duo or AMD Athlon X4 or better recommended)
- 4 GB RAM or more recommended

Ableton Live 9 for Mac OS X (as of this writing):

- Intel Mac with Mac OS X 10.5 or later

- Multicore processor
- 2 GB RAM
- 1024x768 display
- 3GB free disk space

Ableton Live 9 for Windows (as of this writing):

- Windows XP, Windows Vista, Windows 7 or Windows 8
- Multicore processor
- 2 GB RAM
- 1024x768 display
- 3GB free disk space

Software Setup

Assuming all the connections are ready, follow these steps to configure your PreSonus AudioBox hardware in your Ableton session.

- Go to Ableton's "Preferences," and in the "Audio" tab, select the "Audio Input Device" and "Audio Output Device" as the PreSonus Audiobox USB.

This concludes this exercise. Again, all the track/equipment assignments are arbitrarily chosen so you can understand and learn the process of connecting and getting audio signals in Ableton Live. By no means this is the only way to do it, these scenarios are just to practice plugging in your electronic music studio and setting up a session in Ableton Live 9 with your PreSonus AudioBox audio interface. These concepts and steps apply to other audio interfaces and Digital Audio Workstation software programs. See Appendix C for more audio interface options.

Ableton Live Studio

This Ableton Live Setup includes an Apple MacBook Pro laptop computer, M-Audio Trigger Finger, and Monome 40H.

It is a good setup for a composer who likes working with MIDI and working with Controllers in their DAW (Digital Audio Station). Between the Trigger Finger, and especially the Monome 40H, the user has many options for controlling the environment within Ableton Live. This way, the user will not have to rely solely on the mouse and keyboard to make his or her music. For example, the Trigger Finger, with its pads, can be used to "trigger" one-shot samples within Ableton's samplers and instruments. Its knobs and faders can be mapped to any parameters in Live.

The Monome 40H is a re-configurable hardware controller. It consists of an 8 x 8 grid of backlit silicon pads, encased in anodized aluminum. Each of the 64 pads is fully configurable, and the user is able to assign MIDI Continuous Controller (CC), MIDI Note, or OSC messages to each of the individual pads. It communicates serial, MIDI, and OpenSoundControl (OSC) messages over USB 2.0. In this setup, it can be used to launch Ableton clips and sequences. Using Max by Cycling '74, or a Monome application such as Pages, the Monome can be customized greatly to a Live user's specific creative needs.

Equipment List

- 1 – Apple MacBook Pro
- 1 – Monome 40H
- 1 – M-Audio Trigger Finger

Cable List

- 2 – USB cables

Hardware Connections

1. Connecting the Monome 40H to the MacBook Pro

Optional furniture

Ableton Live Studio

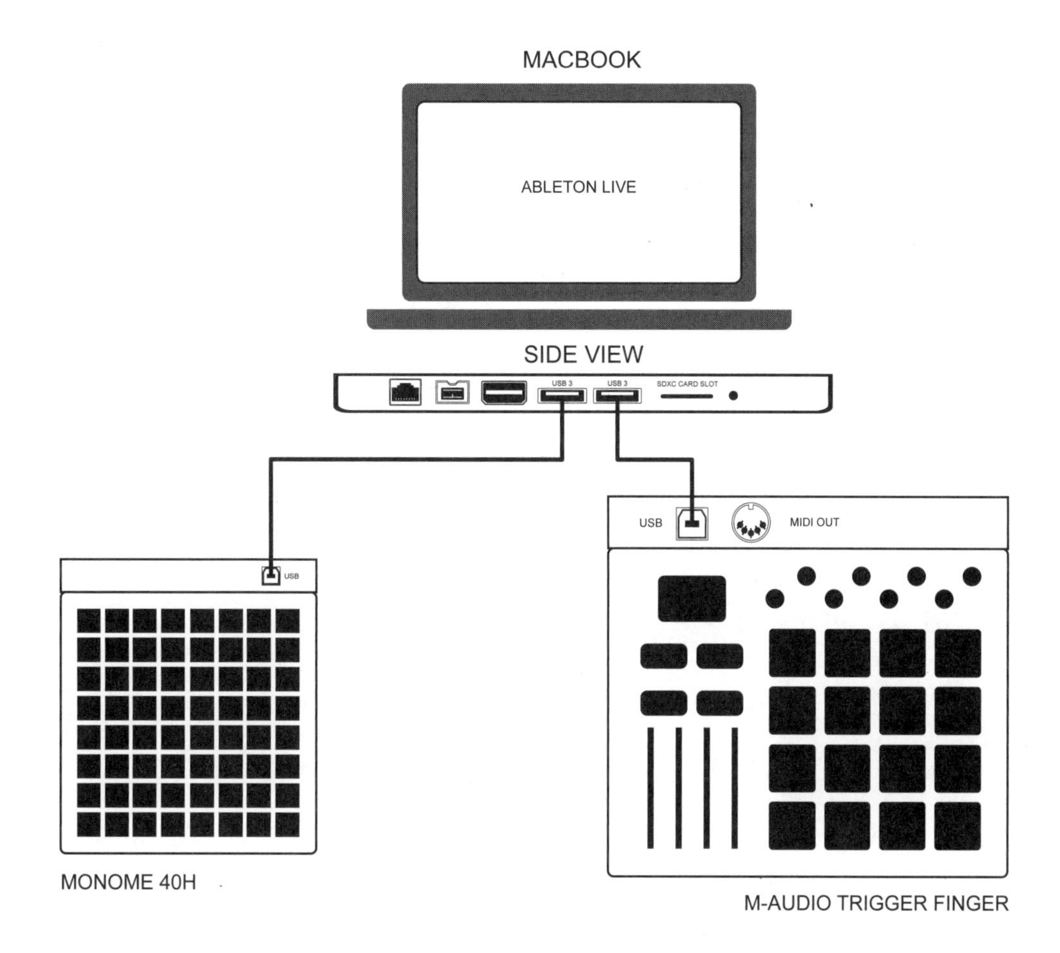

SIGNAL TYPES

- Analog
- Digital
- Snake
- Sync
- MIDI
- Optical
- Video

- Using a USB cable, connect the USB port on the side of the MacBook Pro to the USB port on the back of the Monome 40H.

2. Connecting the M-Audio Trigger Finger to the MacBook Pro

   - Using a USB cable, connect the USB port on the side of the MacBook Pro to the USB port on the back of the M-Audio Trigger Finger.

System Requirements

Ableton Live 9 for Mac OS X (as of this writing):

- Intel Mac with Mac OS X 10.5 or later
- Multicore processor
- 2 GB RAM
- 1024x768 display
- 3GB free disk space

Ableton Live 9 for Windows (as of this writing):

- Windows XP, Windows Vista, Windows 7 or Windows 8
- Multicore processor
- 2 GB RAM
- 1024x768 display
- 3GB free disk space

Software Setup

Configuring the Monome 40H for use with Ableton Live (will cover many steps, but it is a one-time setup):

1. To get the 40H communicating with your computer you will need to first download and install the FTDI virtual COM port (VCP) driver. This driver will

cause the 40H USB device to appear as an additional COM port on your system.

2. Go to the Monome website and download a folder called "base patches." This folder contains utility applications that allow you to route serial, OSC, and MIDI to and from the Monome 40H.
3. Install Serial OSC, which translate between serial data (hardware) and OSC messages (software). You will need to restart your computer once the installation finishes.
4. Install Max by Cycling '74, the most commonly used environment and fastest way to test your setup.
5. Install SerialOSC.maxpat, a Max specific file that allows you to connect and configure your device with an application.
   - Move the file into your /Max 6/patches folder.

   NOTE: If you can't find /Max 6/patches, use /Max6/Cycling '74 instead.

6. Run monome_Test. It is a Max patch designed to test input and output communication with a monome grid or arc.
7. Download the latest version of Pages from the Monome website. Pages is a Monome application that allows the simultaneous execution of multiple other Monome applications on any number of devices. It includes MIDI interfaces (keyboards, triggers, faders, sequencers), Ableton clip launcher interfaces, and a way to script your own programs.
8. Go to the MacBook Pro's "Audio MIDI Setup."
   - Double click on "IAC Driver." An IAC device is a virtual MIDI device, like plugging an app into another app with a MIDI cable. IAC devices are built into OS X, and are used to send MIDI commands between Pages and Ableton, or Max and Ableton, or Max and Pages.
   - In "Ports," add 2 buses. Name one "Clock" and the other "Pages MIDI." Click "Apply." This sets up the Monome 40H as a valid controller in Ableton Live.

9. Installing Live OSC, a python script that lets you use Ableton's controller integration via OSC messages, by copying the LiveOSC folder to the Ableton application package:

    - Open Finder.
    - Go to Applications folder.
    - Find Ableton, right click, "Show Package Contents."
    - Navigate to "Contents/ App-Resources/ MIDI Remote."
    - Copy the LiveOSC folder here, the path should read: "App-Resources/MIDI Remote/Scripts/LiveOSC/__init__.py

10. Install MMJ, which will allow Java MIDI to behave on OS X, and prevent random dropouts.

    - Download MMJ from http:// www.humatic.de/htools/mmj.htm.
    - Unzip MMJ.zip and locate "MMJ.jar" and "libmmj.jnilib"
    - Copy the above files to: /Library/Java/Extension (on the hard drive).

11. MIDI clock sync for Pages and Ableton synchronization

    - Go to Ableton's "Preferences" and "MIDI Sync."
    - Find the IAC Driver (Clock) device, and notice there are both "Input" and "Output."
    - Make sure the Input buttons – "Track," "Sync," and "Remote" are all disabled.
    - On "Output" of IAC Driver (Clock), enable "Sync."
    - Click on the drop down Sync Options for the "Output" of the IAC Driver (Clock), and set "MIDI Clock Sync Delay" to negate the "Overall Latency" in the audio tab.

12. Setting up the MIDI menus in Pages

    - Pages has two MIDI menus. The main program window enables the MIDI device for the program as a whole, while the sub-window enables the device for the current page you have selected.

- In both of the windows above, turn on "MIDI In: IAC Driver (Clock)." Repeat this step for each new page you create.

This concludes this exercise. Again, all the track/equipment assignments are arbitrarily chosen so you can understand and learn the process of a recording session. By no means is this the only way to do it, these scenarios are just to practice plugging in your electronic music studio and setting up a session in Ableton Live with your Monome 40H and Trigger Finger. These concepts and steps apply to other audio interfaces and Digital Audio Workstation software programs. See Appendix C for more audio interface options.

Native Instruments Maschine Studio

This setup is suitable for both electronic and hip hop composers. Native Instruments Maschine comes with a hardware beatbox and integrated software. The package includes an 8 GB sound library and functions with any MIDI keyboard. It connects via MIDI to the MacBook Pro, where it syncs seamlessly with its own software, Maschine 2.0. Also connected to the Maschine 2.0 via MIDI is a MIDI keyboard, for playing samples within Maschine 2.0.

The Komplete Kontrol S49 is Native Instruments' integrated 49-key Fatar controller keyboard with semi-weighted keys and aftertouch. In this setup, it is used as a MIDI keyboard for playing Native Instruments' range of Komplete 10 instruments (and 12,00 sounds). It can be used just as any other MIDI controller keyboard. Since the MacBook Pro only has two built-in USB ports, a USB hub will be necessary.

Equipment List

- 1 – Native Instruments Maschine
- 1 – Apple MacBook Pro Laptop Computer
- 1 – Native Instruments Komplete Kontrol S49 Keyboard Controller
- 1 – Komplete Audio 6 Audio Interface
- 1 – Pair of ADAM A7X Speaker Monitors
- 1 – Pair of Headphones
- 1 – USB Hub

Cable List

- 4 – USB cables
- 2 – MIDI cables
- 2 – 1/4-inch TRS to XLR cables

Optional furniture

Native Instruments Maschine Studio

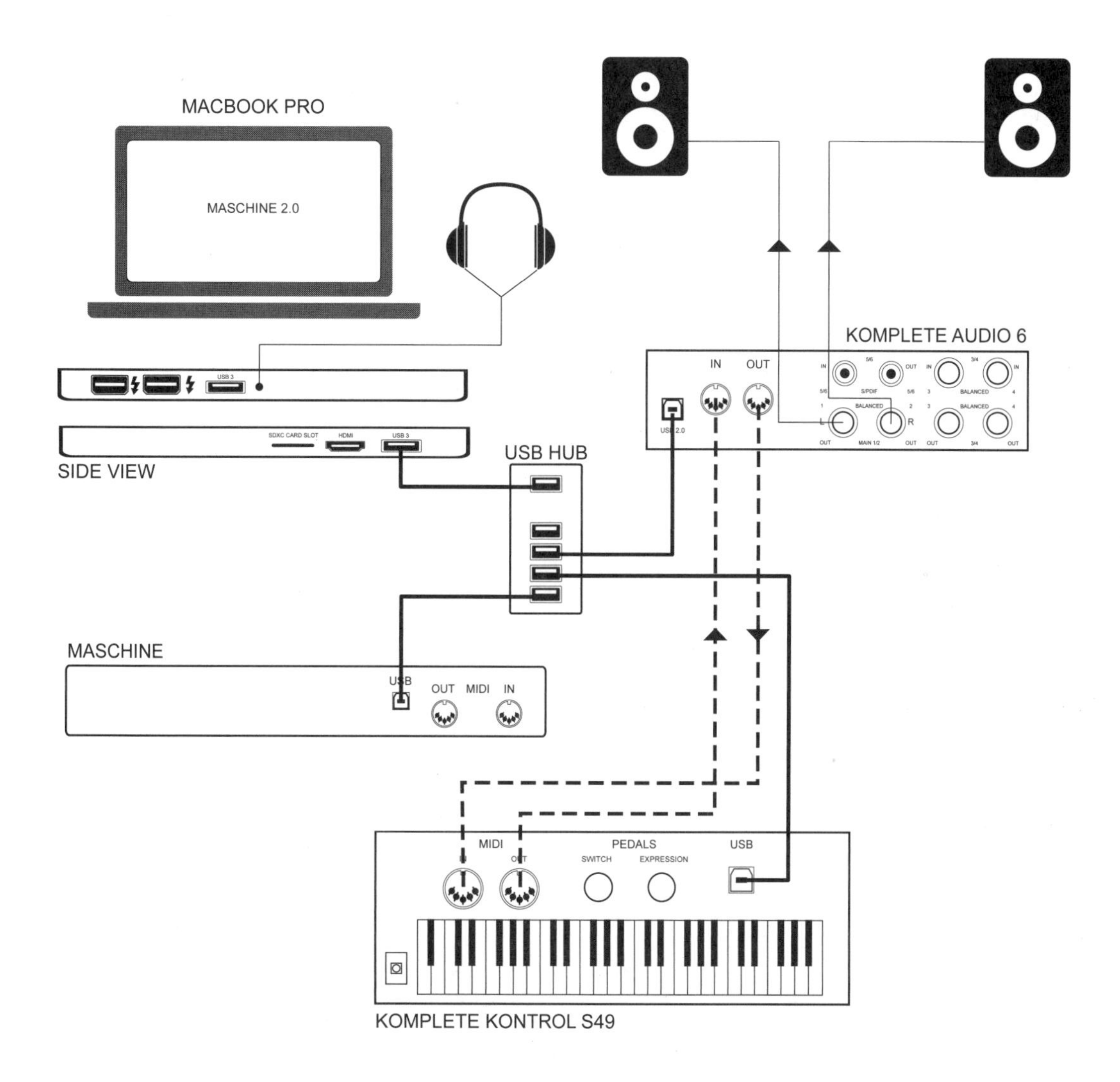

SIGNAL TYPES

- Analog
- Digital
- Snake
- Sync
- MIDI
- Optical
- Video

Hardware Connections

1. Connecting the USB hub to the Apple MacBook Pro Laptop Computer

   • Connect the USB cable provided with the hub to an available USB port on the side of the MacBook Pro.

2 Connecting the Native Instruments Maschine to the Apple MacBook Pro

   • Using a USB cable, connect a USB port on the USB hub to the USB port on the rear panel of the Native Instruments Maschine.

3 Connecting Komplete Kontrol S49 to the Komplete Audio 6 Audio Interface

   • Using a USB cable, connect the USB port located at the back of the Komplete Kontrol S49 to the USB port on the back panel of the Komplete Audio 6 audio interface.

4 Connecting the Komplete Audio 6 Audio Interface to the Apple MacBook Pro

   • Using a USB cable, connect another USB port on the USB hub to the USB port on the rear panel of the Komplete Audio 6 audio interface.

5. Connecting the Speaker Monitors to the Komplete Audio 6 Audio Interface

   • Using a 1/4-inch to XLR cable, connect the "OUT L" of the Komplete Audio 6 audio interface to the Left speaker monitor.

   • Using another 1/4-inch to XLR cable, connect the "OUT R" of the Komplete Audio 6 audio interface to the Right speaker monitor.

6. Connecting the headphones to the Komplete Audio 6 Audio Interface

   • Connect the headphone's 1/4-inch connector into the PHONES jack on the rear panel of the Komplete Audio 6 audio interface.

NOTE: If your headphones have a 1/8-inch connector, you will need to use a 1/8-inch to 1/4-inch adapter.

System Requirements

Komplete Audio 6 for Mac OS X (as of this writing):

- OS X 10.7, 10.8 or 10.9 (latest update)
- Intel Core 2 Duo
- 4 GB RAM or more recommended

Komplete Audio 6 for Windows (as of this writing):

- 7 or Windows 8 (latest Service Pack, 32/64-bit)
- Intel Core 2 Duo or AMD Athlon 64 X2
- 4 GB RAM or more recommended

Maschine 2.0 for Mac OS X (as of this writing):

- Mac OS X 10.7, 10.8 or 10.9 (latest update)
- Intel Core 2 Duo
- 4 GB RAM or more recommended

Maschine 2.0 for Windows (as of this writing):

- Windows 7 or Windows 8 (latest Service Pack, 32/64 Bit)
- Intel Core 2 Duo or AMD Athlon 64 X2
- 4 GB RAM or more recommended

Software Setup

Selecting the KOMPLETE AUDIO 6 as Your System's Default Audio Output Device:

1. Open the System Preferences under the gray Apple Icon menu in the top left corner of your screen.

2. Below Hardware (second row from top), select Sound.

3. In the Sound control panel, select the Output tab.

4. Select the KOMPLETE AUDIO 6 from the list of available soundcards.

5. Close the panel.

6. KOMPLETE AUDIO 6 is now selected as the default audio output device.

Using the KOMPLETE AUDIO 6 as an Audio Output Device with Music Software:

Before using the KOMPLETE AUDIO 6 with music production or DJ software, you will need to set it up as the software's audio output device. Most music production and DJ programs provide direct access to the soundcard properties in the audio and MIDI setup section of their preferences dialog. Please refer to the documentation of your music production or DJ software for more information on how to configure audio and MIDI interfaces.

This concludes this exercise. Remember, all the track/equipment assignments are arbitrarily chosen so you can understand and learn the process of an electronic recording session. By no means is this the only way to do it, these scenarios are just to practice plugging in your electronic studio and setting up a session in Maschine 2.0 with your Komplete Audio 6 interface. These concepts and steps apply to other audio interfaces and Digital Audio Workstation software programs. See Appendix C for more audio interface options.

Propellerhead Reason and Balance Studio

This powerful music writing setup, where one can create, arrange, record and mix MIDI as well as audio, is perfect for a home music production studio. In this setup, a lighter version of Propellerhead's Reason 8 (as of this writing) called Reason Essentials is used along with Propellerhead's Balance audio interface. It comes with a selection of Reason's instruments and effects in a virtual rack, a lighter version of its modeled mixer, and all the recording and sequencing tools needed for writing. Furthermore, this setup is perfect for guitar players, because it contains an integrated virtual guitar and bass PODs from Line 6, which bring a wide range of top quality guitar amps, cabinets, and effects.

Equipment List

- 1 – Propellerhead Balance Audio Interface
- 1 – Apple MacBook Pro Laptop Computer
- 1 – MIDI Keyboard Controller
- 1 – Electric Guitar
- 1 – Electric Bass Guitar
- 1 – AT 4050 Condenser Microphone
- 1 – Pair of Speaker Monitors

Cable List

- 2 – USB cables
- 2 – 1/4-inch TS cables
- 1 – XLR cable
- 2 – 1/4-inch to XLR cables

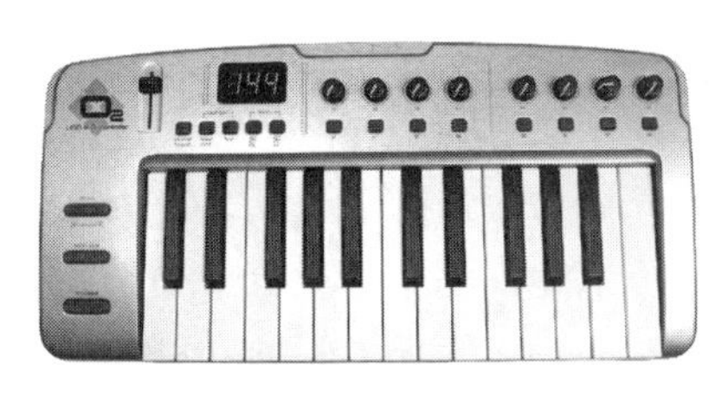

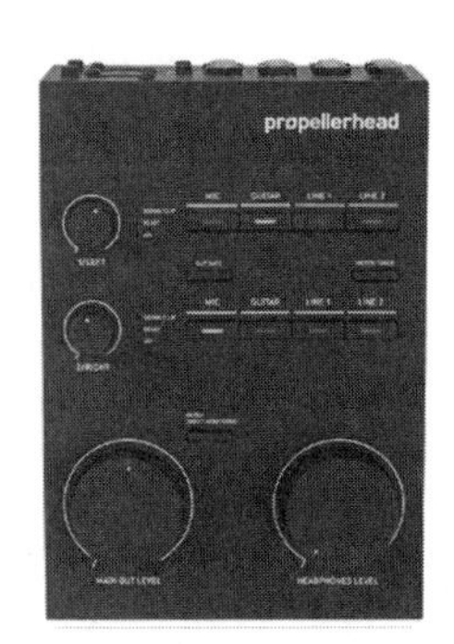

Optional furniture

Propellerhead Reason & Balance Studio

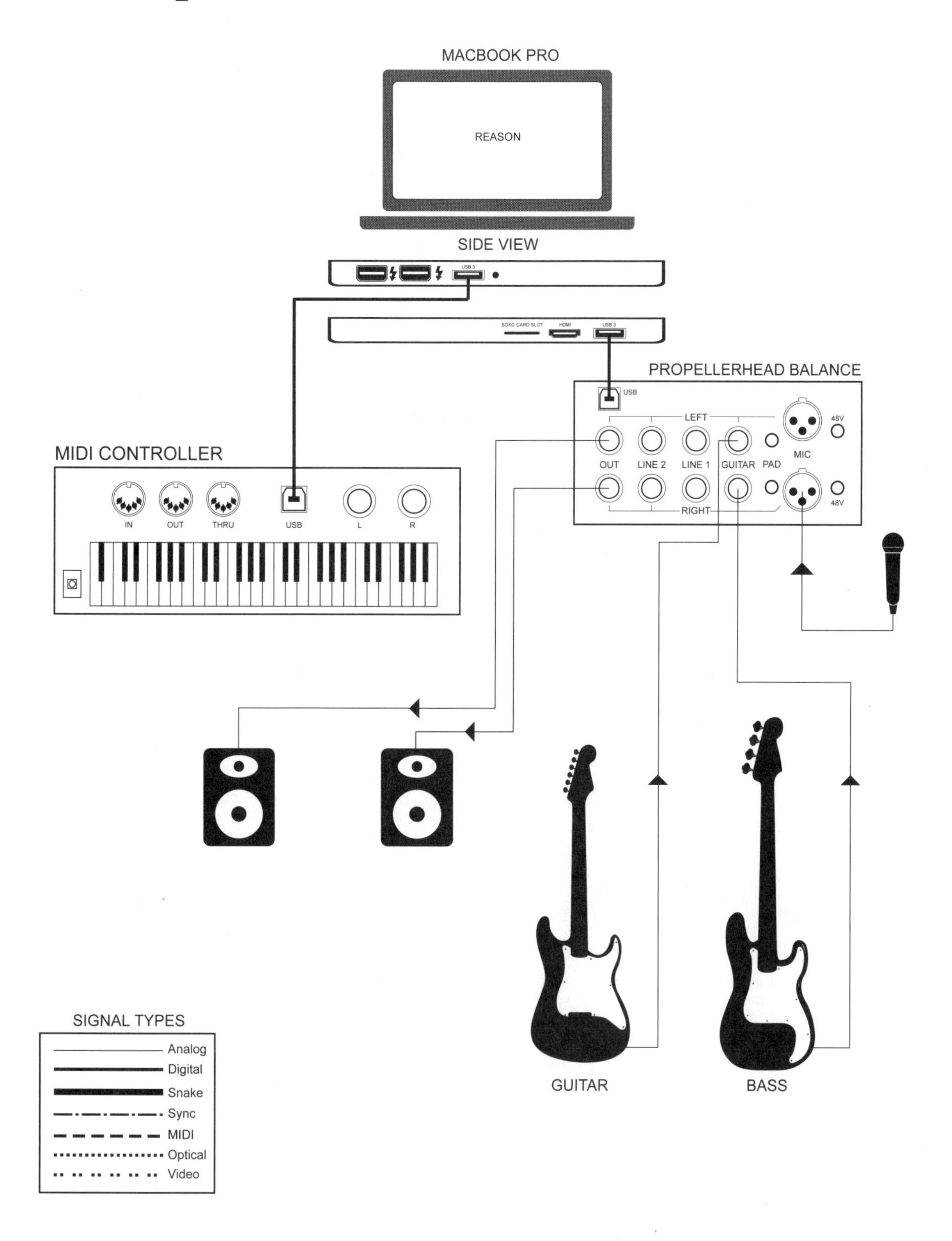

Hardware Connections

Let's take a look at the connections you have to make in order to get this setup working properly:

> *NOTE: It is very important to install the Reason Essentials software first before you connect the Balance audio interface to your computer.*

1. Connecting the Balance Audio Interface to an Apple MacBook Pro Computer

   - Using a USB cable, connect the USB port on the back of your Propellerhead Balance audio interface to an available USB2.0 port on your Apple MacBook Pro.
   - Once you have installed the Reason Essentials software and plugged in the Balance interface in your MacBook Pro computer, the Mac will now recognize it.
   - If you are using a PC computer with Windows for this setup, you will be asked to confirm the audio driver installation.

2. Connecting a Microphone to the Balance Audio Interface

   - Using an XLR cable, connect the output of the microphone to any of the two "MIC" inputs of the Balance audio interface. If you are using a condenser microphone, don't forget to activate the Phantom Power (48V) button on the Balance audio interface. There are two buttons for the 48v phantom power, these are located to the right of each XLR connector on the rear panel of the Balance. Just push the 48V button of the MIC input you are going to be using. Don't activate this button unless you are using a condenser microphone. If you turn the phantom power on in a Mic that is not a condenser microphone, you could damage it, so be careful.
   - Once you activate the phantom power on the input, the next step is to adjust the input signal level by turning the appropriate Input level knob on the left side of the Balance front panel. Test the input signal level of the sound source (voice or instrument). You should notice the SIGNAL/CLIP LED turning on as a signal is coming in. If this indicator turns red, then it means that your sound source is too high, so you need to turn the preamp knob down. A green color light on the SIGNAL/CLIP LED indicates that

the signal has a good input level.

3. Connecting the Electric Guitar to the Balance Audio Interface

- Using a 1/4-inch TS to 1/4-inch TS cable, connect the output of the electric guitar to the top "GUITAR" input of the Balance audio interface.
- These unbalanced GUITAR jacks are designed especially use for passive electric guitar or bass signals.
- Once you plug the guitar in, you need to press the top GUITAR button on the front panel of the Balance interface and adjust the input signal level by turning the top input level knob located on the left side of the front panel of the Balance interface. Play the guitar as you turn the top level knob clock-wise, you should notice the SIGNAL/CLIP LED turning on as the signal is coming in. If this indicator turns red, then it means that your sound source is too high, so you need to turn the preamp knob down. A green light on the SIGNAL/CLIP LED indicates that the signal has a good input level.

NOTE: If your guitar uses active electronics, you should push the PAD button to make it active to better adapt the signal to the specifications.

4. Connecting the Electric Bass Guitar to the Balance Audio Interface

- Using a 1/4-inch TS to 1/4-inch TS cable, connect the output of the electric bass to the bottom "GUITAR" input of the Balance audio interface.
- These unbalanced GUITAR jacks are designed especially use for passive electric guitar or bass signals.
- Once you plug the bass guitar in, you need to press the lower GUITAR button on the front panel of Balance and adjust the input signal level by turning the lower input level knob located on the left side of the front panel of the Balance interface. Play the bass as you turn the lower level knob clockwise, you should notice the SIGNAL/CLIP LED turning on as signal is coming in. If this indicator turns red, then it means that your sound source is too high, so you need to turn the preamp knob down. A green light on the SIGNAL/CLIP LED indicates that the signal has a good input level.

NOTE: If your bass uses active electronics, you should push the PAD button to make it active to better adapt the signal to the specifications.

5. Connecting a MIDI Keyboard Controller to the MacBook Pro Laptop

    - Using a USB cable, connect the USB port on the back of your MIDI Keyboard controller to an available USB port on your MacBook Pro.

6. Connecting the Speaker Monitors to the Balance Audio Interface

    - Using a 1/4-inch TRS to XLR cable, or a 1/4-inch TRS to 1/4-inch TRS cable (depending on the input jacks of your speaker monitors), connect the "OUT L" output jack of the Balance interface to the Left speaker monitor.
    - Using a 1/4-inch TRS to XLR cable, or a 1/4-inch TRS to 1/4-inch TRS cable (depending on the input jacks of your speaker monitors), connect the "OUT R" output jack of the Balance interface to the Right speaker monitor.
    - If you are using only headphones for monitoring your sound, then, just plug the 1/4-inch TRS (stereo) headphone connector to the headphone jack located on the lower right side on the front of the Balance interface. Use the "Big Knob" on the right side of the Balance to adjust the head phone level. Be careful when you wear the headphones as the knob can be set to its highest position and it can hurt your ears.

NOTE: There would be no problem if you happen to connect an electric guitar, a line mixer, an external synthesizer, or any other unbalanced (TS) signal to the "LINE 1" or "LINE 2" balanced (TRS) input jacks, just make the proper signal button selection on the front panel of the Balance audio interface.

System Requirements

Reason Essentials for Mac OS X (as of this writing):

- Intel Mac with dual cores (or better)
- 4 GB RAM or more

- DVD drive
- 3 GB free hard disk space (program may use up to 20 GB)
- Mac OS X 10.7 or later
- Monitor with at least 1024 x 768 resolution
- CoreAudio compliant audio interface, such as Propellerhead Balance, or built-in audio hardware
- A free USB2.0 port is necessary when using the Propellerhead Balance audio interface
- Internet connection for registration and Rack Extension installation
- MIDI interface and a MIDI keyboard recommended

Reason Essentials for Windows (as of this writing):

- Intel Pentium 4/AMD Opteron with dual cores (or better)
- 4GB RAM or more
- DVD drive
- 3 GB free hard disk space (program may use up to 20 GB)
- Windows 7 or later
- Monitor with at least 1024x768 resolution
- Audio Interface with ASIO driver, such as Propellerhead Balance
- A free USB 2.0 port for the Propellerhead Balance audio interface
- Internet connection for registration and Rack Extension installation
- MIDI interface and a MIDI keyboard recommended

If you launch Reason Essentials with an authorized Ignition Key hardware connected, the program will simply start without further ado. From now on, always connect your Ignition Key hardware before starting your computer and launching Reason Essentials. This way Reason Essentials will start up immediately, without the Application Authorization procedure. When you have an authorized Ignition Key hardware connected to your computer, it's no longer necessary to have an Internet connection when running Reason Essentials.

NOTE: Don't forget to always keep the "Ignition Key Hardware" USB key connected in an available USB port of your MacBook Pro or PC computer. If you don't have enough USB ports in your computer, you can purchase a USB hub to add more USB ports in your system. If you unplug the Ignition Key Hardware or lose Internet connection while working with the Reason Essentials software, the software will automatically enter in the Demo Mode. The software will let you keep working and will allow you to save your work. When you reconnect the Ignition Key Hardware USB key, the software will automatically revert to the Authorized mode, and the Demo Mode alert will disappear from the transport panel in the software.

Software Setup

Once you have made the proper hardware connections, installed and authorized the software, there are tasks you still will have to perform before you can record in Reason Essentials using the Balance audio interface.

After you have launched the Reason Essentials software in your computer do the following:

1. Setting up the Balance audio interface

   - Download and install the drivers for Balance if you are working on Windows. If you are using Mac OS, you don't need any drivers. This audio interface is Core Audio compliant. Also, Balance requires Mac OS X 10.6.3 or higher to run efficiently.

   - Make sure you are not connecting Balance through a USB hub, it has to be connected directly to your computer.

   - While in Reason, create a new session. To accomplish this, go to the File menu and select "New" or press the Command + N keys on your computer keyboard.

   - Then, go to the Reason > Preferences menu and from the drop-down menu select Audio.

- On the Audio Device selector choose the Balance audio interface and then, close the pop up window.

2. Setting up a MIDI keyboard controller:

   - Go to the Reason Preferences menu and from the drop-down menu select Keyboards and Control Surfaces.
   - Then, press the Auto-detect Surfaces. Reason will be able to detect the surface you are connected to. But if this does not work, then you will have to add it manually by pressing the "Add" button on the same menu. Another dialog window will appear and you will have to select the Manufacturer and Model of the device you have plugged in. Once you have done that, press the "Find" button on the "In Port" option and press any key or control from your device, this will detect the port you are using to get the communication among the devices. Finally, select the same option for the "Out Port" option and then, click on the OK button.

3. Setting up the tracks to record audio:

   - Go to the Create > Audio Track menu or press the Command + T keys on your computer keyboard. An audio track is created in the sequencer, an audio track device on the rack and a channel strip on the main mixer window.
   - Now, to route the instrument or microphone signal to the track, you have to choose your audio interface input from the selector located at the bottom left corner on the track list. Also, there is a section to select if you will want a mono or a stereo setting.
   - Finally, as soon as you notice a signal registered by Reason Essentials, then you will have to adjust your Balance audio interface input levels in order to avoid clipping and get great sound quality.

This concludes this exercise. Again, all the track assignments are arbitrarily chosen so you can understand and learn the process of a recording session. By no means is this the only way to do it, these scenarios are just to practice plugging in your home studio and setting up a session in Reason Essentials with your Balance audio interface. These concepts and steps apply to other audio interfaces and Digital Audio Workstation software programs. See Appendix C for more audio interface options.

DJ Studios 5

Photo courtesy of Hoerboard

The simplicity of the DJ studio impresses me. Tracing back to the roots of DJing to the '50s in Jamaica, where that time, the "selector," as Jamaicans called the DJ, played music from a vehicle filled with speakers to entertain street parties. Later, this culture was brought to America, specifically to the Bronx in New York, by a 15 year-old Jamaican named Clive Campbell. It became the foundation of what today is known as Hip-Hop. It is interesting to witness how something so simple as it was then in the '50s to entertain people in the streets, can still be as simple, casual, and effective by using vinyl records and CDs, and current digital equipment. This chapter focuses on connecting and combining past and present DJ equipment

Vinyl DJ Studio

This is the most classic DJ studio there is, due to its simplicity and effectiveness. As the most analog of the DJ setups, it combines two Technics 1200 turntables with a two-channel Vestax PMC-06 Pro DJ mixer. This is the DJ setup used before there were digital DJ options: vinyl turntables, a mixer, headphones and occasionally a microphone. To this day, some DJs still prefer this setup when using vinyl records; especially scratch DJs that perform scratching techniques.

Since there is no software involved in this setup, the DJ must manually load vinyl records onto the Technics 1200 turntables, as well as unload the records when he or she wants to change songs. The DJ will also need to learn how to cue up the points of the records he or she wants to mix in with the stylus (needle) of the turntable.

Moreover, the Vestax PMC-06 Pro DJ mixer's simple controls means that the DJ in this setup can master the most fundamental mixing controls, such as levels and EQ. On a mixer, the main controls are EQ controls, gain knob, volume faders, crossfader, and volume controls for the cue, main and booth monitors. Typically at the very top of the mixer is the gain or trim knob for the overall gain of the track, followed downwards by the EQ controls for high, mid and low frequencies, and finally the volume fader to control how much of the total output of that channel will go to the main output; all channels are identical and have the same controls.

Below the individual channel strips is the crossfader, which mixes the outgoing signal from the corresponding channels. Finally, the cue knob is the volume control for the outgoing signal to the headphones for the DJ to listen to the track without actually playing it through the master output; the cue will normally be pre-fader. A mixer will tend to have two different outputs, one referred to as the Master output, which is what will be outputted as the main signal through the PA system, and the other is the Booth output, which is for the DJ to listen to. Connecting a QSC power amplifier to speaker monitors correctly allows the DJ to carry out his function, which is to play for an audience.

Equipment List

- 2 – Technics 1200 Turntables
- 1 – Vestax PMC-06 Pro DJ Mixer

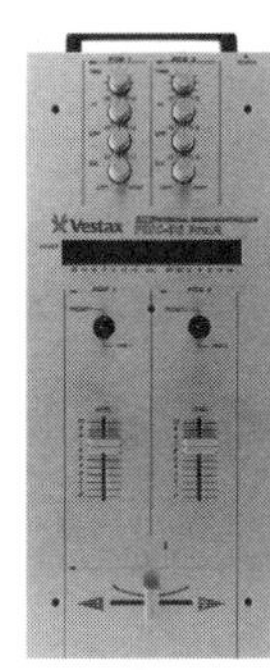

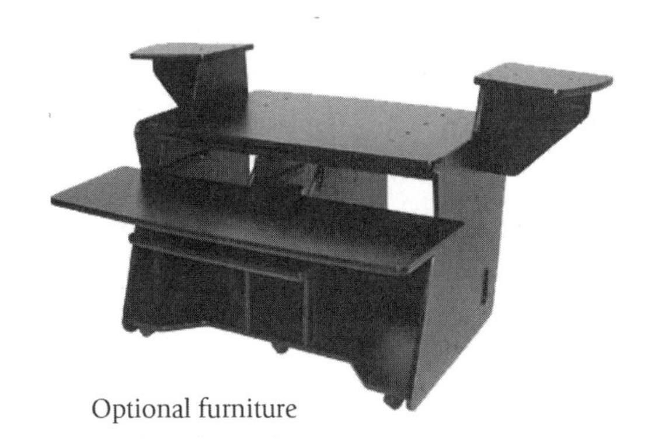

Optional furniture

Vinyl DJ Studio

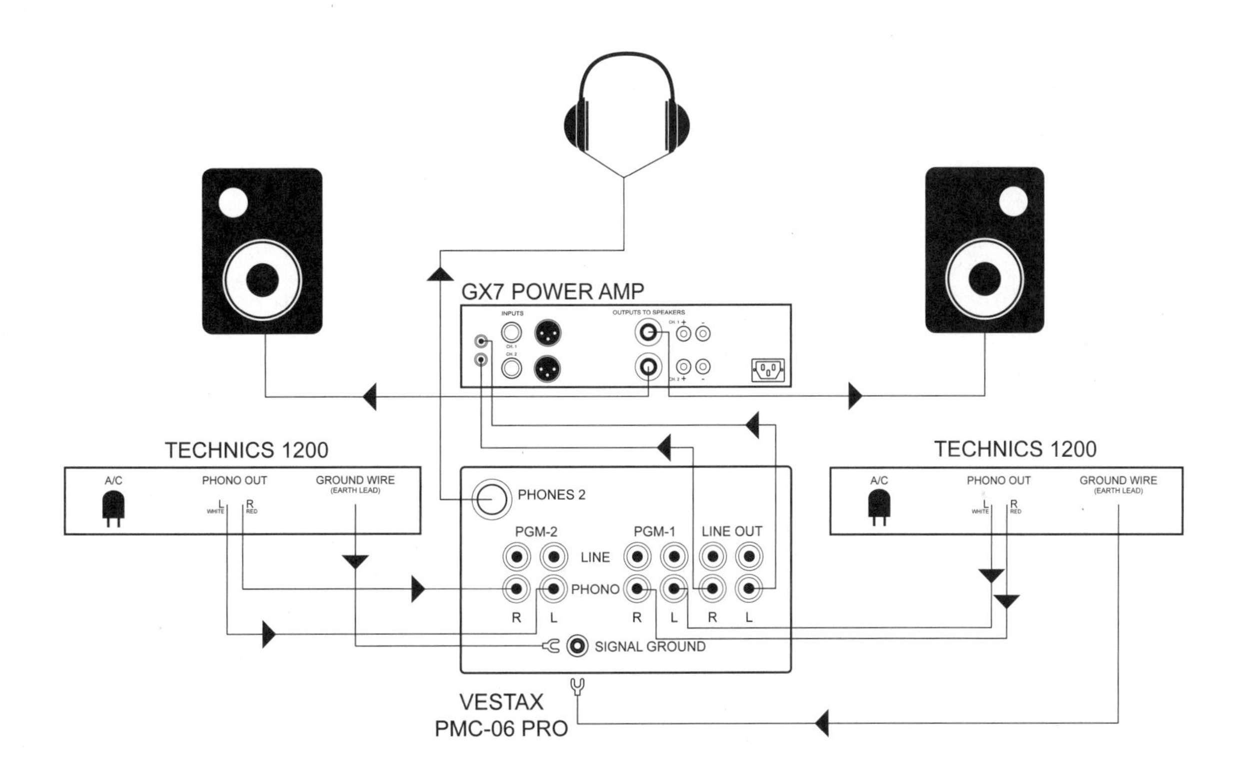

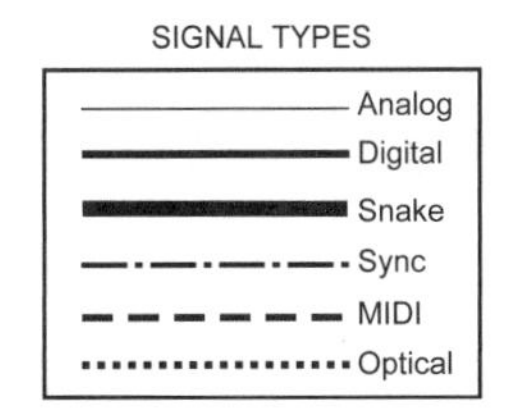

- 1 – QSC GX7 Power Amp
- 1 – Pair of QSC Speaker Monitors
- 1 – Pair of Headphones

Cable List

- 2– RCA to RCA cables
- 4 – RCA to RCA cables (already attached to the turntables)
- 2 – 1/4-inch TS to XLR (or 1/4-inch TS) cables
- 2 – Ground wires (already attached to the turntable)

Hardware Connections

1. Connecting the Technics 1200 Turntables to the Vestax PMC-06 Pro DJ Mixer

    - Using the RCA cable attached on the rear panel of the left Technics 1200 turntable, connect the Left and the Right channels to the "PGM-2 PHONO Left and Right Inputs" of the Vestax PMC-06 Pro DJ Mixer.
    - Using the RCA cable attached on the rear panel of the right Technics 1200 turntable, connect the Left and the Right channels to the "PGM-1 PHONO Left and Right Inputs" of the Vestax PMC-06 Pro DJ Mixer.
    - Attach the ground wire of each turntable to the Ground Wire knob on the rear panel of the Vestax PMC-06 Pro DJ mixer.

2. Connecting the Vestax PMC-06 Pro DJ Mixer to the GX7 Power Amplifier

    - Using an RCA to RCA cable, connect the "LINE OUT 2 L" of the Vestax PMC-06 Pro DJ mixer to the "CH 1 INPUT" (Left channel) of the QSC GX7 Power Amplifier.
    - Using another RCA to RCA cable, connect the "LINE OUT 2 R" of the Vestax PMC-06 Pro DJ mixer to the "CH 2 INPUT" (Right channel) of the QSC GX7 Power Amplifier.

3. Connecting the Speaker Monitors to the GX7 Power Amplifier

   - Using a 1/4-inch TS to XLR or 1/4-inch TS to 1/4-inch TS cable (depending on your speakers), connect the "OUTPUTS TO SPEAKERS CH 1" to the Left speaker monitor.

   - Using another 1/4-inch TS to XLR or 1/4-inch TS to 1/4-inch TS cable (depending on your speakers), connect the "OUTPUTS TO SPEAKERS CH 2" to the Right speaker monitor.

4. Connecting Headphones to the Mixer

   - Connect the 1/4-inch TRS (stereo) headphone connector into the "PHONES" jack on the front of the Vestax PMC-06 DJ mixer. You can also connect the headphones to the "PHONES 2" jack on the rear panel of the Vestax PMC-06 DJ mixer.

NOTE: If you use headphones with a 1/8-inch connector, you will need a 1/8-inch TRS to 1/4-inch TRS adapter

System Requirements

Since there is no software in this particular setup, there are no system requirements to meet.

Software Setup

In this particular setup, there is no need for software.

This concludes this exercise. Remember, all the equipment assignments are arbitrarily chosen so you can understand and learn the process of a DJing session. By no means is this the only way to do it; these scenarios are just to practice plugging in your DJ rig, as well as refining your skills.

Traktor DJ Studio

This is a Native Instruments DJ setup. The Native Instruments Traktor S4 totes a "new level of Kontrol," and is a 4-deck controller with a 24bit/96kHz soundcard and TRAKTOR software. It is a controller that works as an interface for Traktor, simulating a pair of decks and a mixer. To add a track to a deck, use the Browse knob in the middle of the controller and after selecting the track, press the load button on the deck you wish to play it through, dragging and dropping the track from the library into the deck also works. Its interface gives easy access to transport controls, cue points, and trigger loops or Remix Decks. Remix Decks let you slice, loop, edit, and deconstruct tracks— allowing you to create remixes on the fly.

The Traktor Kontrol F1 is a DJ controller that gives the DJ control over Traktor Pro's Remix Decks. Any sound imaginable becomes a building block for the DJ's remixing masterpiece. Each one of its sixteen colored pads, used with its four volume faders and dedicated filter knobs can add spontaneity to your DJ sets. Moreover, each channel has 4 pads that each activate a loop or one shot as specified on the computer and can be synced and quantized to the master tempo by activating the "SYNC" and "QUANT" buttons. To load sounds on the pads, drag and drop the loop or one shot into the pad desired or use the browse button on the Kontrol F1.

A Technics 1200 turntable adds an analog touch to this setup, and is perfect for those rare vinyl records (i.e. a record that is not available digitally) a DJ may want to throw in the Native Instruments Traktor system.

Equipment List

- 1 – Native Instruments Traktor S4
- 1 – Apple MacBook Pro Laptop Computer
- 1 – Native Instruments Traktor Kontrol F1
- 1 – Technics 1200 Turntable
- 1 – Pair of YAMAHA Powered Speaker Monitors
- 1 – Set of Heaphones

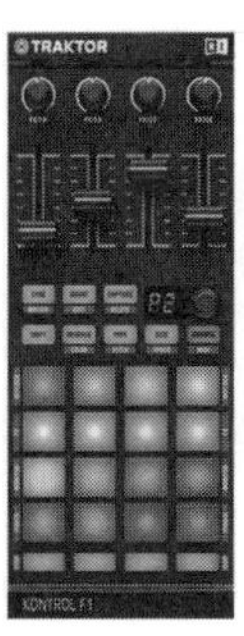

Optional furniture

Traktor DJ Studio

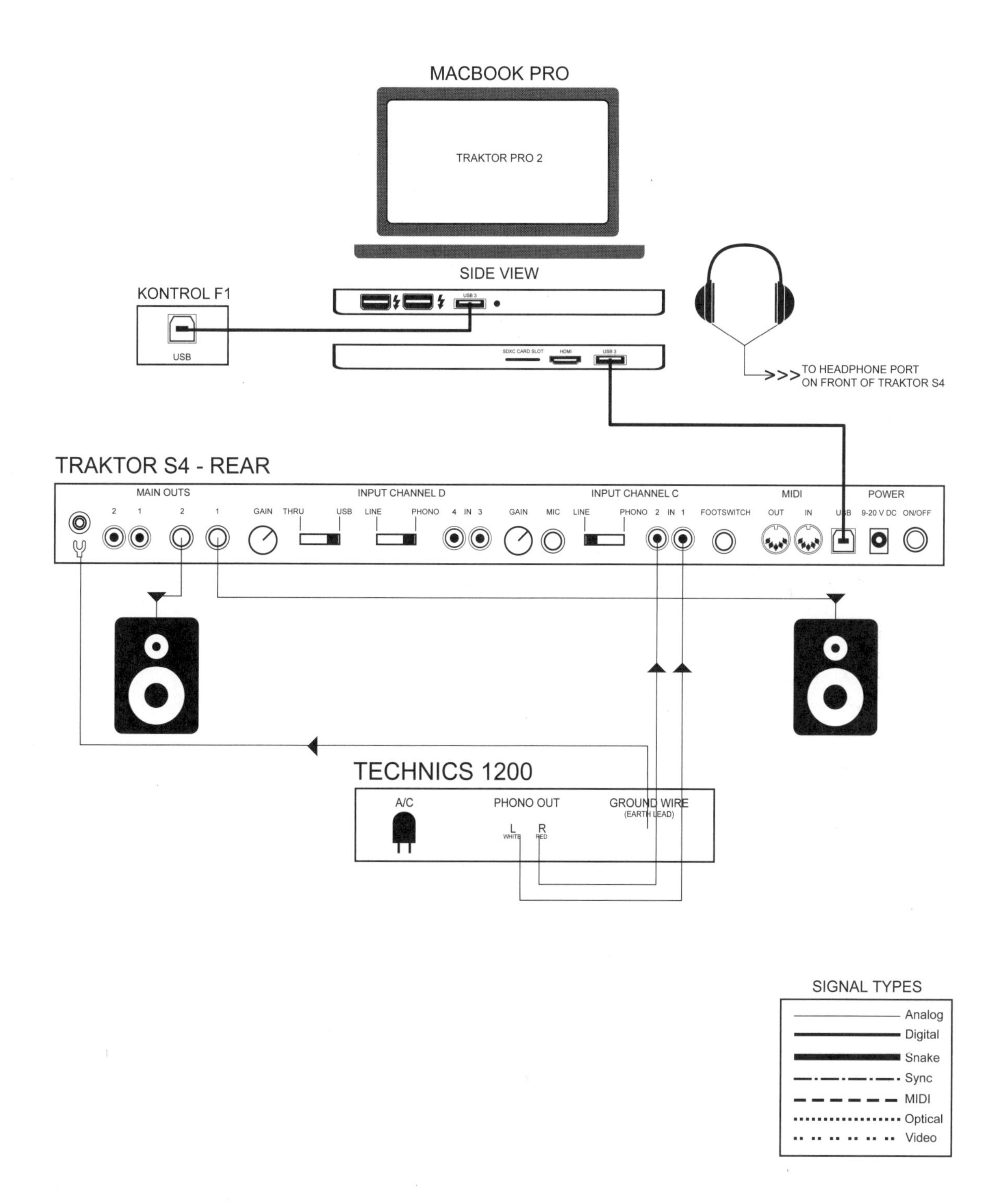

Cable List

- 2 – USB cables
- 2 – 1/4-inch TS to XLR (or 1/4-inch TS) cables
- 2 – RCA cables (already attached to the turntables)
- 1 – Ground wires (already attached to the turntable)

Hardware Connections

1. Connecting the Technics 1200 Turntable to the Native Instruments Traktor S4
   - Using one of the RCA cable attached on the rear panel of the Technics 1200 turntable, connect the Left channel to the "INPUT CHANNEL C - IN 1" on the rear panel of the Native Instruments Traktor S4 (make sure that the input switch is switched from "LINE" to "PHONO").
   - Using one of the RCA cable attached on the rear panel of the Technics 1200 turntable, connect the Right channel to the "INPUT CHANNEL C - IN 2" on the rear panel of the Native Instruments Traktor S4 (make sure that the input switch is switched from "LINE" to "PHONO").
   - Connect the ground wire cable from the Technics 1200 turntable to the ground knob on the rear panel of the Traktor S4.

2. Connecting the Traktor to the MacBook Pro
   - Using a USB cable, connect the USB port of the Traktor S4 into a USB port of the Apple MacBook Pro.

3. Connecting the Kontrol F1 Effects Box to the Apple MacBook Pro
   - Using a USB cable, connect the USB port of the Kontrol F1 into a USB port of the Apple MacBook Pro.

4. Connecting the Headphones to the Traktor S4
   - Connect the 1/4-inch TRS (stereo) Headphones connector to the "PHONES" jack on the front panel of the Traktor S4.

NOTE: If you use headphones with A 1/8-inch TRS (stereo) connector, you will need a 1/4-inch TRS to 1/8-inch TRS adapter.

5. Connecting the YAMAHA Powered Speaker Monitors to the Native Instruments Traktor S4

    - Using a 1/4-inch TS to XLR or 1/4-inch TS to 1/4-inch TS cable (depending on your speakers), connect the "MAIN OUT 1" of the Traktor S4 to the Left speaker monitor.
    - Using a 1/4-inch TS to XLR or 1/4-inch TS to 1/4-inch TS cable (depending on your speakers), connect the "MAIN OUT 2" of the Traktor S4 to the Right speaker monitor.

System Requirements

Traktor Pro 2 for Mac OS X (as of this writing):

- Mac OS X 10.7, 10.8 or 10.9 (latest update)
- Intel Core 2 Duo
- 2 GB RAM (4 GB recommended)

Traktor Pro 2 for Windows (as of this writing):

- Windows 7 or 8 (latest Service Pack, 32/64 Bit)
- 2.0 GHz Intel Core 2 Duo or AMD Athlon 64 X2
- 2 GB RAM (4 GB recommended)

Software Setup

Install the Traktor 2 Pro software from the Native Instruments website. To setup the Traktor 2 Pro software with the Traktor S4, do the following:

1. Open Preferences > Audio Setup.

2. Choose the audio interface of your MIDI controller as Audio Device, in this example: Traktor Kontrol S4 (ASIO).
3. Open Preferences > Output Routing
4. Choose Internal Mixing Mode.
5. With the S4, the outputs will be auto-configured. If you use another MIDI controller, select an output pair for Output Master and one output pair for Output Monitor.
6. If your audio device provides another output, assign this to the Output Record.
7. Connect the respective outputs accordingly, i.e. use a cable (usually RCA) to connect the Master Output of your MIDI controller with your amplifier or speakers and plug your headphones in the Monitor Output.
8. Open Preferences > Controller Manager
9. Click Add > Import, then navigate to Default Settings > Controller and choose your controller from the list.
10. Move a fader or knob on the MIDI controller (e.g. the crossfader) and observe the CTRL status indicator. Whenever you move anything on the MIDI controller, it should show activity by glowing blue.
11. You'll also notice that the corresponding control in TRAKTOR (in the above example, the crossfader) will also move as you manipulate the MIDI Controller.

This concludes this exercise. Remember, all the track/equipment assignments are arbitrarily chosen so you can understand and learn the process of a DJing session. By no means is this the only way to do it; these scenarios are just to practice plugging in your Traktor DJ rig, as well as refining your skills. See Appendix C for more audio interface options.

Serato DJ Studio

This DJ studio is more elaborate in design, and gives the DJ more creative options. It is great for the DJ/Producer. It has the traditional two Technics 1200 turntables setup, and they are used with Serato Control Vinyl and the Serato DJ software.

Serato DJ was one of the first DJ software programs to appear in the digital DJ world and became an industry standard for clubs primarily because of the time-coded vinyl used to control the software, which made it easier for DJs to just bring their laptop with their Serato Scratch Live boxes and play tracks from their digital music libraries.

The turntables are connected to the four-channel Rane Sixty-Four DJ mixer, which, like the DJM-900SRT, has an in-built Serato soundcard for use with the Serato DJ software. The Rane Sixty-Four has full integration with the functions within the Serato DJ software. It controls functions like looping, samples and even allows the use of two virtual decks with just one turntable with its time-coded vinyl. It is also possible to use it as an analog mixer without the need to use Serato DJ, but the advantage is that it permits two computers to be connected at once.

In addition to this setup, a Native Instruments Maschine is connected to the Rane SIXTY-FOUR mixer via MacBook Pro's headphone jack giving the DJ the ability to add samples or effects to his DJ performance using its own standalone software.

Equipment List

- 1 – Rane Sixty-Four DJ mixer
- 2 – Technics 1200 Turntables
- 1 – Native Instruments Maschine
- 1 – Apple MacBook Pro Laptop Computer
- 1 – Pair of YAMAHA Powered Speaker Monitors

Technics
Technics
Technics
Technics
MASCHINE

Serato DJ Studio

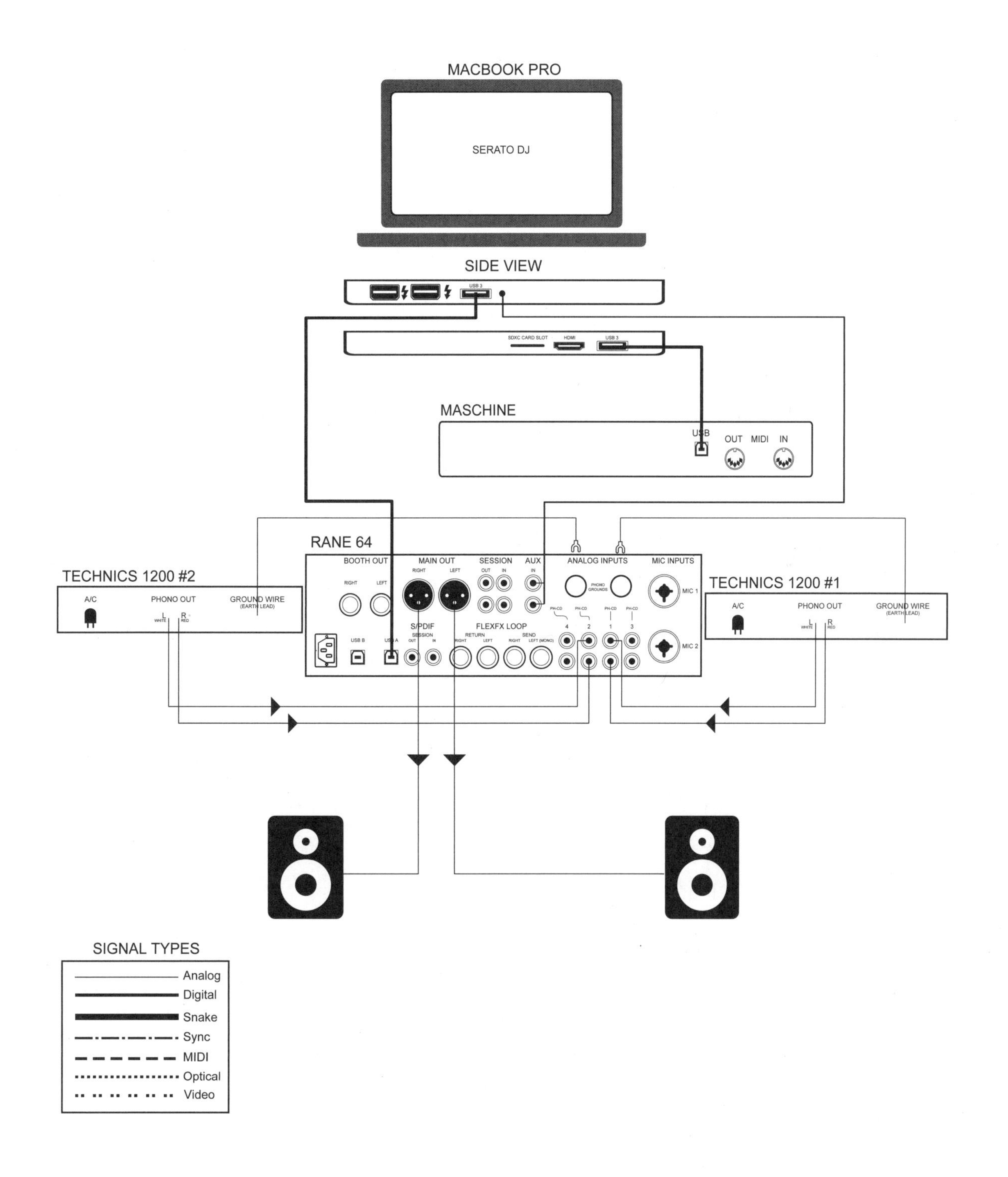

Cable List

- 2 – USB cables
- 2 – XLR cables (or two-1/4-inch TRS to XLR cables)
- 1 – 1/8-inch TRS (Stereo) to two-RCAs cable adapter
- 4 – RCA cables (already attached to each turntable)
- 1 – Ground wires (already attached to the turntable)

Hardware Connections

Serato Scratch Live:

1. Connecting the Technics 1200 Turntables to the Rane Sixty-Four Mixer

    - Using the RCA cable attached on the rear panel of the left Technics 1200 Turntable, connect the Left and the Right channels to the second set (from left to right) of the "ANALOG INPUTS L and R PH-CD" inputs of the Rane Sixty-Four Mixer.
    - Using the RCA cable attached on the rear panel of the right Technics 1200 Turntable, connect the Left and the Right channels to the third set (from left to right) of the "ANALOG INPUTS L and R PH-CD" inputs of the Rane Sixty-Four Mixer.
    - Connect the ground wire (earth lead) from the rear of both Technics 1200 Turntables to the "PHONE GROUNDS" knobs on the rear of the Rane Sixty-Four Mixer to properly ground the turntable.

2. Connecting the Native Instruments Maschine to the Apple MacBook Pro

    - Using a USB cable, connect the USB port of the Native Instruments Maschine to an available USB port on the side of the Apple MacBook Pro.

3. Connecting Audio from the Apple MacBook Pro to the Rane Sixty-Four Mixer

    - Using a 1/8-inch TRS (Stereo) to two-RCAs cable adapter, connect the Headphones port on the side panel of the Apple MacBook Pro to the "AUX IN L and R" of the Rane Sixty-Four mixer.

4. Connecting the Rane Sixty-Four Mixer to the Apple MacBook Pro

    • Using a USB cable, connect the USB port on the rear panel of the Rane Sixty-Four mixer to an available USB port on the side of the Apple MacBook Pro.

5. Connecting the YAMAHA Speaker Monitors to the Rane Sixty-Four mixer

• Using an XLR to XLR or 1/4-inch TRS to XLR cable (depending on your speakers), connect the "MAIN OUT L" of the Rane Sixty-Four to the Left speaker monitor.

• Using an XLR to XLR or 1/4-inch TRS to XLR cable (depending on your speakers), connect the "MAIN OUT R" of the Rane Sixty-Four to the Right speaker monitor.

6. Connecting the Headphones to the Rane Sixty-Four mixer

    • Connect the 1/4-inch TRS (stereo) connector of the Headphones to the "HEADPHONES" jack on the front panel of the Rane Sixty-Four mixer.

NOTE: If you use headphones with a 1/8-inch connector, you will need a 1/8-inch to 1/4-inch adapter.

System Requirements

Serato Scratch Live for Mac OS X (as of this writing):

- Mac OS X 10.7,10.8,10.9
- Intel Processors: i3, i5 or i7, 32 & 64 bit: 1.07GHz+
- Core 2 Duo: 32 bit: 2.0 GHz+, 64 bit: 2.4 GHz+
- 32 bit: 2 GB, 64 bit: 4 GB
- Available USB 2.0 port

Serato Scratch Live for Windows (as of this writing):

- Windows 7, 8, 8.1+
- Intel Processors: i3, i5 or i7, 32 & 64 bit: 1.07GHz+
- Core 2 Duo: 32 bit: 2.0 GHz+, 64 bit: 2.4 GHz+
- RAM: 32 bit: 2 GB, 64 bit: 4 GB
- Available USB 2.0 port

Software Setup

Once you have installed the latest version of Serato DJ (1.5 or above), the software will automatically read and register the Rane Sixty-Four DJ mixer. It is simple as "plug and play." However, in this setup, to connect to the Native Instruments Maschine to the Serato system for synchronization, the following steps must be made:

1. Configuring Rane Sixty-Four:
   - In the Sixty-Four Audio Control Panel (Windows Control Panel for Windows and System Preferences for Mac), click on the tab until the MIDI Configuration page appears, click on the checkboxes for "Receive MIDI Beat Clock" and "Send MIDI Beat Clock."
   - On Serato DJ, load two tracks to be able to turn on the sync and press the "SYNC" button from one of the decks.
   - Play one of the tracks, press and hold the "TAP" button on the Sixty-Four and nudge the "BEAT" joystick until a letter "s" appears in the display in order for the mixer to receive the BPM from Serato.
   - Press the "FLEXFX" button in the channel running the audio so the letter "s" will start flashing. Afterwards, the FLEXFX button can be turned off.

2. Configuring Maschine:
   - Once the Maschine software has been open, in the "Audio and MIDI Settings", select "Rane Sixty-Four" as the Audio Device.
   - On the "Routing" tab, click on the "Outputs" tab. Select corresponding

outputs for Maschine OUT 1 L and Maschine OUT 1 R, in this case we will set Maschine OUT 1 L to Rane Sixty-Four OUT 3, and Maschine OUT 1 R to Rane Sixty-Four OUT 4.

- Click on the "MIDI" tab and then the "Inputs" tab, change the Status for the Device "Sixty-Four" to "On" while the other devices remain off.
- Check that on the "Outputs" tab, all devices are off. Afterwards click OK.
- Click on the File tab and select "Sync to External MIDI Clock."
- Send a MIDI Start Message from the Sixty-Four to the Maschine by pressing the Shift and Tap buttons (preferably on a downbeat).

Calibrating your Serato Control Vinyl:

1. With music playing in the background through your system or booth output, put your needle on the record with the turntable stopped. If you are using CD players, the same rules apply. Have the CD deck paused or stopped while calibrating.
2. Click and hold the Estimate button until the slider stops moving. Moving the Noise Sensitivity slider to the left will make Serato DJ more sensitive to slow record movement, but also more sensitive to background noise.
3. Repeat the process for each deck.

Things to remember:

- Your needle must be on the record.
- Your turntable (or CD player) must be stationary.
- The background music playing must be at a similar level to which you will play your set at.
- Calibrate Serato DJ every time you play.

NOTE: If the slider jumps to the far right, then you have a problem with noise in your turntables/CD players/mixer. Check all your connections and make sure your equipment has a solid connection to the Ground (Earth).

Basic CDJ Studio

This DJ setup requires two Pioneer CDJ-2000 CD turntables, which are the most common types of CD turntables you will find in clubs and festivals around the world, due to their professional DJ features. The Pioneer DJM-900SRT is a new version of the equally ubiquitous line of DJM DJ mixers by Pioneer. It has a built-in "Serato Soundcard," for native control of the popular Serato DJ software.

This way, you will not need to have a wallet full of your CDs, you can just play the music off of your computer's hard disk (using Serato Control CDs). This technology is called "DVS," or Digital Vinyl System. This setup is most useful for the gigging DJ who needs professional quality practice and performance.

The Pioneer DJM-900SRT has six sound color effects, including filter, space, dub echo, bitcrush, and a gate/compression effect for individual channels as well as a main effects section for individual channels or master output. These include delay, filter, flanger, phaser, reverb among others.

Equipment List

- 2 – Pioneer CDJ-2000 CD Turntables
- 1 – Pioneer DJM-900SRT DJ Mixer
- 1 – Pair of YAMAHA Powered Speaker Monitors
- 1 – Pair of Headphones

Cable List

- 2 – RCA cables
- 2 – 75-ohm RCA cables
- 2 – XLR cables (or two-1/4-inch TRS to XLR cables)
- 1 – USB cable

Optional furniture

Basic CDJ Studio

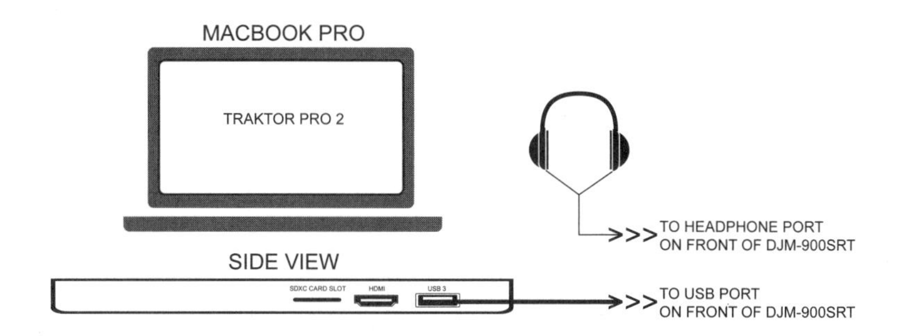

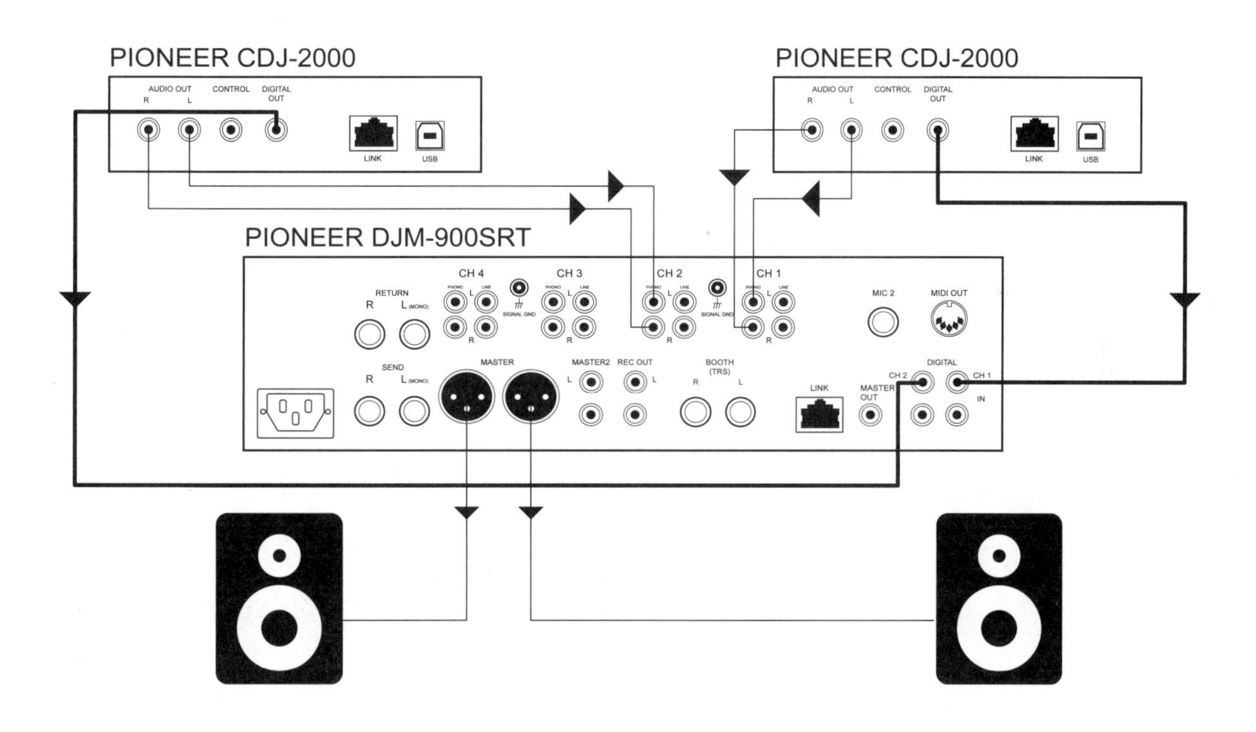

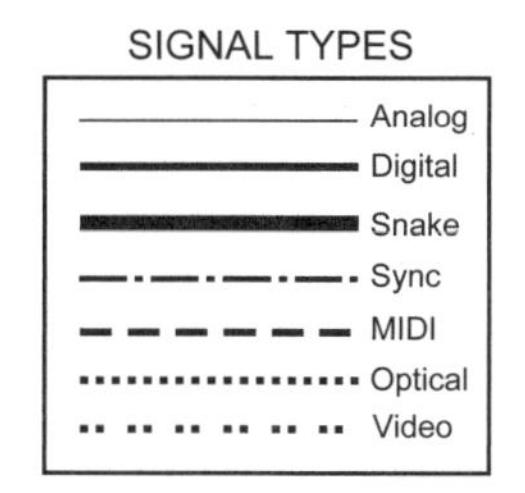

Hardware Connections

1. Connecting the Pioneer CDJ-2000 Turntables to the Pioneer DJM-900SRT Mixer

    - Using an RCA cable, connect the "AUDIO OUT" Left channel of the first Pioneer CDJ-2000 (the left CDJ-2000 in the diagram) to the "CH 2 PHONO CD/LINE" Left Input jack of the Pioneer DJM-900SRT.

    - Using another RCA cable, connect the "AUDIO OUT" Right channel of the first Pioneer CDJ-2000 (the left CDJ-2000 in the diagram) to the "CH 2 PHONO CD/LINE" Right Input jack of the Pioneer DJM-900SRT.

    - Using a third RCA cable, connect the "AUDIO OUT" Left channel of the second Pioneer CDJ-2000 (the right CDJ-2000 in the diagram) to the "CH 1 PHONO CD/LINE" Left Input jack of the Pioneer DJM-900SRT.

    - Using a fourth RCA cable, connect the "AUDIO OUT" Right channel of the second Pioneer CDJ-2000 (the right CDJ-2000 in the diagram) to the "CH 1 PHONO CD/LINE" Right Input jack of the Pioneer DJM-900SRT.

2. Connecting the DJM-900SRT DJ mixer to the Apple MacBook Pro Laptop

    - Using a USB cable, connect the USB port at the top of the DJM-900SRT to the USB port on the side panel of the Apple MacBook Pro.

3. Connecting headphones to the DJM-900SRT DJ mixer

    - Connect the 1/4-inch connector of the Headphones to the "PHONES" jack on the front panel of the DJM-900SRT.

    NOTE: If you use headphones with a 1/8-inch connector, you will need a 1/8-inch to 1/4-inch TRS adapter.

4. Connecting the Yamaha Speaker Monitors to the DJM-900SRT DJ Mixer

    - Using an XLR to XLR or 1/4-inch TRS to XLR cable (depending on your speakers), connect the "MASTER 1 OUT L" of the DJM-900SRT to the Left speaker monitor.

- Using another XLR to XLR or 1/4-inch TRS to XLR cable (depending on your speakers), connect the "MASTER 1 OUT R" of the DJM-900SRT o the Right speaker monitor.

System Requirements

Serato Scratch Live for Mac OS X (as of this writing):

- Mac OS X 10.7,10.8,10.9
- Intel Processors: i3, i5 or i7, 32 & 64 bit: 1.07GHz+
- Core 2 Duo: 32 bit: 2.0 GHz+, 64 bit: 2.4 GHz+
- Screen resolution: 1280 x 720
- 32 bit: 2 GB, 64 bit: 4 GB
- Available USB 2.0 port

Serato Scratch Live for Windows (as of this writing):

- Windows 7, 8, 8.1+
- Intel Processors: i3, i5 or i7, 32 & 64 bit: 1.07GHz+
- Core 2 Duo: 32 bit: 2.0 GHz+, 64 bit: 2.4 GHz+
- Screen resolution: 1280 x 720
- RAM: 32 bit: 2 GB, 64 bit: 4 GB
- Available USB 2.0 port

Software Setup

Serato DJ software with DJM-900SRT:

1. Download the latest version of the Serato DJ software to connect and use DVS (Digital Vinyl System) with the Pioneer DJM-900SRT.

2. When you connect for the first time, Serato will ask you to install drivers for the Pioneer DJM-900SRT. Follow the on-screen steps and do so.

3. Once you are connected, select whether you are using Control Vinyl or CDs as your DVS source. Open the setup screen, go to the Audio tab, and choose from TURNTABLES or CDJs in the Deck Setup area.

4. In the upper left corner of the Virtual Deck is the Playback Control mode selection. If using DVS, choose either ABS (absolute) or REL (relative) mode. If you want to mix internally, select INT (Internal Mode).

Calibrating the Serato DVS system:

1. Turn the sound system up the level you will be playing at during your performance.

2. Play a track from an audio CD or from the other deck in internal mode.

3. Place the needle on the record but keep the turntable stopped.

4. Click and hold down the Estimate button for a few seconds – Scratch Live will estimate the optimal threshold setting for the current environment. Alternatively, you can try manually moving the Estimate slider to the right until you notice the number in the upper-right corner of the scope view stops fluctuating. You should be at the best point for good tracking of the vinyl movement and ignoring noise.

5. Repeat this process for each deck.

6. Once you have set the threshold, start both turntables. For optimal performance, the inner ring should be as close to circular as possible. Use the scope zoom slider (1x to 16x) to zoom in or out as necessary. Use the scope L/R balance and P/A balance controls to adjust the shape of the inner ring. The number in the top left corner of the scope view gives the current absolute position within the control record or CD. The number in the top right corner is the current speed in RPM.

7. In the bottom left is the current threshold setting, and the number in the bottom right shows the percentage of readable signal – this number should be at least 85% when your system is calibrated properly.

Laptop DJ Studio

This Laptop DJ studio is for DJs who want to bypass the traditional use of turntables and a mixer, and who favor an all-in-one type of mixing experience. This setup revolves primarily around the Apple MacBook Pro and Traktor Pro 2 software. As such, it is very portable. The Traktor Kontrol X1 controls the decks and effects within Traktor Pro 2. The X1's multi-purpose touch strip delivers precise command over track position, pitch bend, and FX. From nudging or needle dropping, to track seeking or loop length, the LED-guided touch strip's settings adapt to match your needs. The Kontrol X1 adds physicality to this laptop DJ setup, and lessens the need to use the laptop during the DJ set. Multiple Kontrol X1 units can be chained together to expand the control of Traktor Pro 2.

Equipment List

- 1 – Apple MacBook Pro Laptop Computer
- 1 – Traktor Kontrol F1
- 1 – Traktor Audio 2 DJ Audio Interface
- 1 – VESTAX PCM-06 Pro Mixer
- 1 – Pair of Headphones

Cable List

- 2 – USB cables
- 2 – 1/4-inch TRS (stereo) to two-RCA cables

Hardware Connections

1. Connecting the Traktor Audio 2 DJ Interface to the MacBook Pro Laptop
    - Using a USB cable, connect the USB port from the Traktor Audio 2 DJ interface to the USB port on the side of the MacBook Pro.

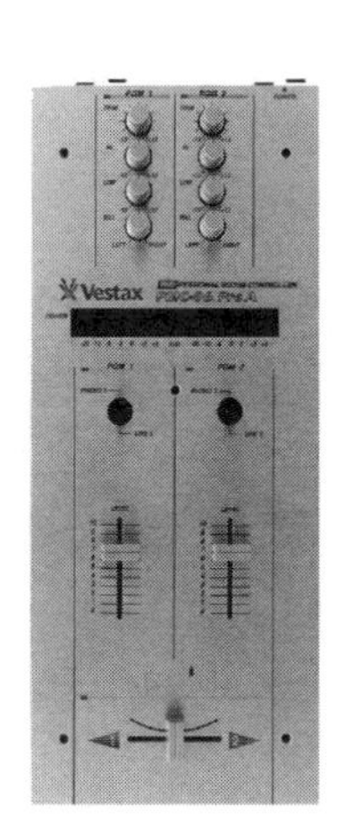

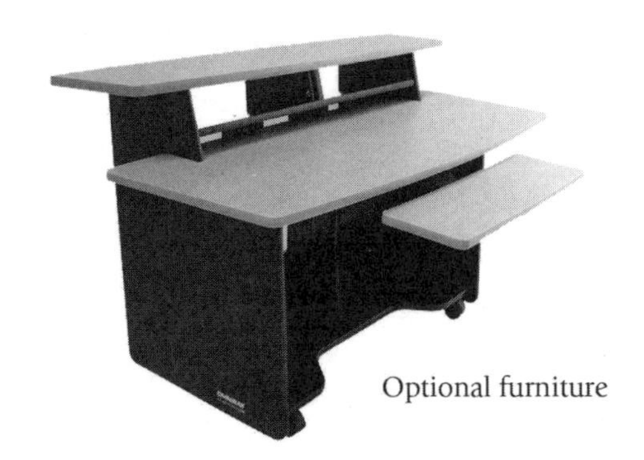

Optional furniture

Laptop DJ Studio

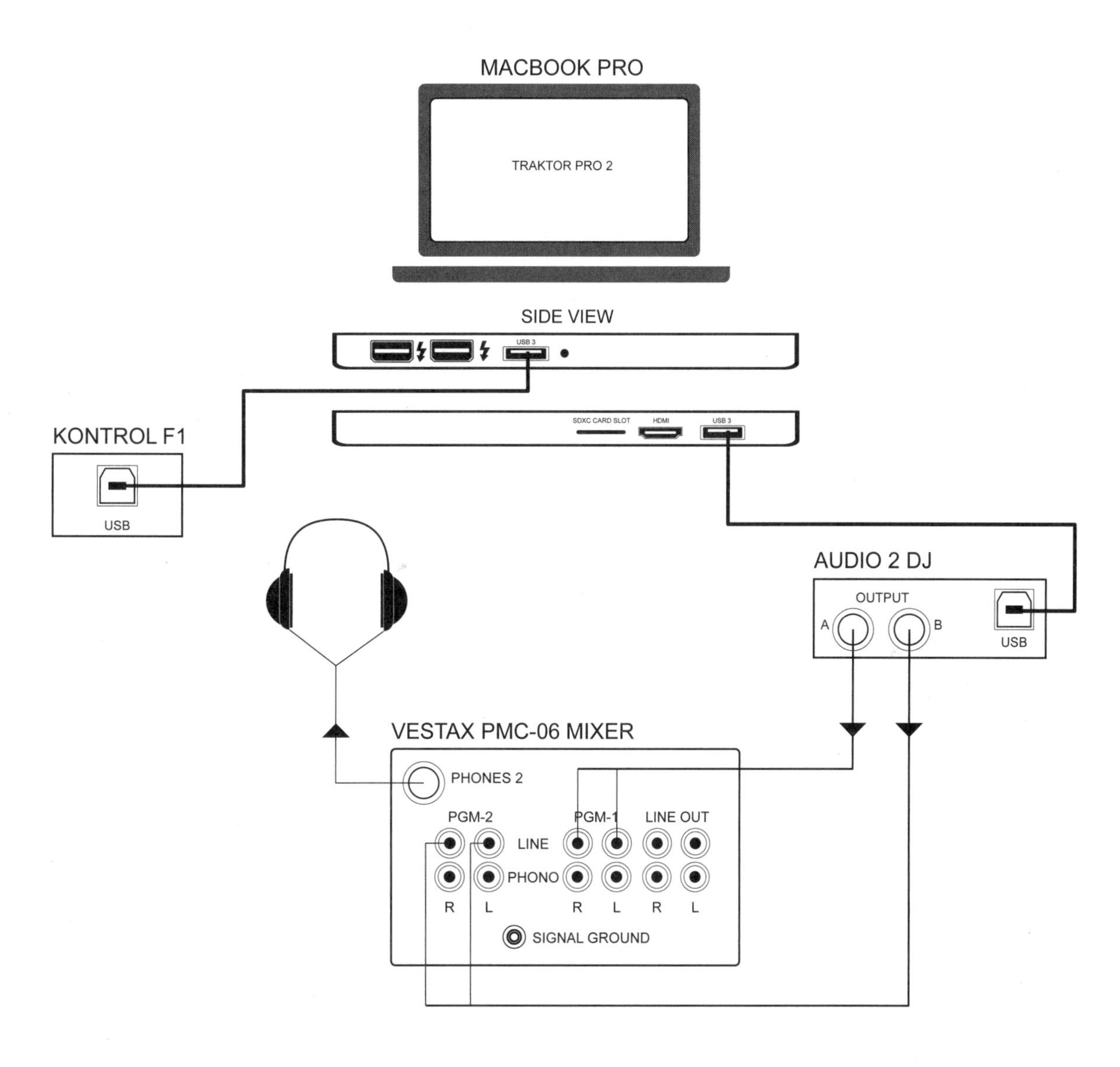

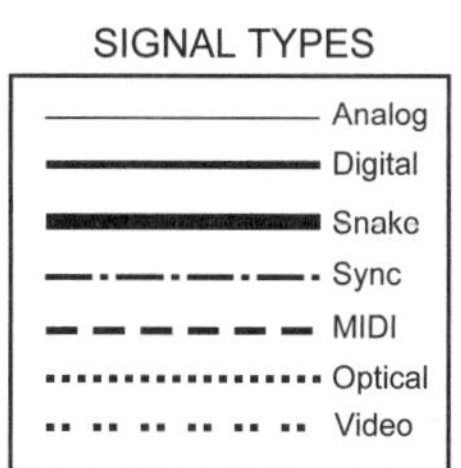

2. Connecting the Traktor Audio 2 DJ Interface to the External Mixer

- Using a 1/4-inch TRS (stereo) to two-RCA cable, connect the 1/4-inch TRS "Output A" from the Traktor Audio 2 DJ interface to the PGM-1 Left and Right input jacks of the VESTAX PCM-06 Mixer.
- Using a 1/4-inch TRS (stereo) to two-RCA cable, connect the 1/4-inch TRS "Output B" from the Traktor Audio 2 DJ interface to the PGM-2 Left and Right input jacks of the VESTAX PCM-06 Mixer.

3. Connecting the Kontrol F1 to the Apple MacBook Pro Laptop Computer

- Using a USB cable, connect the USB port from the "Kontrol F1" to an available USB port on the side of the MacBook Pro.

4. Connecting the Headphones to the VESTAX PCM-06 Mixer

- Connect the 1/4-inch TRS connector from the Headphones to the "PHONES 2" output of the VESTAX PCM-06 Mixer.

NOTE: If you use headphones with a 1/8-inch connector, you will need a 1/8-inch stereo to 1/4-inch TRS adapter.

System Requirements

Traktor Pro 2 for Mac OS X (as of this writing):

- 10.7, 10.8 or 10.9 (or the most recent update)
- Intel Core 2 Duo
- 2 GB RAM (4 GB recommended)

Traktor Pro 2 for Windows (as of this writing):

- Windows 7 or 8 (With the most recent Service Pack installed, 32/64 bits)
- 2.0 GHz Intel Core 2 Duo or AMD Athlon 64 X2
- 2 GB RAM (4 GB recommended)

Software Setup

1. Open up the Traktor Pro 2 software and click on "Preferences."
2. Click on "Setup Wizard."
3. The program will ask you if you are using a controller, click on "Yes."
4. Traktor will show you a list of different companies that produce controllers, select "Native Instruments," and it will show you a list of controllers- choose Kontrol F1.
5. It will show you the type of "TimeCode" you can use, select "No TimeCode Control."
6. It will ask you how you prefer your "Deck Layout," select "2 track Decks."
7. When you finish the "Setup Wizard," it will show you a summary of the setup, if you wish to make a change you can still go back, if not press "Finish." Everything is now configured.
8. Go back to the preferences menu and select "Audio Setup," where you will select the audio card that you will be using (in this case it's the Traktor Audio 2 DJ). The recommended sample rate for a MacBook Pro is 44.1 kHz with a latency of 11.6 ms.

This concludes this exercise. Remember, all the track/equipment assignments are arbitrarily chosen so you can understand and learn the process of a DJing session. By no means is this the only way to do it; these scenarios are just to practice plugging in your DJ rig, as well as refining your skills.

CDJ Studio via Ethernet Link

This DJ setup requires two Pioneer CDJ-2000 CD turntables, as we have seen before, but they are configured a little differently, as they use Ethernet link. An Ethernet link will make it possible for both CDJs to play music off of one source, such as one Flash Drive, or one SD card. The two CDJs will link via Ethernet cable to the Pioneer DJM-900SRT, and the system will use Serato. When the DJM-900SRT is linked with the CDJ-2000s, the mixer will read the BPMs of the CDJs, thereby syncing the effects to that BPM automatically, without the use of software. The jog wheel of each CDJ will turn red, indicating that the Ethernet link is up and working. This is called "On Air" status. When synced via Ethernet link, the CDJs can also be "quantized" using the "QUANTIZE" button, making sure that loops stay on beat no matter when you trigger them.

The Pioneer DJM-900SRT has six sound color effects, including filter, space, dub echo, bitcrush, and a gate/compression effect for individual channels as well as a main effects section for individual channels or master output. These include delay, filter, flanger, phaser, reverb among others.

Equipment List

- 2 – Pioneer CDJ-2000 CD Turntables
- 1 – Pioneer DJM-900SRT DJ Mixer
- 1 – Ethernet Switch
- 1 – Pair of YAMAHA Powered Speaker Monitors
- 1 – Pair of Headphones

Cable List

- 4 – RCA cables
- 2 – 75-ohm RCA cables
- 2 – XLR cables (or two-1/4-inch TRS to XLR cables)

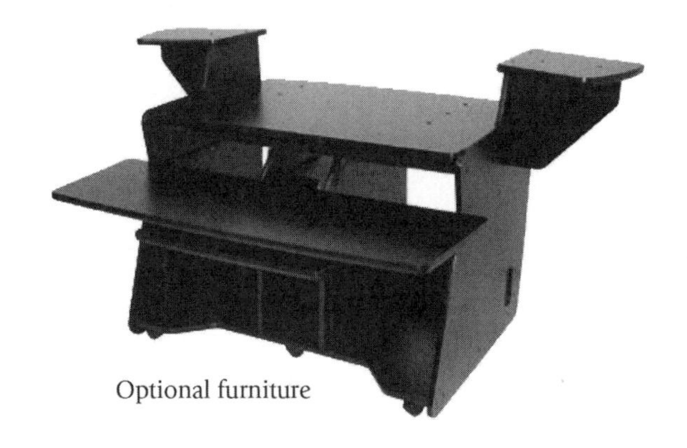

Optional furniture

CDJ Studio via Ethernet Link

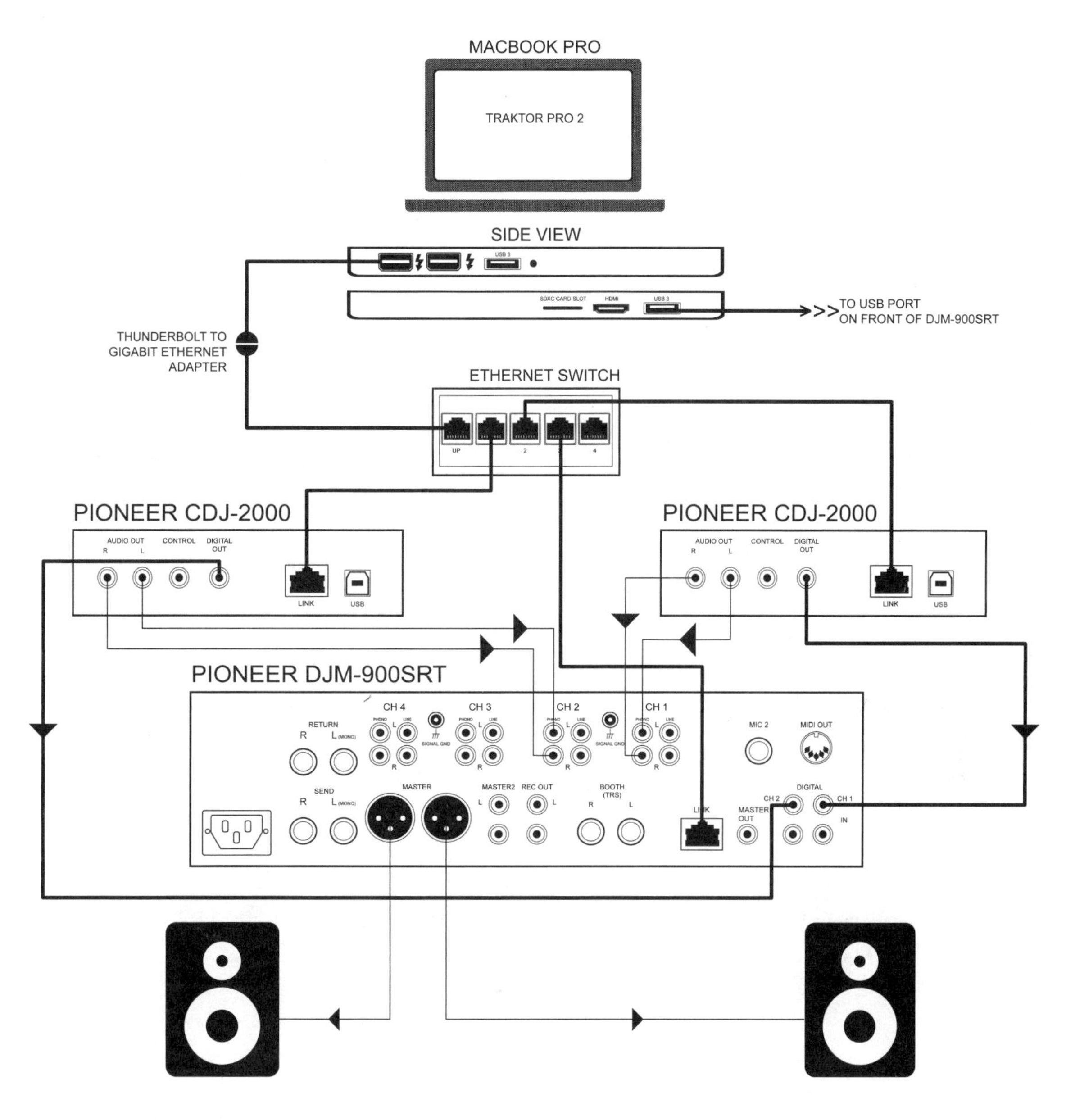

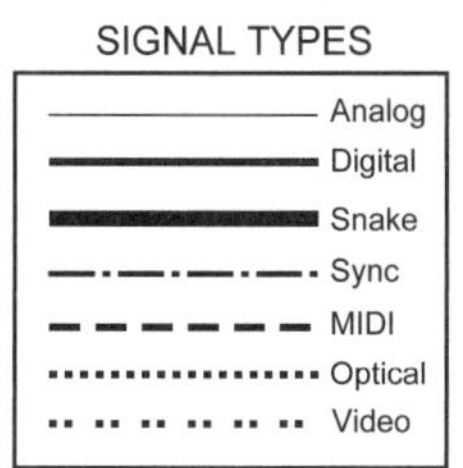

- 2 – USB cable
- 3 – Ethernet cables
- 1 – Thunderbolt to Ethernet cable adapter

Hardware Connections

1. Connecting the Pioneer CDJ-2000 Turntables to the Pioneer DJM-900 Mixer

    - Using an RCA cable, connect the "AUDIO OUT" Left channel of the first Pioneer CDJ-2000 (the left CDJ-2000 in the diagram) to the "CH 2 PHONO CD/LINE" Left Input jack of the Pioneer DJM-900SRT.
    - Using another RCA cable, connect the "AUDIO OUT" Right channel of the first Pioneer CDJ-2000 (the left CDJ-2000 in the diagram) to the "CH 2 PHONO CD/LINE" Right Input jack of the Pioneer DJM-900SRT.
    - Using a third RCA cable, connect the "AUDIO OUT" Left channel of the second Pioneer CDJ-2000 (the right CDJ-2000 in the diagram) to the "CH 1 PHONO CD/LINE" Left Input jack of the Pioneer DJM-900SRT.
    - Using a fourth RCA cable, connect the "AUDIO OUT" Right channel of the second Pioneer CDJ-2000 (the right CDJ-2000 in the diagram) to the "CH 1 PHONO CD/LINE" Right Input jack of the Pioneer DJM-900SRT.

2. Connecting the DJM-900SRT DJ Mixer to the Apple MacBook Pro Laptop

    - Using a USB cable, connect the USB port at the top of the DJM-900SRT to the USB port on the side panel of the Apple MacBook Pro.

3. Connecting the CDJ-2000 Turntables to the Ethernet Switch

    - Using an Ethernet cable, connect the "LINK" jack of the of the first Pioneer CDJ-2000 (the left CDJ-2000 in the diagram) to the second port of the Ethernet Switch.
    - Using another Ethernet cable, connect the "LINK" jack of the of the second Pioneer CDJ-2000 (the right CDJ-2000 in the diagram) to the third port of the Ethernet Switch.

4. Connecting the DJM-900SRT DJ Mixer to the Ethernet Switch

   - Using an Ethernet cable, connect the "LINK" jack of the DJM-900 SRT DJ mixer to the fourth port of the Ethernet Switch.

5. Connecting the Ethernet Switch to the MacBook Pro Laptop Computer

   - Using a Thunderbolt to Ethernet cable adapter, connect the Thunderbolt port from your MacBook Pro to the first port of the Ethernet Switch.

6. Connecting the Headphones to the DJM-900SRT DJ Mixer

   - Connect the 1/4-inch TRS connector of the Headphones to the "PHONES" jack on the front panel of the DJM-900SRT mixer.

NOTE: If you use headphones with a 1/8-inch stereo connector, you will need a 1/8-inch to 1/4-inch TRS adapter.

7. Connecting the YAMAHA Speaker Monitors to the DJM-900SRT Mixer

   - Using an XLR to XLR or 1/4-inch TRS to XLR cable (depending on your speakers), connect the "MASTER 1 OUT L" of the DJM-900SRT to the Left speaker monitor.
   - Using another XLR to XLR or 1/4-inch TRS to XLR cable (depending on your speakers), connect the "MASTER 1 OUT R" of the DJM-900SRT o the Right speaker monitor.

System Requirements

Serato Scratch Live for Mac OS X (as of this writing):

- Mac OS X 10.7,10.8,10.9
- Intel Processors: i3, i5 or i7, 32 & 64 bit: 1.07GHz+
- Core 2 Duo: 32 bit: 2.0 GHz+, 64 bit: 2.4 GHz+
- Screen resolution: 1280 x 720

- 32 bit: 2 GB, 64 bit: 4 GB
- Available USB 2.0 port

Serato Scratch Live for Windows (as of this writing):

- Windows 7, 8, 8.1+
- Intel Processors: i3, i5 or i7, 32 & 64 bit: 1.07GHz+
- Core 2 Duo: 32 bit: 2.0 GHz+, 64 bit: 2.4 GHz+
- Screen resolution: 1280 x 720
- RAM: 32 bit: 2 GB, 64 bit: 4 GB
- Available USB 2.0 port

Software Setup

Serato Scratch Live with DJM-900SRT

1. Download the latest version of the Serato DJ software to connect and use DVS (Digital Vinyl System) with the Pioneer DJM-900SRT.
2. When you connect for the first time, Serato will ask you to install drivers for the Pioneer DJM-900SRT. Follow the on-screen steps and do so.
3. Once you are connected, select whether you are using Control Vinyl or CDs as your DVS source. Open the setup screen, go to the Audio tab, and choose from TURNTABLES or CDJs in the Deck Setup area.
4. In the upper left corner of the Virtual Deck is the playback control mode selection. If using DVS, choose either ABS (absolute) or REL (relative) mode. If you want to mix internally, select INT (internal mode).

Calibrating the Serato DVS system:

1. Turn the sound system up the level you will be playing at during your performance.
2. Play a track from an audio CD or from the other deck in internal mode.

3. Place the needle on the record but keep the turntable stopped.

4. Click and hold down the Estimate button for a few seconds– Scratch Live will estimate the optimal threshold setting for the current environment. Alternatively, you can try manually moving the Estimate slider to the right until you notice the number in the upper-right corner of the scope view stops fluctuating. You should be at the best point for good tracking of the vinyl movement and ignoring noise.

5. Repeat this process for each deck.

6. Once you have set the threshold, start both turntables. For optimal performance the inner ring should be as close to circular as possible. Use the scope zoom slider (1x to 16x) to zoom in or out as necessary. Use the scope L/R balance and P/A balance controls to adjust the shape of the inner ring. The number in the top left corner of the scope view gives the current absolute position within the control record or CD. The number in the top right corner is the current speed in RPM.

7. In the bottom left is the current threshold setting, and the number in the bottom right shows the percentage of readable signal– this number should be at least 85% when your system is calibrated properly.

This concludes this exercise. Remember, all the track/equipment assignments are arbitrarily chosen so you can understand and learn the process of a DJing session. By no means is this the only way to do it; these scenarios are just to practice plugging in your DJ rig, as well as refining your skills.

Cables & Connectors

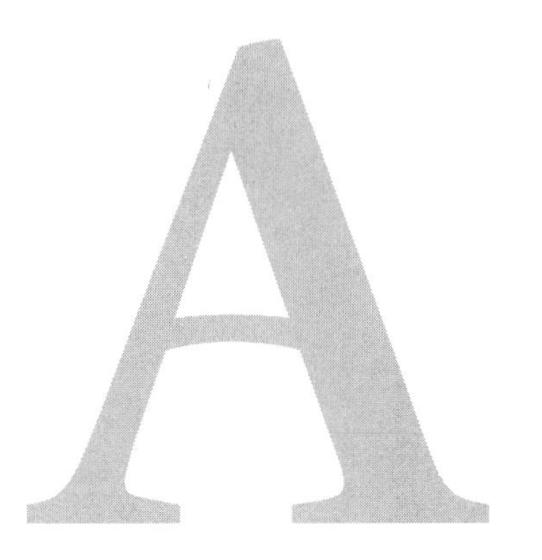

The diagrams contained within this book represent a wide variety of cables and connectors, from Lo-Fi to professional quality. In many cases, you can identify these cables by the connectors used at each end. But in some cases, you may need to know a few more details about these cables, such as length limitations, impedance, etc. This addendum will introduce to you the most commonly used cables and connectors used within this text.

- DigiLink and DigiLink Mini Interface Cables
- TDM FlexCables
- TDM Ribbon Cable
- 9-Pin Serial Cables
- BNC Cable
- ADAT/Optical Cables
- DB-25 Connector
- RCA Connectors
- XLR Connectors
- 1/4-inch Plug Connectors (TRS and TS)
- 5-pin DIN MIDI Connector
- USB Connectors
- FireWire Connectors
- Ethernet Connector
- HDMI Connector
- Thunderbolt Connector
- Banana Plug Connectors
- Binding Posts Connector
- Breakout Cable
- 8-Pin Mini DIN Serial Connector
- Mini DisplayPort to HDMI Adapter

DigiLink Interface Cables

If you have a Pro Tools | HD 1, HD 2 or HD 3, depending on your system, you will need at least one standard DigiLink Interface Cable (Figure 6-1) to connect the HD Core and/or an HD Accel PCIe cards in your computer, to your audio interface (192 I/O or 96 I/O). Now, with the latest Avid HDX, HD Native PCIe cards, and the HD Native Thunderbolt system, the standard DigiLink cable wont work, what you need, is a DigiLink Mini cable (see both in Figure 6-1) to connect these PCIe cards to your audio interface such as: the HD I/O, HD OMNI, HD MADI or the Symphony I/O among others. A 12-foot long DigiLink or DigiLink Mini cable is included with your system. To add a second audio interface you will need another short DigiLink or DigiLink Mini Interface Cable, or even a DigiLink to a DigiLink Mini adapter, depending on the audio interface you are connecting in your Pro Tools system.

Figure 6-1

TDM FlexCables

A multi card Pro Tools HD system (HD2, HD3) will need a TDM II FlexCable (Figure 6.2A) to connect the cards. This is a short, flat, custom cable used to connect HD PCI cards together inside your computer or expansion chassis. You will not need a TDM II FlexCable if you own a single card system (HD1). A Pro Tools | HD 2 system will include one cable, and a Pro Tools | HD 3 system will include two. You will also need a FlexCable-jumper TDM 3 to connect multiple HDX PCIe cards together, up to three HDX if them (Figure 6.2B).

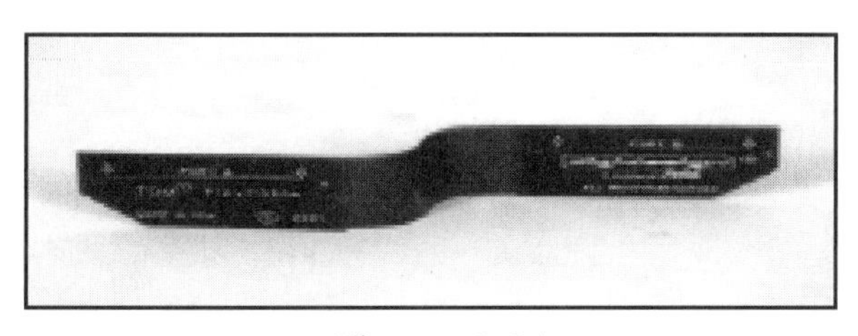

Figure 6-2A

Figure 6-2B

TDM Ribbon Cable

If you have a Mix Series Pro Tools TDM system, you will need to interconnect all the Mix Core and Mix Farm series PCI cards inside your computer or expansion chassis using a TDM Ribbon Cable as shown in Figure 6-3. A 5-node TDM Ribbon Cable is included in a Pro Tools | 24 MIX Plus system. Expanded systems that require an external Expansion Chassis, either 7 or 13 slots, will need a 7, 8 or 10-node TDM Ribbon Cable from Digidesign.

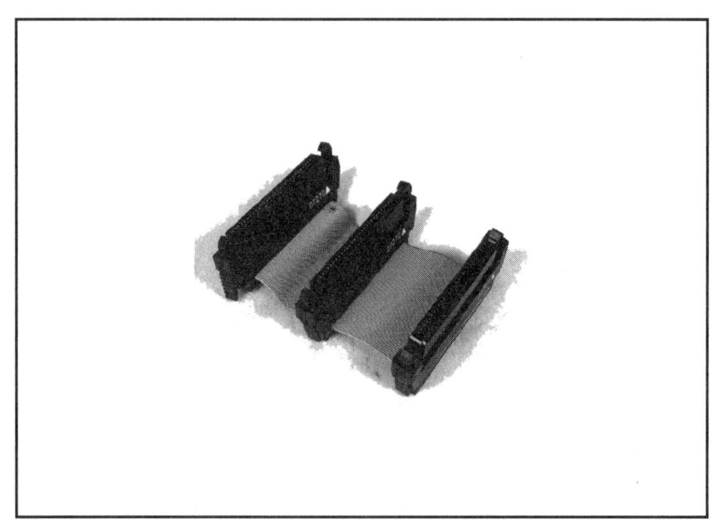

Figure 6-3

9-Pin Serial Cables

This type of serial cable (Figure 6-4) is used by Avid's Sync HD and Sync I/O synchronizers to interface them with the Sony 9-pin protocol to be able to use the Machine Control option in a Pro Tools HD system. They are also used to synchronize two or more ADAT (Alesis Digital Audio Tape) modular recording machines. And furthermore, this serial cable is used on Avid's control workstations such as the S6, D-Control, and the D-Command to communicate with the monitor section, such as the X-MON, in a Pro Tools HD studio setup.

Figure 6-4

BNC Cable

A BNC cable is used to convey "clock" information between digital devices in a studio. In essence, this timing information allows your digital electronic components to march in step with one another. Timing issues are critical in the digital realm so BNC cables (Figure 6-5) are included with any Avid or third-party audio interface. Always use high quality 75-ohm RG-59 cable, and keep the length of these cables under nine feet because of the crucial timing data passing through them. This type of cable is used to make the Word Clock In/Out, or Loop Sync In/Out connections between the audio interfaces and synchronizers used in a Pro Tools HD studio setup. They are also used to transfer digital audio via the MADI digital audio transfer format.

Figure 6-5

Optical Cables

Optical Cables (Figure 6-6) use laser pulses to digitally transfer information through a thin fiber-optic cable with Toslink connectors at both ends. Avoid looking at the red laser light coming out of the Toslink connectors when your equipment is turned on. Optical Cables are used in Pro Tools and other DAW systems to transfer data digitally among digital devices. When used with Pro Tools you can transfer up to eight digital audio tracks from an ADAT device to Pro Tools using the digital audio transfer format know as Lightpipe. You can also transfer two digital audio tracks via S/PDIF optical to Pro Tools. You will find Toslink connectors in many audio interfaces such as the Symphony I/O by Apogee, the RedNet 6 by Focusrite, the HD I/O, HD MADI, and the 192 I/O from Avid, among many others

Figure 6-6

DB-25 Connector

DB-25 Pin Connectors, aka 25-in D-sub multi-pin connectors, are used in a wide range of computer applications—from SCSI connections to printer cables. HD-series Pro Tools systems use a special cable with DB-25 pin connectors (Figure 6-7) to do digital audio transfers using the AES/EBU and the T-DIF digital audio formats between Pro Tools and other digital devices. Also, these type of connectors are used on each end of an audio cable snake to plug a set of eight balanced analog inputs or outputs at the time through patch bays or among analog devises.

Figure 6-7

RCA Connectors

You can use RCA connectors for digital transfers using the coaxial S/PDIF digital audio transfer format. Make sure the cables you use for S/PDIF digital transfers have an impedance rating of 75 ohms. You will be fine if your cables are gold-plated RCA connectors (Figure 6-8 and Figure 6-9). If you have to choose between analog or digital transfer, you should stay in the digital domain. Connecting a CD player, DVD player or any external signal processor via an audio interface will degrade your audio with each transfer. Your original signal will be preserved when kept in the digital domain. Never plug a digital output into an analog input, the results would be loud, unpleasant, and perhaps even destructive to your equipment.

Figure 6-8

Figure 6-9

XLR Connectors

XLR connectors, aka Cannon connectors (Figure 6-10), are typically used for microphone cables. Although there is no industry standard for the assignment of the 3 pins on these connectors, usually pin 1 is connected to ground, pin 2 is the 'hot' or the '+' signal, and pin 3 is the 'cold' or '-' signal. You should check the pin out arrangements whenever you connect any professional equipment. Some companies assign pin 2 to be the '-' signal, and pin 3 the '+' signal. If you don't pay attention to this, you could end up with audio signals 180° out of phase. Besides using this type of connectors to plug in microphones in a recording studio, they are also used for an AES/AES digital audio transfer between audio devices. When you use XLR cables for AES/EBU digital audio transfers, be sure they have an impedance of 110 ohms.

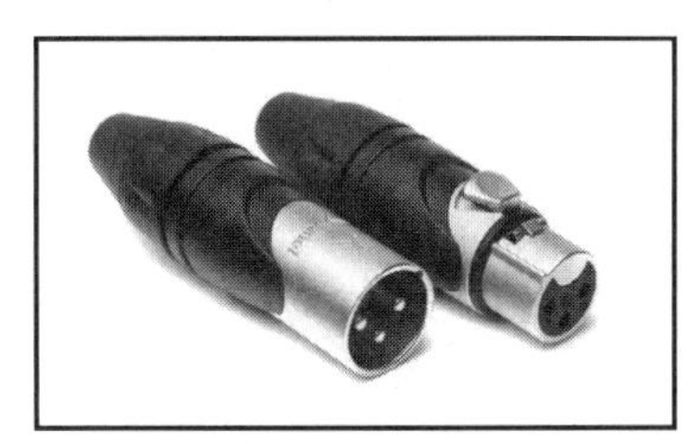

Figure 6-10

1/4-Inch Plug Connector (TRS and TS)

1/4-inch Plug Connectors are used almost exclusively for analog audio transfers, and come in two different configurations, TS and TRS. A ¼-inch TS (Tip-Sleeve) type of connector (Figure 6-11) is used for unbalanced audio lines (-10dBv), such as the level signal from an electric guitar or bass guitar, for example. You will find ¼-inch TS type of connectors on audio devices such as a direct box to convert your line level (Hi-Z) signal to a Mic level (Lo-Z) signal, guitar amplifiers, audio mixing boards, and audio signal processors among others. The ¼-inch TRS (Tip-Ring-Sleeve) connectors (Figure 6-12) are used for balanced analog audio inputs and outputs (+4dBu). They are usually used on insert points (in/out) for effects loops, on audio mixing boards, audio interfaces, professional signal processors, and for headphone outputs (stereo), among other audio devices.

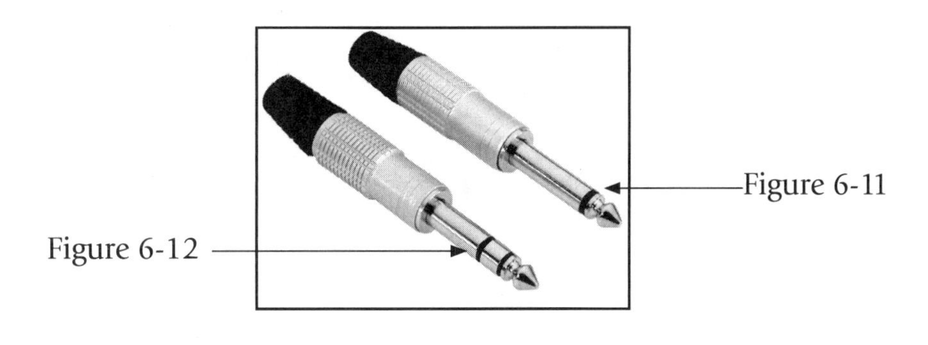

Figure 6-11

Figure 6-12

5-pin DIN MIDI Connector

The 5-pin DIN connector (short for Deutsche Industry Norm) also known as a MIDI connector (short for Musical Instrument Digital Interface), is used exclusively for MIDI applications (Figure 6-13).

Sixteen MIDI channels pass through this connector when use on a MIDI cable. MIDI is used by Pro Tools and other DAW (Digital Audio Workstation) to control MIDI sequencers and synthesizers, and to control digital data via MIDI controllers, such as keyboard controllers from M-Audio and Novation, the Command | 8 by Avid, and the HUI from Mackie, among others. These connectors are typically used on hardware synthesizers and other electronic music devices, as well as audio interfaces, digital signal processors, digital mixing boards, etc.

Figure 6-13

USB Connectors

The Universal Serial Bus or USB is easy to use. USB devices can be connected and disconnected without having to power your computer off and/or on. If your computer runs out of USB ports, you can add ports by buying a 4 or 7 port USB hub. USB lets you connect up to 127 external devices such as keyboards, computer mouse, microphones, smart telephones, and storage devices among other devices. USB provides data transfer rates up to 12-megabits-per-second (12Mbps), which is over 50 times faster than traditional serial ports. As of this writing, there are three different data transfer speeds of USB, these are: USB 1.0 rate is 12Mbps (Figure 6-14), USB 2.0 rate is 480 Mbps (Figure 6-15), and USB 3.0 rate is 5Gbps (FIgure 6-16), a little over ten times faster than USB 2.0

Figure 6-14

Figure 6-15

Figure 6-16

FireWire Connectors

The FireWire connector, also known as a IEEE 1394 bus, was designed to inexpensively interconnect a wide variety of devices. A FireWire connection can be made and broken without powering your computer off and on, which can be a real time saver. FireWire also allows you to connect consumer electronic devices such as: computers, hard drives, digital camcorders, printers, and scanners, among many other types of consumer electronic devices. In the audio industry has been used to interconnect audio interfaces to computers and hard drives, among other applications. The FireWire data transfer rates are up to 400 Mbps, 30 times faster than the USB standard, and up to 63 FireWire external devices can be chained together. As of this writing, there are two FireWire standards, the FireWire 400 or IEEE 1394 (Figure 6-17), and the FireWire 800 or IEEE 1394b (Figure 6-18). Their data speeds are 400Mbps and 800Mbps respectively. Different than a USB connection, the FireWire bus speed does not decrease when a FireWire 400 shares a FireWire 800 bus. Currently, the maximum cable length is around 15 feet long or 4.5 meters.

Figure 6-17

Figure 6-18

Ethernet Connector

Ethernet Connectors (Figure 6-19) are widely used in local area networks (LAN) to connect computers together and to share devices. If you have internet cable or DSL connection, this is the connector you use to plug your computer to the modem. Audio companies such as Focusrite, MOTU, and Avid among other companies use Ethernet cables to connect their control surfaces (Avid's S6 and D-Control), their modular Ethernet-networked audio interfaces (Focusrite RedNet and MOTU's AVB Ethernet Networks), and synchronization among audio workstations such as Avid's Satellite Link HD.

Figure 6-19

HDMI Connector

HDMI stands for High Definition Multimedia Interface (Figure 6-20), and is a compact audio/video interface capable of sending uncompressed video along with digital audio information from a source to a smart, television, computer monitor or audio device. It transmits all ATSC HDTV standards and supports 8-channel, 192kHz, uncompressed digital audio. HDMI is a digital replacement of the transmission of analog audio and video signals.

Figure 6-20

Thunderbolt Connector

Thunderbolt is a dual protocol connection that combines PCI Express (PCIe) and DisplayPort into a singular connection with DC for electric power. Thunderbolt (Figure 6-21) was developed in conjunction between Apple and Intel to act as both optical and electrical cable. It sends data at a speed of 10 Gigs/sec per channel, with 2 channels per cable delivering up to 20 Gigs/second. This connection is used in newer Macintosh computers and PCs in Home and Professional studios as a means to connect them to an external chassis, such as the Magma ExpressBox 3T to interconnect a Pro Tools HDX or Pro Tools HD Native PCIe cards, as well as several newer interfaces, such as the Apollo Twin from Universal Audio. Now with Thunderbolt 2 built into the new Mac Pro and MacBook Pro with Retina display, you can connect the latest 4K desktop displays and get double the bandwidth for your peripherals. And the two generations of Thunderbolt technology are compatible with each other.

Figure 6-21

Banana Plug Connectors

A Banana connector (Plug for a male connector and Socket or Jack for female connector), are also know as a 4mm single wire connector that is normally used to connect high fidelity speakers to external amplifier or a receiver. In audio, you will probably use a Banana Plug (Figure 6-22) to connect power amplifiers and loudspeakers such as the NS-10 from Yamaha and the Reftones reference monitors, as well as Hi-Fi consumer systems.

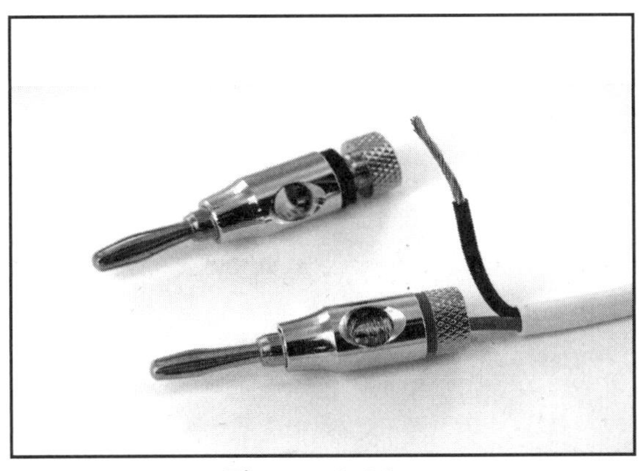

Figure 6-22

Binding Post Connector

A Binding Post is a connector commonly used on electronic test equipment to attach a single wire or test lead. A Binding Post (Figure 6-23) has a central threaded metal rod and a cap that screws down that rod. The cap is typically insulated or color-coded. In audio you will find them on loudspeakers, amplifiers and receivers, from low-fi, mid-level and up to professional levels. A red cap in a binding post commonly means that is the active or positive terminal. A black cap means the it is the inactive or negative terminal

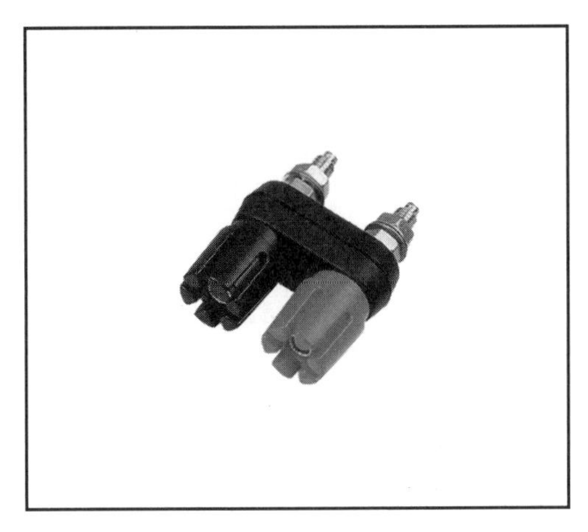

Figure 6-23

Breakout Cable

The Breakout Cable (Figure 6-24) is commonly found in the Duet and Duet 2 audio interfaces from Apogee Electronics. There are optional breakout cables that offer more inputs and outputs, but the standard cable with 2 inputs and 2 outputs is what comes with these devices.

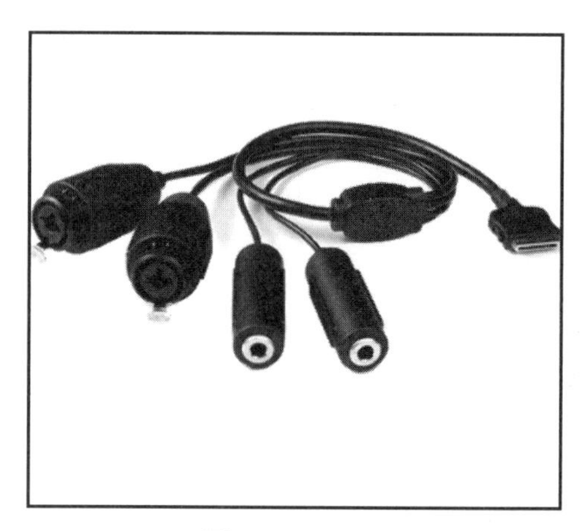

Figure 6-24

8-Pin Mini DIN Serial Connector

The 8-pin Mini DIN connector (Figure 6-25) was used on older Apple computers to connect printers and modems to the computer. Nowadays, the serial connector is used by Pro Tools to connect an Avid Sync HD or Sync I/O synchronizer to the DigiSerial port on a Pro Tools HDX card, Pro Tools HD Native, Pro Tools HD Native Thunderbolt or the "older" HD Core PCIe card (Pro Tools HD-series).
The serial connection enables Pro Tools to synchronize with external video or audio devices via SMPTE time code or MIDI Time Code (MTC).

Figure 6-25

Mini DisplayPort to HDMI Adapter

A Mini DisplayPort is a miniaturized version of the DisplayPort audio-visual digital interface. This port is capable to drive display devices with VGA, DVI, or HDMI interfaces. You will commonly use them to connect newer video monitors with a VGA, DVI, and or HDMI connectors to a computer via a Mini Display adaptor (Figure 6-26).

Figure 6-26

Studio Furniture

B

Here are a few studio furniture options from Omnirax Furniture Company that may inspire you to create, adjust, or customize your ideal studio setup. You can visit them at www.omnirax.com for more details and a list of the latest available products.

Audio Interface Options

This Appendix, shows other audio interface options available in the market (as of this writing), in case you are looking for different options that fits your home studio setup and more importantly, your budget.

Steinberg UR-22

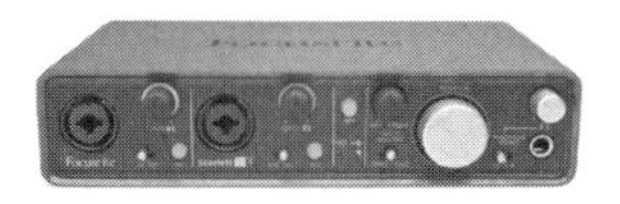

Focusrite Scarlet 2i4

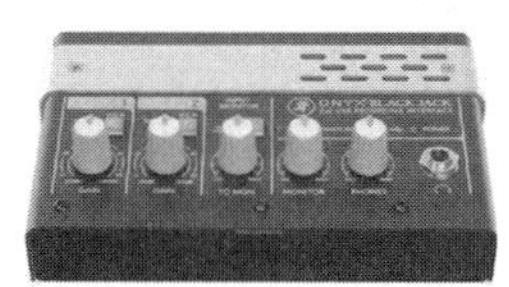

Onyx Black Jack 2x2

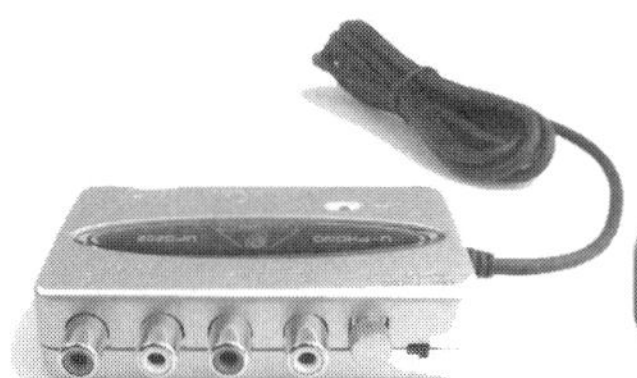

Behringer UFO 202

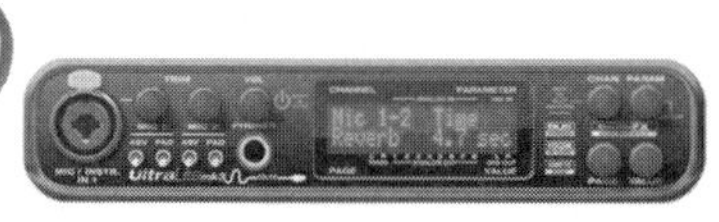

MOTU UltraLite-mk3 Hybrid

MOTU 4pre

Avid Mbox Pro

Avid Mbox 3G

M-Audio M Track

Line 6 Sonic Port VX

Focusrite Forte

Roland Duo Capture EX

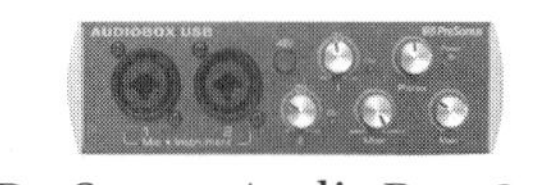

PreSonus AudioBox 2x2

Universal Audio Apollo Twin

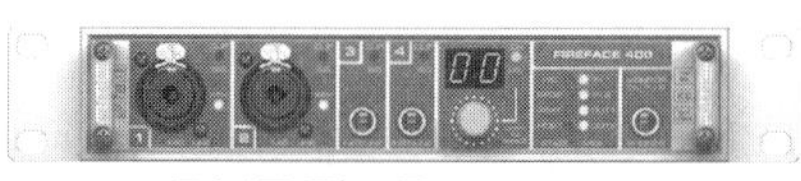

RME FireFace 400

Directory

D

Ableton Inc.

36 W. Colorado Blvd. Suite 300
Pasadena, CA 91105, USA
Tel: 646.723.4550
www.ableton.com

ADAM Audio GmbH

Ederstr. 16
D-12059 Berlin
Germany
Tel: +49-30 / 86 30 097 - 0
Fax: +49-30 / 86 30 097 - 7
www.adam-audio.com

Alesis

InMusic
World Headquarters
200 Scenic View Drive, Suite 201
Cumberland, RI 02864, USA
Tel: 401.658.5760
www.alesis.com

Automated Processes, Inc.

8301 Patuxent Range Road
Jessup, MD 20794, USA
www.apiaudio.com

Apple Inc.

1 Infinite Loop
Cupertino, CA 95014, USA
Tel: 408.996.1010
www.apple.com

Apogee Electronics Corp.

1715 Berkeley St
Santa Monica, CA 90404, USA
Tel: +1 310.584.9394
Fax: +1 310.584.9385
www.apogeedigital.com

Arturia

5776-D Lindero Cyn Rd #239
Westlake Village, CA 91362, USA
www.arturia.com

Audio-Technica U.S., Inc.

1221 Commerce Drive
Stow, Ohio 44224
Tel: 330-686-2600
www.audio-technica.com

Avalon Design

14741-B Franklin Avenue
Tustin, CA 92780, USA
Telephone: 949.492.2000
Fax: 949.492.4284
www.avalondesign.com

Avid Technology, Inc.

65-75 Network Drive
Burlington, MA 01803, USA
Tel: 978 640 6789
www.avid.com

Burl Audio LLC

240 Feather Lane
Santa Cruz CA, 95060
Tel: 831.425.7501
Fax: 831.621.076
www.burlaudio.com

Burst Electronics, Inc

PO Box 65947
Albuquerque, NM 87193, USA
Tel: 505.890.8926
Fax: 505.898.0159
www.burstelectronics.com

Dorrough

5221 Collier Place
Woodland Hills, California 91364, USA
Tel: 818.998.2824
Fax: 818.998.1507
www.dorrough.com

Fender Musical Instruments Corporation

17600 N. Perimeter Drive, Suite 100
Scottsdale, AZ 85255, USA
Tel: 480.596.9690
Fax: 480.596.1384
www.fender.com

Focusrite Novation Inc.

Focusrite Novation Inc.
840 Apollo Street, Suite 312
El Segundo, CA 90245, USA
Tel: 310.322.5500
Fax: 310.426.9508
us.focusrite.com

Fostex Company

Foster Electric Co., Ltd.
1-1-109 Tsutsujigaoka, Akishima, Tokyo, Japan 196-8550
Tel: +81 42 546 4974
Fax: +81 42 546 2335
www.fostex.com

G-Technology

Sales and Marketing
3528 Hayden Avenue
Second Floor, South
Culver City, CA 90232, USA
www.g-technology.com

Genelec Inc. / U.S.A.

7 Tech Circle
Natick, Massachusetts 01760, USA
Tel: 508 652 0900
Fax: 508 652 0909
www.genelec.com

Kaotica Corp.

www.kaoticaeyeball.com

Line 6, Inc.

26580 Agoura Road
Calabasas, CA 91302-1921, USA
Tel: 818.575.3600
Fax: 818.575.3601
www.line6.com

M-Audio

200 Scenic View Drive
Cumberland, RI 02864, USA
Tel: 401.658.5765
Fax: 401.658.3640
www.m-audio.com

Mackie.

LOUD Technologies Inc.
16220 Wood-Red Rd. N.E.
Woodinville, WA 98072, USA
Tel: 800-258-6883
Fax: 425-487-4337
www.mackie.com

Magma

9918 Via Pasar
San Diego, CA 92126, USA
Tel: 858.530.2511
Fax: 858.530.2733
www.magma.com

Manley Laboratories, Inc.

13880 Magnolia Ave.
Chino, CA 91710, USA
Tel: 909.627.4256
Fax: 909.308.2482
www.manley.com

MOTU, Inc.

1280 Massachusetts Ave
Cambridge MA 02138, USA
Tel: 617.576.2760
Fax: 617.576.3609
www.motu.com

Músico Pro Magazine

Music Maker Publications, Inc.
5408 Idylewild Trail
Boulder, CO 80301
Tel: 303.516.9118
Fax: 303.516.9119
www.musicopro.com

Mytek Digital

148 India Street
Brooklyn, New York, 11222, USA
Tel: 347.384.2687
Fax: 347.202.5331
www.mytekdigital.com

Native Instruments North America, Inc.

6725 Sunset Boulevard
5th Floor
Los Angeles, CA 90028, USA
Tel: 866.556.6487
Fax: 866.556.6490
www.native-instruments.com

NETGEAR

350 E. Plumeria Drive
San Jose, CA 95134, USA
Tel: 408.907.8000
Fax: 408.907.8097
www.netgear.com

Omnirax Furniture Company

P.O. Box 1792
Sausalito, CA 94966, USA
Tel: 800.332.3393
www.omnirax.com

Pioneer Electronics (USA) Inc.

1925 E Dominguez Street
Long Beach, CA 90810, USA
Tel: 310.952.2000
www.pioneerelectronics.com

PreSonus Audio Electronics Inc.

18011 Grand Bay Court
Baton Rouge, LA 70809, USA
Tel: +1 225.216.7887
Fax: +1 225.926.8347
www.presonus.com

Propellerhead Software

Hornsbruksgatan 23
SE-117 34 Stockholm
Sweden
www.propellerheads.se

Rane Corporation

10802 47TH Avenue. W.
Mukilteo, WA 98275-5000 ,USA
Tel: 425.355.6000
www.rane.com

Recording Magazine

Music Maker Publications, Inc.
5408 Idylewild Trail
Boulder, CO 80301
Tel: 303.516.9118
Fax: 303.516.9119

Reftone Speakers

www.reftone.com

Roland Corporation U.S.

5100 S. Eastern Ave.
Los Angeles, CA 90040-2938, USA
Tel: 323.903.3700
www.rolandus.com

TEAC America, Inc.

1834 Gage Road
Montebello, CA 90640, USA
Tel: 323.726.0303
www.tascam.com

T.C. Electronic

TC Group
335 Gage Ave., Suite 1
Kitchener, N2M 5E1, Canada
Tel;:+1 519.745.1158
Fax: +1 519.745.2364
www.tcelectronic.com

Technics

Panasonic Corporation of America
Two Riverfront Plaza
Newark, NJ 07102
www.panasonic.com

Universal Audio, Inc.

4585 Scotts Valley Dr.
Scotts Valley CA 95066, USA
Tel: 877.698.2834
Fax: 931.461.1550
www.uaudio.com

Vestax Corporation

World Headquarters
2-16-15 fukasawa Setagaya- Ku
Tokyo Japan 158-0081
Tel: 800.431.2609
www.vestax.com

Waves Inc.

2800 Merchants Drive
Knoxville, TN 37912
Tel: 865.909.9200
Fax: 865.909.9245
www.waves.com

Whirlwind Music Distributors, Inc.

99 Ling Road
Greece, New York 14612, USA
Tel: 800.733.9473
Fax: 585.865.8930
www.whirlwindusa.com

Yamaha Corporation of America

6600 Orangethorpe Ave.
Buena Park, CA 90620, USA
usa.yamaha.com